Tears Are Only Water

J. Herman Kleiger

TEARS ARE ONLY WATER
By J. Herman Kleiger

First Edition
Copyright © 2023 by J. Herman Kleiger

JAMES KLEIGER PC

All rights reserved. No part of this publication may be reproduced, distributed, or transmitted in any form or by any means, including photocopying, recording, or other electronic or mechanical methods, without the prior written permission of the publisher, except as permitted by U.S. copyright law.

The story, all names, characters, and incidents portrayed in this production are fictitious. No identification with actual persons (living or deceased), places, buildings, and products is intended or should be inferred.

ISBN# 979-8-88862-011-3
Printed in the United States of America

Dedicated to indigenous people worldwide
whose suffering and wisdom are too easily forgotten;
to healers no matter their teachings and traditions;
to the visions and humanity of the International Council
of Thirteen Indigenous Grandmothers;
and finally, to the grace, mystery,
and majesty of birds.

Table of Contents

PART ONE SLEEPING COMPARTMENTS 1

Chapter 1 When the Numbers Disappeared 3

Chapter 2 E 11

Chapter 3 Dihn 20

Chapter 4 Reading Codes 27

Chapter 5 EEP! 37

Chapter 6 This is Anne 45

Chapter 7 Overhead Compartments 52

Chapter 8 The Sociologist & the Bookkeeper 62

Chapter 9 Blue 68

Chapter 10 Mile High 77

Chapter 11 Cinnamon Gummies 89

Chapter 12 Messes He's Made 97

Chapter 13 Following Breadcrumbs 104

Chapter 14 Semper Fi 117

Chapter 15 Dr Hazel 125

Chapter 16 Misdeeds of a Troubled Soul 128

Chapter 17 Dimitri Onboard 136

Chapter 18 The Old Woman in the Garden–Nicola 144

Chapter 19 The Old Woman in the Garden–Anne 147

PART 2	AWAKENING	159
Chapter 20	Sacred Birds	161
Chapter 21	Beelzebuffo	163
Chapter 22	*Non Compos Mentis*	167
Chapter 23	Off the Grid	173
Chapter 24	Tallulah	180
Chapter 25	Messages From the Dead	183
Chapter 26	Apache 11 Eagle Down!	190
Chapter 27	Woman in the Window	198
Chapter 28	2 Kings 14	202
Chapter 29	The Magic of Pi	213
Chapter 30	A Long Blue Feather	218
Chapter 31	BOB	224
Chapter 32	Tears Are Only Water	229
Chapter 33	Hijo Prodìgo	237
Chapter 34	Hall of Mirrors	242
Chapter 35	Myth of the Sleeping Boy	245
Chapter 36	Song of Death and Renewal	253
Chapter 37	Balancing the Books	262
Chapter 38	Kelly, Casey, Bowman, & Young	266
Chapter 39	Must Mean Somethin'	274
Chapter 40	Colorful Constants	281
Chapter 41	*Ahéheé*	288

PART ONE

SLEEPING COMPARTMENTS

"Honestly, we've been force-fed the Freudian fairytale that it's better to recover memories, process, and work through the past and that this will somehow set us free when, in truth, we are better off exhaling the mental detritus, finding a secure overhead compartment, and tucking away the past with all its warts, bruisings, and imperfections. Without such compartments, we're doomed to endless claims of victimhood. Then, and only then, will we be set free and finally able to sleep soundly."

–ANNE SCHIVALONE
Unmasking the Cognitive Orchestrator of Maladaptive Thought and How to Silence Him, 2012

Chapter 1

When the Numbers Disappeared

Sunday, March 16, 2014, 11:45 PM

Pale moonlight stalked the warped blinds, casting ragged shadows in the corner of an inconsequential office. Hunched over his desk, the bookkeeper had grown accustomed to working through the night. Gulping coffee, bitter and black, he scrolled down pages of spreadsheets, frantically searching for those numbers that had disappeared.

Faint tapping at the window broke his concentration. The bookkeeper tried to ignore it. When it grew louder, he spun around to see the luminous face peering in. Hungry eyes searching, always searching for him.

She came at night in his dreams, but he couldn't be sure because the edges between sleep and wakefulness were soft. Paralyzed by a fear that she would find him, the bookkeeper closed his eyes like a child hoping not to be seen. He couldn't remember when she had first appeared. Maybe she'd always been there. He rubbed his eyes, looked at his hands, and clenched his fists. "Wake the hell up!" He willed himself to awaken but realized he was not dreaming. His heart pounded as the tapping grew more urgent. He needed to hide, now!

A month earlier, his boss had permitted Carmine Luedke to use the office at night to work on his accounts. Before this arrangement, his workday was interrupted by loss of bodily control and "cut-outs"––the name he'd given to his narcoleptic attacks––which snuck up on him without warning. Moreover, working alone through the night allowed him to avoid the hushed comments and open mockery of his co-workers.

During normal office hours, co-workers had snored and bobbed their heads when he passed, while others giggled and pointed to the bandages on his forehead––a tell-tale sign that he'd gone limp, banged his head on the computer keyboard, and once again, broken his glasses.

A thirty-something man of average height, the bookkeeper wore drab-colored sweater vests and t-shirts that hung loosely around his neck. His trousers, always baggy and gray, flashed a hint of brightly colored socks at the cuff line. Completing his ensemble was a pair of square-toed black leather shoes, polished to such a fine sheen that they reflected the overhead lights and trumpeted his polychromatic socks. He stepped softly in a slightly slouched posture as if wishing he could shrink out of sight. Carmine wore a mop of red hair pushed into place but never combed. His glasses were meticulously taped together, and his ears a tad too big for his face.

Officemates referred to him as "Shiny Shoes." Others called him "Sleepy" or "Rain Man" because he carted around obscure math books, appeared to have an eidetic memory, and avoided eye contact. They didn't understand that looking people in the eye brought too much sensory information. So, he looked down when others walked by. The name-calling was nothing new. He never reacted, but their comments burrowed beneath his skin.

Reconciling cash accounts at the end of the month had always been a simple task for the man who romanced numbers and remembered everything. Still, his easy dance with simple accounting procedures somehow lost its rhythm two months ago when he couldn't reconcile the books for one of his accounts. Numbers appeared and then were gone as if they had never been there.

But tonight, the bookkeeper vowed he would find them. He had arrived at his office at 9:00 PM determined to end this game of hide-and-seek. The end of the month brought yet another chance to balance the books and reconcile the $250,000 variance that kept coming up.

Another 30 mgs of Adderall, chased by caffeine, sharpened his focus and narrowed his attention. Rubbing his hands together, he knew he could coax the numbers back and balance the figures for Tawney-Banks Commercial Fishing Company.

"Routine accounting practices," the CFO said in her last email. "There's nothing to worry about. Surely you understand such matters." But he didn't.

He nosed closer to the monitor and strained to see, but the screen was blurry, and the numbers were beginning to float from their columns. He rubbed his eyes again and looked for another pill as he cursed the numbers on the screen.

"Where the hell are you? Why are you doing this to me?" He squinted and reached out to steady the monitor as if this would keep the numbers from floating off the screen. "Found you!"

Buried in the bowels of the ledger was a quarter of a million-dollar payment to a company called BOB that he didn't recognize. He searched feverishly for corresponding bank deposits or assets to balance the books but found none. Then, hidden in the back pages of the spreadsheets itemizing the company's revenue and expenses for the month, a deposit of $150,000 disappeared while another $100,000 payment showed up. This is how it had been for the last three months. Numbers would vanish and then suddenly reappear--gone one month and mysteriously present the next. In his final calculations, the figures didn't add up, and once again, the earth tilted on its axis. How could the bookkeeper live in a world where the numbers didn't make sense?

Before the bookkeeper turned five, he began reciting the digits of pi. He liked counting as high as he could, first forward, then back. Counting all the time, he added numbers by two, then subtracted by three. Numbers and calculations demanded his complete attention. They awakened him in the morning and put him to sleep at night when they crept into his dreams. His mind had yielded to an imperative of complete immersion in numbers--learning their tricks and the secrets they kept. Becoming both puppet master and puppet of numbers, he could not stop, nor did he want to. Without the insulative magic of numbers, his mind might wander into realms too dangerous to contemplate.

Carmine saw colors in numbers. He also saw colors in the sounds and voices around him. As a boy, he became obsessed with abstract theories, square roots, complex equations, and arcane proofs. While other boys daydreamed about sports heroes like Nolan Ryan, Pele, Joe Montana, or Dr J., it was an Indian mathlete named Srinivasa Ramanujan who inhabited Carmine's thoughts. Before turning ten, he'd consumed the crimson equations from Ramanujan's Lost Notebook. He took comfort in knowing that Ramanujan's first job had been as a bookkeeper in Madras's Accountant General's Office. He then felt compelled to learn about the colorful Bernoulli numbers.

In the summer of his twelfth year, Carmine found tattered boxes of old books in the wooden shed behind his house. On an earmarked page in one of those books, he discovered an underlined passage about a unifying equation created by Leonhard Euler, an 18th-century Swiss mathematician and physicist. Settling into the musty shed, Carmine read about Euler's Identity. This equation, $e^{i\pi} + 1 = 0$, was described as the jewel of mathematics. What was so remarkable about this equation was how it connected essential constants across different fields of mathematics. Something about the simplicity, purity, and orderliness of the equation deeply touched a lonely twelve-year-old who found comfort in knowing about constancy and connectivity. Like reliable friends, constants could be trusted--they never changed and never left. If Euler's simple formula, with its two constants, e and π, could connect essential mathematical truths and reduce them to a simple equation, then maybe it could help him make connections, find truths, and simplify the complexities in the world around him. Since his discovery on a sultry summer day, in a dilapidated shed, this equation provided Carmine with reassurance and clarity. He developed such an attachment to Euler's Identity that it became his mantra for self-soothing and sleep: $e^{i\pi} + 1 = 0...e^{i\pi} + 1 = 0... e^{i\pi}$.

. . .

TEARS ARE ONLY WATER

His passionate compulsion for numbers with their myriad colors never wavered. Numbers demanded his complete attention and, in exchange, became his constant and loyal companions. Numbers had never given up on him.

Until now.

Three months ago, he started having trouble with Tawney-Banks, one of his firm's largest accounts. The numbers and their radiant colors, with their soothing charm and power to focus his mind, began to disappear. His unique form of chromesthesia was gone too. His world faded and leadened to gray. Voices became drab and translucent. He felt a sickening torment like oxygen being sucked from your lungs when you fall into an icy river.

The first casualty of his numero-chromatic crisis was existential. He felt alone and unmoored. How could he live in a colorless world where the numbers didn't add up? Then, he began to have trouble sleeping. Not only had sleep abandoned him at night, but his daytime sleeping attacks had worsened.

For over twenty years, he'd suffered from a virulent form of Type 1 Narcolepsy. Five years earlier, he had to surrender his driver's license after his fifth accident. Six months ago, he gave up his bicycle after repeatedly falling asleep while riding home from work. The final effect of his multiple ailments was that he'd become dependent on stimulants to help him work into the night. He found them easy to obtain on the Internet and even easier to buy on the street.

Shrenklin's Tax & Accounting was a dingy office in a strip mall behind an industrial park. His boss, the colorless Marvin Shrenklin, had hired him when no other company would. Shrenklin recognized the bookkeeper's prodigious talent with numbers and hired him at a ridiculously low salary. But now, Carmine worried he might lose his job. On several occasions, he thought about telling his boss he couldn't reconcile T-B CFC's cash accounts.

Two months ago, he told Shrenklin that the Tawney-Banks numbers were wrong.

"Like I've told you before, Luedke, you're the bookkeeper. Get on the damn phone with their Finance Department and see what gives. And don't screw this up with anything weird. We need this account."

The "anything weird" reference had to do with the fact that the bookkeeper had always struggled with words. Thinking was one thing, but talking was another. Second only to falling asleep during employment interviews, his long pauses, stuttering, and clumsy syntax had been responsible for having countless employment interviews prematurely terminated.

Because phone conversations were hard, the bookkeeper finally emailed Misha Horvath, the CFO at Tawney-Banks.

It took her days to respond. "Well, hello, Mr Lusky. You're the bookkeeper, so you should understand routine accounting procedures. You're worrying needlessly. We're dealing with the encumbrance value of absorption costs, so naturally, this incorporates the asset turnover ratio and variance accruals. These are things I'm sure you're well aware of."

But he was not. He had never heard these terms. A more confident person would have questioned her and asked what the fuck she was talking about. But sadly, these words were not in his vocabulary, and this is not what introverts, filled with doubt and self-loathing, did. He thought it must be him. *He* was missing something. *She* must know something he didn't. *He* was just a bookkeeper, not a CPA, much less the CFO.

The bookkeeper paused searching through spreadsheets and went to the T-B CFC website. Maybe he'd missed something on their webpage that would help explain the variance, but all he found in a recent update was an announcement that they'd nominated a new Chairman of their Board. Then he pulled up Horvath's last email as if rereading it a tenth time would make it any clearer. But her words on the screen began to spin.

He heard movement outside his door. That would be the office manager, LuCinda, trundling around the secretaries' desks, organizing schedules, and scanning the premises for anything untoward. She began showing up at odd hours after he started working nights. He suspected she came in to keep tabs on him. Carmine tried to steer clear of this woman with her condescending tone, hidden behind a dishonest smile and the cloying scent of perfume, which made his eyes water.

It was nearly midnight. The bookkeeper tried to refocus on the moving numbers, but the screen appeared farther away as if his office had grown longer and narrower. That's when he first heard the tapping.

His heart pounded as the tapping grew louder and more demanding. The eyes searched for him. Realizing that no matter where he hid, she would find him, the bookkeeper stepped in front of the window and looked directly into her eyes. Emboldened by the stimulants in his system, he shouted, "Enough! This ends now." He would not turn away, but tonight would confront his stalker. Carmine moved closer and studied the face. Her eyes locked onto his....*No! It can't be.*

But there she was ...E. Just as he had last seen her 20 years ago with the same hint of a smile and riddle in her eyes. He recalled the siren sound of her voice that promised rosy hues which always faded too quickly.

The bookkeeper stared, heart pounding, stunned. Catching his breath, he couldn't believe what he saw. *A ghost? Alive after all these years?* His thoughts were catapulted back to her sudden disappearance, which occurred under circumstances he had long ago buried in a locked compartment. The mind helps put to sleep that which needs to be forgotten. It places the pain and fear into little boxes, squeezes them into paper-thin folders, and files them away. Yet, here she was, the face at his window, bringing back all the gut-wrenching emotion he'd locked away.

He froze. His throat tightened, and his pulse quickened. Heat radiated from the back of his neck, and water pooled in his eyes. The bookkeeper sought refuge in the Banach-Tarski Paradox, but he couldn't envision the bounded subsets of Euclidean space. He desperately recited Euler's formula, his steadfast guardian, but it came out as a jumbled mess: $e^{i\pi 2}$ + 1 ... $= \emptyset + 1 = 0$... $e^{i\pi}$.

His botched chant was fractured by the sound of a voice outside his window last heard 20 years ago.

"Hey Carm, ya gonna let me in?"

Chapter 2

E

Monday, March 17, 12:45 AM

Carmine trembled as he motioned for her to come around to the front door. She nodded. As the stunned bookkeeper maneuvered through the darkened reception area, he noticed light and muffled voices coming from LuCinda's office. He stumbled down the stairs, pushed open the outside door, and stared.

"Well...are you going to ask me in, Carm? Sorry, I know you weren't expecting this. I've been looking, trying to find you." Her breath turned to vapors in the frosty air.

Nodding as if in a trance, he stared in disbelief at the ghost before him.

The long scar running down the right side of E's face had faded with time. She was wearing a fashionable trench coat with a matching cashmere scarf. She followed him through a maze of desks to his office.

"Hmm, your office?"

He detected a tone of disapproval.

She took off her gloves and placed them on his small couch. If seeing her face––an older version of what he'd remembered––unleashed pictograms from his past, the familiar scent of her lavender perfume tickled long-forgotten memories.

"I'm so sorry. I know, you have a gabillion questions." He noticed she was still using that time-worn phrase from high school. "I know I won't be able to answer all of them. I'm not sure I really can. You're probably wondering why I'm here now after half a lifetime. I wouldn't have come, but it's urgent."

She began speaking more rapidly than he remembered. Always so calm and collected, E never broke a sweat. "I have so much to tell you, and time is short, Carm. Things are going to change forever! It's all going to be different, for sure. Nothing's ever going to be the same. That's totally why I had to see you now."

Feeling disoriented, he recognized the trace of "valley-speak" in her voice, a bizarre contradiction to her intellectual gifts and Phi Beta Kappa talents. His attention shifted to the lines creasing her left eye but not the surgically repaired area around her right. The scar swayed slightly as she spoke, while the faint line tracing her cheekbone gave way to unbidden images of how she looked that day when he peeked at her through the window of the ICU. All he could envision now was the red, swollen gash disfiguring her velvety complexion––a billboard that announced to the world that he was a worthless fool. Her scar had faded with time, and although he'd locked the memories of the accident in a vault, his shame and self-loathing had not aged a day. Then, suddenly released from their cave, memories rushed back and returned him to the time when their hearts shared a beat, or so he wanted to believe.

She found him at a tenth-grade science fair––E, the straight-A-student-destined-to-become-valedictorian, and he, the nerdy math geek who couldn't string more than two words together or look anyone in the eye. How two souls from different planets became friends was the eighth wonder of the world. But, unfortunately, his mother and sister, Anne, were convinced that E saw him as nothing more than a novelty, her own personal Elephant Man.

Anne harangued him. "Can't you see, you're the community service project she'll write about in her college essays? She cares nothing for you. Wake the hell up, brother!"

Carmine heard but tried to ignore her words. Even back then, his sister's cynicism, always justified as protectiveness, cut like rusted barbed wire.

Now, known as Dr Anne Schivalone, the famous psychology professor who thought she knew more than everyone else, his sister's words left burn marks. But he knew better. She––none of them––knew E the way he did. When this painfully shy boy made himself look at E, he'd always seen kindness and warmth in her eyes until it was no longer there....

The bookkeeper's attention shifted back to the ghost in front of him.

"And that's why it is vital that I came tonight. We, the international team of scientists I'm heading, need people with amazing mathematical talents and computer coding skills. You see, this is why I've been looking for you. We need people like you. *I* need you, Carm––*you're* one of the only people I can trust."

He listened and blinked as numbers danced in his head, flashing shapes and colors that brought back long-forgotten yearning and unsealed memories.

E had transferred to East High School from California. Her corporate executive father recently moved the family to Denver. The day after seeing Carmine at the science fair, E boldly broke social mores in the cafeteria when she strode to his table, where he always sat by himself. Then, glowing iridescent indigo, she asked, "Mind if I join you? Remember me? We met at the Science Fair. Your proof of Cantor's Diagonalization Argument was totally rad, by the way."

Back then, no one understood why a girl with her spectrum of luminous colors, classic bone structure, athletic talents, and brains had given a boy with his spectrum of oddities a second look. E quickly became popular, and when her friends mocked the size of Carmine's ears or his taped-together glasses, she silenced them with a glare. She routinely joined him at lunch or sought him out in class. Among her myriad talents, E had a scientifically curious mind and was bewitched by his facility with numbers and his description of the shapes and colors he saw when he recited pi to the 300th digit. They sat together silently in study hall, reading and researching genetic theory––her passion––or mathematical mysteries––his. When they did speak, it was usually about mapping the genome, solving exponential equations, or memorizing mathematical constants. He hoped she enjoyed the quiet when they sat together and liked being with someone different than her other friends.

One day he asked, "Why me? I d-don't get it. That's all."

E smiled and said, "Oh Carm, most kids are posers and ignoramasaurs. You're different. I like that about you. You can really see colors in numbers?"

"It's called synesthesia," he explained. His halting stutter began to disappear when talking to E as he spoke with normal fluency and cadence. She was his Dorothy, and he, her Tinman whose jaws she oiled with an invisible can.

A couple of years later, she became valedictorian and gave a graduation speech that was written up in the papers. A tour de force, an original "Yes We Can" speech that some said inspired a young African American community organizer to make his mark on the world. Everyone expected E would go on to become something special. Their AP Chemistry teacher beamed after her speech, "That one's gonna blast out of here and not stop until she's in orbit. A cure for cancer or dementia? Take your pick, but hopefully not politics. We need medical saviors like her, not more crooked politicians."

Carmine realized that E had continued talking about her vital project and that his reverie had distracted him from what she was saying. He forced himself to listen to her words, which sounded like a garbled recording.

"As I mentioned...hey Carm, you've got to.... Look at me! ...a critical point in our protein sequencing research. The mRNA permutations... immense, but my team thinks...find the key within the next...months... came tonight because...approved bringing you on board...need you... time is short...team arriving from MIT this week."

E had been an obvious choice for MIT, but no one expected Carmine would also receive an admissions letter. His grades were decent, and his SATs perfect, which was nothing unusual for MIT applicants. But the Admissions Committee was gobsmacked by his mathematical wizardry and compelling personal story––having been raised by a single mother, an early feminist poet, and his father, a deceased concentration camp survivor.

His guidance counselor told him, "You need to find your voice. Just write about something you know deep in your gut. Tell us about your passions."

So, he wrote about finding order, beauty, constancy, and companionship in the colors and shapes of numbers. Somewhere between admiration and pathos, his essay awakened the Committee members from their mind-numbing stupor after reading thousands of applications.

E left MIT in her sophomore year, long after he dropped out. By then, she was known as the wunderkind of the Ivy circuit. Several senior faculty members, plus the crew coach, were apoplectic when she announced her plans to transfer. How could E leave the vaunted halls of MIT, for Stanford no less? They'd all fallen in love with pieces of E–– her scientific mind, alluring beauty, athletic frame, boundless charm, and Mona Lisa smile––but none of her legion of admirers had really known her as he did.

After she left, E contacted Carmine in Denver, urging that he pack up and bring his mathematical brilliance to Palo Alto. She was working in a lab and could find him a job as a research assistant. "They'll be blown away by your essay on the majesty of Euler's identity and your proof of Fermat's little theorem," she wrote.

Unable to resist her scarlet siren song, the future bookkeeper packed a small suitcase, ignoring his sister's stern warning.

"Don't be an idiot chasing a golden fleece. She cares nothing for you. Wake up, Carmie. Don't go!"

But he did.

During that bus ride, visions of E danced through his dreams, and her words formed a bewitching array of crimson equations he hoped to solve with her. Carmine had always seen the amber softness in her eyes but mistook it for something more. His brief stay in her dorm room had been awkward and confusing. He'd never tasted alcohol, but E insisted it would be alright. She wanted her friends to hear him recite pi, which he did like her dancing bear. With so little understanding of what she really wanted, he misread her enigmatic smile and tried to kiss her that night. She'd recoiled. Was it the putrid green of disgust he read in her eyes? Carmine had bolted from the dorm, drunk with shame, found a hiding place, and watched as she followed, calling for him.

"Come back! Please!! Carm, please. I can explain."

From the bushes, he watched her wander into the darkness, heard the violent screech of tires, and saw her struck down by a hit-and-run driver. Unable to move or scream, he did what he always did to soothe himself: summon Euler's formula and fall asleep.

They found her unconscious on the side of the road, with a severe head injury and lacerations lining the right side of her face. He'd awakened to the blaring of sirens and flashing strobe lights of the ambulance, which took her to the Stanford Trauma Center. He tried to visit her in the ICU, but her family, who never understood what their talented and beautiful daughter saw in such a social misfit, would not let him near her. Instead, they blamed him when they found out what happened that weekend. The closest he got was to view her face through the window of the ICU room, where he strained to see her lying unconsciously among the tubes, monitors, and bandages.

After a record-setting recuperation, she returned to Stanford, graduating at the top of her class and taking a fellowship there, where she headed up her own biogenetics lab. Later, she tried to contact him with occasional letters or rare phone messages, saying she wanted to apologize and didn't blame him for her accident. But he never returned her letters or calls, trying to find comfort in numbers instead. Over time, the trickle of cards, notes, and phone messages stopped.

Finally, months later, choking on the loneliness of isolation and missing the one person he could look in the eyes, he tried to contact her.

Dear E, It's me. I miss you. I'm sorry. Maybe I can come to California to see you. I could help in your genetics lab. That's all.

Your friend forever,

C.

P.S. I think I can solve the Poincaré conjecture now.

Then came the note from her friend Mary Beth––E had disappeared. She'd been acting strangely, and one day was gone. She'd left all her belongings in her apartment and a cryptic note that only read, "It's time."

They suspected she'd traveled to San Francisco and jumped off the bridge. Her body was never recovered. She'd vanished. The newspaper wrote about "another tragic suicide by a brilliant Icarus who had burned too intensely and flamed out."

The bookkeeper forced himself back into the room to hold onto the music of her voice. But the light grew dim.

Her truncated words turned frantic. "Oh my God, Carm, everything... change, and you can be...need you...in a world without Fleming's discovery...or life before mapping...genome. Everything changed ....This will be bigger...stumbled on...combination of amino acids in one of the codons... an accident...miracle...manipulation...nucleotides on that spot... eluded everyone about the genetics...Parkinson's, Alzheimer's, Schizophren...tweaking of the combinations ...the 13th codon...key that unlocked it all."

As she talked, the light extinguished in his eyes. Her words, written with invisible ink, dropped like grains of sand.

"Have to listen! Don't have that much time! Send a signal...come for you...watch for the signs. You'll know when it's time."

And, at that, the bookkeeper fell asleep. That's how it always happened––a candle in his mind snuffed out. As one doctor described, his sleep disorder was a temporary death, *la petite mort*. When he was out, others couldn't rouse him from the depths of his narcoleptic attacks. But in his deadened state, a more insidious parasomnic intruder often visited the somnolent bookkeeper.

Among his other anomalies, the neurologist called it Narcolepsy-Cataplexy Syndrome, commonly known as sleep paralysis with visual hallucinations. Unlike his routine narcoleptic attacks, sleep paralysis froze every muscle. Unable to move, he always felt a threatening presence in his room. Fear swelled to panic. His words were slurred as he tried to call out for help. With immobilized limbs and an anesthetized trachea, he thrashed about and moaned.

Sophia Griavkas, the office cleaner, found him at 5:30 AM. Unlike many who gossiped, averted their gaze, and avoided him like he had a contagious disease, the housekeeper had kind eyes that never looked away. Kneeling at his side, she gently touched his shoulder and said quietly, "I hear you moaning and groaning again, mister. Do you have another bad dream? Poor man. Here, let me help you up. You sit, yes? I bring water. Then you will feel better, okay?"

Carmine sat for another hour watching the sunrise and hearing the clatter of morning sounds in the reception area as the office came to life with greetings and muffled exchanges. The hangover of the night before began to set in. A visit from a phantasm he'd long thought was dead. Gone from his life, she'd returned to find him and bring an urgent message about something he couldn't quite recall. Something about a fantastic discovery, something about her needing him. But like before, E had gone, leaving nothing but memory crumbs behind.

He caught a whiff of the office manager's perfume, stood, and stumbled into the main reception area. The officious woman was busy posting something on the bulletin board while answering questions from one of the secretaries. She turned as the disheveled bookkeeper approached and eyed him disapprovingly.

"Sleeping in again, hmm? Do we need to get you jammies and a bathrobe, dear?" Chuckles from across the room. "Maybe you should take some time off. But, really dear, you don't look well."

The bewildered bookkeeper forced a smile and inched closer to the woman, who looked uneasy and backed up. "Is there something more? You seem––"

"Last night...um, th-th-there was a woman here. C-came to see me. We passed your office. I-I saw your light was––"

"What? Get it out, dear. Speak clearly so everyone can understand what you're trying to say."

"Just n-need to know...uh...did she leave a card, this woman. Did she leave anything for me? That's it. Did she, you know, s-speak to you?"

Pausing, she replied with a startled look, "What woman, dear? There was no one else here last night."

Chapter 3

Dihn

Monday, March 17, 8:30 AM

The office manager directed the confused bookkeeper into her office, sharply clapping her hands at the gawking office staff and sniping, "Back to work now, chickens." They instinctively obeyed, part out of habit, part out of fear. The lyrical folksiness of her voice belied the steeliness of her intent. LuCinda Pelcovey was not a person to cross.

Carmine's eyes burned as he followed her into an office thick with the noxious scent of perfume and the cobalt muddiness of her voice. Iterations of pi pushed to gain admission into his conscious mind to calm and protect against assaults to his senses. Her windowless office was tidy, buttressed by two large file cabinets adorned with a fan and a collection of small potted plants. On her desk was a clutter of tchotchkes, book-ended by neatly arranged pictures of children with oversized, silver-bracketed teeth and hair ribbons.

LuCinda signaled for him to take a seat, not with words, but with a glance and downward gesture of her meaty hand, for she was a large woman who used her commanding size and body language to intimidate and control.

"Dear, you don't seem well. Just look at you. I'm afraid that working late into the night has altered your perspective. My Uncle Roland, God rest his soul, never slept a wink after the war, and what a mess he was–– seeing things no one else saw, talking to the dog, and all such nonsense. Point is, you need to rest. I'll talk with Marvin. Let him know that you've come down with the flu or the likes. For all I know, that's what this is, hmm? The flu or some such virus that's gotten you stressed. We'll just tell him that you're out for a few days. It'll be between us, dear. You're overwrought with those nasty accounts that have gotten the best of you, hon."

He nodded, looking down at his mismatched shoes, one brown and the other black.

The office manager continued. "Maybe those pills you're taking are the problem, or perhaps you need to take more to help you correct your mistakes. Like Grandmother Pelcovey used to say, 'Mistakes are our teachers.' Most people here make those kinds of accounting errors, you know. I'm sure in your exhaustion, you misplaced a number here and added it over there. You really need to put all this out of your mind. Just go home, dear. Get into a real bed and sleep. Momma always said there's nothing that can't be fixed with a good night's sleep. Make sure the room is dark and cool. Now off you go, dear."

She spoke like a stage hypnotist inducing a trance. His thoughts remained jumbled, and not even Belphegor's prime number could rescue him. Words dribbled out.

"Okay. I guess... maybe I just, you know, got sort of mixed up. That's it. Tell Mr Shrenklin I can reconcile those accounts. Um, maybe a b...b...b-reak will help.... That's all."

"Yes, dear, that *is* all. Oh, you don't have to worry about Marvin or your little accounting error, dear. Not to worry. We'll deal with that nasty T-B CFC matter. I'm sure the naughty little figures will eventually balance out. I'll have Deena take a look. And as far as Marvin goes, I'll just wear something a little low cut, and he'll agree to whatever I tell him."

With a wink and reek of her rank cologne, the office manager leaned in and flashed her ample cleavage, which made the weary bookkeeper nauseous. "Your job is to go home. Sleep, now. Good lord, you need to sleep, dear, and forget about all this nonsense. Now scoot, off you go." With that, she steered him out of her office, turned her back, and shut the door.

He shuffled back to his office and grabbed his tattered coat and backpack. No one looked up or spoke as he walked through the reception area. All he heard were whispers he could not make out. He walked from the parking lot to the bus stop. He waited for Number 10, his mind unfocused yet restless, as unbidden images of E and LuCinda flashed through his brain. Maybe she was right. Exhaustion made sense. People make mistakes when they're tired. They even see things. He just needed to sleep, but what no one seemed to understand about narcolepsy was you're always tired, always in need of rest. She was definitely right about his mega doses of Adderall. Maybe he should take more or perhaps cut down. Pills kept him alert, but he needed to sleep, especially if he wasn't returning to work. He didn't like LuCinda Pelcovey but thought it was true that he needed a break. Maybe he could even sleep.

In his sparse studio apartment, unopened mail sat on the table. From the corner, a tawny-colored cat approached, stretched, and mewed.

"Hey, Raman, did you miss me, boy? You hungry, huh? See what we got here." Raman followed his best friend to the small pantry, where a box of Kibbles awaited. The cat sidled up and purred. Next to mathematics, Raman helped soothe his frazzled nerves.

The bookkeeper had arranged his life neatly into a single room––his bed next to a small closet, old couch, chair, lamp, table, and a massive bookcase, which took up most of the wall. The shelves were lined with volumes of obscure mathematicians and their proofs. There was a single shelf devoted to books about Srinivasa Ramanujan. On the bottom shelf sat several dusty accounting books and a battered binder containing Wiley CPA Exam review materials. After his 3rd attempt to take the exam, he accepted that he could not remain awake through all four sections and would never become a CPA. Instead, he would stay a bookkeeper, as Ramanujan had once been.

Time to try to sleep. He lay down and shut his eyes, hoping to trick his brain into thinking that sleep would come naturally.

But after 20 minutes, he was up again; his brain suddenly powered on, and his thoughts were captured by E.

TEARS ARE ONLY WATER

"She *was* real," he said to the cat. "Not imagined. E came back to me after all these years. Not dead, but alive, hidden away, making incredible discoveries, and changing the world, And she found me, *needed* me. I need to be ready."

It was so much like E to have fooled the world and disappeared to work secretly in a hidden lab doing research that would change the world. And now, they, no, *she* wanted him. He searched his memory to piece together fragments of what she'd spoken so urgently.

"A combination of amino acids...on the 13th codon...your amazing math talents and coding skills...everything will change...watch for the signs... I'll come when it's time."

Meanwhile, he should try to summon the magic of numbers once more and reclaim what had been lost. But first, he would need more pills.

The bookkeeper splashed water on his face and gobbled several loose capsules beside Ramanujan's Collected Works on his nightstand. There were things he must research. He bounded over to his table and opened his computer. Raman jumped on his lap and put his tiny paws on the keyboard. Until now, he'd promised sister Anne to never search for E online. The professor had urged him to file those memories away and move on, reminding him that he'd never been more than E's science project.

As usual, he'd begrudgingly heeded his sister's cautions and stayed away from late-night searches on the internet. Besides, he'd figured that Googling E would only bring up information until her disappearance. To go beyond the public record, he needed a more powerful search engine like the one on the discs he'd gotten from Dihn.

Dihn, whose real name was Carl Carothers, lived in a one-room apartment surrounded by computer screens, where he and a small group of misfits sometimes hung out, worshiping numbers, data sets, 0's and 1's.

Although the others seemed a colorless composite of computer nerds, Dihn was the closest thing Carmine had to a true friend. An ex-marine with a sandy brown aura, he'd once worked as an analyst at NSI but was fired for doing personal data searches on company time. Dihn had become obsessed with discovering his roots and was one of the first to send his saliva to a startup company called Ancestry.com. The results came back that his family, the Dihns, originated in Can Tho, Vietnam, and he had many relatives in surrounding villages. Though there was nothing remotely Asian about the Oklahoma Native, Carl became obsessed and began calling himself "Dihn." Soon, others in his small band of brothers followed suit. He began writing to a Dihn Van Duc in Can Tho, who said he knew nothing about a familial connection with anyone from Oklahoma and that Carl should stop writing. Undeterred, Carl bought a ticket to visit his family in Can Tho but received an urgent call from an executive from Ancestry before he left. The man sheepishly apologized, saying they'd somehow mixed up his saliva sample with that of a Vietnamese registrant from San Jose. If Carl signed an NDA, they agreed to quietly wire him a five-figure settlement for any inconvenience. He agreed. The family connection to Can Tho was severed, but the name stuck.

Inserting one of the special discs Dihn had lent him when trying to find Ramanujan's unpublished letters to Hardy, Carmine anxiously typed in E's name and began his search. *Sorry, Sister, just a peek.* The screen lit up with links to stories and pictures of Elizabeth Hooper Covington. He clicked on a link, and there was the face lodged in his memories––E in all her splendor, quizzically smiling in the camera's direction. No one knew what was hidden beneath her inscrutable smile.

The bookkeeper read about her becoming a Davidson Fellow in high school and then remembered that she'd won an AAN Neuroscience Research Prize for her paper on codon capture theory. Link after link appeared attesting to her academic, scientific, and athletic achievements. Each hit hollowed out his stomach as he tried to shake off feelings that trailed behind. He rapidly scanned through scores of press links chronicling her notoriety. Articles from the Boston Globe––"Covington

Dominates IC4A Pentathlon;" "MIT Freshman Takes to the Charles in Harvard-MIT Regatta;" "Say it Ain't So: Covington to Take Her Talents to Palo Alto;" "Ex-MIT Stanford Fellow to Head Genetics Lab;" and finally, "Covington Becomes Youngest Member of the Human Genome Project."

Everything he read, he'd known before and effectively had managed to forget. The professor would have been proud. He was never sure how much his sister's indoctrination efforts were for his benefit or hers. For all he knew, she was guinea-pigging him to develop a new psychological theory. Anne's words came back. "Find a compartment and file it away, Carmie. Remembering is your enemy now." Bracing himself for what would come next, the bookkeeper forced himself to read articles in the Denver Post and Palo Alto Daily News about her hit-and-run accident in February 1995.

He kept hearing his sister's warnings. "For God's sake, brother, stay away from the internet. Too much information about a past you can't change will toxify your brain." The bookkeeper felt the weight of her words as he opened each link. A gnawing in his gut brought a thought about Freud's Ratman, with his fantasies of vermin crawling through his intestines. Was this hunger or fatigue? Was he overdosing on these pills, or was it something else?

The articles beckoned long repressed images while the bookkeeper recited his mantra, $e^{i\pi} + 1 = 0$, $e^{i\pi} + 1 = 0$. He reached for another orange pill and pressed on. The final few links were to articles about her disappearance in 1998. Mary Beth Hanson and others from her lab talked about changes they'd noticed in her appearance and behavior. "It's as if her bright light burned out. Elizabeth just changed. All that was left was her scribbled note, which read, 'It's time.'"

That was it. They'd never found her body. She vanished, leaving no trace or trail of crumbs. Her family, seeking closure, finally accepted the narrative that she was bipolar and had chosen to end her life by jumping off the Bay Bridge. Even with Dihn's enhanced search tools, the stories ended with her sudden disappearance. And that was it. Nothing hidden had been revealed, only the traces of E that had escaped their compartments.

He got up and looked at the titles in his bookcase, hoping to bury the stroboscopic afterimages under the weight of byzantine equations and abstruse proofs, but it didn't work. He was not finished. If anyone could find someone off the grid, it was Dihn, who'd worked on Freenet and helped develop Tor, which opened a portal to the internet's dark underbelly. No one could navigate the waters of the dark web and find traces invisible to more conventional searches like Dihn.

Because Dihn stayed up through the night and didn't respond to texts before 2:00 PM, the bookkeeper would have to wait for an answer. Meanwhile, there was more he could research on his own. Although he'd missed much of what E was trying to tell him last night, he remembered the embers of her fiery appeal. He took another pill, made a pot of coffee, and then reviewed all he'd learned long ago about genetic sequencing and codon theory. How could he have dreamed about something he knew so little about? He spent another two hours poring over articles about genetic codes and the advanced math in sequencing research. The bookkeeper searched for the numbers in the codes; the answer would be in the numbers. He sat back and rubbed his eyes. Isn't this why she came to him? A riddle hidden in the codes that she knew only he could solve.

Chapter 4

Reading Codes

Monday, March 17, 2:00 PM

"Tired and wired" was one of the few phrases the bookkeeper remembered from his semester at MIT. In the dining room, when people would ask each other if they were ready for an exam, the standard answer after pulling an all-nighter was, "Tired, but cylinders are wired."

The rest was a blur. Long ago, he'd found a compartment to stuff most of his memories of those unhappy months in Cambridge. After the first quarter, he'd stopped attending classes. Despite E's goading, he couldn't keep up, nor was he particularly interested in doing so. Instead, he spent his nights reading old mathematics tomes unearthed from the musty stacks of Hayden Library, which left little time for reading assigned texts or keeping up with his labs. The gray November sky and chill from the Charles River matched his mood and cooled his desire to stay, even if it meant being close to E. He withdrew before January.

He felt that wired, tired feeling now. Exhausted, every cell slavishly begged for rest while the overlord cracked his whip and commanded, "More! There is more you must do!" Ignoring the ache in his shoulders and neck, he feverishly read article after article on genomic sequencing, codon theory, and trinucleotide repeat expansion disorders. Finally, he remembered that the DNA sequence of a gene gets written into RNA and becomes processed as a messenger, or mRNA. The messengers carry a code of three nucleotides, which the cells must decipher. The three nucleotides are the "codons." There are a total of 64 possible patterns of codons. Hadn't she said something about the 13th codon?

The sun was high overhead and peeked through his drawn blinds. Raman wanted attention and crawled up on his lap. "That's right, Rama. It's here, what she was trying to tell me." Reaching for another pill, he opened the next batch of articles.

Fragments of E's words lingered. She said international research teams had already amassed information about genetic components of major mental health conditions like Autism, ADHD, Bipolar Disorder, Schizophrenia, and Major Depression. Still, no available genetic tests or scans could predict or prevent these conditions. So, what her team had discovered was utterly unknown and projected years into the future.

His search was halted by the sound of a car outside his apartment. Vigilant by nature, the bookkeeper noticed the comings and goings outside his apartment. The infusion of Adderall into his system made him startle easily. He peered through the blinds. A white Nissan with a dented fender drove slowly by his apartment. Odd that a car he'd never seen would be circling his parking lot.

A loud buzzing from the alarm he'd set for 2:00 PM alerted him it was time to awaken Dihn.

He texted, "It's me. Need help to find someone who's disappeared. A ghost, maybe. Your super discs came up empty."

Another 30 minutes passed before Dihn responded, "Come on over, and we'll take a peek."

Carmine took the Number 10 and transferred at Alameda and 4th. His second bus was late. A regular patron of the RTD, he'd come to recognize most of the bus drivers but not this one. With her long reddish hair and stylish nail art, she looked out of place. He stepped onboard as she glanced at him and winked, further unnerving his wired and tired brain. He found a seat in the back where he could keep an eye on her.

Dihn had few visitors to his cramped apartment. A droning hum vibrated throughout the dingy room, lit only by the unnatural light from multiple screens fixed on every wall and surface. Dihn always dressed in an old military fatigue jacket. He had a patchy gray beard and long, stringy hair tied in a ponytail. He never bothered with small talk. Their conversation was largely transactional––long on problem-solving and short on chit-chat and back story. But Dihn never refused a request to help his "pals" with background searches.

Cracking his knuckles, he said, "What'ya got for me, Carm?" His head vibrated almost imperceptibly as he spoke. "Man, you feelin' alright? You're not lookin' too good."

Stories about personal relationships and feelings rarely gained admission into Dihn's small group of like-minded travelers. Once, a group member had too many beers and spilled his guts and tears about an old girlfriend who'd left him for a sailor. The group, collectively high on IQ but low on EQ, listened as the man sobbed. No one moved or interrupted. When he'd finished, the bookkeeper blurted out how he once had feelings for a woman who killed herself long ago.

There was a long pause until Dihn said, "Hey, fellers, got ahold of some classified shee-it from the Pentagon that'll make yer eyes bug out." The others moved in close, and that was that.

The bookkeeper stammered through the events of the last 14 hours–– an account that wouldn't balance, money out and money in, a visit from a dead woman with a message about the 13th codon, an office manager's strange denial, a white car circling the parking lot outside his apartment, and a peculiar-looking bus driver.

Dihn knelt by a small safe and spun the dial until it clicked open. He pulled out a lock box, which he opened with the key he wore around his neck. Using two gnarly fingers, he fished out three discs and, with a lover's gentle touch, placed them in his palm.

"There ya are, my darlin's. Come to Papa." He put them one at a time on the velvety pad next to his computer. After adjusting his wrist splints, he gingerly inserted the first into his massive CPU. "Hmm, this'll take some time, Carm. You can stay if ya want, but it's better you head on out. I'll text when I've got something. If she's out there, we'll find her. Can't hide from ol' Dihn and his darlin's."

The bookkeeper returned to the bus stop. The late afternoon sun warmed his face as he searched for an old equation or two to settle his mind, but all formulae led back to E and her late-night visit. On the bus, he tried mulling over what he'd read about the genetics of mental illness, but his twitchy mind would not allow for an inward gaze. Instead, he scanned the other passengers, looking for a sign or pattern hidden in plain sight. And there it was. A man who'd gotten on after him, wearing a long coat, a black ballcap, and dark sunglasses, which didn't seem of much functional use as the sun was low in the sky. Usually, passengers shut their eyes, read, looked at their feet, or gazed mindlessly out the window, but this man seemed to be looking at the wary bookkeeper. The man got off but stood watching as the bus pulled away.

Carmine tried to compose himself. He shut his eyes and began to count, much as he had when he was a child before he'd learned anything about the complexities of higher mathematics. But, when he opened them, it was dark. He'd fallen asleep and was in an unfamiliar part of town with a grouchy bus driver trying to wake him.

"Hey, buddy. HEY! Mister sleepy. At the end of the line here. You gotta get up and get off. I got my own life to live, ya know."

The somnolent bookkeeper exited and wandered into a Denny's. It had been 24 hours since he'd eaten anything more than Adderall chased down by caffeine. He found a booth in the back and ordered a bowl of soup and a pot of coffee. He swallowed two more pills and checked his phone. Nothing from Dihn. On full alert now, he surveilled the surrounding tables and booths. Finally, around 10:30 PM, Dihn texted and told him to call. "Better talk straight up on this one, pal."

Carmine started to dial Dihn's number but was distracted by loud laughter from the other side of the restaurant.

A woman was sitting with the man in the black ball cap, who was still wearing his sunglasses. Both turned their heads toward the bookkeeper.

TEARS ARE ONLY WATER

E had said she'd send a signal. Seeing this man twice in one day was no coincidence. Carmine found himself walking over to their table. His movements felt pre-programmed, as if he were being willed by an external agency. He heard the distant echo of his sister's annoying voice, "Just let this go. Take a breath and count or factor some polynomials, for God's sake, Carmine."

As he approached their table, the woman turned toward him and giggled. She had dark hair and a sleeve of garish tattoos. She looked back at the man and whispered something. Both seemed startled by the appearance of a disheveled bookkeeper standing at the edge of their table.

"Um, 'scuse me. I would like to say, um, I saw you on the b...b...b-us earlier...."

The man stared curiously and shrugged, "And?"

"I, um, thought you might have something you needed to tell me, like, you know... I'm not sure, but is there a m-m-message?"

The man looked at the woman and then sized up Carmine from head to toe. "Yeah... sure, d-d-d-dude. There is something I'd like to say. Take your shiny-ass shoes and leave us the fuck alone, creep! There's the door."

"B...b...b-ut, I saw you on the Number 10. That's all. Sorry...but−−"

The tattooed woman snickered. "Hey, Stuttering Stephen, get the 'ell away from us, ya bloody nonce. You heard 'im dumbo!"

C-C-C-Carmine, Bunny-ears, Mickey, Earmuffs, Bugs, Lop-ears, Frisbee head, Jar Jar Binks, and always, Dumbo. Yes, he heard them all before.

The guy laughed. "Fuck off, mutant!"

The ordinarily taciturn bookkeeper swung his hand and slapped the black cap off the man's head. Black Cap leaped to his feet, but the woman restrained him, "Hey luv, not worth breakin' a sweat over this nutter here."

Carmine stumbled as he backed away, hurried to the front door, and ran to the bus stop. Panting heavily, he looked to see if the man had come after him. He tried to seek safety in Euler's number but, in his frenzy, couldn't find it. He took a deep breath and dialed Dihn.

"Man, I got nothin' for you. Either she never died like they said she did, or she was scrubbed by pros." Dihn sounded deflated. He and his darlins had met their match––been defeated. "Maybe ya dreamed this all, ya know. Just sayin'. You said you haven't been sleeping. The mind can play tricks. That shit happens. Either that or...no one ever wants her to be found. If she's out there, I can't find her. Sorry, Carm...sorry."

This was not what he wanted to hear. But maybe all this with E was just a crazy dream. Too little sleep and too much Adderall had addled his brain. The dead don't come back. Death is a constant, not a variable. Like the numbers he couldn't coax back, E was gone and had been gone long before she ever disappeared. None of this was real. It was time to go home.

As he unlocked the door to his apartment, he spotted the same white Nissan parked on the street. The driver flashed the lights. Another sign? This time the disillusioned bookkeeper decided to heed his sister's words, "Let this one go and lock it away. Don't tilt at windmills, Carmie." He was exhausted.

Carmine put some food out for Raman and lay fully clothed on his bed. Sleep finally visited, but it brought with it the dreaded paralysis. He was trapped and couldn't move or sound the urgently needed warning. Asleep but awake, dreaming yet terrified. The face at his window peered in, searching for him. Frozen in place as if poison darts of curare had been blown into his skin. He moaned, but no one could hear––only Raman, who jumped onto his chest when the cat heard his best friend's slurred cries for help. With a start, the bookkeeper was freed from his paralytic prison.

It was beginning to get light. After a shower and a bowl of cereal, he decided to go back to Shrenklin's. He would explain to the office manager that he was feeling better. He'd gotten the rest she'd prescribed and knew he could lure the numbers back and close out the books for Tawney-Banks. So, he poured coffee, downed a few more pills, and took the bus to work. There had been no white car in front of his apartment and no strange people getting on and off the bus.

It was early enough that he could slip into the building unnoticed. He walked through the dark reception area and felt the way to his office. Once there, he shut the door and refocused his mind as he prepared to re-examine the T-B spreadsheets. Fresh air would sharpen his senses. He opened the window, and the crisp pre-dawn air cleared his mind. The numbers would return as they always had. His friends would not abandon him for long. His mother had taken him to see therapists as a child because he had stopped talking. His sister always said, "Numbers are my brother's muse. Don't talk to him about his feelings; just count with him."

Sunlight peeked through his blinds, and there was a rustling in the office beyond his door. He heard the chatter of voices and the clicking of keyboards and inhaled the aroma of coffee brewing. He sat at his desk to begin working but was locked out of his computer. Unsuccessful after several attempts to log in, the bookkeeper recalled a company memo that the IT system was being updated. Yet...why could he hear keyboard strokes in the outer office if this was so?

He listened.... Wait, what was that? The patterning of the keyboard strokes. Why had he never paid attention to these before? He listened. They were different this morning.

"Tap...tap...tap, tap, tap." Then, a "click, click...clickety, clickety." A code! This was it. He reached for a pen and paper and wrote down the sequence of taps and clicks. There had to be a message of some sort hidden in the pattern of keystrokes. *Just like E. How ingenious!* No one would ever notice. Hidden in plain sight. No one could detect that these were anything but random sounds from an office coming to life. But the bookkeeper knew differently now. He was fully wired and on fire to crack the code he knew was being sent. It was time. As he leaned in, he saw something lying under his couch. Squinting, he knelt and reached for the object partially obscured by the front of the sofa, lifting it to the light. In his hand...he held a glove.

He inspected it for a full minute. Bringing it close to his nose, he inhaled the lavender scent. Then, the bookkeeper remembered. Hadn't E taken off her gloves and dropped them on the couch? One must have fallen before she left.... Proof that she had been here! LuCinda lied about this. What the hell was she hiding!? He had to find her and confront her with his evidence.

The bookkeeper never moved quickly, but he did now. He charged out of his office. Heads turned as he bumped into the water cooler and found the office manager pinning a schedule on the bulletin board. She turned as he approached, looking both startled and displeased that he had returned so soon.

"Excuse me?" She lowered her voice. "I thought I told you, dear, that you needed to go home and get well." She continued to speak quietly through her teeth. "You shouldn't be here. Now, gather your things and leave. Chop, chop now! Out you go. You need rest."

For the second time within eight hours, the bookkeeper made the mistake of abruptly invading another's physical space, first with the black-hatted stranger and now with the irritated office manager. He shoved the glove toward her face.

"W...w...w-hat the hell is this?! I-I found it in my office."

"A g-g-glove," she mocked as others giggled. "Oh good, you found it. Sophia's been looking all over for that. Thank you. I'll make sure to give it to her. Now, you need to leave. Do you hear me? Now!"

He knew she was lying. Every word from her thin-lipped mouth was a deception. He moved a step closer. Speaking with volume and intensity that no one had ever heard, Carmine shouted,

"IT'S NOT THE HOUSEKEEPER'S G-GLOVE! E WAS here last night! The woman you said wasn't here. She left this. Why are you doing this to me?"

TEARS ARE ONLY WATER

The office manager glared and spewed a rush of burnt charcoal threats. "Back off now and get the hell out of here! I will call the police! Oh, and you can leave your keys on the desk. You're done here." She turned to the crowd of sycophants, "Do you believe this idiot, this lunatic, this stuttering piece of--"

Before she could complete her scathing rant, the bookkeeper mindlessly lunged at her, his fingers closed around the fleshy folds of her neck.

Deafening shrieks pierced his eardrums and rattled the rafters. Though in that awful moment, the unhinged bookkeeper shocked the onlookers with his frenzied attack, her monstrous screams assaulted their collective senses. His fingers acted under their own command and held firmly to her neck. He willed them to let go, but before he could loosen his grip, he was tackled by one of Shrenklin's hefty interns. Corbel Cornsmooth, a hygienically-challenged man-boy with a rust-colored aura, had been an all-conference tackle for the Broomfield Eagles before he'd blown out his knee and put on an extra 80 lbs. Called "Doughboy" by the secretaries and accounting staff, Corbel's sluggish movements would have typically eluded time-lapse photography. But not today. Like a beefy panther, he flattened the unsuspecting bookkeeper, who broke like a plywood plank. Another intern piled on and positioned himself firmly on the breathless bookkeeper's chest. When it was clear he'd been subdued, the second intern delivered a sucker punch and shattered Carmine's glasses.

With one good eye, he watched the crowd huddle around the office manager, whose screams had softened to a loud whimper. Disembodied chatter in the room sounded a chorus of shock and contempt.

"Hooollly crap, I knew ol' Rain Man would lose it!"

"It's always the quiet ones. You could tell he wasn't right."

"Wouldn't look you in the eye. Did ya ever see him crack his head on the keyboard when he zonked out?"

The office manager's assistant tried to comfort her boss. "Shh Shh, hon. Lemme see your neck now, Lu. Ooh, that's ugly. Would someone call 911? Call–call the goddam police!"

Time loses its linearity in moments like these. The bookkeeper's eyes stung, and his chest had collapsed. A large intern called "Doughboy" had broken his ribs and another his glasses. For a moment, the panic of suffocation was all there was. Other feelings——shock, humiliation, and a realization of what he'd just done——had to wait their turn. Gasping for air took precedence as the light faded from his one working eye, and then whoosh, the candle was blown out.

Chapter 5

EEP!

Tuesday, March 18, 8:30 AM

The bookkeeper regained consciousness as he felt a thick hand slapping his face. Someone had propped him against a file cabinet like a limp hand puppet. Two deputies knelt in front of him. A bald officer smacked him again and said, "We're taking you into custody, dimwit."

The other deputy, a tall Black woman with a sympathetic look, grabbed her partner's shoulder and said, "Cut the crap, Jerry, enough!" She lowered her voice, "You don't wanna make me write you up for this shit again." She leaned over and placed her hand on the bookkeeper's limp arm. "Sir? Sir! Can you hear me? Lotta witnesses here say you assaulted that woman over there." Two EMTs placed the large office manager on a gurney. "I'm Deputy Kitts. Can you tell us what happened? Why'd you go after her like that?" Fifteen pairs of eyes pointed toward him like daggers. "Sir? Hey. Sir. What gives?"

Carmine tried to speak, but words were always challenging. Each breath brought searing pain. He was desperate to explain how the office manager had lied and how others were tapping out codes on their keyboards, but all he could do was gasp an incoherent sputter of para-noid-sounding gibberish. That was all the deputy needed to hear.

"Okay, my friend, we'll take you in for more questions. See if we can sort all this out and get you some help." He winced, and she said EMTs would check him out at the station.

She turned to her heavy-handed partner, "I don't like the looks of this crowd. We gotta get him out of here now. Watch his ribs when we lift him." They helped him to his feet and shuffled him toward the door. "The backup can take statements when they get here. Let's get him into the cruiser."

The glaring light and cool air intensified his pain. Finally, they steered him into the back seat of their vehicle. The bald deputy picked up the radio, "This is 451. We have a nutcase from the 10-46 assault at 600 Devils Horn Rd. ETA in 15. Over and out."

He reached for the siren, but the female deputy stopped him. "Really? Come on, Jerry."

He smirked, ignored his partner, and turned on the siren.

They drove to the Arapahoe County Sheriff's Department and parked the cruiser. Jerry opened the back door and grabbed the prisoner's arm. The female nudged him aside, gently eased Carmine from the back seat, and guided him to the interview room. "Okay, Jerry, you got the paperwork on this one. I'll find the sheriff and tell him what we got." She leaned over to Carmine and said, "So this is where I get off. The rest of these guys'll take you to your next dance. Hope you can get all this sorted out. See if I can find a medic to check you out."

He nodded, and a river of pain flooded from his cheek to his right flank. The bookkeeper searched for Euler's formula to anesthetize the pain. Finding nothing but a yawning void, he stammered his thanks. Through one eye, he surveyed her face. There was something in the lines around her eyes, but he had no idea what it was.

She left, and five minutes later, the sheriff lumbered in. He wore his uniform as neatly as his bulky frame and stooped shoulders would allow. His pants were baggy and hung on the floor. A button was missing from his shirt, which had a stain on the collar––a souvenir from breakfast or last night's dinner? The sheriff's impressive belly hung over his belt line. Pulling his pants up and his glasses down on his nose, he looked through the papers he'd brought in.

TEARS ARE ONLY WATER

The bookkeeper attempted to speak, but the sheriff silenced him with his hand as he flipped through the arrest papers. When he finished, he set them down and, with a cigarette voice, coughed and said,

"I'm Sheriff Burwinkle. What do they call ya, son?" He glanced down at the pages and stumbled with the name. "What is it––Carmen, somethin' like that?" Sounds I-talian, huh?"

Not waiting for a response, he continued, "Okay, son, here's the deal, we're looking at some pretty serious assault charges. Open and shut, looks like to me. Couldn't ask for any more witnesses, all sayin' the same thing. Got two of 'em sayin' they heard you threaten to kill her. That right? Cuz, it looks like we got ya dead to rights, son. And, oh, you attacked the wrong woman. LuCinda Pelcovey's been an upstanding friend of this department for quite some time now. Yep, yep, ya don't go messin with LuCinda. Nope, ya really crossed the line on that one. So, we got her statement. By the way, EMTs had to go take her to the ER, and you can be sure she's pressin' charges. It looks like a slam dunk assault in the 1st degree. All that's missin' here is your statement. So, why'd you go after her like that? Ya coulda killed her. Had somethin' against her, I reckon. So, what gives here, son?"

As he tried to answer, Carmine felt a bolt of pain, not all of which came from his broken ribs and bashed-in eye. Under the best circumstances, people paid more attention to how he spoke than what he had to say. His typically tortured speech became more tangled and sputtered when he was anxious. So, he'd learned to hide in silence. But he desperately wanted, no, *needed* to tell anyone who would listen what had happened. His speech became pressured. With a flurry of words, he tried to explain it all––the numbers on the accounts that kept changing ––a visit by a woman who'd committed suicide many years before but hadn't really–– people watching and following him––an office manager who was hiding something––officemates sending coded messages on their keyboards–– and how he was about to figure it all out.

As expected, his staccato spew of misshapen sentences was disastrous. The goulash of words and half-finished conspiratorial charges sounded the alarm of incoherence and delusionality.

The sheriff's expression softened as he sat back and took a deep breath.

"Okay, son.... I got ya now. Seen this kind of thing before. Had me a brother, but that's a story for another day. Get ya some water or somethin'? Sounds like maybe yer either on somethin' or need somethin' to help with all this." He picked up the phone, "Hey, hon. Yeah, can ya bring us all some water or a Coke, maybe, and get an EEP ready? And while yer at it, give ol' Judge Rainsford a call and tell him we're gonna need some paperwork. Yeah, I also need ya to arrange a prisoner transport to MCA, would ya, Marlene, hon. Oh, and see about gettin' contact information for his next of kin. I'll plan to be giving 'em a call later."

He hung up and stood. "Don't think we can help ya here right now, son. Seems ya got some bigger fish to fry before we can get to yer other shitstorm with LuCinda." With a sorrowful smile, he trudged out into the hallway. Twenty minutes later, a female officer brought a Coke, but his hands were still cuffed.

"I'll try to find you a straw. But, sorry, the cuffs have to stay on."

As she was leaving, Carmine asked, "What's an EEP?"

"Emergency Evaluation Petition. They're taking you to the hospital."

It took more than an hour to arrange for transport, and no one came to check on his ribs. His escorts were the same two deputies who'd brought him in earlier. The female deputy didn't look surprised when she came to pick up her prisoner.

"Well, I guess that wasn't our last dance." Deputy Kitts glanced at the papers to read his last name. "So, Mr Luedke, looks like we're taking you to the Emergency Department for them to check you out. They can look at your ribs at MCA. Sorry, doesn't look like anyone here has gotten to you yet."

The other one, Jerry, the slapper, grabbed the bookkeeper by the collar with one hand and tugged at the handcuffs with his other. "C'mon, Nicola, let's just get this done. Don't coddle him, for Chrissake. You

TEARS ARE ONLY WATER

know the sheriff wants you to be more of a cop and to stop this sociologist crap. Are you forgetting what he did to poor Mama Lu back there? Kooks like him get what's coming to them."

Kitts sighed and quietly said, "Moron. No siren this time."

Together they stood in the ER waiting room with the handcuffed prisoner between them. No words passed until a nurse arrived and directed the trio to an examining room. A young Middle Eastern doctor entered and asked the deputies to wait outside.

"No can do, Doc," Jerry said. "He might be here on an EEP, but he's facing assault one, so we're sticking to him like white on rice. So just get your examination thing done so we can get on with this, okay, Haji?"

The doctor stared uncomfortably at Jerry, who glared back.

Nicola tried to deflect her partner's racial slur. "Look, ignore my partner's bad manners. We'll just sit back here while you do your examination, Doctor, but we can't take his cuffs off and leave this room. He was complaining about his ribs, so you'll want someone to check those too."

The doctor wore an ill-fitting white coat with a name tag that read "K. Kashimi, M.D. Intern." A stethoscope draped his narrow shoulders, framing a pocket with note cards and too many pens. A large pair of horn-rimmed glasses dwarfed his tiny face. A thin grove of facial hair lined his upper lip. New to the Psychiatry Service, this was Kaspar's first shift on call in the ER.

His hands shook as he pulled open a metal chart, clicked his pen, and cleared his throat.

"So, they say you assaulted this woman at your place of work. Is this so?" The doctor waited uncomfortably for a response, which was not forthcoming. He pulled a stack of index cards from his pocket with notes he'd scribbled after his supervision session with the esteemed Chief of Psychiatry, Dr Jonas. He fumbled through the cards and dropped them.

The female deputy bent to pick them up and got a good look at the notes before returning them.

41

J. HERMAN KLEIGER

- *Engage senses when assessing a patient. What do we know from how he looks?*
- *Notice shoes and his fingernails.*
- *Clothes washed? Most importantly, how does he smell?*
- *Anxiety smells different from depression, and rage has a burning, pungent odor.*
- *Listen to sound of patient's voice and register cadence of speech.*
- *Pay less attention to the words. They will trick and mislead.*

The young intern cleared his throat again and began to sniff loudly. "It says here that you believed your co-workers, and this woman you assaulted, were trying to play tricks on you." He looked for a reaction and jotted a note.

"Yes, I see. The report from the sheriff's department says that it was also your belief that the others in your office were sending coded messages to each other on their computer keyboards and that you concluded they were hiding something, possibly wanting to hurt you. Is this true?"

Carmine became agitated and pulled at his restraints. His speech was loud and frenzied. "THERE WAS T-TAPPING. I know codes and ciphers, I found her g-glove, they were sending messages, I had p...p-roof, she knew it but was lying. That's all."

The intern continued to sniff while feverishly jotting notes. "Yes, yes. Go on. Tapping and hidden codes, you say. Very good. Yes, and you thought they were out to get you. Is this correct? Tell me about the glove." But it was too late. His patient's head drooped, and he began to snore.

The intern turned toward the deputies and shrugged. He reached over and tapped the man's feet, but to no avail; his patient remained unconscious.

"Excuse me, Doctor," the female deputy said. "This man needs to have someone look at his ribs. He's been in a lot of pain, but I'm not sure why he's fallen asleep."

TEARS ARE ONLY WATER

The intern responded, "Yes, yes, most assuredly. Of course. But first, I must establish a differential diagnosis--a classical form of paranoid schizophrenia--for his admission papers. Then we'll do a tox screen and all the laboratory studies, I assure you."

Kashimi completed the admission papers, only to have his patient suddenly awaken with a jolt. Slurring his words, Carmine thrashed his arms violently against the restraints. He arched his back and frantically tried to move his legs. It had been too long since his last dose of Adderall, and unbeknownst to the young intern, his patient was showing signs of withdrawal.

Taken aback by the frantic movements of his patient, the intern scribbled more notes in the chart. The patient is showing signs of agitated catatonia--a condition Jonas had recently described in his seminar. He called the nurse to arrange for the patient to be taken to inpatient psychiatry. Then, with a self-satisfied nod to the deputies, he left the room.

The bookkeeper was restrained to a gurney and wheeled upstairs. The female deputy stood at the nursing station, arguing that the patient was still a prisoner and that they would need to post a guard outside his room.

Several nurses and aides transferred him to a bed and attached a new set of restraints. A tech rolled a cart in, tried to find a serviceable vein, and drew several vials of blood. Another placed a line in his arm and hung a bag on an IV pole. The drugs dripped in, burning at first, then cooling to an even flow. He was determined not to lose consciousness again. $e^{i\pi} + 1 = 0...e^{i\pi} + 1 = 0... e^{i\pi}....$ This was no time to pass out. But that's what he did.

Delta brain waves signaled a deep slumberous state, which, aided by the Ativan drip, brought paralysis of his limbs and larynx while he remained mentally alert and agitated. The threat felt immediate. A sharp awareness. The paradox of a wakeful sleep while unable to wake, let alone move. Known but unknown. Carmine willed himself to hide so she

43

couldn't find him in the room. It was always the same terror with the woman at the window and his urgent need to escape her gaze so she couldn't find him. *Must move NOW!* His silent words sounded an alarm, but his lifeless limbs could not respond.

Yet, tonight, there was something new, something different from before. In her searching eyes, he sensed a soft familiarity. In his dreamer's vision, he saw a faded scar aside one eye. At once, he knew whose face was at his window. She is searching for him! He remembered E's words, "It's time." He knew why she had come! He struggled to form the words and cry out, but all he managed was a drooling, babbling slur. "P...p...p-lease...Pease. Hep me...Peeasse...E... EEEEEEEE. Pease...EEEEPPPP!"

Chapter 6

This is Anne

Tuesday, March 18, 11:47 PM

A ringing phone in the middle of the night never foretells anything good. Unless you've given birth and calls are made to expectant family members, she knew that no one calls at midnight to bring you good news. Someone's in trouble--Uncle Mortie's had a heart attack; there's been a terrible accident; a tree's fallen onto the garage. It's never anything good.

Such was the case tonight when she was awakened by the clatter of her phone. She'd purposely set the ringer on her new iPhone 6 Plus to a raucous tone. If someone tried to reach her, she didn't need to be regaled by some sweet melody or riff from a popular tune.

The professor reached for the phone, trying not to wake the snoring woman beside her. Noa had crawled into bed after her PM shift in the ER, leaving her scrubs in an untidy pile on the floor.

"This is Anne Schivalone," she whispered, "and who the hell is calling at this ungodly hour?"

"Anne Shivolino? Not sure I'm sayin' it right." A male voice. Midwestern twang.

Oh great, a new butchering of her name. "It's Professor Schivalone, but that's close enough. So, who is this?"

"Oh, Sch-va-lone, kinda like the actor, Sylvester Stallone, ol' Rambo. Gotcha. This is Sheriff Oliver Burwinkle, ma'am, from the Aurora

County Sheriff's Department out here in Colorado. We got yer name from yer brother, Carmen, who we had to bring in this mornin'."

Anne shot up in bed. "Oh my God, Carmie! What's wrong? Is he okay!?" Adrenaline shot through her veins, temporarily distracting her from the hangover that lay in waiting. The police calling in the middle of the night about Carmie! *For Christ's sake, what was wrong with him now?!*

"Well, ma'am, Yeah, I guess you could say he's all right, but he was involved in an incident at his place of work this mornin'. Wanted to get to you earlier but took us a while to track down his next of kin."

Her head began to pound. "Sheriff, for God's sake, what happened to him?"

Noa stopped snoring and moaned her discontent with the midnight clatter. She turned over and snapped a pillow over her head.

"Yeah, well, like I said, he's basically okay. Got some bruises in the take-down after the incident, but he'll live. Seems like this brother of yers attacked a woman at work. Just went off on her. Bunch of witnesses saw the whole thing. Have all their statements. They're sayin' he assaulted her plain as can be. We got a pretty big deal on our hands, Miss Shivalin. Figger she'll be pressin charges. So, tween you and me, yer brother Carmen will be facin' a pretty serious situation."

Anne tried to settle her tattered nerves. Deep breaths. In and out. Just focus and get rid of the emotional detritus. But intrusive images of a shy and awkward brother elbowed their way in, making it difficult to focus.

Before, it had always been calls from doctors but never the police. Carmine's lifelong problems were rivaled only by his gentleness and quiet brilliance. Never any violence, even when faced with the taunting of cruel bullies. Carmine would never hurt a fly. She flashed back to an image of an 8-year-old boy who didn't even know how to swim, rescuing insects from a neighborhood pool.

. . .

Such memories never did any good. The professor put the intruders back into their compartments, so she could refocus on the slow-talking sheriff from Colorado.

"Okay, Sheriff. I'll catch the first flight out. This isn't like him at all."

"Sure, but there's another thing here, ma'am.... Yer brother seemed to be hearin' or seein' someone and was actin' real paranoid-like. Figgered we needed to get a hold and treat order pronto and get him some care. I'll have someone from Aurora Medical Center give ya a call. That's where they took him. I'm sorry, Miss Shivalen. Had me a brother like that. I know, this can be kinda tough."

Anne hung up. Trying not to disturb Noa, she got out of bed, took a bag from the closet, and started to pack some clothes.

Noa stirred. "Aye Blanca, what is so important that you insist on making so much noise? This rackety-rack. It's dark out. Mother of Mary, I swear to you, if I don't get some sleep, you will not be happy, Cariña."

Anne explained. As Dr Moreno, Assistant Chief of Emergency Services at Cooley Dickinson Hospital, Noa had treated her share of assault victims in the ER. Her sympathies were always with the victims, and contempt was reserved for the perpetrators of such heinous acts––weak men, threatened by strong women; small men, looking to control the mothers they blamed for their failures. But this was Carmie. He'd never hurt anyone in his life.

"Have to go to Denver," Anne said, shoving clothes into the bag. I'll catch the first flight tomorrow. Something's terribly wrong. There must be a mix-up."

The harried professor caught a glimpse of her reflection in the mirror. Worry was written in bold font on her forehead. If she was going to be of any use at all, she must quash the internal chatter before she lost her grip. What she needed more than anything was a drink. But, instead, she thought of years of Carmine's puzzling symptoms and a parade of doctors and clinicians–– "the fraud squad," as she called them. There had been misdiagnoses, medical "mix-ups," and multitudinous medications, followed by long periods of unemployment and, in recent years, a spate of car and bicycle accidents. During the ritual of his medical appointments, she'd acted as a translator because her brother was allergic to words. But through it all, he'd never lifted his hand to anyone. *God, this made no fucking sense.*

Anne grabbed a satchel and stuffed it full of students' papers. She bent over, kissed her partner's forehead, and whispered, "I'll text when I know something."

The air was cool and brought clarity to her jumbled thoughts. Streetlights on South Prospect St. illuminated the sidewalk towards Amity. It was easier to catch a cab than call an Uber. Even at this ungodly hour, plenty of cabs drove down Pleasant and Main looking for students returning from late-night grazing and guzzling at the Spoke or Moan & Dove.

The professor had taught at Amherst College for 20 years. Their three-room townhouse on South Prospect was an easy walk to Amherst and a quick commute to the hospital for Noa. Her favorite kind of driver pulled over--a middle-aged man, short on small talk, asking only for her destination. No mindless chatter or feigned interest, just a ride. She'd be at the airport in about 40 minutes. Navigating apps on her new phone, she saw no nonstops to Denver International, so she booked a flight out of Bradley with a connection in O'Hare. Her flight left at 8:30 AM and, with a change of planes, she should arrive in Denver around 2:00 PM MST.

With six hours before her flight, she could wait comfortably in the Delta Lounge. Hopefully, she could find someone to serve a glass of wine or two to steady her nerves and thwart the hangover that was crashing cymbals in her brain. She could pass the time digging into her backlog of work, like finally looking at her students' paper proposals she'd managed to avoid all semester. The Department Head, Braden Holmes--a classical male hysteric in Chicken Little disguise--had been chirping about this for the last few weeks. But she regarded this as his issue, not hers. Papers would eventually get graded on her time, not his.

TEARS ARE ONLY WATER

The professor's stomach was twisted in knots, and her breathing was shallow. She had to slow down, dammit! *Breathe from the diaphragm. Just focus and compose yourself already, for God's sake, already.* In the rearview mirror, she caught sight of a scared mouse looking at her. God, she looked awful. She tried making a mental list of things she needed to do.

1. Text Noa
2. Make sure the sheriff sends information about where Carmine is being held

That's as far as she got with the list before her mental projector unspooled long entombed scenes from half a lifetime ago.

Three-year-old Carmine––the chatty little kid who was into everything–– playing in front of that old duplex in East Denver. An Easter morning when little brother devised an algorithm to search their backyard for a few colored eggs and later sobbed as crows feasted on them. That Halloween party when he kept tripping over his baggy ET costume that Mother, or Maimie, as Carmie always called her, had made. A Christmas memory when he was four and gripped his new abacus while doing a slow-motion dance with roller skates fastened to cowboy boots. Mother was laughing loudly while Vati tried to read a book by their droopy little tree.... *Oh, Vati.*

Her father had left so little behind. A quiet, gentle soul whose time was too short, Emil Lüedke's silent presence seeped through the floorboards of her normally stoic and rational mind.

She shook away the reverie and sadness. The professor preferred life with all such matters neatly boxed up. It was only when she was tired or had too much wine that Vati haunted her thoughts, bringing unwanted achiness that she would have to cram back into the cellar boxes. After all, that's how the sane must function. Find a sturdy compartment for all the unnecessary baggage from the past and dump it in.

The driver switched stations and bobbed his head to the sounds of Led Kaapana, one of Mother's favorites. The lilting notes of Waimea Lullaby helped loosen the knot in her stomach. *Keep breathing from your diaphragm and clear your mind*. But the slack key melody brought back more clutter.

Long before The Descendants popularized Hawaiian style, Mother collected records, cassettes, and finally, CDs of Gabby Pahinui, Leonard Kwan, and Ray Kane. Mother had never been your typical love-being-at-home-raising-the-kids type. Born Regina Magdalena Schivalone, she chose uncharted paths while remaining oblivious to where others were walking. Mother–Gina, to her few friends–broke eggs wherever she went, and her omelets were not that tasty.

Her parents had emigrated from a coastal village in the Abruzzo region east of Rome when Europe smoldered in the aftermath of World War I. Like other immigrants, they pioneered west, settling in downtown Denver's growing suburbs. Grandfather, Galo Schivalone, worked long hours as a mechanic until he injured his back. He spent his remaining days sitting by the garden drinking vino behind their small house. Their Nonna, like many Italian grandmothers in those days, lived in the kitchen cooking, cleaning, and trying to read the moods of her ill-tempered husband. Only later did it become clear that one root of his meanness and irritability was the constant pain, which tortured him and led him to share his suffering with others as if they were somehow the source of his unrelenting agony.

Mother had two older brothers, both of whom worked at the garage along with Nonno Galo. Uncle Mario had some business sense and saved enough to buy his own small garage, which employed many cousins, some of whom were true *cugini*, but most were unrelated neighbors and friends. Then there was Gina, the Bella Dona, always intent on being the center of attention, having the last word, and not accepting anything at face value. A small group of followers thought of her as a feminist visionary, but most viewed her as a vainglorious kook.

Her poetry would inspire a handful but irritated those with a more cultured ear.

The driver's voice brought her back to the present. "What airline?"

Anne told him Delta and took a deep, slow breath, counting to herself as she exhaled. Veering towards Departures, he pulled over and got out to help with her bag. The professor waved him off and gave him a $10 tip for his quiet indifference and taste in music.

Chapter 7

Overhead Compartments

Wednesday, March 19, 2:30 AM

The bright lights inside the terminal emitted a noxious hum. The airport was unusually crowded for this ungodly hour. She joined the zombie apocalypse, elbowed through ticket and security lines, and headed straight to the Delta Lounge. Once she was away from the plebians, she searched for a coffee station, and stopped the woman setting out dried pastries. "Excuse me, would you bring me a glass of chardonnay?"

The woman raised an eyebrow and checked her watch. "If you say so, ma'am."

"I just did, didn't I? Be a dear and bring it to me over there." She found a comfy and secluded alcove and waited for her morning medicine to arrive––the hair of the dog. *Note to self, must look up the origin of that vile expression.*

She forced herself to begin reading her undergraduates' paper proposals, which she'd put off far too long. Other matters had been more pressing––speaking engagements, book signings, and a contract for a new book she called *Booo! Trick or Treatment.* Yes, she was quite the one in demand.

Her wine arrived, and she opened her email. There was another annoying message from Holmes about her midterm grades for the Freshman Seminar. Though a graduate school faculty member, she was still compelled to do some undergraduate teaching. This year, she'd gotten stuck with a Freshman Seminar on Models of Psychopathology in the 21st Century. Finding no way to dodge Holmes' exhortation to run the seminar, she negotiated a reduced teaching load by one course. Still, she'd fallen behind in posting her midterm grades and had to deal with the department head's annoying emails and complaints about her missing appointments during office hours. True, this had happened twice, maybe three times over the semester, when her agent called about a book signing or radio interview. Still, she did her best to meet with her needy students when possible.

The competition to get into her freshman seminar had been fierce among incoming students. Even graduating high school seniors had heard the Amherst psychology professor on *Good Morning America* speak about "how to ignore our most unpleasant thoughts." That's how GMA host Lara Spencer described her book.

Unfortunately, from that interview forward, no one learned the title of her book, *Beliefs, Misbeliefs, and Aberrations: Unmasking the Cognitive Orchestrator of Maladaptive Thought and How to Silence Him*. Instead, it was known as "The Handbook on Learning How to Compartmentalize," or for those focusing more on style over substance, "Lessons on Forgetting the Bad Stuff." Whatever the title, her work had created quite a stir. A self-proclaimed disrupter, Anne had taken on the therapy establishment and their antiquated doctrine that getting in touch with one's feelings was necessary for psychological health, which she regarded as rubbish.

She'd experienced this firsthand as a graduate student with her department's requirement for personal psychotherapy, which she considered a violation of a student's right to privacy. But her aversion to traditional therapy was born in the crucible of her childhood with her mother, the poster child for psychotherapy, who insisted that everyone, except herself, needed treatment. Anne had managed to resist this inexorable pressure to see a therapist, so her mother set her sights on Carmine, whom she sentenced to an endless line of therapists, all trying to get to the core of his refusal to speak. Her mother finally tricked

Anne into seeing someone, so she decided to emulate Carmine and refused to talk. Instead, she focused on the giant mole on the therapist's neck and let his words disappear into the ether.

Later as a graduate student at Penn, she'd completed the mandatory 30 sessions with an analyst named Salma Kahn, whom she'd derisively dubbed "Swami Salami." With her Boston Psychoanalytic pedigree, Salma had been on a mission to link Anne's pursuit of a Ph.D. in psychology to the loss of her father. The professor remembered her words.

"We all seek ways to bring back those we cherish most, Miss Schivalone." Perhaps your decision to enter the field is a belated drive to master a grief you felt overwhelmed by as a child."

Well, barf to that. The professor always recalled this scornfully, chuckling to herself that this Salami caused her heartburn. She would later write that all such therapies were unnecessary hogwash.

Her temples pounded, her stomach curdled, and her fingers tingled. Another chardonnay would fix things. Deep breaths, in and out, through the diaphragm to eliminate the hyperventilation that creeps up on you. Put the useless droppings of the past away.

She texted Noa that she was waiting in the Delta lounge, then searched her purse for more Tylenol, washing it down with wine. The Sky Lounge was filling up as the walking dead shuffled through the line for coffee and wilted crudité. She watched as they robotically filled their tiny plates. *Honestly, people looked so strange at this hour. Too few seemed as concerned about their appearance as they should be.*

CNN was on with Alison Camerota interviewing someone about that Malaysian airliner that had vanished last week. She felt a momentary twinge of something approaching empathy––a rare visitor to her inner sanctum––for the family members left wondering what had become of their lost loved ones. But her poor, lost brother was her only concern. To her dismay, thinking of Carmine rattled her mental compartment doors. She forgot to breathe again, *Goddammit. Get a grip. Focus. Let it go. Find the damned compartment and make a deposit. The past is history, and tomorrow will be a shitshow. It's today that demands complete attention.*

She needed a distraction. Grading student paper proposals would get the twit Holmes off her back and turn down the volume of the mental noise. The eight students—or was it nine?— in the seminar had submitted their proposals for a major paper they needed to write. Their midterm grade was based chiefly on their proposals. The professor reached into her satchel and felt for one that would take the least amount of time to peruse.

She pulled out one written by a heavyset, dark-skinned boy named Gerardo. His proposal was titled "Psychological Maiming: A Form of Self-Deadening?" But, unfortunately, Gerardo's choice of the word maiming immediately cued a tumbling of memories of her mother.

Anne refused to refer to her as anything but Mother. It was her little brother's attempt to say Momma that came out "Maimie." The laughter of her uncles and cousins shamed her poor brother further into silence. Mother's response was to slice these bullies with her tongue.

"Why do you *idioti* laugh when you have butchered the English language so magnificently your entire lives!?"

"Maimie" caught on and stuck after Carmine stopped speaking at age five and lived on long after her uncles were dead and buried.

Rosalind Russell made the character "Auntie Mame" a household name in the 1960s. An independent and plucky woman during the 1920s, Russell's eccentric and independent Mame character fused with Mother's indomitable spirit, which, although admirable to many, could quickly flatten those left in her wake. Sadly, this had been Carmine's fate as their mother nagged, ignored, and dragged him behind her for far too long.

If the younger child faded and grew silent in their mother's presence, her firstborn learned by example. As a child, Anne became a worthy counterforce within the family. Yet despite their conflicts, Mother taught her the power of words, the impact of modulating volume and cadence, the advantage of a fixed glare, and the need to question everyone about everything. But, as often happens, the teacher becomes the primary target for the student to question, criticize, and oppose. Anne took pride in parrying Mother's verbal attacks with an effective riposte, which allowed her, not her mother, to have the last word.

Even before she became a student of human behavior, she regarded her mother as the portrait of maternal narcissism. Mother treated others not as complex subjects but as objects of convenience, providing they held her interest or served her needs. When they no longer did, she discarded them. Moreover, she was skilled in steering any conversation back to herself. If she had a momentary insight that she'd gone on too long about herself, she would ask the listener a question, which invariably would be a springboard for a more self-focused monologue. It was as if she said, "Enough talk about me; let's talk about you. What do you think of me?"

As an adolescent, Anne vowed that she'd never take anything from her mother. But she took her name, Schivalone. Although she had an easy answer for most things, Anne could never explain why she let go of her father's name. Salami had her theories, which her skeptical patient regarded as typical bullshit shrink-speak. Salma said maybe choosing her mother's name in the 1970s was an easier way of pushing back and rejecting society's low expectations of women, or perhaps it was an effort to gain her dear mother's love and admiration. As always, Dr Salami's interpretations fell on deaf ears. Even if they made sense and resonated, Anne would never acknowledge it. She told herself that she liked the lilting, glittering sound of Schivalone more than Luedke's harsh, Germanic dissonance. Loved the man but not his name. She certainly wasn't going to take the name of her creepy stepfather, Jasper Bilkes, or the Bilker, as she called him.

How Mother, the fiercely independent, self-styled feminist poet, who had never been one to suffer fools, fell for an alcoholic con man like Bilkes, was a puzzle. After Vati was gone, Mother withered for a few months then leaped at the first man who looked her way. Whether it was loneliness or Bilkes's smarmy country songs, Mother made excuses for his short temper and lack of regular work. Bilkes gave the impression that he was listening and taking in your words, nodding at the right moments while scanning the room or bathing in some self-absorbed fantasy. Mother would talk, and he would not hear a word she said. When she'd ask his opinion, he would say, "Oh, darlin', I agree with what you said." Mother wanted to be with a sophisticated and intelligent gentleman. But the Bilker was a shallow and stupid man, and Mother saw only what she wanted to see.

For one thing, Bilkes lied like a worm spins silk. He said he would cut a country album as he tried to Travis pick his way through two gigs at the Cozy Inn, a dive on E. Colfax Ave. He wrote a song called "Lord, Why Me" that was utterly gag-worthy. When they met, he told Mother he worked as the senior executive in charge of marketing at KLZ, a radio station in Denver. The truth was, Bilkes was never an executive. Instead, he wrote jingles for radio ads.

The Jingler lied with conviction, bypassing Mother's radar for detecting lying bullshitters and scam artists. Then, he lied to her about being laid off after she got sick.

"The company's downsizing, darlin', and they told us to reduce our staff, so I volunteered to protect the troops. I just told them I'd step down so they could all keep their jobs."

In fact, Jasper the Jingler was fired for having sex with one of the interns in the recording studio. The sad thing was that Mother didn't toss him out. Instead, she made excuses even when the Bilker ran off with this woman after draining one of her bank accounts.

The professor felt lucky to have escaped the worst of the Bilkes' era. A scholarship to Choate in her sophomore year was a ticket out, but poor Carmie was only seven then and had to suffer the brunt of the Bilker's meanness.

Anne snapped the rubber band around her wrist to silence the leakage of unbidden and unwanted memories from the crypt. This thing with her brother had strained her much-heralded theory of adaptive compartmentalization.

She scolded herself. For the love of God, what the hell was wrong with her? Seriously, she'd allowed a bottom-feeder like Bilkes out of his cage to rummage about her psyche? Chapter 2, just breathe. Chapter 3, let all the past garbage disappear with a breath; breathe it out now, dammit. Find a compartment and lock it before you start hyperventilating again, you big phony.

She glanced up at the clock. Good time to walk to her gate. There was still an hour before her flight, but she always liked to settle in before boarding. She bought a latte and scone and waited to board her flight.

Boarding with Group 2 gave her plenty of time to find her seat, stake out her territory, grab her folder of papers, and don her noise-canceling headphones to ward off any seatmate who might try to strike up a meaningless conversation. Settling into 18C, she found her favorite whispering piano music and began looking through her students' paper proposals. She asked for another coffee and pulled out the next proposal, this one from a diminutive girl named Nomi.

Her proposal, "Does Selective Mutism Attract Bullies?", unfortunately transported the professor to more intrusive memories of her wordless brother, the bully magnet, and his odd fascination with esoteric mathematical proofs.

Mother used to joke about measuring little brother's growth, not in inches or pounds, but by how many words he said per month. Although more exaggeration than fact, Mother liked to tell the story about how he hardly spoke until he was ten. With a shrug here and an "I d-d-dunno" there, he was the invisible boy around the house. Carmie had a way of letting you know when he was done talking. His signature lines of "That's it" or "That's all" were shorthand ways of saying, "I'm done. Conversation over. No more questions because you're not getting anything more from me." Mother refused to see that his silence might have something to do with his self-consciousness about his stuttering, for which she had neither patience nor empathy.

The truth about Carmie hadn't been discovered until he was in the 5th grade when he was finally diagnosed with Selective Mutism. Up to then, the assembly of shrinks and speech pathologists said he had a speech impediment––gee, ya think that's it, Captain Obvious? Some said he was mentally retarded or suffered from depression. One crank said he was autistic and asked if he had been vaccinated. That wasn't the only so-called expert who thought out loud that he was on the spectrum, which may have been more on target than not. When his 1st-grade teacher told Mother that he might be mentally retarded, she reacted by taking him out of school and teaching him at home. When he eventually returned to public school in the 3rd grade, his teacher complained that he sat with his head down, never participating in classroom discussions. Then, she discovered that he was reading a high school calculus textbook. He had found some old books somewhere and was always reading them. After that, teachers no longer questioned his intelligence, but few grasped how advanced his mind was.

Somewhere over Illinois, Anne began recalling her brother's peculiar interests and symptoms. She visualized him sitting silently, writing equations, and poring over obscure mathematics books. In elementary school, he announced that all numbers and sounds had their own colors. They had known about his synesthesia, but signs of narcolepsy didn't appear until high school when he started nodding off on the school bus, in class, or at the dinner table. If speech pathologists misunderstood Carmie, shrinks fared no better. Social workers, psychologists, and psychiatrists practicing psychoanalytic therapy, CBT, behavior therapy, play therapy, and family therapy all had trouble connecting with him. They couldn't resist imposing their pet diagnostic theories and prescribing a ridiculous pharmacopeia of on- and off-label medications because they couldn't get him to talk.

The attendant appeared over Anne's shoulder with coffee. "Refill, Miss?" She glanced at the sheath of papers on her lap. "Oh, you're a teacher?"

"No, I'm a tenured professor and want something stronger. A glass of chardonnay, please." The attendant nodded and moved up the aisle. The professor was disappointed by her defective filter, leaking unbidden mental pictures from her past. She flipped through a couple other proposals before stopping on one by Jansey Combs, titled "Do Mental Health Professionals Secretly Pathologize Homosexuality?"

The professor chuckled. *Why, yes, Jansey, they do; and in case you didn't know, you are my favorite student. An A for you.* How did these students all choose topics that resonated with her personal experiences? Anne liked this girl even before she read her paper proposal. Jansey had a bright-eyed quietude about her. She wasn't obsequious or toady-esque like some of her classmates. The professor assumed that her own sexual orientation was not the best-kept secret, so it didn't surprise her that one of her students would choose to write about this.

Anne hadn't always gone by Schivalone. For three years, she'd taken her husband's name. Like Mother's blind spot with Bilkes, the professor, too, had violated her rules and given into convention. Following one drunken fog in graduate school, she married a man she didn't love and took his name because that was easier than facing the truth about herself. Salma Kahn had a field day with that one. Jude Harrington was a handsome second-year law student at Penn, from the right family, and with the right friends. But more than having all the "right" boxes checked, he was wrong for Mother, making him right for Anne. Their last battle of wills concerned her relationship with Jude. Mother was convinced Anne had been gay all along. She essentially dared her to marry Jude, proclaiming that she would be lying to herself if she did.

"You don't know what it is you want or who you really are, Angelina." Simply calling her "Anne" was never enough for Mother. "This man, this family, really? Is this your final form of defiance against me?" Notice how it always had to be about her? "But, if you marry this person, you'll rue the day, I promise you that. When you were a teenager, remember I was the one who told you not to expect much development in the bosom department. You know I've always told you the truth. So, when will you stop lying to yourself about your sexuality?"

Beyond stubborn defiance, though, there was another reason Anne had decided to marry Jude. If she could be with a man, no one, especially herself, would have grounds to question her sexuality. Despite the sexual liberation of the late 60s and 70s, attraction to members of one's own gender was not widely accepted. Unfortunately, it took way too long to emerge from her cloistered closet. Whatever her problems with Salma Kahn, it was Kahn who recognized the truth and invited her patient to set herself free. Despite Anne's wish to discredit her therapist in every way possible, Dr Kahn had seen a self in hiding and invited her to come out.

The pilot's muffled voice came over the loudspeaker, announcing that they would encounter turbulence, a darkly comical foreshadowing if there ever was one. The professor tried to shut her eyes and doze. Her compartments, usually tightly sealed, had developed gaping cracks. She switched playlists and drifted to the jazz piano of Diana Krall, only to have her brief respite rudely interrupted by the attendant's piercing announcement that they were beginning their descent into DIA. "Place your seats in the upright position and return your carry-ons to the overhead compartments."

The professor was past the point of compliance. She had carried on too much mental baggage that she couldn't return to their compartments. The pounding in her head and knotting in her stomach returned. She willed herself to slow her breathing. *Just breathe, for fuck's sake!*

But it was too late. Her fingers had already gone numb.

Chapter 8

The Sociologist & the Bookkeeper

Wednesday, March 19, 9:05 AM

Deputy Nicola Kitts took another sip and grimaced as the gritty liquid snaked down her throat. The coffee, a lukewarm and translucent gruel, was always the same. Who made it didn't matter; the Maxwell House was never good to the last drop. Mississippi John Hurt had a song about Maxwell House Coffee that her grandfather always played. Every time she saw that red can, Mississippi John's old song, "Lovin' Spoonful," came to mind, and with it, memories of Bub.

She was looking forward to a week off. After mandatory roll call, she would spend a few hours cocooning in her garden before driving to a little cabin in Redwood for some alone time. Kitts craved solitude; burnout was closing in. Graduate school brochures and postings for law enforcement openings across the state cluttered her desk. She had to decide soon.

Morning call always began the same. When all the deputies were seated, Sheriff Burwinkle penguin walked to the front. Her partner sat with his buddies toward the back of the room, bringing back memories of social studies class in high school when a cluster of jerks yukked it up in the back row. Unlike high school, everyone quieted up when the sheriff entered the room.

An introvert with an edge, Deputy Kitts sat alone with a notebook and pen in hand. After almost three years in the department, she hadn't really bonded with any of her fellow deputies, but that was nothing new. She had little interest in socializing or small talk.

Burwinkle's girth filled the podium. His large hands and stubby fingers shuffled through pages of updates, status reports, and assignments for the day. "I trust yer all rested and on yer toes." He coughed away the night's accumulation of cigarette residue in his throat and rubbed his chest as he read through the assignments, informed them of any changes in who was riding with whom, and summarized any open cases that required attention.

"This bookkeeper fella that a couple of ya collared on Tuesday, he's gonna need him another escort from MCA down to Pe-eblo, to the State Hospital 'round noontime."

Jerry snickered from the back of the room. "Knew he was a whack job when we picked him up, Sheriff."

Burwinkle didn't find this funny. "Goddammit, Jerry. How many times I have to tell ya we got protocols to follow here, and calling our prisoners those kinds of names don't cut it. You just can't seem to get that through yer thick skull, can you, Jerry?" He rubbed his chest and shook his head. "Chrissake, you'll drive me to an early grave."

After Nicola's third transfer request, the sheriff had called her in for a heart-to-heart.

"Look, Cole, yer a good deputy, maybe the best we have here. Jerry's an ass, but we can't go shuffling the deck every time the two of ya don't see eye to eye. But if he gets racial with you, come and tell me that, and I'll see what I can do."

The thing was, Jerry walked up to the line of blatant racism and sexism but always left enough room for plausible deniability. The department was small, and Burwinkle would not want to lose a deputy, no matter how much of an asshole he was. So, Nicola had to put up with him. Jerry discovered she'd filed an anonymous complaint about his tactics a while back. He never said a word about it, but she could feel his hatred whenever he looked at her. They continued to ride together, sitting silently in the cruiser, only speaking when necessary.

. . .

Sheriff Burwinkle coughed and continued, "Need to pull only one of ya to accompany the bookkeeper. Got him pretty sedated, and course, he'll be cuffed, so shouldn't be much of a deal. Let's see, gonna send...." He paused, flipping through his papers, "Depety Kitts. Ya collared him and took him over to MCA on that EEP, so I figger that'll do just fine. Know ya got yer leave planned. We can push that back a day. I'll find somethin' else for you, Jerry."

Someone chortled from the back of the room, "Yeah, Sheriff, this is a good one for the Sociologist."

Burwinkle's glare silenced the muffled laughter in the room. "Goddammit, do we have to have this conversation again? Boggs, I know that was you."

Nicola turned to see Cletus Boggs trying to wipe a grin off his baby face. He'd been her first partner, a less intelligent, less sadistic, and unfiltered version of Jerry.

After Burwinkle had heeded her request not to ride with Boggs, Jerry and Boggs rode together, and all hell broke loose. The complaints from the community almost doubled in the two months they were partners. Boggs followed Jerry around like a pup, often echoing, or worse, saying out loud the racist shit Jerry whispered. She relished not having a partner for those few months, but after the shit hit the fan with those two, the sheriff called her into his office and pleaded that she ride with Jerry.

"Cole, need some adult supervision here for these knuckleheads. It's just fer a while, mind you. Don't know what I'm gonna do with Boggs. He can't pass the stupid test cuz he don't even know just how stupid he really is. But look, I need ya to ride with Jerry fer a while, just til we get that boy straightened out a bit."

It was Burwinkle who first referred to her as the "Sociologist." He reviewed the previous week's arrests in a morning meeting some years back. The deputy questioned the increased number of Black motorists being pulled over for bogus reasons just to search their vehicles. She

TEARS ARE ONLY WATER

wondered whether this was profiling and thought the department would attract unwanted attention if this practice continued.

"Goddammit, Depety Kitts, so now yer a sociologist? What happened to depety? Officers make good faith stops fer probable cause. That's the way we do it here. Policin' comes first. Ya wanna be a social worker, Kitts, do it in yer own time, not mine."

The meeting ended, and the sheriff called her into his office before she geared up and left for MCA. "Look, I know this ain't the plan with your leave and what not. Ya been workin' yer ass off, Cole. I know that, and believe you me, I appreciate it. And don't think it gets lost on me what a knucklehead I've got ya ridin' with, but Jerry ain't the worst around here. Hey listen, I know ya been wantin' that transfer to Denver Metro, but, ya know, Cole, I just don't want to lose ya."

Despite his bluster and Country Bob demeanor, she thought the sheriff was one of the good guys. Still, he didn't know she was thinking about leaving the police and going to graduate school in——wait for it——social work. A secret she shared with no one.

If word got out, the taunting would never end. "I knew it! The damned Sociologist's becomin' a bleeding-heart social worker. Out to save the scum instead of fulfilling her duty as an officer of the peace."

Kitts heard all this before——Jerry holding court with his boys, bitching about his goodie-two-shoes, holier-than-thou-ass partner, and how she'd never talk to him in the patrol car.

She saw the "Sociologist" thing as code, a thinly veiled dog whistle that painted her as a Black woman, more aligned with the underclass than the law. But what the moron Jerry said about her wasn't true. The part about her not talking to him in the patrol car was true, but not much else. She had a stellar record. In her few short years with the department, she led the others in making arrests. The part about her talking to people about their feelings was Jerry's simple-minded way of announcing his abject lack of curiosity, compassion, and fair-mindedness––all attributes that unfortunately made her a misfit in the department. Someday, she hoped she'd find kindred spirits in another department, other officers interested in community relations who believed, as she did, that police work was about serving and protecting, not the type of street justice Jerry and Boggs practiced and perfected. She imagined a new way of policing, but then she'd awaken in the middle of the night with the fear that she was only kidding herself, that she'd entered the police academy for all the wrong reasons and had essentially wasted the past few years of her life.

Today, the deputy managed to place all of this into a compartment, something she'd learned well from her father. Today was not the time to figure all of this out. Relieved to be riding alone, she settled into the driver's seat of the cruiser. Jerry's cheap aftershave hung in the air like rotten fruit. She thought how hard it was to escape that bastard even when he wasn't sitting beside her. His words echoed in her head, and his stale odor stalked her senses. She announced her departure time and destination on the radio and set out for MCA.

Kitts entered the sliding glass doors and announced to the reception desk that she would take custody of Carmine Luedke for transport to the Colorado State Mental Health Institute in Pueblo. A distracted woman told her to take a seat while the patient was processed for discharge.

Hospital lobbies are always the same––same receptionists with sequined glasses, same tired-looking attendants, same distracted doctors, and same harried nurses. Oh, how the Sociologist loved these lobbies and waiting rooms. People-watching was her favorite pastime.

Since childhood, she'd loved watching people, imagining their life stories, where they came from and where they were headed, who had loved them, and who had made them cry. Lines carved into faces told stories if only you cared enough to discern the hidden tale. Neither Bub nor her father had been people watchers. But Aunt Rhea, the actual social worker in the family, was. She taught her niece how to observe and ask the right questions.

TEARS ARE ONLY WATER

Like the heavyset man rushing through the lobby wearing a dirty t-shirt with two urchins in tow. *What's your story, Sparky? You look like a Randy, no, more like a Del. Probably visiting the wife after giving birth to yet another mouth to feed. You have that look—more dread than excitement. Facing a layoff maybe or struggling to keep up with rent and your interest-only mortgage?*

Nicola profiled a couple other strangers, maintaining enough humility to keep from sounding like a know-it-all sociologist, even to herself.

The elevator doors pinged. An aide pushed a gaunt man in a wheelchair into the reception area. It took Kitts a moment to recognize the man she'd arrested and taken to MCA the morning before. He didn't look cleaned up, rested, or restored. On the contrary, he was a more shriveled version of the sad-looking man they'd left there yesterday.

"Are you the deputy? Here, I've got Carmine for you. You can pull your car around, and I'll wheel him out. We got him all ready for the trip, isn't that right, buddy? We tried to feed him breakfast, but he's not much into eating. He's had his morning meds, so he should be no trouble for the trip."

The deputy went to fetch the cruiser. The aide unlocked the cuffs and helped her secure the patient in the back of the car. "Like I said, Deputy, he's pretty sedated, and he's got this narcolepsy thing, so you can uncuff him if you like."

An emaciated, sleeping man and a risk for assault seemed oxymoronic, but the deputy was not naïve. She'd seen too many seemingly unconscious suspects suddenly awaken with the strength of Samson. "Thanks," she said. "Not expecting any trouble, but let's leave him cuffed all the same."

Chapter 9

Blue

Wednesday, March 19, 1:00 PM

Turning onto I-25 South, the deputy turned on her GPS and radioed the station that they were enroute, eyeing her prisoner's face in the rearview mirror to monitor his level of consciousness. She hoped he would wake up. Pueblo was close to a two-hour drive, and she welcomed conversation, especially if it satisfied her curiosity about the "why's." Nicola had already seen enough to know the "what" and "how"––an unhinged bookkeeper attacked a woman, who was the darling of the department, with his bare hands––but she was thirsty to know what went on in those private, hidden spaces that gave rise to the "why."

After a few minutes, the bookkeeper opened his eyes and looked to each side, trying to orient himself.

"Good morning, Carmine," the deputy said. "Seems I'm always telling you this is our last dance, but I keep being wrong about that. Know where you are?"

The bookkeeper shook his head and looked directly at her eyes in the rearview mirror.

"I'm Deputy Kitts. We've met a couple of times. Remember me from Shrenklin's and then the hospital? My partner and I picked you up on a disturbance call early yesterday."

TEARS ARE ONLY WATER

There was no response other than a blank stare. Refusing to be discouraged, she continued. Talking was a welcome respite from the monotonous silence when riding with Jerry.

"We're heading to Pueblo. Got an institute there that can hopefully help you feel a whole lot better and get to the bottom of why you went off like you did."

Still, no reaction from the stolid bookkeeper.

"I got you, Carmine. They said you'd be a little sleepy. This is kind of a pretty drive, so try to chill and enjoy the view."

The sound of her voice in the car felt good. "You're a bookkeeper, right? What do they call you? Like I'm a deputy, so they refer to me as Deputy Kitts. They have something they call bookkeepers?"

The prisoner squinted as if he appeared to be listening.

"'Mr Bookkeeper' sounds stiff and too formal, you know. Maybe Mr Books, or how about just plain Books, to your friends. Got a nice ring to it, Books. So, that's what I'll call you then."

Books slowly closed his eyes.

Nevertheless, Nicola continued her monologue. Voicing her thoughts helped center and organize her mind, and sharing her stream of consciousness with a sleeping stranger she'd never see again was a low risk.

"You know, Books, that was some crazy shit that went down at Shrenklin's. Something must have snapped to set you off like that. Old LuCinda P was pretty freaked out. Mind you, I know she's a piece of work, but Mama Lu is kind of a sweetheart with the boys at the station. Man, something must've happened to get you to go all Mortal Kombat on her like that. You lost it pretty bad."

There was no reaction from the back seat. The prisoner remained immobile.

"Hmm, you know, people and their stories amaze me. See, I'm always interested in that kind of stuff, Books, you know, the story behind the story. Don't get me wrong, what you did was bad. No justification, and you're where you are now because of that. Unless they find you *non-compos mentis*, you're gonna have to pay the price, Books. You were saying some even crazier-sounding stuff when we took you in for your EEP at MCA. Remember? That kid doctor, sniffing all up in your face, kept asking what happened, and you launched into some wild-ass story about a dead woman's midnight visit, finding a glove, LuCinda lying, and then something about how they were sending each other coded messages. Man, Books, dude, that's some heavy paranoid-sounding shit. But know what? There's a *why* in there. Way I got it figured, there's always a grain of truth with paranoid folk that no one gets cuz everyone's too busy looking at the *what* or *when* or just the crazy ass paranoid-sounding stuff."

Nicola kept glancing back to see if her prisoner had opened his eyes. If anything, he seemed even more out of it. She raised her voice a decibel, hoping he would respond to satisfy her curiosity. To no avail, the torpid bookkeeper appeared fast asleep.

In the silence, she thought back to her college roommate, Darcy Cummings, who had a psychotic break during the first semester of freshman year at Wichita State. It all began with a breakup and some heavy use of weed. She stopped speaking, then started staying up all night and keeping the shades drawn during the day. Not one to intrude, Kitts observed from a distance. She knew that her quiet demeanor would not pose a threat to Darcy or risk becoming part of her delusional explanations. One night, when it was apparent that Darcy was quickly losing her mind, she asked softly, "Hey, Darce, I can see it's all pretty scary. I'm here to listen if you want to tell me your story. Sup to you, girl."

Like Jane Goodall's patiently waiting for the chimps to edge closer to her, Darcy began to open up about her psychotic terror. She eventually agreed to accompany Nicola to talk with someone at the student health services.

Nicola lowered the guardrails even more and spoke her most private thoughts out loud.

"Yeah, Books, policin's in my blood since you asked. Both my Pops and Bub, what I called my grandpa, retired from the department in Wichita, where I grew up. That was after they served in the Corps—Pops in Nam, and Bub fought at Iwo Jima. Not one of the flag raisers, mind you, but he was there. People always called them 'the Marines.' Man, I grew up around that shit and decided to step right into it, Oorah!"

She kept glancing back to see if the statue man was still breathing. The bookkeeper hadn't budged, opened his eyes, or uttered so much as a groan.

"Mama died when I was little, and Pops got remarried to the bottle. Her dyin' and Nam sure did a number on him. He was there, but I recall mostly his empty, angry looks, and his swapping war stories with Bub. Bub and Mama's big sister lived with us too. If she hadn't been there, man, no tellin' what would have happened. If Bub was a crusty old hoot owl, I guess you could say Auntie Rhea was my north star. Yeah, she kind of saved me. She was more of a mother to my little brother Blue and me after Mama passed. Had a backbone of steel, my aunt did. Hell, no one messed with Auntie Rhea."

She told the sleeping bookkeeper about her aunt becoming one of the first Black social workers in Kansas and how she might decide to follow that path too. "Surprised to hear that, Books? Me becomin' a social worker after the Corp and policing. Man, if they knew, Bub and Pops would do a rollover in their graves." In the spaces between her words, images formed in her mind, transporting her back to a life she hadn't thought about for years.

"They called Aunt Rhea 'the Bleedin' Heart Social Worker.' Though blood ties ran deep, there was always heavy-duty tension in the family between Rhea and the Marines. Once in a blue moon, the tension spilled over."

In the privacy of the cruiser heading south on I-25, she talked about the loud argument between Bub and his "bleedin' heart" daughter Rhea one Thanksgiving when Nicola was in middle school.

"Books, I gotta tell you, that night, Auntie's voice rang out like a bell. She got all up in Bub's face, her own father, mind you. That little woman stood there with her fists clenched saying, 'It's that kind of mentality, Daddy, that leads to more violence on the streets. Of course, policing *is* needed, but you just don't want to look at the lives of the people driven to commit crimes.'"

She talked about how Bub listened quietly, a smirk on his face, as he heard more "damned righteous" words from his daughter. Then, he raised his head and began his rant.

"Daughter, you think yer pretty goddammed smart. Got ya a BHSW degree, a goddam 'Bleedin' Heart Social Worker degree that makes you think you know everything. Hell, Rhea, get with the real world!"

Nicola glanced back. Her prisoner was still asleep. "So, Pops just sat there, staring down at the glass in his hand, leg shakin' a million miles a minute, pouring drink after drink. He finally stood up, smashed a bottle of Black Jack against the wall, and stormed off, muttering, 'Don't mean nothin', none of this shit. Don't mean nothin'!'"

The deputy paused, wondering what had loosened the dam inside her. By now, she was lost in her dark recollections and stopped glancing into the rearview mirror to check on her passenger. If she had looked back again, she would have been met by a pair of eyes watching her intently.

The traffic thickened somewhere south of Castle Rock, and the deputy hit the brakes when the car ahead of them stopped. As the cruiser lurched forward and back, she saw the bookkeeper's head snap to the front and bob backward.

"Blue," she said softly. At that moment, she fell silent as the long-closed curtain lifted in her mind and spilled out the ghostly memory of sweet Blue.

Little brother Bruce Charles was her only sibling. He could never say his name properly; it always came out Bluce. So, they called him Blue. Little brother took heaps of shit from the bully boys when the Marines weren't around. Kids like Blue have a harder road in life, especially when they're short and can't say their "rs." Always carrying around that raggedy, blue Power Rangers backpack everywhere he went, Blue was four years younger and a head shorter than his big sister. Nicola saw herself as his protector after Mama had passed. Auntie Rhea was supposed to fill that role, but she was often at school or work. "Little Mother Hen," Pops and Bub called her as she led Blue around with a gentle push and pull. Blue was known for his sweetness. "My sweet, sunshine apple blossom," Rhea would always say when referring to Blue. If she was Little Mama, then he became Sweet Blue. A study in contrasts, Blue was everything that his big sister was not. She was a daredevil, tough as nails. He was afraid of his shadow. She told no one what she thought; he told everyone everything. She did not give up smiles easily; he gave them freely. Her tears dried up long ago; his flowed like summer rain. When she was a kid and would cry after hurting herself, Pops would say, "Don't mean nothin', Cole. Stop yer cryin'." And she did.

People always thought that the Marines would make life holy hell for the only boy in the family, but Blue melted their hardened exteriors with his wide-eyed innocence. For Blue, feelings were the currency of relating to the world, especially when everyone makes it okay for you to have them. Why they clamped down on Nicola and gave Sweet Blue a pass was a mystery locked away in the clouds. Auntie Rhea tried to stand up to them for their harsh treatment of big sister Nicola, but it was always two against one. The only way to survive was to box up her tears and listen to Pops' voice inside, "Don't mean nothin'."

Over time, her heart, like all her muscles, hardened, and her doting on Blue began to fade. She became busy with school and sports and had less time for a little brother with his silly backpack wanting to follow her everywhere. But something about his innocent, wondering look could still reach her. Sweet Blue could always coax his stand-offish sister into the sunlight.

Then came the day that changed the world forever.

On an autumn day in her freshman year, she was annoyed that she had to pick up her little brother after school. His smiles and wide-eyed looks wouldn't penetrate her resentment that day as she impatiently waited for him in front of the school. He came out late. She was annoyed and walked briskly in front of him. Blue pleaded, "Wait up, Sissy." God, how she hated that name. She was no sissy! They could shave off twenty minutes by taking a shortcut through Matlock Heights, and maybe she could get back in time for practice. But she'd promised Pops, Bub, and Aunt Rhea to never go into that neighborhood because there were "too many knuckleheads looking to settle scores."

But today was different; she had to get to practice because she'd just made varsity, and the coach would be mad if she was late.

Blue protested as they turned onto East 21st North. "No, Sissy, wait, we're not supposa go in there!"

They were deep into the Heights when a car sped by like a bolt of thunder, and shots pierced the calm autumn day. A bullet grazed her left shoulder, another severed Blue's spinal cord, while a third shot lodged in his anterior temporal lobe.

Blue never spoke or walked again. His frame withered down to the size of a miniature scarecrow. The smile was gone, and the light from his eyes extinguished. Bub said he forgave her, but her Pops never did. Even if he had forgiven her, she never would. "Don't mean nothin'."

From that day on, she quit all sports and spent long hours alone in her room. Every weekend, she spent hours wheeling Blue around the campus of the Kansas Neurological Institute in Topeka. His little head would bob and weave like a cork in a choppy lake whenever she would stop. This was all that was left of him––the lurching and sagging motion of his small head.... Her mind flashed to heads...bloody heads and limbs...bodies lying in the sand. Wilson and Peters. Garza, Gonlin. The images flashed before her. Strange how guilt acts as a magnet, drawing to it the failings and sins of a lifetime.

Nicola recovered from what happened to Blue and learned to survive by dulling all the pain and grief. Life lessons learned.

TEARS ARE ONLY WATER

Auntie Rhea was there, always trying to reach her, urging her to grieve.

"Wounds can't heal if you hide them from the light," she'd say. But her words and loving gaze couldn't reach her niece. Tears would not come.

Nicola Kitts followed her familial path and buried her pain behind the eagle, globe, and anchor, and then the badge, all the while maintaining a detached, antiseptic interest in other people's stories, everyone's but her own.

Social work meant learning about other people's lives, their troubles, and their pains. But at some level, it would also mean facing her own pain and opening the door to all her ghosts from the past.

On that afternoon cruising south on I-25, the bobbing head of a scrawny, unconscious bookkeeper beckoned unwanted memories from the shadows, silencing the inquisitive deputy. Having driven the last 30 minutes in silence with a stinging in her eyes, she returned her attention to the GPS, following directions to Colorado Mental Health Institute. She had stopped checking on her prisoner and never noticed that he had been watching her from the back seat.

She parked the cruiser in front of the admissions building and notified them she'd arrived with her prisoner. Aides strapped him to a wheel-chair and wheeled him to the admissions building. The deputy walked behind. She noticed a well-manicured garden with all shades of Columbines in an outer courtyard. An old woman in a white robe danced between the beds of flowers.

The deputy spoke with the receptionist at the admission desk and filled out the paperwork before turning over her charge to the nurse's aide, who had arrived to complete the intake process.

"Hey, Deputy, we've got him and can take it from here." The nurse turned to her new patient, "Hello there, I'm Kittie, and we're gonna take care of you now." As she adjusted the restraints on the wheelchair, the bookkeeper looked toward the silent deputy. Nicola held his gaze and spoke her last words mechanically.

75

J. HERMAN KLEIGER

"Okay, there it is, Books. They'll help you here. Help you see what's going on with you. You know, help you see things more clearly."

He spoke his first words, catching her off guard. "Yes...I can s...s-ee that." Then he added something too softly for her to hear.

She leaned closer. "I can't hear you."

"I said, w...w-ho will help *you* see?.... That's it."

Chapter 10

Mile High

Wednesday, March 19, 3:20 PM

The airport was a bustling mess. The professor cursed under her breath as she was herded onto a tram to the main terminal in DIA. She flashed back to a simpler time when laid-back people in cowboy hats strolled through Stapleton Airport, long before the behemoth Denver International became a hub for travelers flocking to the mile-high city for God knows what reasons.

"Colorado is God's country," her dissertation advisor never tired of saying. But for Anne, Denver was more like Hell, laden with too many undead memories escaping their compartments and coming back to life whenever she returned.

Three months earlier, Colorado had legalized the recreational sale of cannabis, paving the way for commercial licensing of marijuana shops, which turbocharged an influx of out-of-staters responding to the lure of a new Green Rush.

Cursing the numbness in her fingers, Anne phoned Noa, but the call went into voicemail. So typical for the all-important doctor, always too busy to pick up her damn phone. After ordering an Uber to the Medical Center in Aurora, she walked out of Exit 4 and waited for the black Sonata and its driver, Spiro, to pull up to the third island. The air was crisp and thin, but she was sweating like she was in the spa. Fucking menopause.

The black sedan flashed its lights and edged forward. A curly-headed, post-pubescent driver leaned over the wheel, grinned, and waved her in. The car was clean but had an overpowering scent of evergreen. *Hmm, what was Spiro trying to cover up?*

The tanned youngster spoke with an accent she couldn't immediately place, which annoyed the professor because, in addition to her robust attacks against the psychotherapy industry, she considered languages her forte. *He sounds Serbian, perhaps of the Smederevo-Vršac dialect. Then, again, he could be Romanian too, perhaps even Bulgarian, but definitely not Polish.*

Regardless of his nationality, she had no intention of inquiring to satisfy her senseless obsessing. She hoped beyond hope that Spiro, *most likely shortened from Spiridon,* wouldn't try to force a conversation. On a good day, she had little tolerance for mind-numbing prattle. Today, she had none.

Unfortunately, Spiro hadn't gotten the memo. "Welcome to our Mile High City, miss. You know why we call Denver Mile High, hmm?" Spiro continued to wax on about the obvious before she could utter her noninterest and desire to be left alone. "You see, it is because Denver is so high. It is actually one-mile high above level of the sea. So, you see, this is why we call it Mile High City."

A barely audible "Oh Jesus" slipped past her pursed lips. "Yes, I'm originally from Denver." She bit her lip. *For God's sake, don't encourage him. Just tell him you've got work to do.*

"Oh, good, yes, yes. So, you know Denver. But, miss, maybe you don't know another reason we call Denver Mile High, no? You know this?"

Please, God, no; here it comes. After an uncomfortable silence, she breathed a sigh of resignation. "Okay, Mr Spiro, it seems you'd like to tell me." *Christ, am I actually encouraging this jibber.* Her cool indifference must be slipping. Worries about her little brother had ripped a large gaping hole in her armor.

"Well, you see, miss, the use of cannabinoids is now legal in Denver. If you are old enough, this means you can buy weed from shops. I know

TEARS ARE ONLY WATER

we are going to pass one. These places are all over. So you see, miss, Denver is not just one mile high up in the sky but also a place to get one high!" Spiro's sustained laughter was loud and high-pitched.

After a beat, she said, "Okay, Spiro, thank you for that. Interesting factoids, indeed. I need silence now if you please."

Not one to read the room, Spiro continued. "Yes, yes, we are free to buy ganja now. If you want, I can stop for you to buy. I have a place to--"

"No, no, not interested. Nope. Not on the schedule today."

They rode in silence, hearing only the hum of the tires on Interstate 425. Anne belatedly realized Spiro's annoying burble had provided a respite from ruminations about her brother. Still, she was not about to encourage more conversation. Instead, she listened to the voicemail message that had come through during the flight from an annoying-sounding Dr Levine.

The professor's original plan to go directly to the good old boy sheriff was upended by his news that her little brother had been hospitalized the morning after he'd been arrested. God, that was yesterday, and they were just leaving a message now? First, arrest for assault, then a petition for emergency psychiatric admission, and now, there's Miss Noa not picking up. Holy Jesus. She thought of the Bilker's song, *Lord, Why Me* and a wave of nausea washed over her.

The black Sonata pulled into the parking lot of the MCA. The professor scooched forward to exit. Spiro turned around with a faint smile and said, "I hope you be well, miss," apparently referring to their destination at the hospital. She nodded curtly and climbed out, then watched his car with a small Polish flag decal on the bumper disappear in the distance.

The receptionist spent several minutes trying to track down Dr Levine in Psychiatry. Finally, she directed the professor to the 5th floor, where the ward secretary would be of more help. Anne found the nurses' station, where a busy nurse looked up over her glasses and ignored her while she finished typing notes into her computer.

The professor donned her most imperious demeanor. "Excuse me, but as you can see, I'm standing here right in front of you, obviously with a need. Can you please help me now?"

Noa would have said, "Chill the hell out, Blanca," but the professor had little tolerance for rudeness. Her partner may have been raised a peasant and accustomed to waiting for civil servants, but that's not how things are done here.

Having been reminded of her place, the distracted nurse dropped what she was doing and said, "Yes, I appreciate your patience. Now, how can I be of help, ma'am?"

"First of all, I'm a doctor. It's Professor Schivalone, and I believe that my brother was admitted to this ward by a Dr Levine yesterday." She impatiently spelled Carmine's first and last name.

"I see, miss, er Doctor. Are you a relative?"

"You obviously missed it the first time. I'm his sister. Please tell me where I can find him or speak with this Dr Levine."

The nurse scrolled down her screen, making annoying humming sounds. "Hmm, nope, sorry, I'm afraid your brother's no longer here. I see he was admitted yesterday, but it looks like they transferred him a few hours ago to the Forensic Evaluation and Treatment Center in Pueblo, our state hospital. But let me see if I can track down Dr Levine, who might be able to tell you more."

The professor's head exploded, "What!? Not here? You're telling me my brother's been moved to the state hospital?"

Taken aback by the unexpected outburst, the sheepish nurse quickly added, "Let me page the doctor for you right now. I'll get someone down here right away to talk with you, ma'am–I mean, Doctor. Sorry, Professor. You can wait over there."

Anne sat in an uncomfortable chair, then stood and began to pace while reflexively redialing Noa. The screen showed nine calls. She left another voicemail––her tone now desperate and angry––urging her partner to

TEARS ARE ONLY WATER

call and explaining the magnitude of the situation concerning her brother and how tired and distraught she was.

The elevator opened, and a bespectacled young woman in a white coat walked out. True to form, the professor began making disparaging mental notes about this woman: *The stethoscope draped around the neck was no more than an accouterment designed to make this woman appear more important than she was. Most likely, she was compensating for feelings of inferiority, trying desperately to quiet the self-doubt that all imposters carry. The woman's wan complexion and dark circles suggested that this weary-looking underling had been working all night. She'd probably not seen sunlight for a week.*

The young doctor plastered on a smile. "Hello, Ms Shivalon, is it? I'm the Chief Resident, Dr Levine, and I understand you are inquiring about your brother. Glad you received my message this morning. We can talk in the office over here if you like."

The professor, taller by several inches, nodded as she looked down at the woman and followed her into a small, sterile examining room. Anne launched a scathing rebuke that nearly set off the smoke detector when the young doctor closed the door.

"First, young lady, my name is Dr Anne Schivalone, and you may address me as such. Need I remind you that you're still in training? I'm a tenured professor of Psychology at Amherst College and have traveled a long way to see my brother. I'm tired, jet-lagged, and low on estrogen. Now you're telling me he's not even here and has been transferred to the state mental hospital, and I'm only learning of this NOW?" Speaking to her as if she were a student, the professor added, "You can be sure that such indifference will not look good on your evaluation!"

The doctor looked like she'd been singed by a blast of hot air. She adjusted her glasses and cleared her throat. "Okay. I'm sorry for the distress this has caused. Um, you must be exhausted, and I understand your concern about your brother. You see, his clinical condition deteriorated rapidly. An acute paranoid psychotic episode, rule-out schizophrenia, but--"

"But? But what? And don't you dare try to patronize me with your feigned empathy because I'm well acquainted with all your little tricks and this diagnostic mumbo? So, stop the shrink-speak nonsense. I'm tired and only want you to tell me what in fuck's sake is going on with my brother, missy! What was the rush in sending him off to the state hospital when he'd just gotten here? I want to talk with your supervisor, someone who knows what the hell is going on."

The Chief Resident wisely implored the professor to wait "just a minute more" while she called to see if Dr Jonas could meet with them. He agreed, and the two women headed off to the staff psychiatry offices, which were housed on the 7th floor. Dr Levine studied her own shoes during the silent elevator ride. She escorted the tenured professor down the corridor to the office of the Chief of Psychiatry, Roger Jonas. His door was cracked open, and Dr Levine rapped gently. An upper-crust English voice told them to enter. A tall gentleman with salt and pepper hair, wearing a white coat the length of a bathrobe, stood up and walked past the analytic couch to greet them.

"Hello, Dr Schivalone. I trust I'm pronouncing your name correctly. I'm acquainted with your work on unmasking the cognitive orchestrator. Quite brilliant, really. Thank you for coming. I'm Roger Jonas, head of the department. Please have a seat, and we'll talk about your brother. Lindsay, get the professor something to drink. Water? Maybe some coffee or tea?"

Jonas was not alone. A handful of students of various colors and shapes were with him, all in white coats of varying lengths. The professor sized him up. Typically, she would have responded to his buttery tone and efforts to ingratiate with swift condemnation. Yet, his acquaintance with her book cast him in a slightly different light. *Undoubtedly, he is a bright man with a refined taste in popular nonfiction.* But she quickly shook off his flattery.

She gazed around the room, smirking to herself at what she saw. *Like most of his kind, he'd worshiped for years with the high priests of psycho-analysis. How quaint; how trite and anachronistic to find a psychoanalyst serving as department head in 2014. His office looks like a set out of central casting --the faux archeological figures on the shelf behind his analytic couch, a pagan offering to their Freudian deity, then row upon row of books standing at attention in mahogany bookcases. The walls were neatly adorned with framed certificates, all screaming of self-importance.*

Dr Jonas waved a hand at the students. "These are my trainees who examined your brother. He was brought here early Tuesday on an EEP, essentially an emergency evaluation status, but I imagine, Dr Schivalone, that you're acquainted with these types of emergency petitions. Dr Kashimi, here, received your brother in our Emergency Department. It soon became apparent that your brother needed an extended period of observation and treatment. We're a small acute care facility here. His condition became more unstable, and I determined that we needed to seek an involuntary confinement– "

The professor boomed, filling the room with flaming innuendos and accusations. "DID YOU EVEN EXAMINE HIM? Did you even TRY to treat him? And why the rush to ship him off to the state hospital after only a day?"

The room was filled with young deer caught in the headlights of an onrushing Mack Truck. The trainees fidgeted, fingered their stethoscopes, and squirmed in their chairs while Jonas sat calmly and gazed out the window.

"I understand your shock and worry, Professor. Dreadful what you must be going through. You're angry and have lots of questions for us that we hope to be able to answer. Please, Dr Schivalone, let us supply the full narrative and context. We hope you might be able to help us as well, both from a familial and professional perspective."

Fatigue was setting in, and Anne was mildly winded from her Vesuvian explosion.

Jonas turned to one of the trainees. "Kaspar, please tell us Mr Luedke's clinical status when you first examined him yesterday."

Unctuous charm was enhanced by the pompous sound of his Queen's English, which too many Americans mistook for erudition and wisdom. The intern straightened and began sniffing loudly. He nervously described how "the patient" had been accompanied by two police officers, who were present during his clinical interview.

Jonas interrupted. "Uh, Dr Kashimi, remember your patient has a name. We've talked about the importance of humanizing those in our care."

"Yes, of course, sir. I was paged to the Emergency Room to conduct an emergency psychiatric evaluation. The first thing I did was assess the patient's, I mean Mr Ludick's, mental status. In the course of my clinical examination, I considered a clinical delirium or acute confusional state, which is a neurological disturbance in the patient's, uh, Mr uh, Ludick's neurological status resulting in a confused mental state with a lack of orientation to person, place, and time. I concluded that he demonstrated a thought disorder of both form and content." He glanced at Jonas, who nodded for him to continue. "So, I determined a diagnosis of ruling out schizophrenia with a paranoid clarification. I can describe this too––"

Jonas motioned for Kazimi to sit down. The Chief Psychiatrist gazed out the window and pinched the bridge of his nose. The professor knew this affectation well. *It is the ultimate postural cliché of a man wanting to exude wisdom and gravitas.* But in this case, she took it more as a sign of his embarrassment at the word salad that had dribbled from his intern's mouth. Jonas turned to Levine and asked her to describe her emergency call to the patient's room at 1:00 AM Wednesday morning.

Levine cleared her throat. "I was paged because your brother was in acute pain and––"

Anne rounded on her. "He was in pain? I didn't hear a word about that. HE WAS IN PAIN? WHAT IN GOD'S NAME DID YOU DO ABOUT IT?"

Levine took a breath. "Um, his chart notes from Dr Kashimi's intake noted subjective complaints of right flank pain, radiating to his ribs––"

"So, what the hell did your X-ray show was going on with my brother?"

TEARS ARE ONLY WATER

The chief resident looked to her supervisor, who was still gazing out the window, rubbing his brow, and said that X-rays had not been ordered, but she had gotten them immediately with the call to the X-ray Tech. Her voice dropped. "He had severe contusions and two fractured ribs. After he was secured back in his bed, we increased his Ativan, and I ordered something stronger as needed. Your brother had been asleep for much of this. Around 2:45 this morning, I was called back to the ward because he was screaming that someone was at his window. He was highly agitated and said he knew who was coming to get him. The night nurse and tech couldn't make out what he was saying as he slurred and spoke in what sounded like a code. I ordered a CT scan and tox screen, which I thought had been done, but I couldn't find them. They found a high level of dextroamphetamine, or Adderall, in his system. I called Dr Jonas, who agreed that your brother needed a more extensive period of observation and treatment––"

The professor had heard enough. "Really, Dr Jonas? This sounds like amateur hour. These are your best and brightest? My brother was lying there in agony, and you have inexperienced trainees testing out their theories and playing doctor? For God's sake, you left him CHAINED TO HIS FUCKING BED WITH BROKEN RIBS!"

Jonas clenched his jaw. He leaned in and spoke softly.

"Dr Schivalone, this is inexcusable, and I will personally investigate what was clearly our mistake. Please know I will do everything possible to determine how the ball was dropped." He glanced toward Kaspar, who was fiddling with his tie. "Believe me, I understand you've traveled far and are horror-struck by the events leading to your brother's emergency petition. But you're here now and can be of invaluable help in understanding what happened to him. Despite what you've heard here today, we are all concerned and curious to understand more. We need your help."

"Okay, I just want to know what happened."

Jonas leaned in further. "As do I, Professor. I want us to work as a team to piece together the events in the context of your brother's medical and family history, which could provide invaluable clues to understanding and helping him. Your brother was agitated throughout the night and well into the morning and was not responding to our protocols. We couldn't be sure whether this was purely drug-induced or something requiring a longer period of stabilization and treatment."

The professor narrowed her eyes. "What are you getting at? He suffers from intractable narcolepsy, possibly Kleine-Levin Syndrome. No one has ever been sure. He self-medicates with stimulants to stay awake. When he sleeps, he suffers from cataleptic sleep paralysis. We've known this for years. There is nothing else. No other explanation. This is a travesty, a complete waste of time."

"I understand how you feel, Professor. I hear you and rest assured, whatever you can tell us is of tremendous diagnostic assistance, which I shall pass on to the doctors in Pueblo. May I ask about any family history of mental illness, say, schizophrenia? Something that might help us understand your brother's acute agitation and confusion after he'd been on an Ativan drip through the night. Clearly, the overuse of Adderall plays into all of this, but we think there may be something more. So, I need to ask if there might've been a history of mental issues in the family tree, Professor."

Anne sank back into her chair and rubbed her forehead. "Yes...no.... I don't know, but I don't think any of this is relevant to my brother. I've already told you. He has narcolepsy and abuses Adderall. End of story. There's no need to––"

"Excuse me, Professor," Jonas interrupted. "You first said yes. Please tell me about this history. It sounds important but also, perhaps, somewhat equivocal. But anything you can tell us might help his team in Pueblo understand how to reach your brother."

The professor rubbed her hands. She was so tired it was hard to think straight, much less push back at Jonas' persistent questioning. "Well... my, our father...he survived Bergen-Belsen as a child. He was a brilliant physicist but had...something of a breakdown...He talked to ghosts in the evening and needed to be hospitalized. Just that. He went away, but...." Her voice trailed off.

Jonas turned from the window. "Please continue, Professor. This is so important."

Feeling like a fish unable to wiggle free from the hook he had set, she cleared her throat and paused. "Um...his incompetent doctors decided to give him a weekend pass...and he died the next day."

Jonas was not the only one to see the moistness in her eyes. "How very tragic, Professor. I'm so sorry.... Can you remember his diagnosis?"

There was a long pause. Anne's shoulders slumped. "It was paranoid schizophrenia, but that was total rubbish. They were wrong. Idiots, all of them. He'd spent two years in a concentration camp as a child, for God's sake. Have you ever heard of PTSD? My father did *not* have schizophrenia. I've spent my life studying disorders of the mind, and this was *not* schizophrenia. I can assure you of that."

Jonas nodded. "Of course, I'm sure you're right. Thank you, Professor. This is incredibly helpful. I value your expertise in cognitive neuroscience and know you've written in that field. Anyone surviving a death camp would certainly have been damaged by that experience. Because this is so important and due to the legal charges facing your brother, I felt it even more important to transfer him to a top-notch forensic evaluation center where he can get the care he deserves. As I have said, we are an acute care facility and would not have been able to keep him with us for the observational period necessary. He needs more time than we can provide."

Jonas paused and cleaned his glasses. "Judge Julius Rainsford, very respected in our community, had an opening in his schedule so we could expedite your brother's hearing earlier today. We're convinced this is for the best. Your brother is a special man and deserves our best efforts to understand him and help alleviate his pain and suffering. As you've told us, his is a most complicated and vexing case with a neurologically based disorder, coupled with a drug-induced state, against the backdrop of a possible family history of schizophrenia. However, as you point out, that was probably an incorrect diagnosis. I believe it is best to keep an open mind until your dear brother can undergo a thorough work-up at the Forensic Evaluation and Treatment Unit in Pueblo. They have a number of talented clinicians there who will care for your brother. They have a new director who has overseen the development of cutting-edge forms of psychiatric and psychopharmacological treatment."

The room fell silent. She felt depleted and didn't respond. Dr Levine stood and offered to get a map and directions to the state hospital. She said that the unit secretary would help Anne make reservations for lodging and a car if she wished. The professor was beyond exhausted, her venom spent. She stood and followed Levine down the hall.

Chapter 11

Cinnamon Gummies

Wednesday, March 19, 4:45 PM

Whether they were trying to deflect from their screw-ups or because she'd revealed herself to be a paper tiger--*God, I'm so pathetic*--Anne appreciated the department secretary making all her arrangements, including two nights at the Marriott in Englewood, a Hertz rental to be delivered to the hotel, and a taxi to whisk her away from the hospital. The driver found her sitting in the lobby.

Shock and jet lag--not to mention the recently escaped inmates from her psychic prison romping about--had taken an exhausting emotional toll. It had been twenty hours of hell. She'd experienced a kaleidoscope of anxiety quickening to panic, hyperventilation leading to numbness, and anger bleeding to rage. It was always easier for her to channel outrage and indignation than to feel scared and vulnerable. Her blood boiled at the thought that Jonas had played her. His clever ploy to get her to lower her sword and shield had caught her off guard. When he took away her fury, he exposed something softer. Still, tears were a sign of weakness and had no place in a well-ordered life, especially not today. She was raw from fatigue and shocked at her brother's arrest and forced hospitalization because he had gone bonkers. On top of altitude and exhaustion, all this craziness about little brother was compounded by the fact that Goddamned Noa hadn't responded to her umpteen voice-mails. And now, seated in the cab, she felt a faint tapping at her mental compartment door, announcing the presence of yet another unwelcome intruder from the shadows. Fucking Jonas had summoned memories of Vati.

Professor Emil Lüedke had been a physicist at the Colorado School of Mines. Widely respected for his brilliance and kind-heartedness, Vati had the manner and accent of an old European patrician. Given Mother's embrace of all that was different, it was surprising that she decided to drop the umlaut from their last name after the war because it drew unwanted attention to his German heritage. Impeccably dressed in a tie and tweed jacket, with an aroma of Latakia pipe tobacco permeating his clothing and skin, Vati read every book he could touch. Nestled in his chair by the window, his face framed by a carpet of snow-white hair and a neatly trimmed Van Dyke, Vati would sit quietly reading and muttering with his head tilted to the side. With a thick cloud of smoke wafting overhead and a Meerschaum hanging from the corner of his mouth, he sat for hours, pouring over obscure tomes by dead physicists and mathematicians. When anyone entered the room, he'd smile sweetly, relight his pipe, and return to his book and quiet mutterings. This old compartment sealed long ago had not been opened...until today.

Anne rubbed her hands together and shook her head as if this would herd the untethered memories back into their containers. It was not until her cab pulled up to a Marriott on West Colfax Ave. that she was jolted back to reality. It was late afternoon, and the gnawing in her stomach was not simply a sign of tension and disgust. She hadn't eaten anything for almost 20 hours. That, combined with everything else, made her feel faint. After checking into her room, she showered and tried Noa several times. Her final message was an angry ramble of needs and accusations.

"Hey, Tonta." That was Noa's favorite word for the idiots she encountered in the ER. "Why are you not picking up, for fuck's sake? The almighty doctor's just too important to answer her damn phone? Can't you see I need you? So, have some courtesy and call me. And quit being so self-focused and ADD."

The professor glanced out her window. One of the stores in the strip mall across the parking lot was quaintly called Cora's Weed Garden, Smokes, Vapes, and Edibles. How long had it been since she'd smoked pot? There was that one time when Noa rolled a joint, and they coughed out smoke together. Noa couldn't stop talking and suddenly passed out, but Anne became more hypervigilant and paranoid. *But that was from smoking pot, right? Marijuana candies might be different. It couldn't hurt.*

The inside of the Weed Garden was as she had imagined, cluttered with paraphernalia, t-shirts, and cases of cannabis buds and oregano-looking leaves. Anne wandered around feeling as if she'd stumbled into an episode of The Twilight Zone.

A tattooed woman with a pronounced nose ring, presumably Cora, looked up and asked if she could help.

With a hint of embarrassment, the professor said, "Um, I'm looking for something edible. Feeling some stress and a touch of the altitude."

"Cool. As you can see, we have quite a mega selection. The cinnamon gummies are my fave, and I get raves from customers."

Hunger made the professor lightheaded, and she found herself transfixed on the movement of Cora's nose ring as she spoke. Anne detested facial jewelry and had displeased the department head once by making her students take out facial piercings when they entered her classroom. The ring's movement reminded her of that bouncing ball accentuating the lyrics of a silly song.

"They're real smooth. One or two'll round the edges off. Like to try one?"

"Sure," the professor said, biting into the tiny bear. *Well, damn, Nose Ring Cora, that was heavenly.* She bought two packs because she was hungry. On her short walk back to the motel, she downed two more. The little cinnamon bears went straight to the lateral hypothalamus and amplified her hunger.

The professor checked with the pimply front desk fellow, first about when her car would arrive and then about a place to eat. He said Hertz would deliver a Toyota Corolla in the morning and that their restaurant, the Jester's Room, was "Purty good, they say."

Who says that? Why do people speak this way? More times than she could remember, she had dressed down a student for importing vacuous clichés into their lexicon. But she was too tired and hungry to ask for names and directions to other places, so she followed the hall to the Jester's Room.

A too-young and perky hostess asked, "How many?"

"Do you see anyone standing next to me?"

The young hostess looked around for others. "Oh, okay, ma'am. This way, please."

Apart from an old couple occupying a booth at the back, the place was empty. "Purty good, hmm," the professor snarked under her breath. The hostess led her to a booth.

An annoyingly cheerful waitress approached with a prepared "Welcome to East Englewood Marriott" speech. The impatient professor stopped her mid-sentence with a wave of her numbed hand, said she was tired and hungry and wanted to see a menu; thank you very much. The woman's smile faded as she handed over a glossy menu.

The hungry professor chewed on another cinnamon bud. She signaled to the smiley waitress—*what's behind that smile, Missy?* A smirk maybe, and why was the girl staring at her? She ordered a Manhattan and some hummus. Her senses heightened, she looked over her shoulder and wondered why the old couple seemed to be looking her way. She perused the menu. In defiance of Noa, with whom she was thoroughly pissed, she ordered the Betsy Heifer Special––a bloody rare eight-inch filet––, a Caesar salad, and baked potato. Noa was an avowed vegan for health reasons, and the professor begrudgingly followed suit. She was tired of being called a control freak, so she went along with her partner's dietary mandate. Besides, neither Noa nor Anne had time or interest in cooking, so they subscribed to several

TEARS ARE ONLY WATER

plant-based meal delivery plans. But God, the professor wanted to eat an animal tonight.

Beef was not served when she was growing up. Mother said it was a savage practice reserved for cannibals and Republicans. Instead, she prepared mystery tofu dishes, masquerading as casseroles.

After gulping down the watery Manhattan, the professor ordered another before her Betsy Special arrived. The drink went straight to her head, dancing the paso doble with the little cinnamon bears. Goddam Noa! She hit speed dial. Another call went straight to voicemail. She punched in the number to the Emergency Room. If Noa were there, they would page her.

"Emergency Department, this is Rochelle."

The professor knew Rochelle socially. A senior nurse in the department, she'd been over for one of Noa's work parties. "Hi, Rochelle, Anne here."

Speaking deliberately and trying not to slur her words, she said, "Lissen, I'm trying to reesh Noa, but she must have her phone off. Can you find her for me, please?"

"Hey, Anne...Yeah, we've been just slammed here. Place is a train wreck. But, um, yeah, she's been running around, you know. Next time I catch up with her, I'll let her know you called. K? Hey, sorry girl, gotta go." The professor detected a hesitation in the nurse's voice.

The Betsy Special arrived with another Manhattan. She carved into the overdone filet and took large sips of her drink. The food quieted her roaring hunger, but the call with Rochelle had set off a chain of tender memories about Noa.

They'd first met when Anne had broken an arm in a yoga class. *Note to self, don't do yoga when you're tipsy.* A Latina doctor wearing purple scrubs, Dr Moreno maintained a hardened demeanor that belied her humor and kindness. She'd approached with a physicianly swagger and picked up the chart while maintaining an implacable expression before bursting out in laughter. "It says here you fractured your radius by... yoga-ing. Is this true?"

Anne had felt more embarrassment than pain, but the laughter that lit up the physician's face was an instant analgesic. Doctors aren't supposed to laugh at their patients, but this one did it in a way that invited her not to take everything so seriously. Noa's soft, firm touch communicated competence and caring as she hummed while tending to the broken arm. Later that night, she called to ensure her patient was feeling okay.

Anne didn't see Noa again until they bumped into each other at a Pride event four months later. When their eyes met, Noa smiled and wrapped her arm around her neck, mimicking a yoga position she had termed "the pretzel" that day in the ER. They spent the rest of the afternoon together, walking the botanical gardens around Amherst. They started seeing each other weekly––grabbing an espresso and, whenever Noa was free, meeting at their favorite wine bar. After a six-month courtship, they moved into a condo together before buying the house on South Prospect.

Before Noa, there had been a few girlfriends, all in the same mold of an over-educated Ivy League academic, who'd stepped out of the closet too late in their lives. Noa and the professor couldn't have been more different. The professor was the offspring of an Italian atheist and a German Jew but exuded the White privilege of a blue-blooded wasp. She tried to speak softly so that others would be forced to listen closely, choosing words they would need to look up, scoring points, not by talking loudly but by deploying her rapier wit and logic. Her hair was short and brown, fiercely competing against encroaching strands of gray claiming eminent domain. She was a quiet, cerebral, bony-elbowed academic who others saw as overly severe and laugh-deprived. Yet, despite her brashness and ostensible self-assuredness, her sexual identity still felt new and uncertain. Noa was her opposite. An open book––loud, intuitively intelligent, impatient, passionate, and dark-skinned. She always knew and never hid who she was.

Anne stopped taking Prozac after she fell in love. Noa became her mood stabilizer, but something was up with her. Noa had grown distant and moody recently. True, her schedule was killing her, but it seemed there might be something more. Really, if there were, Noa would have to figure that out. Right now, there were more important problems to solve, and Noa needed to step up and be there for her.

The professor's ravenous hunger satisfied by the Betsy Heifer, she ordered a cognac and a decaf, then returned to her room. She would try Noa again tomorrow. Her annoyance had mellowed. She reminded herself that Noa often got slammed at work and either misplaced or forgot to charge her phone. She smiled at the thought of her lovable ADD Noa. Her little bear buddies from the Weed Garden had smoothed out her anger. *Purty good, huh?*

Feeling the effect of two, or was it three, Manhattans, a brandy, and the edibles, she lay on the bed and shut her eyes to the spinning ceiling. It was at that moment the day caught up with her. Betsy was mooing in her stomach, and the gummies had walked off the job, leaving a sickening feeling in their wake. She staggered to the bathroom, splashed cold water on her face, and searched for the Tylenol she'd stashed in her purse. Her head throbbed. A hot shower helped some. She tried to reassure herself. After sorting out all this mess, she'd set things right with her Noa. She crawled into bed and began to drift off when her phone pinged. A voicemail message.

"Lo siento, Blanca. Sorry, it has been crazy today with gunshot gangsters and car crashes. But, Annie, I have to tell you that living with you and your moods and constant drinking is starting to suck the air out of my lungs. Everything has to be the professor's way. You always have to get the last word in. You criticize everything about everybody, including me, but you are like a closed box. You complain that I don't tell you my feelings. Ha! Are you serious, Blanca, when you share nothing? And you talk, talk, talk about this mother of yours. Really, Annie, you want to see your crazy mother? I suggest you just look in the mirror. But I know you can't see that. Why do you work so hard to make people not want to be around you? It's like you try to get people not to like you. This is very sad. And, for me, I'm like your brown-skinned charm on a bracelet that you like to show everyone, but I don't think you know me at all. Really, Querida, I need a break. I need my spaces for a while. Please, give me that, Annie. Maybe I will call sometime. I just cannot go on with this."

Instantly sober, the professor began chanting frantically. "Please, you have to stop doing this to me! Please, you have to stop doing this to me!"

In a rush of rage and nausea, all her compartments collapsed as she ran to the bathroom and heaved up the day's horrors--a mile high in the sky.

Chapter 12

The Messes He's Made

Wednesday, March 19, 5:30 PM

Carmine watched the deputy walk away, wondering why she had fallen silent during their trip. All he knew was her voice was now flat, and her eyes had grown dark. From when he was five, he'd been watching people from the quiet corners of a room. He coded what they were saying, first using numbers and then with colors, which he assigned to their voice tones and facial expressions. He paid less attention to the words they spoke and more to the light patterns in their eyes and the prosody of their speech. Though his understanding was unconventional, he surprised people with his intuitive grasp of emotion.

Yes, something had unmistakably changed in the deputy during their drive to this strange place. Like a sudden modification of a variable in an equation, the bookkeeper detected a shift in the code sequence of her speech after the spark in her eyes was extinguished. The air of confidence encased by her words had disappeared in an instant. The deputy had openly shared parts of her private world with a silent man she assumed was asleep. Even the crispness of her uniform and sharpness of her movements couldn't hide the vulnerability she had exposed. Now, she was gone, with whatever secrets had frozen her in place.

The aide left him strapped to his wheelchair while she went to speak with the admissions secretary. He felt sleepy and alone--a familiar feeling for a strange man in a strange place. Yet his mind was restless.

. . .

He had felt out of place his whole life. People glanced at the books he carried, like *Ramanujan's Lost Notebook* or Hardy's essay, *A Mathematician's Apology*, and then winced or furrowed their brows with puzzled looks. No one understood him. At one time, he thought E saw him; but in the end, he couldn't be sure. The bookkeeper was as inscrutable as his impenetrable books for the few who knew him.

It had been this way with Maimie, who tried to read him like an inkblot, always assuming things about him that were merely her projections. "My brilliant boy, you're just like your mother, thinking marvelously deep thoughts that will change the world." When others commented on his silence, she would answer, "You're just too dense to understand. My boy Carmine is a genius. He's incubating thoughts that you can't begin to fathom." But she never came close to knowing who he was.

The events of the last three days left a muddy residue in his mind. His strange encounter with E had awakened dormant longings.

Clever E, who'd tricked the world into believing she was gone, had returned to him with an urgent message: "Carm, we want you to join us. We need you. *I* need you. Watch for the signs." She had finally come for him. But then, hearing the tapping code and finding the glove she'd left behind led to that awful moment he was trying to erase from his mind––his hands around that loathsome woman's throat, squeezing tightly, hating her for attempting to take E away from him.

He reached deeply for numbers to replace the unwanted memories that were returning––

$e^{i\pi} + 1 = 0...e^{i\pi} + 1 = 0....$ But the numbers had lost their magic. His fingers tightened as he recalled the terror in the office manager's eyes.

The bookkeeper vomited on the floor in the admissions area. The aide came running over when she saw her new patient leaning to the side of his wheelchair and retching.

"Oh dear, look what you've done. Now I've got to clean all this up. Oh my, what a mess you've made!"

TEARS ARE ONLY WATER

. . .

For much of his life, he'd been told about the messes he made. When his wordlessness extended into his eighth year, Maimie took it personally, and her adulation turned to criticism and scorn. "Why won't you speak or look at me?" When he'd embarrassed her in front of her poetry group with his stuttered response to a question, she cornered him and lashed out, "You're a mess, Carmine. What have I ever done to you? I gave you life, and you've given me nothing but the shame of your oddness and your retreat from the world. You either refuse to speak, or you talk like an idiot." All he could see was the harsh glare of her orange and purple accusations, and all he could do was look away and surround himself with a shield of numbers.

With E's coming back into his life, this all could change. No more messes with accounts not balancing and no more feeling useless and invisible.

As she cleaned up his mess, the aide mumbled to herself with disgust before taking him to the admissions window for processing. The young woman asked for his name, date of birth, living relatives, social security number, and insurance. The bookkeeper answered the first three questions, enough to complete the processing. Another aide wheeled him onto the elevator, then up to the observation ward on the 4th floor, where he would spend the next 24 hours in isolation. The aide made sure his restraints were secure and left him alone. The shadows on the wall grew longer while he waited for someone to notice he was there.

An older nurse wearing glasses on the tip of her nose arrived carrying a chart. She motioned to an enormous man. "Julio, we'll do the admissions interview now. Afterward, you can take him to the observation ward. I assume the doctor will be by sometime to check on her new patient."

As the nurse was shuffling through her papers, Carmine fell asleep. Awakened by a loud voice and a finger jabbing his shoulder, he opened his eyes to see the bespectacled nurse sitting across from him and the super-sized aide standing at her side. Her nametag read Olive Astracides, R.N. The aide's ID, draped around his thick tattooed neck, read Julio Garza. The nurse pulled out a pen and began flicking through the chart.

"Julio, you may loosen his restraints, but I'd like you to stay with us." Julio's giant hands adjusted the restraints and gently patted the bookkeeper's shoulder.

The nurse raised her eyebrows. "Let's keep our distance. We don't know what we're dealing with."

The interview with Nurse Astracides lasted a little over 30 minutes. She asked the new patient about his medical history and family background. Carmine answered her initial questions with minimal elaboration. But he became agitated and protested when the nurse said he would spend the next 24 hours in the observation ward before being transferred to the forensics unit.

"I c-can't be here! She can't, won't f-f-find me. Don't you see? Why are you doing this t-to me?"

The nurse asked a series of follow-up questions, each with a sharper tone. When she'd finished, she voiced her frustration. "Mr Luedke, you'll find that your treatment will require more active participation and a different tone. Your irritability is not an excuse. We're here to help, but that depends on your cooperation and clear communication." She stood up and pushed through the door as a nursing tech with a cart entered to take his blood.

Julio remained with him, once again patting his shoulder with his beefy hand while the tech drew several vials of blood.

"It's okay, ese. You be alright." Julio wheeled the bookkeeper to a barren seclusion room. "You should just chill out in here until tomorrow, bro." He left and came back with some orange juice and graham crackers. "Figure after all the buzz, you gotta be hungry. Here, it'll help you feel better, bro, yer blood sugar and whatnot."

Julio brought in a chair and took a seat. The chair disappeared under his oversized frame. "Damn, homes, those are some shiny shoes, bro. *Nice*. I been reading the discharge notes from the last hospital they had you at. Man, you had one hell of a week." His eyes lit up with interest and then sympathy. "Somethin' must've tripped for you, bro. Says you were seein' and hearin' some things and went after a lady you worked with. Sorry life's been so dark, bro. What went down with all this?"

The long pause would have told most people that it was time to move on, that a response was not forthcoming, and that there were more important things to do than wait for the silent to speak. Instead, Julio continued to look at him, not with a menacing stare but with patience and interest.

"I get it, bro. Too many questions and not enough listening. First the cops, then the doctors and nurses, and now you got big Julio in yer face. Hey, it's all right. Save yer energy. You'll need it, bro." He got up and started to leave when Carmine pulled at his restraints and stammered a panicky response.

"They're t-trying to....Think I made a m-mess. Can't sleep but can't stay awake. Can't fix accounts at work. BUT SHE C-CAME. They want to HIDE this. It will all c-change now. That's it....I t-think I k-k-killed someone. Messes because the numbers didn't add up. She's LOOKING to FIND me. Have to tell her. CAN'T be here."

With a benevolent smile, Julio nodded. "Yeah, bro, but you *are* here. Don't know about your messes, but I didn't see nothin' about a murder, homes. Messed her up some but didn't kill her. But you're here now. Maybe a good thing, bro. Get all this sorted out. Got all kinds of folks here. Tween you and me, some are fools, but that's not for me to say. Some good folks too. You'll see when you meet Doctor Hazel, homes. She sees like a hawk, bro." He pulled up his shirt sleeve to look at his watch, revealing a gallery of artwork on his heavily inked forearm.

"She's doing her rounds, but she'll be in later for a short meet-up. Tomorrow, I'll come and take you to your room. I'll leave you some more OJ. Adios."

The bookkeeper closed his eyes as more jumbled memories began to return. Replaying the events from Monday night, his heart quickened at the thought that E had returned to him, that she needed him, wanted him. How could she find him now? She'd brought something so vital and secret that it needed to be guarded and hidden in a code. Something so important that others would go to great lengths to deny her return to him. LuCinda had found out. Yeah, she knew that he knew about her coverup. Something awakened deep inside. Longing? Anger? Shame? His stomach turned at the thought of how he'd lunged for the office manager's throat. Throughout his sad life, he'd never laid his hands on another person, animal, or insect. Now he was in this strange place because he had. Yet, his shame for having lashed out could not silence his rage, and his fingers tightened into fists.

For the bookkeeper, candles of consciousness are too quickly extinguished. Thoughts, sensations, longing, sadness, and rage are all blown out in an instant. Carmine drifted as the room darkened beneath his closed eyelids. The restraints, even loosely bound to the arms of the chair, constricted his movements. Uncertain about whether his eyes were open or shut, he saw in the window a face looking in. There she was...found him, coming again to make things right. As dread mixed with hope, he watched the light play around her face and recognized the luminosity of her hair. And there she was...peering in, trying to find him. He could hear her voice in his head, "You're the one, Carmine. It's time!" He tried to call out to her, but his words were reduced to the sounds of a wounded animal. "E! EEE...EEE!"

The door suddenly opened, and in walked his doctor. Behind her stood the mountainous aid, who gently roused the bookkeeper.

"I see we startled you," she said. "I'm so sorry. I'm your doctor, Hazel Lukachunai. Mr Garza said you are having some difficulty settling in. I came to introduce myself and begin our conversation. I would like to understand, Mr Luedke." She leaned forward with her soft words.

Carmine looked up, transfixed. Her umber-shaded eyes held his gaze. Deeply etched lines danced in rhythmic movements as she spoke, communicating a warmth and understanding that made it difficult for him to look away. He felt a stirring, unfamiliar, yet not wholly unknown.

A voice inside sounded an alarm. "Pull back, look away. You can't trust her." A scent, faint yet sweet and herbal, filled his nostrils, tempting him to engage his senses. "No, look away," the voice cautioned, and he repeated his mantra embedded in the tissues of his mind, $e^{i\pi} + 1 = 0...e^{i\pi} + 1 = 0.$

Yet the bookkeeper could not make himself look away. Nor could he make himself invisible or disappear from her knowing eyes. Unexpectedly, he held her gaze, and, at that moment, his frozen words thawed.

"She's found me because it's time. I can't be here. Everything will change. They need mathematical brilliance, she said. Me. No more messes. That's all."

She motioned to Julio that it was time to leave him with the staff on the observation ward. "Tomorrow, we'll go outside and enjoy the lovely day. The sky is a canvas of blues and pinks the great spirit has painted for our delight. Then we'll start talking about these messes of yours."

Chapter 13

Following Breadcrumbs

Thursday, March 20, 10:00 AM

Dry heaves continued throughout the night. The professor's jet lag was compounded by shock, outrage, indignation, and heartbreak. As hangovers go, this ranked among the worst. The past 24 hours had been a nightmare, with one vulgar surprise after another. She decided not to try to contact Noa. The message was clear. She'd honor her partner's wish for space, at least for now. The thought of driving two hours to the state hospital and dealing with more medical quackery sickened her sickness. She felt she couldn't face more psychiatric dumplings, at least not for another day. Carmine was not going anywhere. They'd told her at the state hospital that she might not even be allowed to see him for up to a week after his admission, which was outrageous. No, she needed to calm her nerves and try to piece together what had happened to her brother. First, she needed coffee, then wine, to make her feel normal again.

She vowed to do her own investigative work and gather the data. That's what she always preached to her first years. It was a matter of following the breadcrumbs. Be like Hansel and Gretel, but don't get lured off your path of discovery by the easy promises of the witch. She wasn't sure that the metaphor held water. Still, no matter what, she always enjoyed the sound of her voice, and her students always assumed there was great wisdom in anything she said.

So, the professor mapped out a plan. She would spend a day or so in Denver trying to piece things together while processing the shocks to her system. First on her list was to visit Sheriff Burwinkle, who had started all this madness with his unwelcome midnight call. She wanted to learn more about her brother's state of mind when he was picked up and taken to jail. This would be the place to start--find out about his mental state and what in God's creation had happened to put this unholy episode in motion in the first place. The next stop would be to the place where all this supposedly happened, the company where he worked. She looked up the address. She would find the owner--Shrenklin if there was such a person--and, of course, confront the woman her brother had allegedly attacked. She decided she would play the role of the overwrought sister, conveying equal parts apology and worry.

After a fourth cup of coffee and two more Tylenol for her pounding headache, she restlessly flipped through the Denver Post, skimming articles about the crackdown on pro-democracy protests in Hong Kong and one about ISIS beheading journalists. Turning the page, she saw a headline about Russia annexing Crimea and this ongoing thing with the Malaysian airliner, which has been freaking everyone out. The world is falling apart, and the madness has hit home with her brother. The mayhem of the last few days brought to mind a singer named Barry McGuire and his song in the '60s called "Eve of Destruction."

She picked up her car and found the address for the Arapahoe County Sheriff's Department. Her GPS mapped out the route. Burrowing into this mess with her brother would focus her mind and provide an antidote to the helplessness she'd felt yesterday. It would also allow her to put Noa into a box and shut the lid on the hole she left, if only for a while.

The officer at the front desk immediately called Sheriff Burwinkle, who looked like she'd pictured him from their call—a Wilford Brimley clone with countrified mannerisms and a lip-obscuring mustache.

"Howdy doody, Miss, uh, Stalone. Sorry to meet under these circumstances."

Tired of correcting his butchering of her name and the Miss instead of Professor, she implored the good sheriff to tell her everything he could about her little brother's condition the day he was brought in. He described Carmine as agitated with a "wild look about him like a rabid mud cat" talking about "some kind of conspiracy thing at work."

The sheriff leaned back, rubbing his chest, and reached for a bottle of pills, "I figgered he just wasn't right. Seen it in my own family if you want to know the whole truth."

The professor didn't care to know an iota of truth about his family. Still, a wave of nausea silenced her from voicing an objection.

The sheriff continued. "Would've been inhumane to hold him in a cell when anyone could plainly see he belonged in a hospital where they could keep an eye on him and tend to his needs better than we coulda done here. You should talk to the depety who was on the scene and brought him in. Depety Kitts also escorted him to MCA. Yesterday, I sent her to accompany yer brother to our state facility in Pe-eblo after the judge did an involuntary commitment on him. If anyone knows what he's got goin' on in his head, it's her. She's a pretty sharp gal. Likes to think about things real deep and figger out what makes people tick, more than I reckon she should, just tween you, me, and the wall there. Too bad, though, cuz she's probably headin' out of town fer the next week."

The professor politely asked for the deputy's phone number or address so she could meet with her. Maybe there was a chance she was still around.

Massaging his chest again, he replied, "No can do. Strictly against departmental policy to give out any personal info on anyone who works here. Just leave yer phone number, and I'll have her give ya a call when she returns."

Anne got in her rental and began to sweat. Goddammit. Now this. She turned on the AC, which was not working. "Perfect shitshow. Now I'll cook inside this cheap car. I am being punished," she cursed. She entered the address to Shrenklin's and continued to review her list of complaints as she drove.

The faded green awning read Shrenklin's Tax and Accounting. She shook her head. There would be no awards given out for euphonious business branding. The location was no less lackluster, nestled in a strip mall adjacent to an industrial park. The professor pushed open the glass door and walked up a flight of cement steps leading to a lobby with a clump of desks in front of some nondescript cubicles. Toward the back, three or four offices flanked the cubicles––a boringly geometric and unimaginative floor plan. A heavyset woman wearing an orthopedic Victorian collar flitted from desk to desk then back into one of the offices. She resembled the Dustin Hoffman character in the '80s movie *Tootsie*.

Assuming the role of the worried and contrite sister, the professor exhaled and knocked on that office door with the sign, "Office Manager LuCinda Pelcovey." The high-collared woman opened the door. Before she could speak, Anne stepped into the office, stared into the manager's eyes, and filled the air with a barrage of contrition.

The professor once took a seminar on the techniques of a charismatic master hypnotherapist named Milton Erickson, who taught a confusional technique. The idea was for the hypnotist to flood the subject with lilting, repetitive verbiage while fixing their gaze directly on them and then planting suggestions for what they wanted their subject to do.

"Ms Pelcovey? Hello, I'm Anne Schivalone, the older sister of the man who did this dreadful thing to you. First, let me say I'm beyond horror-struck by his actions. I'm so terribly, terribly, terrribbly sorry, Ms Pelcovey, for the pain he must have caused you and sooo grateful that... you will talk to me now and tell me everything you know....I've flown in from the East Coast, from the EEEast Coast, to try to piece together what in God's eternal plan got into my brother and to offer my sincerest, sincccerest apologies. However, I realize that cannot hold a candle to the pain and suffering you've undoubtedly endured. I'm heartsick, Ms Pelcooovey, and obviously very worried about my brother, who has no history of anything remotely like this. If it isn't asking too much, perhaps...you will help me understand what happened *to my little brother*...leading up to this horrific event that caused you so much pain. Only you can help here; you can help me...help me now."

The office manager stared wide-eyed, stunned by the professor's odd cadence and unnerving stare. Her reaction gave the professor hope that her suggestions had landed and made the office manager pliable.

The truth was the professor had fallen asleep in the Ericksonian hypnosis seminar and never finished the training, so she shouldn't have been surprised that her trance-inducing efforts failed miserably.

LuCinda blinked and, with a scarlet flush around her cheeks, unloaded. "Well, I never! How DARE you march in here and presume to tell ME what to do! You have some nerve showing up here after what that maniac brother of yours did. I knew there was something off about him from the beginning. I don't know why Marvin ever hired him to begin with. He's got a soft spot for oddballs, but your brother never belonged here. Anyone could see something was horribly wrong with a man who could only work at night. Mr Shrenklin asked me to stay in the office the nights he was working late to keep an eye on him. Kept to himself and gave everyone the creeps, your brother did. Then all this absurd nonsense about some woman coming to visit him Sunday night. That was a feeble lie on his part to cover up whatever he shouldn't have been doing. COMPLETE POPPYCOCK, his claiming I'd let this woman into his office. He'd imagined the whole thing or invented it as an excuse to blame someone else for his miserable failings. Didn't surprise me. Your brother was unfit and unstable from the moment he started working here. And when he accused *ME* of lying about this glove he found in his office, he suddenly snapped and ATTACKED ME!" LuCinda began to cough and reflexively reached for her orthopedic collar.

With all her restraint and resolve, the professor asked what had become of the glove, that maybe she could speak with its owner and apologize to her as well. LuCinda looked confused and blurted out, "It belonged to our cleaning woman, and I gave it BACK to her! Now, as you can plainly see, we have lots of work to do here. Your brother belongs behind bars, and if I have any say, that's exactly where he'll go after all this hospital foolishness."

TEARS ARE ONLY WATER

The professor was not one to be bludgeoned in verbal combat. "I see. Let me just say--"

But the horse-collared office manager cut her off. "Oh, and there's more to your little innocent-looking, sick brother than meets the eye, you know. Not only is he a violent psychopath, but we have reason to believe he stole from one of our accounts. We have our own people beginning an investigation, so if I were you, I'd get back on a plane and go back to wherever it is you're from. And while you're at it, you should get him a criminal defense attorney, because, I assure you, he will need one. Off you go. Tick tock. I have work to do here. Now, shoo."

The pounding in Anne's temples and screaming in her brain made it hard for her to take in what the office manager was saying. Struggling to regain her composure, she dug her fingernails into her palms and forced herself to sound reasonable.

"Um...I completely understand your feelings, Ms Pelcovey. Honestly, I'd feel the same way if this had happened to me. I'd like to apologize to Mr Shrenklin and offer my gratitude for hiring my little brother in the first place. I'd also like to offer an apology to your cleaning woman."

"Impossible," the office manager fired back. "In case you don't know, this is tax season. Mr Shrenklin's working out of the office, and our cleaning woman has left for the day. Now, you've overstayed your welcome. I have no more to say to you, miss!" She lifted her chubby index finger and pointed to the exit.

The professor bowed her head, thanked the office manager for her time, apologized twice more, and backed out of her office. Anne's ulcer was spewing acid. Distracted, she left the office, searching her phone contacts for her brother's address as she exited the building. Not paying attention in the parking lot, she nearly knocked over a man wearing sunglasses and a black ball cap. He seemed to appear out of nowhere. When she turned around to apologize, he had disappeared.

Sitting in her car, she found an address for Carmine's apartment and entered it into her GPS. Her expectations about his living situation were low and were not inaccurate. She parked her car in front of a badly neglected row of townhouses. Anne found the manager, a young kid her students' age, and explained that her brother was in the hospital, and she'd flown in from the East Coast to help. If she could get into his apartment, she'd be able to pick up his medicine and bring him some things before his heart surgery. The wily professor flashed him her driver's license and a twenty, which he pocketed, and let her in.

The stale odor of cooking oil and cat litter greeted her as she pushed open the door against a small pile of mail. The shades were drawn. Newspapers were strewn about and dishes stacked in the sink—no doubt incubating various forms of undiscovered bacteria. She checked the refrigerator on the off chance that her brother might have an opened bottle of wine. She was disappointed but not surprised to find nothing worth drinking in the fridge.

She found his calendar on the desk by his computer. Nothing much there, just a couple of phone numbers in the back. One name seemed curious, Dihn.

His computer screen lit up as she pressed Enter. Damn, she needed a password to get into the thing. Then, she remembered her brother's fascination with numbers and that he had once used a 5-digit square root of pi on his devices. She Googled the number and tried it, smiling as the computer whirred and clicked. *Little brother was so predictable.* He'd left several pages open. Why was he searching for information on the human genome and something called codons? Link after link on the genetic basis of mental and neurological diseases. If he'd wanted to know something about this, he should have come to his big sister, who had more than a passing familiarity with such matters. After scanning ten or so articles, she came upon a new search. Her eyes widened, and her stomach dropped. Elizabeth Covington. Another ghost back from the grave. Articles about her academic awards, reports of the wunderkind beginning a laboratory at Stanford, stories of the accident, and news of her suicide flooded the screen.

Her brother had always referred to her as E. *How quaint.* Anne had met her on several occasions when he was in high school. Why a future socialite like Elizabeth would have given Carmie a second look never made sense. She was one of a long line of people who'd taken pity and saw him as a human reclamation project. Elizabeth had obviously been in it for herself. She must have had an angle and seen Carmie as an easy mark. Maybe she was secretly getting community service credits for befriending this odd, friendless boy. They somehow ended up at MIT together, but all that came crashing down after the accident. It still made her blood boil that the parents blamed everything on her brother. Then, the so-called E disappeared before breaking her brother's heart. *Karma's a bitch, right, Lizzy? You had plenty of your own issues, or you wouldn't have ended up doing a nosedive off the Bay Bridge, and that was that. But why in the kingdom of God was he searching for her now? Did Miss E have something to do with the mysterious night visitor with the glove? Why was this ghost returning to haunt Carmie now if she was a ghost?*

Luckily, he'd left his phone by the computer. Typical Carmie, leaving his cell phone behind with no way to contact him. Voila. The same password opened his ancient Android with a cracked screen. Scrolling through his emails and texts, she kept finding the name of his Vietnamese friend, Dihn. An animal leaped onto the keyboard and emitted a pathetic yowl during her search. It looked more rodentian than feline. This scrawny thing probably hadn't eaten since Monday. Finding cat food in the kitchen, she poured a bowl for the grateful creature.

The professor had no use for pets, which had been a sticking point with Noa, whom she had managed to block from her mind until now. The only pet she ever had was a goldfish named Goldilocks, who died days after Anne carried it home in a little baggie. She cried when her mother refused her wish for a burial service and flushed Goldilocks down the toilet.

Time stamps on his texts to Dihn lined up with little brother's misadventures earlier in the week. So, who was Dihn, and why had her brother sent him so many texts on Tuesday? She returned to Carmine's calendar and found a phone number and email address for a Carl Carothers, but nothing for someone named Dihn. Looking through his emails, she opened one from Carothers that was signed "Dihn." So Dihn and Carothers were the same person. She called the number he'd been texting. An older-sounding man answered, "Yup," and she identified herself, saying it would be beneficial if they could meet. She always favored in-person meetings over those on the phone. He agreed with her request and gave her his address.

As she drove through his neighborhood, she wondered if everyone her brother knew lived in rundown buildings adjacent to industrial parks. Dihn's was a small wooden framed house that probably saw its last coat of paint during the Ford administration. A short, bespectacled Caucasian man in his 60s wearing a military jacket invited her in. He had a gray, patchy beard and long, thinning hair--*clearly a man unconcerned about his appearance and personal hygiene.* He had a head tremor, an unmistakable sign of neurodegenerative disease. Parkinson's, maybe. She had neither the time nor inclination to ask about the pseudonym Dihn, figuring he was one of those vets who'd never completely left Vietnam behind.

"Come on in. You're his sister, you say. Well, I'll be. Never knew Carm had a sister. I'm Carl. Been a friend of your brother's for some time now."

The room was cluttered with computer screens atop every surface in his tiny house. The odor was musty but tolerable. *Predictable for a straight man who lives by himself.* Dihn's place exuded organized chaos, its clutter neatly ordered. No doubt Dihn knew where everything was in his tiny universe. She could feel the electromagnetic radiation seeping into her skin in the cramped living room. A droning hum vibrated throughout the dingy room, lit only by the unnatural light from the multiple screens fixed on every wall and every surface. Her reward for this cursed trip to Denver would be death by radiation poisoning.

She told Dihn what had happened to her brother and why she was there. "Besides the people he worked with, you may have been the last to speak with him. You're his friend. He needs your help. Why did he come to see you? I know he was looking for a woman named Elizabeth Covington. Why? And what did this have to do with codons and whatever other nonsense he was looking into?"

TEARS ARE ONLY WATER

Dihn took an unnatural amount of time to answer, convincing her that he was in the early stages of Parkinson's. Soon it became clear that this was just his style of communicating.

"Yeah...well, didn't see that coming.... Poor guy.... He come to me hoping I could help him find out anything on the dark web about this woman he called E, this Elizabeth woman. He was real worked up, not like him, you know. Said he'd seen her the night before, that she appeared in his office out of nowhere and then disappeared.... Couple years back, we got wasted here, me, Carm, and our band of brothers....Course, Carm wasn't much for drinking and never said much. Most of the guys just called him the bookkeeper. Not sure they bothered to learn his name. You know, a bunch of computer nerds and hackers. Anyway, some guy started talking about how his girlfriend left him, and no one knew what to say, except your brother said something about a woman.... I think it was E. He said she got herself run over or some such because of him, and later she killed herself. We weren't into asking too many questions. That's all I know. Didn't say nothing about condoms or whatever. I told him I'd take a peek and let him know when I found anything about her.... But the search came up empty, just a ghost. A trail leading no wheres––Nada, bubkas. Bottom line, if I can't find her, she probably ain't out there. Trust me. But hell, I ain't the sharpest tool in the shed, and maybe this gal really didn't want to be found and could have scrubbed her digital fingerprints pretty good. Guess that's possible, but I doubt it."

The professor read no hint of emotion on the man's face. Dihn was a loyal friend, a technician made up more of microchips and semiconductors than human mirror neurons. She thanked him and told him she'd keep him posted if she learned anything else.

"Well, anything for your brother. Carm's good people. If you need anything, you know where to find me."

As she approached the door, she turned and asked, "Dihn, there is something. Can you get me a home address for a Deputy Nicola Kitts at the Sheriff's Department in Arapahoe County?"

113

It was late afternoon, and the professor drove back to the Marriott to rest while waiting for a text from Dihn. Time was short because Burwinkle said the deputy was going away. She also wanted to talk to Carmine's boss——this Marvin Shrenklin person——to see if he knew any more about her brother's mindset and behavior before Monday. Dropping by again in person risked creating a scene with Tootsie. She decided to call. She would disguise her voice and have a plausible reason for talking to the boss. The office manager would, no doubt, keep tight control of his schedule and calls. She would have to speak with this woman again to talk to him. In the meantime, she texted Dihn to ask if he could provide the names of Shrenklin's clients, especially the ones her brother was working on. In less than ten minutes, he texted back with the deputy's address and a list of 20 accounts.

The professor chose Shreveport Medical Waste and called Shrenklin's main number. The office manager picked up on the second ring, "Shrenklin's Auditing & Accounting, you can count on us. This is Miss Pelcovey, and how may I brighten your day?"

'Well, hi there, Miss Pelcovey. I'm Joanna Budreau from Shreveport. How are y'all doin' out there? I just started working in our financial department. I needed to go over some of our accounting figures with Mr Shrenklin. Would you be a peach and put me through?"

Her stomach burned with the pause on the other end. Then, that annoying voice that had eviscerated her earlier spoke.

"Oh, you can just give me those figures, and I'll ensure that Marvin gets them, dear. No need to bother him."

Needing to improvise, the professor said, "I see, but I'm new here and was strictly instructed to speak directly with Mr Shrenklin. My boss is just awful about these things. Could you help a girl out? I'm afraid if I don't do exactly as he instructed, he'll be really upset. Please, I don't want to mess this up, y'know. I really need this job."

Another silence. Then, "This is highly irregular. We have a protocol here, which we expect all support staff to follow. In the future, I expect you to observe the appropriate chain of command, Miss."

"Oh yes ma'am, I certainly will. I promise you that. I'm so grateful for this one exception. Thank you kindly."

After a pause, LuCinda answered, "Okay, but ignorance is no excuse and will not be tolerated....Hold. I'll see if he's available."

Yes! Damn Horse-Collar was not the brightest bulb in the packet.

There was a click, and a man's voice came on the line. "Hello, this is Marvin Shrenklin. With whom am I speaking, and how can I help? LuCinda said something about verifying accounting figures. You know Miss Pelcovey can take care of all of that."

The professor apologized for the ruse and told him the truth about being Carmine's sister and how she was afraid Miss Pelcovey wouldn't put her through. Then, she repeated the parts about her regret and grief over the mayhem that her brother had caused.

"The only way I can help him is to find out why he acted as he did and attacked poor Miss Pelcovey. She said something about him embezzling from one of his accounts. That seems so preposterous. It's completely out of character for Carmine."

Shrenklin paused. "I'm sorry, but I'm afraid all this is a matter for the police. I don't have much to tell you except that your brother is in a lot of trouble." Shrenklin was obviously the kind of person who told you he couldn't talk about things and then began talking about what he said he couldn't. "Truth be told, I liked your brother. Might have been the only one here who did. He minded his own business. Not into social-izing on company time. I kinda felt sorry for him with that narcolepsy thing. He was a good worker, razor sharp with the numbers, so I gave him keys and let him come in at night to work on his accounts. What-ever happened earlier in the week came out of the blue."

He'd provided an opening, so she pushed a little harder. "You're saying he hadn't behaved this way before, aggressive or, you know...paranoid?"

"Nope. Like I said. Your brother was a loner and kept to himself but always got his work done on time until recently. It's busy season, and end-of-year statements are due. I was on him about finishing his audits of some of our accounts. He kept telling me that the numbers were off. That's the only thing, but now, it looks like he might have been monkeying around with one of those accounts."

Sickened by his words, the professor couldn't picture her brother ever embezzling or, for that matter, assaulting anyone. She rubbed her fingers and reminded herself to keep breathing. *Focus, filter, breathe out, and press on.*

"Yes, that's very disturbing and, like I said, completely out of character. But I also understand that you felt that Miss Pelcovey should stay late just to keep an eye on things, to make sure he was doing what he needed to be doing."

He paused. "Well, I don't know about that. That's what she told you? Maybe she felt the need to check on him herself. I never told her that. She's inclined to take charge, if you know what I mean."

"So, Mr Shrenklin, it sounds like you trusted him, then?"

"Yeah. Until he went full metal jacket on LuCinda, that is. He just kinda snapped. And we'll have to see about this other matter under investigation."

The call with Shrenklin was upsetting, but at least the professor had gotten a piece of critical information that contradicted the office manager. Shrenklin had NOT instructed Pelcovey to keep an eye on her brother at night. Anne felt so pleased with scoring another point that she didn't notice the click on the line an instant before their call ended.

Chapter 14

Semper Fi

Thursday, March 20, 5:30 PM

There was a gnawing in the professor's stomach—this time hunger, not dread. The hotel restaurant was handy, and the food was passable. She limited herself to one glass of wine and a salad, girding herself for the challenging evening ahead. Next stop, drop in on the deputy at her home, 445 Happy Canyon Road. *What a silly name. Was the canyon really all that happy? And people didn't just drop by anymore. Why was that? Why did they feel the need to text first to make sure it's okay to call and then call if it's okay to come over? Such nonsense. This is a prime example of what has killed spontaneity and thickened the walls between people.*

The deputy lived in a small rambler at the end of Happy Canyon Road. *Ha! Finally, no industrial park in sight.* The professor tapped on the door. She could hear music inside, Nina Simone singing "Hard Times."

A Black woman opened the door. She wore a faded, sleeveless KU Jayhawks tee-shirt, accented by well-chiseled shoulders, one with a prominent Semper Fidelis tattoo imprinted above the USMC emblem. The other shoulder was adorned with a 4-inch scar. Her short afro was parted on one side. Perched on her left shoulder sat an enormous blue bird of some sort. In her right hand, she held a pistol.

The professor remembered how Burwinkle said the deputy liked to "think about things real deep and figger out what makes people tick." Anne needed to appeal to the deputy's curiosity about her brother's psyche to avoid coming off as a deranged stalker and keep from getting shot.

"Deputy Kitts, excuse me for the intrusion," she said. "My name is Anne Schivalone. You arrested my brother and took him to the state hospital yesterday. I realize I look like a crazy person and that it's incredibly rude for a stranger to pop in on someone, but I'm overwrought and quite desperate to find out what might have happened to my little brother to make him snap as he did. It's not like him. Please believe me."

The deputy eyed her the way any person would when sizing up a stranger who suddenly appears on their doorstep at night. Finally, she said, "Oh, I'd say you don't just look like a crazy lady, you pretty much are. How the hell you get this address?" She glanced down at her gun.

"I-I apologize for finding your address. Look, I know how this appears, but I'm not a stalker, really, Deputy, and I've been told I'm a lot of things, but crazy isn't one of them. I got your address from a hacker friend of my brother. I'm sorry, really, really sorry for intruding into your private space, but I'm going out of my mind with all that's happened this week. So I'm only asking for a few minutes of your time to find out what you saw and heard that might help me understand what happened. Only then can I help my brother."

The professor told of her conversation with the sheriff, who said that if anyone had any insights, it would be Deputy Kitts. After another moment of silence, the wary deputy motioned with her gun for her visitor to come in. The pterodactyl on her shoulder squawked menacingly.

"Be nice, Langston. We've talked about how we treat guests. Just have to figure out if this lady is a guest. Okay, talk fast, Sis. You've got five minutes starting now." She set the timer on her watch. "Go."

The professor stepped inside and scanned the small living room. There were plants and candles in every corner, prints of Monet's *Garden at Giverny*, and *Water Lily Pond* on adjacent walls. She recognized a few others that looked like Kandinsky's or Pollock's. A duffle bag sat on the floor next to a set of dumbbells, an enormous perch for the bird, a

TEARS ARE ONLY WATER

shadow box with a folded flag, and what looked like a small case of service medals beneath a plaque on an antique-looking secretary. The professor was intrigued by the room's contrasting stories about this woman.

The deputy pushed one of her bags off the couch and told her "guest" to take a seat. "Okay, Books' sister, clock's counting down. Better start talking." She sat across from the couch and rested her pistol on her lap.

The professor wasn't sure who Books was. Still, she began with her conversation with Burwinkle, her visit to Shrenklin's, and the strange encounter with the office manager.

"Yep, know all about her. But this little brother of yours sure did a number on her neck. No getting around that one, Sis. No matter what kind of demons he was fighting, he's now facing assault one. And if I know Mama Lu, she'll take it all the way to the Supreme Court if she has to."

The deputy told Anne about the arrest, the examination at MCA, and the trip to the state hospital. "There was some kind of sadness in your brother. Like he was all alone in the world. Not a soul taking up for him, 'cept you being here now. Where I'm from, that's not right. Your brother did a bad thing, but that doesn't automatically make him bad. People get that kind of thing mixed up."

"That sounds like my brother's life story. He was always different-- loner, awkward beyond belief, silent, genius--but misunderstood and taunted by the world. Yet, he never hurt a fly. That's why all of this confuses me so much. As a kid, he vowed never to kill a bug. Way before anyone thought about becoming a vegan, he decided it was wrong to eat animals."

Kitts nodded and put her pistol on the side table. "Hmm, okay, now you got me a little interested in this story you're telling. But first, I think we need wine."

She placed Langston on his perch. "Don't bite her yet, Langs. But, Sis, don't try anything cuz he'll kill on command." The deputy headed off into the kitchen.

"Okay. Hey, do you mind if I look at your artwork?" The professor, a world-class snoop, wanted to look at the case of medals on the secretary. She stood slowly, watching the bird watch her, and tiptoed to the plaque with the recognizable eagle, globe, and anchor insignia at the top. It read:

Gunnery Sergeant Nicola C. Kitts, USMC

"Strike of the Sword"

Operation Khanjar, Helmand Province, Afghanistan

Alpha Company, 1st Battalion, 5th Marine Regiment

FET-1

For Exemplary Service, 2009-2010.

First to Fight.

The professor recognized one of the medals in the small case on the table, a Silver Star, like the one Noa's brother had earned in Iraq, only his was bronze. So, the deputy was the real thing, a bona fide war hero. Anne remembered reading about the hell the marines went through in Helmand Province.

She took her seat when she heard the ex-Gunnery Sergeant coming from the kitchen. The bird had been observing her every move. No doubt, he would tell Kitts of the professor's snoopery.

"You said your name was Schivalone. I got that right?" The professor nodded, accepting a glass of red wine. "No relation to some poet from way back, I suppose. Had to read some of her shit back in a college feminist lit class. What was that one, 'It's All We Have'?"

"Shit is the correct term indeed. Yes, that was my dear mother, I'm afraid. The grande dame herself. Gina Maria Schivalone."

The deputy jumped in. "Well, just between us girls, and don't take offense, but since you just barged into my house, I think I got a license to say what I think. I always thought her poems were, um, a bit--?"

"Rubbish?" the professor shot back.

TEARS ARE ONLY WATER

The deputy laughed, "Yeah, thought she was a bit full of herself. How did it go? Something like,

'And in the end, what are we left?

A life that's been lived,

Oh, welcome, ye, bitter messes and blemishes, along with the sweet nectar,

Into your heart.

Gifts, all.'

Anyone who wrote that never lived *my* life, that's for goddamn sure."

It felt good to laugh, and Mother was an easy target. Taking a sip of wine, the professor said, "If you must know, she was not easy on Carmine. I don't think she ever understood him, not that he was easy to understand. Not only did he stop talking for a long time, but he amassed such a strange collection of symptoms as a kid."

"Like what?"

"To begin with, he slept all the time. Whenever he was awake, he was reading old books on math theories, and he didn't have friends until high school, but that was just one person. If speech pathologists misunderstood my brother, shrinks were pretty clueless. Oh God, there was an endless line of social workers, psychologists, and psychiatrists practicing all forms of useless therapy. None could really connect with him, and all of them imposed their pet theories. And then there were the drugs prescribed by quacks of all shapes and sizes."

Kitts poured another glass of wine. As the professor reached for it, she could feel the sizable blue bird watching disapprovingly. The wine began to loosen her inhibitions as she told stories about the relentless bullying that began in the 3rd grade. Being a quiet, skinny kid with coal-black eyes, glasses, and overly large ears attracted bullies like a magnet. The name-calling, shoving, and laughing behind his back brought her to his defense more times than she wished to remember.

"Yeah. I know something about that. Here's the thing with bullies. When those assholes grow up, they just become bigger bullies. But the stink of cowardice never wears off. Trust me."

"Mother insisted that I needed to learn self-defense to be a liberated middle-schooler. So I took Tae Kwon Do and got pretty good. Although my sensei would have kicked me out if he knew I was beating the crap out of all these grade school bullies. Truth is, I enjoyed punching out those little monsters."

Somewhere into their third glass of Pinot, the deputy's demeanor became more solemn.

"Your brother didn't say a word the whole way down to Pueblo. I thought he was out of it, but I think he was watching and listening to me going on about this and that. I was just kind of enjoying letting it all out to someone who wouldn't interrupt or judge. Funny thing, because I thought he was asleep the whole way, it felt safe to say whatever––even some stuff that came out of nowhere. I stopped paying attention to him and forgot he was even there. But you know what he said when we got to the hospital? I was saying goodbye, acting all professional, like how we'd come here so these folks could help him out, you know, help him to see what was going on so he could feel better, you know some shit like that. Then, your brother, Books, pipes up in that little ass voice of his for the first time. I thought there was a ghost in the car, but he says, 'Who will help you see?'.... Who will help *me* see?" Her voice trailed off and grew softer. "Huh, man, that's some deep and heavy shit. Still thinking about that crazy day."

It was getting late, and they'd both had too much wine. The professor hadn't expected to like the deputy, but she did. A diamond in the rough, full of contradictions and surprises, like pieces of a jigsaw puzzle from one box that got mixed in with another. She got up to leave and shook her hand. The deputy's grip was firm but not overbearing. Anne glanced down and did a quick upside-down reading of the calligraphic tattoo on her ebony-toned forearm.

"Tears Are Only Water."

TEARS ARE ONLY WATER

She thought it must be some military version of "Big Girls Don't Cry," like tears can't hurt you because they don't matter. Yeah, she'd got that right. This woman had figured out that tears are just salty liquid from the eye, no more, no less. So, you suck it up, mop the salt water, and move on.

As she was leaving, the professor asked about the graduate school brochures she'd spotted on the desk.

Kitts shrugged, "Could say they belong to my alter ego. Policing over here and social working over there. Can't figure out which way to turn."

"Well, I'm a psychologist, actually a tenured professor. I know something about the programs on the East Coast. If you ever need someone to talk to, I owe you."

The deputy lifted Langston off his perch and placed him on her shoulder. "Thanks, might take you up on that someday. You take care, Books' sister. Oh, and don't go knocking on any other strangers' doors."

Langston ruffled his feathers, still eying her suspiciously. He wasn't ready to lower his guard.

Giddiness is too strong a word to describe how the professor felt upon leaving the deputy's house. Her head was spinning, partly from the wine but more from a rush of half-baked thoughts about the day. The sky was a pallet of chiaroscuro shades. As she drove off, absorbed in her thoughts about the encounter with Kitts, she paid no attention to the couple sitting in a white car, watching her from the shadows.

Another night, another bender, but at least no cinnamon gummies tonight. Hopefully, she wouldn't feel as wretched in the morning for her trip to the state hospital. The Jester's Room was still serving, so she went down for a cup of decaf to sift through her breadcrumbs. The professor reviewed her conversation with the overpowering office manager and these new accusations about the embezzlement. She made a list of questions.

Why did Horse-Collar lie about Shrenklin's instructing her to keep tabs on her brother when he was working at night?

The quick signing of an involuntary commitment by a judge friend of Jonas––what was that all about?

Why the hurry to ship Carmie off to the state hospital? Jonas sounded so convincing, so empathic, peddling the lie about how it was in Carmie's best interests to be committed.

Then, enter E, with her mystery glove, into all of this. Really? Elizabeth the fuck Covington? Of all the characters to make an appearance, why choose a woman who killed herself 20 years ago?

Things didn't add up, but the problem was these idiots were all sticking to their stories.

The professor's carefully orchestrated plan to follow the trail of breadcrumbs hadn't worked. She found herself in a box canyon. *Not a happy place to be...Happy...Canyon.* Suddenly, she was struck by an idea that ran contrary to every instinct she had. If she was Hansel, she needed a Gretel. Clarity cut through the haze of inebriation. Anne ran to her car, sped back to the deputy's, and knocked on the door. A sleepy-looking Kitts appeared in the doorframe.

"Sorry, I know you think I'm crazy, and I suspect I might be, but I need your help!"

Chapter 15

Dr Hazel

Thursday, March 20, 5:40 PM

Carmine's 24-hour observation was uneventful. Julio arrived at the end of his shift and escorted the bookkeeper to his room on the forensic unit. Dr Hazel soon joined them. After a short meeting, they filed out of Carmine's room——the doctor followed by the tattooed giant pushing the small man in a wheelchair. Nurse Astracides looked up from her precariously positioned eyeglasses as they passed the nursing station.

"Oh, Doctor, I didn't realize you'd finished your rounds and gone to see the new patient. His transfer orders specify that he remain in restraints. Need I remind you, we have a protocol to follow?"

"Yes, Ms Astracides," the doctor responded. "I'm always grateful for your attention to detail, but I, too, am aware of the orders he came in with. He is here now, and we will make our own determination. I'm sure you also noticed that the timestamp on his orders indicates that Mr Luedke has been in restraints for more than 48 hours. So, I have decided, for now, we can remove them while we talk. I have Mr Garza here, so we should be fine. We'll be in the garden for a short conversation. You know this settles our patients when they are agitated."

With that, Dr Lukachunai walked to the elevator with Julio close behind. Nurse Astracides scowled and pulled a file out of her purse. Julio wheeled his patient onto the elevator as the nurse began to jot down notes.

Carmine felt the cool air on his skin. The sky was painted orange and amber as the sun hung over the Rockies. The bookkeeper had known only darkness for the last week and maybe much longer. He'd lived in tiny boxes—his office, apartment, holding cell, hospital rooms, and the cramped quarters of his mind. He recognized the sweet fragrances he'd detected on his doctor and inhaled the scents of rosemary, lavender, and sage. They strolled past beds of newly planted roses and white, orange, and purple mums surrounded by millet grasses.

The doctor sat on a bench beneath the umbrella of a white weeping cherry tree. Julio pulled the wheelchair next to her and set the brakes. "I'll be over there, Doctora. Wave if you need me."

He stepped away, but not with the lumbering gait of a man his massive size. No, Julio Garza first bent down to inhale the roses, turned his face to the sun, and walked with unexpected grace to the bench at the far end of the garden. Seated, he remained focused on the doctor and her frail-looking patient.

The doctor sat quietly for several minutes, her eyes closed as if in meditation or prayer. Carmine watched as she opened her eyes and spoke.

"To have wanted to hurt this woman, you must have felt injured yourself. You know, Mr Luedke, we judge the actions of others in narrow terms. We say, 'he acted badly; therefore, he must be a bad man. Or how kind she is; she is truly a saint.' In truth, people are far more complex. Though our actions belong to us, they are not the essence of who we are. So, Mr Luedke, I think you have a story to tell that your actions do not reveal. I do not entirely understand why they sent you to us, but you are here now, and we want to hear your story."

After a few minutes with her, Carmine sensed something different. Not since E, with her infinite patience, had he sat with someone who seemed so comfortable with his silence and stammer. Lukachunai asked about the events of the last week. His tone softened and became less urgent. He did his best to respond and thought of others who'd tried to help but grew impatient with his shyness and halting words.

Some had previously voiced hollow words of comfort, understanding, tolerance, and empathy. "Tell me how you feel, Carmine." "Oh, that must have hurt or frightened you." "You can take your time. I'll be here." But they really weren't. They soon grew restless if he didn't respond or couldn't find the words to begin or finish his thoughts. Their eyes would bounce from one object to the next, first down at their feet and then out the window. They'd clear their collective throats. The less experienced would begin to strum their fingers on the arm of the chair while others would attempt to answer for him. Occasionally, they betrayed their impatience and discomfort in sitting with his stuttered words by speaking loudly, slowly, as if he lacked normal capacities or was unfamiliar with the English language.

None of this happened with Dr Hazel Lukachunai. Instead, she looked at his face when she spoke and gave him the space she sensed he needed. She had time. When she looked away, her gaze drifted to the flowers before slowly returning to him.

He stared at her before replying. "When you c-called me that, Mr Luedke, I didn't know who you meant. Sometimes p-people call me the bookkeeper, but my name is Carmine."

She nodded and said, "Yes, it startles us to be called the names used to address our parents. Mr Luedke might well have been the name they called your father. But I will call you Carmine, as you wish....Tell me, Carmine, do you like birds?"

Chapter 16

Misdeeds of a Troubled Soul

Friday, March 21, 7:00 AM

Deputy Kitts shivered with pleasure. His morning kisses were soft and warm. He gently nuzzled her neck, beckoning her to wake up. Oh, Ray. He'd come back. Feeling the weight of his strong arms on her chest, she forced her eyes open to gaze at this beautiful man who was with her again, only to see the large blue bird standing on her chest as he pecked and nuzzled his black beak into her neck.

She'd been dreaming of Raymond more frequently. The breakup three years ago after she got out of the Corps had been painful. But with all such harsh realities, Papa's mantra, 'Don't mean nothin', helped silence the sadness and longing that occasionally visited at night.

"G'mornin' to you, Langs. Love you too, boy, or is it just breakfast you want?" Nicola sat up, and the bird climbed onto her shoulder. Moving more slowly than usual, she made her way to the kitchen to brew a pot of strong coffee. "Some crazy business with all that shit last night, huh? The look on that sister's face when she got one look at you and my Glock. Man, she didn't know what she was getting into, did she? Think you scared her more than the gun. Yeah, you're such a badass, Langs."

The bird bobbed his head and waved an enormous talon toward her as she prepared his morning fruit bowl. Unlike Ray, the bird accepted her for who she was. It didn't matter whether she was a soldier, cop, sociologist, or gardener. Ray cared more about what she did than who she was. Not so with her bird. Loyalty among people was conditional, but in the world of animals, loyalty knows no conditions.

Langston had come into her life after the Corps, a gift from her friend Marni, who told her, "Sister-girl, a man will leave you, but a bird like this will be your partner for life." And so it was that this brilliant blue hyacinth with solid dark eyes, encircled by yellow rings, became her constant companion. His massive black beak––strong enough to crack the hardest of nuts––was fixed in a constant smile that gave him both a friendly and impish appearance. Macaws are not known for their talking ability, which suited the deputy fine. She would have found mimicking words or silly sounds annoying. But her bird brought constancy into her life and an unspoken comfort. He watched her leave in the morning and waited for her to return at night, always flying from his perch to greet her as she walked through the door. He watched her from his perch when not cracking a large nut or preening his tail feathers. The macaw knew all her moods in the ways large birds learn to read their human companions, listening to voice tones and watching movements, some so subtle that most humans would miss.

The bird bobbed his head to the mellow, bluesiness of Mississippi John Hurt while the deputy poured herself a bowl of cornflakes and a large mug of black coffee. Hurt sang out about

Stag O'Lee, the bad man.

"Yep, plenty of bad men, Mississippi John, you're right about that one," she said. Nicola continued mulling over snippets from her two-part meeting with the bookkeeper's sister on Thursday. The sister was sure about some nasty goings-on with this whole thing, and she had some good points, starting with Mama Lu. Since coming to the Aurora County Sheriff's Department, Kitts had several encounters with LuCinda Pelcovey, who had been clearly adopted as a stepmother by some of the good ol' boys at the department. Jerry and Collins loved her ass and started calling her Mama Lu, or quaintly, Big Mama, which made the deputy want to throw up on herself. That alone was enough reason to be suspicious of her. LuCinda had even fooled the sheriff, who appointed her as head of The Aurora Society of Law & Order Boosters, fittingly known as A-SLOB. The group was essentially a group of local business owners in Aurora who liked to curry favor with the police. They, too, fell for whatever LuCinda was peddling. Still, the deputy knew that, beneath her sweet smile and folksy-sugared words, the office manager was basically a mean bitch who would smile while she pushed the knife a little deeper into your chest.

Then there was the whole EEP thing. Again, Books' sister had a good point. From what Nicola had heard and witnessed, the bookkeeper probably had some major psych issues, and there was no doubt that he'd assaulted Big Mama. Still, they usually kept prisoners on EEP orders for at least a couple of days. The commitment to Pueblo had definitely seemed rushed. She didn't know the doctors at MCA. The nervous, sniffing intern she'd encountered that day in the ER seemed fresh out of Psych 101. Maybe they all saw something she didn't, but that would be something she could check out. She stumbled on the thought "something to check out" and realized...she was really going to do this.

Langston flew over to her. Together, they glanced at her camping gear on the floor and then back at each other. She sighed. Yep, that trip wasn't gonna happen.

A few hours later, the deputy was on her way to Shrenklin's. There was a good chance the office manager would be in because it was tax season. She didn't relish seeing Mama Lu first thing in the morning, or if truth be told, any time of the day. Her uniform, back from the cleaners, was clean, crisp, and creased in all the right places. Though not on official duty, no one would know this. Just some routine follow-up after the incident on Monday. Just the facts, ma'am.

A large fan blew stale air through the lobby while one of the outer office staff went to fetch the manager. Nicola took a seat on a cracked vinyl sofa which promised a backache for those who sat for more than a few minutes. It was more official-looking to stand anyway, so she stood up with her thumbs hanging from her belt and holster.

After another ten minutes, Pelcovey appeared, moving a hand to her neck collar to punctuate the point that she'd suffered an assault. Her smile, cracked like the vinyl couch, preceded her words. "Why, Deputy Kitts––that's right, isn't it dear? This is a surprise. The others took all our statements, so I don't see how there's any more I can tell you." With this curt proclamation, she turned and began to walk away.

TEARS ARE ONLY WATER

"Hold on. Please, Ms Pelcovey, this is just a routine follow-up. You know how Sheriff B. will eat my lunch if I don't do the paperwork to close out this case. I'm supposed to be going on leave tomorrow and gotta finish my report. Sorry to bring up all this mess again. I can see that you've already been through a lot." She cringed. "...Mama Lu." Kitts knew the office manager loved being called Mama Lu.

LuCinda pivoted as the harsh lines around her mouth softened into a smile. "Why yes, Deputy Kitts, I do understand. My years as Chair of A-SLOB have taught me a thing or two about the process, and I do know Oliver well enough. Okay, Deputy, I have a few minutes. Let's see if we can wrap this up, dear."

The deputy followed the manager into her office and was immediately met with the asphyxiating scent of her Eau de Yuck. LuCinda sat at her desk, ready to hold court, tugging at her collar again to leave no doubt that she was the victim of an unspeakable crime.

"Now, dear, I can't imagine I have anything to tell you that hasn't already been covered. So, let's get on with your questions and not wait for the grass to grow. Hmm?"

"I know. We've got the statements after your assault, but I'd like to see if I can get some context, you know, what went on before all this happened. Like, can you sketch out the assailant's movements or demeanor the day or so before the assault?"

"Honestly, Deputy Kitts, I've already stated that this man is a deranged lunatic who suddenly turned violent and tried to kill me. He was hired about 18 months ago to do a job that, in my opinion, he never did all that well. Marvin, err, Mr Shrenklin ignored my reservations and hired him anyway. He's a softie, you know, and felt sorry for this pathetic creature. Truthfully, this wretched man couldn't even stay awake during the day. Can you imagine? Marvin hired a bookkeeper who spent more time with his head resting on the keyboard than with his fingers doing the job he was being paid to do. My staff was uncomfortable when he was around. He wouldn't look anyone in the eye and seemed to be living in another world. He'd bring in strange math books written by foreigners and read them during lunchtime. Honestly, he was a misfit from day one, so help me, as Jesus is my witness. I thought it was a big mistake for Mr Shrenklin to allow him to work at night, but I bit my tongue. I came in to make sure he was doing what he was supposed to be doing. Uh, that is, Mr S. asked me to check up on him when he was in at night. Really, I had no earthly idea what he was doing with his accounts. Deputy Kitts, this isn't rocket science. It's basic accounting, and he couldn't manage it. That's when I got suspicious and started poking around."

Nodding while jotting her notes, the deputy encouraged Big Mama to continue. "Did you find anything? I mean, when you started poking around."

"Did I find anything, Deputy Kitts? Did I *find* anything? Well...yes, I did. That's when it became clear that this dangerous lunatic was also a criminal. You see, his accounts weren't balancing because he was funneling money into an offshore account. I've got the paperwork, and we're going to have some forensic people in Denver come to take a look. So, you see, not only is he deranged, but he's also a criminal, all the while acting all quiet and innocent. I think it's pretty obvious. He's a bad man and needs to be locked up for the rest of his life."

Ba-dum. Mississippi John's words danced through her mind. *A bad man, oh cruel Stag O'Luedke.* The deputy caught Mama Lu looking down at her watch, indicating that her time was almost up. "Thank you, Miss Pelcov–uh, Mama Lu. One more question. Any odd behaviors besides the ones you've already reported? Someone said something about his pills."

"Oh, yes, Deputy. He was also a pillhead. When I asked about the pill bottles on his desk, he said he was taking some such drug to stay awake. Said Mr Shrenklin had approved. Yes, lunatic, criminal, and drug addict." LuCinda checked off imaginary boxes in the air. "Is that enough for you, Deputy? We're quite busy here."

"Sure, thank you for your time. This has all been helpful. I can see myself out." Craving fresh air to cleanse the toxic fumes of the office manager's perfume, the deputy stood and opened the door, then stopped and asked, "Oh, yeah, final question, ma'am. The bookkeeper

TEARS ARE ONLY WATER

said a woman had visited him the night before he attacked you and left a glove in his office. Know anything about that?"

LuCinda's vinyl smile cracked. "*This* nonsense again? Really, Deputy Kitts, I've gone over this a hundred times. No one visited him that night, and the glove belonged to Sophia, our cleaning woman. But honestly, this is becoming tiring. Enough now. Off you go."

"Gotcha, ma'am. So, no woman visitor and no gloves." She scribbled her final notes and thanked the visibly annoyed office manager one more time.

As she walked through the lobby, Nicola saw an older woman vacuuming the back hallway. The woman glanced toward the deputy, stopped her machine, and motioned for her to come over. The deputy looked over her shoulder to see if the woman was signaling to someone else. Seeing no one there, she approached the cleaning woman.

"Em, I was the one who found him Monday. This happen before. He fall asleep and have bad dreams. I hear what they say now, that he is bad and not right in the head. He is not bad. Is quiet and, how you say, em... shy? Yes, shy. Not bad. And Miss Pelcove say he find my glove. No, no that not true. I have no glove."

The deputy thanked the office cleaner and turned to leave, nearly bumping into a blonde woman in a red suit on the narrow staircase. She got into the cruiser and picked up a message on her phone. It was Burwinkle. The deputy had guessed he would find out about her off-the-books investigation but not this quickly. Big Mama had wasted no time reporting that Kitts had been asking questions.

"Depety Kitts." She could hear the irritation in his voice. Burwinkle spoke in a lower register when he was pissed. "Yer gonna need to come in here pronto. And ya better bring yer revolver and badge cuz I jest might have ta keep em.... Goddammit, Cole. What the hell ya think yer doin'? Just got a call from Shrenklin's that you been pokin' round there, asking all sorts of questions. Yer supposed to be gone. Dammit, girl, you got some mighty big explainin' to do, and I ain't feelin' very charitable 'bout any of this."

Maybe getting mixed up in all this was a mistake, but the deputy was puzzled by the cleaning woman's comment about the glove. That meant the office manager was lying and trying to cover something up. It made no sense but had gotten her attention.

The sheriff's secretary gave the deputy a sympathetic look when she approached the front desk. "Sorry, he's on the warpath today, Nicola."

Burwinkle sat in a rumpled repose, looking out his window as she entered the office. "Better shut the door behind ya," he said, motioning her to sit.

The deputy began to explain, but he silenced her with the palm of one hand while he rubbed his chest with the other. He popped a couple of pills in his mouth and swallowed hard. "Just what the hell is this all about, Cole? Who in God's green acre gave ya permission to think ya could conduct this rogue investigation? Yer not even supposed to be here. Yet ya take it upon yerself to go over to Shrenklin's and harass poor ol' Mama Lu by tellin' her ya were there conducting a routine investigation? What the hell, Nicola? This ain't like you at all. Now, say yer piece cuz I'm 'bout an inch away from putting ya on leave without pay, young lady, if my ticker holds out, that is. Goddam ya, Kitts!"

Nicola apologized, acknowledging that she was wrong to conduct an off-the-books investigation, but she told the sheriff that some things did not add up. Hesitant to admit she'd already met with the bookkeeper's sister, she decided to use some of the information she'd discovered anyway. She told him that Mama Lu might not be telling the truth about a couple of things, like being instructed to keep tabs on the bookkeeper and the glove thing.

Burwinkle leaned forward. "Well, hell. That all ya got? That glove thing? Who the hell knows why she said the glove belonged to the cleaning lady? Didja ever think that woman might not be telling the whole truth either? Seems they got the goods on this bookkeeper fella, thinkin' now he was doing some embezzlin' from one of their companies. I just don't get why this crazy bookkeeper has ya all up in a bundle. We're talkin' bout the misdeeds of a troubled soul, plain and simple, Nicola. If ya value yer job, ya got to let this whole thing go."

TEARS ARE ONLY WATER

The sheriff's fondness for his deputy was revealed first in his eyes, then in a softening of his tone. "Why's this one so important that ya gotta be pokin' all around like this and even putting yer career in jeopardy? Just plum don't make sense."

He was right. It didn't make sense. Call it a gut feeling, but something was off here. She said she knew the evidence was scant but asked if he'd give her a few more days to check out where the bookkeeper lived and talk to some folks at the hospital.

"Sheriff, you ever heard of an EEP moving through the system this fast? Maybe you're right and there's nothing to this, but I got these hairs beginning to dance around on the back of my neck. Something doesn't feel right."

He rotated his chair back to the window and paused before he spoke. "Okay, Cole, I hear ya. Just gotta get this one outta yer system. I don't agree, but tell ya what, I'll authorize this for two days tops, so ya kin finish up whatever ya started here. Then yer gonna owe me, Cole, and I mean big time."

Chapter 17

Dimitri Onboard

Friday, March 21, 3:25 PM

The deputy maneuvered through the station, hoping she wouldn't have to answer questions about why she hadn't left on vacation. The sheriff's words, "You're gonna owe me big time," hung in the air. *What bargain did he have in mind?* She feared she just gave away whatever power she might have had.

Back in the cruiser, she did a mental checklist of who she wanted to talk to. Chances were that the sheriff was right, and there was nothing to any of this. Yet for some reason, this case had gotten stuck inside, and she couldn't let it go. She knew herself well enough to follow her instincts and see this through.

There were people to check in with at the hospital. First, she wanted to find the sniffing intern. Maybe he knew something. Then, she'd meet with the head shrink and find out about the EEP and the rush to ship him off to Pueblo. After the hospital, she'd pay a visit to this guy Dihn, the bookkeeper's hacker friend the sister told her about. The deputy could picture him. She knew his type. *You're a secret keeper, aren't you? But you also can decode secrets that others want to keep hidden.* After meeting with the hacker, who knows? She'd keep her options open to see what other leads might surface. The deputy felt focused, like when she used to walk patrol––primed and on the lookout.

She found a seat in the hospital lobby, one of her favorite people-watching domains. Lucky girl; second time in one week. She told the

TEARS ARE ONLY WATER

receptionist that she was doing an official investigation into the matter concerning the bookkeeper, whom she'd brought in on an EEP on Tuesday, and would need to speak with the staff who handled his admission. She had only a few minutes of reverie before a woman approached her.

"Are you the one looking into a patient who was here last week? I'm Dr Levine, the Chief Resident. I attended to him after he was admitted. I guess I could answer some of your questions, but maybe you should talk with Dr Jonas first. He's the Chief of Psychiatry and told...um...advised us on the patient's treatment and disposition."

"Perfect, Doctor. He is at the top of my list. Also, the Middle Eastern physician who saw him in the ER the night we brought him in. Where can I find him?"

Dr Levine's sideways glance was a tell that the mention of the sniffing intern had hit a nerve. "That would be Dr Kashimi. Sorry, he's no longer in the department, but we can go upstairs and look at Dr Jonas' schedule. Maybe he's between meetings and can squeeze in time to see you."

Odd that this particular intern had been transferred. Possibly a coincidence, but good police work left little room for coincidences. Following an awkward elevator ride, Levine chatted with the secretary overseeing the Chief's schedule.

Turning back to the deputy, she said, "You're in luck. Looks like he's finishing up a staff meeting and can answer some of your questions."

Some of my questions? The deputy thought to herself. *What about the ones he won't answer?* A skeptical mind is an investigator's compass. People rarely disclose everything they know.

Dr Levine nodded at her. "If you don't mind, Deputy, I have patients to see. Dr Jonas is better placed to answer questions about this patient. I just saw him that one night."

"Duly noted, Dr Levine, but I might need to check back with you if I have more questions, so don't wander off too far." The deputy smiled as

J. HERMAN KLEIGER

she reflexively put her hand on her holster. People always get the nonverbals at times like this.

The Chief Resident nodded, backed away, and pivoted towards the elevator, leaving the deputy to survey the odd assortment of visitors, nurses, and patients as they paraded past. The door to his office popped open. Five white-coated doctors emerged, chatting this or that.

"Brilliant as usual."

"Need to get Grand Rounds scheduled."

"I'm starved. How about Italian?"

A well-dressed blonde woman in a splashy fuchsia suit lingered behind the others. Wasn't that the same woman Nicola bumped into when leaving Shrenklin's? She was finishing a private conversation with a tall man, presumably Jonas. The deputy made a mental note of this odd coincidence. The woman headed for the elevator. Jonas turned and approached with a polished smile, exuding cordiality and command.

He extended his large hand, which was smooth and bone-dry. "Why, hello there, Deputy Kitts. I'm told you're here to ask some questions about one of our recent patients, the gentleman who was here on an EEP. Please, come in. You've caught me between meetings, but perhaps I can spare a few minutes to tell you what I know."

Jonas motioned toward his office and invited the deputy to sit in front of his large desk. His walls, one plastered with certificates and another with pictures of him shaking hands with presumably important people, told Kitts that Dr Jonas considered himself a VIP by his association with the famous and well-heeled. She knew his type.

"Thank you, Doctor. Just have a few questions. First, I'm curious about the other doctor who saw him in the ER––what's his name? Kashimi? He no longer works here?"

Jonas wrinkled his brow. "You're asking about *him*? Those are routine educational and administrative decisions, Deputy. They have nothing to do with the man you've come to ask about. Now, what can we tell you about this patient, Luedke?'

She'd let the matter rest for now. Still, she made a mental note about the dismissal of her question.

"Okay, thank you. I'd like to ask you, Dr Jonas, about the transfer to Pueblo state hospital. I can't ever recall seeing a civil commitment completed so quickly. Seems highly unusual, wouldn't you say?"

Jonas stiffened and shifted uneasily. A slight crack in his smarmy manner? "I'm of the philosophy, Deputy, that criminal matters are best left to law enforcement and medical issues are most expertly addressed by doctors."

He recounted the main findings from their emergency evaluation the day the bookkeeper was admitted, including evidence of psychosis and lab studies finding high levels of amphetamines in his system. The Chief Resident reported that the patient had further deteriorated during his first night on the ward, leading Jonas, as head of the service, to decide that a civil commitment and expedited transfer to the state hospital were clinically indicated, especially considering the patient's recent history of extreme violence.

"So, in case you're unaware, Deputy, those patients who are both psychotically impaired and violent warrant an expedited transfer to a contained forensic evaluation facility better suited to their needs and those of the community. Our unit is not a long-term evaluation and treatment facility, nor does it have the security protocols needed for patients who've demonstrated violent proclivities. This patient was an unfortunate man in the throes of a psychotic decompensation exacerbated by his over-usage of amphetamines. We could not be sure that his psychosis was induced by these drugs or if the drugs triggered an underlying condition such as schizophrenia. As I'm sure you're aware, Deputy, amphetamine psychosis is a serious matter, but then again, you might not have ever dealt with such an individual in your routine police work. As healers, we ensure these individuals are well cared for, no matter their crimes. You're no doubt familiar with the Hippocratic Oath, Deputy. We always have our patients' best interests in mind, and it was medically necessary for Mr Luedke's well-being to transfer him to Pueblo sooner rather than later."

His words, like an overdone British Christmas pudding, were pleasing to the senses but got stuck in the throat. Jonas, the medical authority and concerned public servant, was equal parts patronizing spin doctor and sanctimonious snob. However, she was not in a position to challenge his decision. He was the head shrink, and she a cop with a college degree in sociology. He had the clout to make a plausible-sounding case about why the bookkeeper had to be transferred ASAP.

"So, as I'm sure you can see, Deputy, to delay his transfer even a day later would have been unconscionable."

Unconscionable.... Now there's a cringe-worthy word. She always tensed when people spoke like this. *The man was a pompous ass. Time to bring this interview to a close.*

"Thank you, Doctor. You've been helpful, but I may have some follow-up questions later. I'd still like to talk to the young intern we met the night this man was admitted, but I'll let that rest. For now, that is." *Za-zing!*

Jonas looked at his gold Rolex and began to rise. "Yes, I think it's best you do. Thank you for coming in, Deputy. As you can see, we're swamped here but always eager to assist your department in such matters. I'm glad I've answered all your questions." He directed her out of his office, bid her a curt farewell, and shut his door with more physical force than necessary.

Though most people would have found these explanations, delivered in an impeccable upper-class English accent, satisfactory, the deputy was unconvinced. He was too ready with answers to questions that hadn't even been asked. Nicola wasn't naïve about the suspects she arrested. Even the meekest of people could turn violent, but she didn't get that vibe with the bookkeeper. Kitts wasn't buying it despite Jonas explaining the speedy court order for a transfer. The courthouse would have records about the bookkeeper's commitment hearing, so she'd swing by there to check. The deputy also thought about trying to track down Kashimi. It seemed fishy that he disappeared right after the bookkeeper was shipped off.

TEARS ARE ONLY WATER

It occurred to her that an old marine buddy from Alpha Company FET-1, Kermit Froggie Milbane, worked in the lab at the hospital. Froggie had been the medic for their Female Engagement Team. Kitts had been the NCO who took charge of the team. When they returned from Afghanistan, she and Milbane had a drink together a time or two, but Froggie was one to cry in his beer when he talked about Afghanistan, and the deputy was not. She didn't talk about any of that, especially Khanjar. They were just names and faces to her. *Don't mean nothin'. Don't really mean shit.* Still, she and PFC Milbane had bled in the dirt together. Nicola could count on him for information.

She took the elevator to the basement and followed the signs to the Laboratory. Kermit, with his Muppet-like mustache, was sitting at a monitor, munching a sandwich.

"Brother Frogman, drop and give me 50!"

With a well-oiled startle response, the lab technician turned around and grinned as he saw Kitts leaning against the wall.

"Whoa, sup, Gunny. Oorah! Man, you're sure as shit a sight for these failing eyes. My God, look at you. All high and tight in your deputy suit. Knew you'd never be able to take off a uniform. Hey, why don't you answer my calls and come to one of our groups? Lots of brothers and sisters come to talk about their shit. You know you can let go of that whole shit show over there... S'ok, Gunny, really."

Nicola grinned at him. "Aww, Froggie, yeah, that's right. Shit sure does happen. Don't think much about any of that, but sure, we'll get together sometime. Hey, I need your help with a patient I'm investigating. Need to double-check the lab results after his admission. This would've been Monday-Tuesday. We brought this guy in on an EEP. He was admitted to psychiatry, and the head shrink said he was hopped up on speed. If I give you his name, can you check it out?"

"Sure, Gunny. If it was anyone else asking, I'd have to call upstairs to get the go-ahead but let me have a looksee." He squinted and whistled as he accessed coded records. "Oh yeah, this guy. Man, he was pretty jacked up. The tox screen showed dextroamphetamine levels off the charts."

Froggie fell silent and leaned in, his face inches from the screen. "Hmm, that's odd.... Looks like someone did some extra testing here, but...they don't show up in his lab report or...in his electronic chart."

The deputy stood up straighter. "You gotta translate for me, Frogman. I'm not sure what you're saying. Someone did some extra tests, but they aren't showing up in his record?"

"Yeah, Gunny. Don't make much sense. See this line here shows someone was looking for something that wasn't picked up by a routine tox screen." He pointed to the monitor, "Look here, they used the Ehrlich reagent to look for something in your guy's pee but seems the results got erased from his chart the next day. Some of my lab guys are stoners, but they are pretty darn good. They don't just go around deleting test results. That'd be bad juju if they did."

The deputy cleared her throat. She'd known something was off, and this could be it. "Frogman, can you find out what they were looking for? Would those test results show up somewhere else?"

"Yeah, that's why you was the Gunny and me the grunt. Sure, lemme... just...." He made a few more clicks and keystrokes, scrolling up and down from one database to another. "Just wanna check who logged this in."

Kitts leaned in to look at his screen. She caught a glimpse of the faded scar behind Milbane's ear and tried to muzzle the intrusion of painful memories of the second-worst day of her life. A suicide bomber and an ambush in the Musa Qala District. Her team, slaughtered. She survived without a scratch after taking out a Taliban hit squad.

"There! It was during one of Stenna Marks' shifts. She's a pretty sharp cookie. She was working the night your guy came in. Wow, there was something else. Looks like he had Dimitri onboard. Your dude wasn't just speeding, Gunny. His pee was sparkling with some pretty high levels of dimethyltryptamine, you know, DMT. We're seeing more of this shit show up. Good old street-cut Dimitri, they're calling it. God bless the mile high city. Problem is you don't wanna mix this shit with something like Adderall. This Dimitri shit can produce some wild-ass hallucina-

TEARS ARE ONLY WATER

tions, euphoria, agitation, and pretty intense paranoia. Speed'll do that too, but the two of them together...Prrggh!" Froggie motioned with his fingers moving away from his head. "Dude's lucky to be alive. Yeah, Gunny, looks like Stenna found something but then erased it from his chart. Totally not like this gal unless someone told her to, but even that goes against protocol. That's major incident report shit. Man, this ain't cool at all."

On high alert, the deputy asked where she could find Stenna Marks.

"Funny thing about that, Gunny, ol' Stenna has kinda disappeared. She hasn't come into work for the last few nights. So, there you go...damn."

Chapter 18

The Old Woman in the Garden-Nicola

Saturday, March 22, 6:30 AM

Early morning fog had moved in, engulfing the deputy's yard in a cottony glow. The last few days left her unsettled. Kitts' trademark cool had been disturbed. Why? She felt a searing in her gut and tightness in her chest like in Afghanistan but without the adrenalin rush. *Easy, girl, there is no threat here. Just too much wine on top of the whisky.*

But she knew there was something. Something about the odd bookkeeper had troubled her––his silence in the car and his parting comment to her, as if he had been listening and reading her mood all along. Then the visits from his sister––tight-assed and high-strung but not wholly unlikeable. Nicola wanted to shake all this off. *I seriously need to get away from this shit. Oh, and how about the crazy sister showing up like that?*

She picked up her bird. "Scared her good, didn't we, Langs? She didn't expect to be greeted by a Glock-22 and a monster bird. You did your part, boy."

The bird cocked his head, extended his talons, and liberated another black nut from her hand. As outrageous as that woman's unannounced visits had been, Nicola admired her moxie.

"Sister lady's got some big brass balls, doesn't she, Langs?" The deputy nuzzled against Langston's ominous-looking black beak. "The sister's story was wild, huh; some wild ass shit. But the way she told it, the

TEARS ARE ONLY WATER

pieces don't add up. Someone's lying and hiding something. How come? And now this shit with the missing lab tech and the DMT, come on."

Still, the cabin in Redwood beckoned, offering quiet to numb her twitchy mind, but the hook had been set, and she couldn't wiggle free. She tickled the back of Langston's ruffled neck and said, "That cabin will just have to wait for us. Gotta keep going with this. What do you say, Langs? You know, continue to poke around some, ask more questions of these yahoos."

"Graak."

"Dude, deal with it, okay? Just a couple more days, and then we'll take off. Promise."

The bookkeeper's sister had given her names and contact information for the key players. But it wasn't just that she'd been hooked by the puzzle, or by her admiration of the sister's gutsy play, or even the fact that the woman had an annoying charm. Something else stuck at the edge of the deputy's mind—an uncanny connection that didn't make much sense.

The track switched from Billie Holiday to John Hurt. The old voice rang out

about walking that lonesome valley for yourself. *Words to live by*, she thought, as she walked around her living room. The small room's walls encapsulated her life: part museum, part time capsule, full-time tomb? Monet's gardens and Georgia O'Keefe's orchids, so pleasing to the eye, abutted by a wall of police commendations and medals from the Corps. Nicola and Cole. Yin and yang. Where did one stop and the other begin?

The room began to spin. Nothing an early morning stroll through her garden in the crisp March air couldn't cure. As she walked to the back door, she saw a small, framed poem embroidered in purple stitching. On a small table was Aunt Rhea's poem about tears being only water. She remembered when her aunt gave her this and how she'd reached out her hand and said, "Nicola, my dear, don't be ashamed to weep. You've got

145

to grieve, girl, to grow." Aunt Rhea had never given up. She'd sewn this poem about tears and water for her niece a few months before she died.

Nicola's garden was a sanctified place, her refuge when her compartments were overcrowded by feelings she couldn't contain. The weather was changing. A front was moving in. Cool, foggy Colorado air sobered her senses as she sat on the wooden bench by the daffodils. This was her favorite spot to rest, sometimes with Langston but often alone, savoring the quiet voices of her plants and flowers. The fog obscured the clean lines of the dogwood. Shadows took form as shapes stepped out from the dim light. Nicola squinted to see. There was Auntie Rhea, trowel in hand, tending her garden, gently whispering, as she always had, to the wildflowers and hyacinths.

Chapter 19

The Old Woman in the Garden-Anne

Saturday, March 22, 8:30 AM

The professor awakened with another headache, though not as bad as the morning before. The trumpeting in her temples had softened. Her sleep had still been fitful but was not punctuated by emergency trips to the bathroom. Hangovers came in different shapes and sizes. This one was a petite or junior miss. Still, she'd have nothing more this morning than black coffee and a glass of wine or two later.

The meeting the night before last with the deputy continued to inhabit her thoughts. Nicola Kitts was different than she'd expected––the opposite of the redneck sheriff. The deputy had listened to her rantings and seemed genuinely intrigued with Carmie's case. She was an imposing figure but soft around the edges––hardened and combat-tested but intelligent and intuitive. The professor was glad Kitts didn't shoot her on the porch. *Still, what was with that parakeet of hers with the glandular problem?*

More planning time was needed, so she decided to push back her drive to Pueblo for later that day. She phoned the state hospital and got an annoying recording about visiting hours beginning at 1:00 PM. Then, she remembered that the Aurora hospital had warned her she probably wouldn't be able to see her brother for a few days, maybe longer.

When the professor finally stopped ranting about this outlandish policy, she called the central number for the Community Mental Health Institute in Pueblo. She left a message with her name and number, adding that she was a tenured psychology professor, was driving down from

Denver Friday afternoon, and expected to meet with the doctor in charge of her brother's care.

Bypassing the hostess, she found a booth in the Jester's Room. True to form, she complained that the coffee was weak. She'd been too nice to too many people. Note to self; you're slipping. Time to get back to business. Her cell pinged as she read a message from AT&T that Dr Noa Morena had been removed from the Schivalone family plan per her request. Determined not to darken what felt like a brighter mood, she trashed the message, vowing to place all things regarding Noa in the trash bin. Then, she saw another message that came in late last night.

The subject line was overdone in bold caps, even without the superfluous exclamation marks. Who would send such a dramatic message? Why, of course, none other than the peapod, Braden Holmes.

"URGENT! NEED TO TALK! WHERE ARE SEMINAR GRADES!!??" It was signed by the Dean of Academic Affairs and cc'd to several Trustees.

The snare drum beat quickened, and the La Brea Tar Pit in her gut opened for business. What to rub first, temples, hands, or stomach? She hesitated to open her department head's email. Braden, you're such a Grade-A twit. Though she was far too refined and cultured to use vulgar names, she considered Braden Holmes a real pussy.

She knew what the desperate message would say. Grades were overdue; students were complaining, and other faculty members were grumbling that they had to cover her classes, blah, blah, blah. But, like any glad-handing bureaucrat, Holmes cared less about academic freedom and maintaining standards than he did about pleasing the Trustees and wealthy donors to the university. Typical Chicken Little move, always looking for who to blow next.

Opening the email, she expected another carefully worded so-as-not-to-offend message about needing to get her grades in as soon as possible, but she read this instead:

Dear Professor Schivalone,

TEARS ARE ONLY WATER

Though we are all aware of your family issues and wish you the best, your callous disregard for your students and teaching responsibilities cannot continue. We've looked the other way on more than one occasion when you've come to class with alcohol on your breath. As you know, we've given you a long tether to pursue your work and acknowledge that the department and university have benefitted from your scholarship and recent notoriety. However, need I remind you that you are not on sabbatical and have pressing teaching responsibilities that are clearly spelled out in your contract. This is my third reminder that your grades are overdue. Unfortunately, you've either not thought it essential or overestimated my patience with this matter.

Having received numerous complaints from your colleagues, students, and even their parents, I had no choice but to consult with Dean Henry, who promptly convened a meeting of the Disciplinary Board to determine how best to respond to what can only be termed woeful academic neglect. A range of options was placed on the table, from some hardliners who wanted to consult our lawyers about terminating your tenure, to some of the cooler heads who recommended a probation period. We eventually reached a decision to place you on administrative leave without pay. We consulted the legal team, who assured us this met the necessary clauses in your contract with the university.

Drs Hartfield and Maetia will take over your classes. If you value your connection to the university, it is imperative that you FedEx your Freshman Seminar paper proposals to me ASAP. We are turning over your seminar to Dr Maetia. Anne, I worked hard to remove this Sword of Damocles hanging over your head as certain members in attendance today pressed to rescind your tenure. We are also considering the possibility of you accepting an early retirement, which I hope you'll seriously consider.

I expect to hear that you've received, read, and comprehended the gravity of this situation.

Furthermore, I expect to receive your students' papers by Monday. Anne, please do not turn your back on this matter. You have literally reached the end of your truss. Get some help, please. This is serious!

With grave concerns,

J. Braden Holmes, PhD

Chair, Psychology Department

Willard Henry, PhD

Dean of Academic Affairs

Ba Dum Tum. The snare drum hit a rim shot, and the throbbing in her temples grew louder. She was stunned. *Okay, okay, attach a feeling. Concerned, yes; disappointed, sure; but furious, you're Goddamn right. How dare that overly-dramatic bovine convene a meeting with the dean and trustees without any notification?*

In her outrage, the professor thought about her recent messages from the universe. A few people were not too happy with her–first Noa, and now this mess. Without missing a beat, she exhaled and said, "Find a fucking compartment for this one too." Like the mess with Noa, she would deal with the university later. For now, she curtly responded to Holmes: "Message received." Then, she would spend the next few hours grading the proposals and FedEx the lot to Holmes per his spineless request. As for being placed on administrative leave, fine; early retirement––not the end of the world either. She had money in the bank and more important things to deal with. The professor would do as she had always done when faced with bad news––file it away and ignore it. It was certainly not worth losing sleep over. Her sleep was too important; it always had been.

"How to Sleep at Night: Compartmentalization in the Service of Adaptation" was a paper she had written years ago. It created quite a stir in the professional community. It got the professor her first gig on a talk

TEARS ARE ONLY WATER

radio show. She had argued that recovering repressed feelings and memories or working to integrate disparate parts of the self were myths propagated by generations of psychoanalysts who had never resolved their idealization of Papa Freud. As a grad student, she'd studied under Gerta Gelman, the iconoclastic feminist psychologist who devoted her career to eviscerating everything Freudian. Gelman, regarded as a virago by the men in the department, wrote that we function optimally when we selectively ignore and utilize adaptive compartmentalizing. Like pain——we do best when we ignore it.

Anne found Gelman's theories a good fit with how she'd learned to deal with the world——maximizing attention and energy on one thing while ignoring and shutting the door on another. That's how she survived the drama of a narcissistic mother and her revolving door of relationships—— just tune out and ignore the noise. As a grad student, she worshiped Gelman and was excited when the middle-aged professor asked that she join her for a summer in Nantucket.

As Gerta's reputation suffered one scandal after another, her interest in Anne faded. Questions about academic integrity and inappropriate relationships with students eventually led to her dismissal from the college. However, by this time, her former student, now Associate Professor Schivalone, was making a name for herself. She'd researched and revised Gelman's theory and then repackaged it as her own. In addition, she proposed new terminology for Gerta's radical views on defense mechanisms, which had traditionally been viewed by the psychiatric community pejoratively. Relabeling them "sectionalization strategies," the young associate professor described various forms of selective ignoring.

To her critics who argued that she was encouraging splits in the personality, the professor answered, "Splits aren't so bad, that is, unless you're bowling." She preached that as long as one is cognizant of what one chooses to ignore and locks it away in a psychic compartment, the personality can thrive with its energies freed up to invest in what was truly important. Surprisingly, a lot of people bought what she was selling.

· · ·

She'd spend the rest of the morning working on her students' paper proposals. Then, she would find a FedEx drop-off on her way out of town to wash her hands of this unfortunate business with the university and the invertebrate Holmes.

Next on her list was to check in with Deputy Kitts. Anne was grateful that the deputy seemed sincerely interested and had agreed to help investigate the events surrounding this imbroglio with Carmine. The war hero, Kitts, had probably learned to treat tears as nothing more than excess liquid dripping from the eyes. What's not to like about that one? When her thoughts strayed to the deputy's square jawline and sinewy shoulders, the professor quickly opened a compartment to toss in these dangerous associations. *Don't go there, Anne. No needless distractions.*

After Anne dropped the papers at the closest FedEx office, she mapped a route to Pueblo. ETA was roughly two hours if she stopped for lunch. The professor focused her mind on the two battlefronts––first, the investigation with Kitts, and second, the medical charlatans she expected to encounter at the state hospital. Both concerned her brother's mental state, the motives of the shady characters, and their rush to ship him off to the state hospital. Kitts seemed hungry to do real detective work. With her interest in figuring people out, she'll have a field day with Carmie. Good luck with that one, Nicola.

The truth was that the professor never understood her brother all that well. She knew all the technical lingo, all the labels and DSM diagnoses, but she never really knew him. Sure, he was introversive and a mathematical savant, but not entirely on the spectrum because he had that uncanny way of reading emotions on faces and in voice tones. Some thought him a genius, but his life had always been a mess. Who knows? Mother had always been clueless. Although confident that the Narcissistic Drama Queen, or NDQ for short, caused most of her children's problems, Anne couldn't blame her mother for not understanding Carmine because no one had.

But the unsentimental professor was sure of one thing. Despite the ice in her veins and contempt for the softer range of human emotion, she loved her little brother and would travel to the end of the world to protect him. She never considered herself to have much in the way of a maternal instinct. Still, she felt something approaching that with Carmine. In her cynicism, she wondered whether her protective urges were nothing more than penance for leaving him to the wolves after she'd escaped to Choate all those years back. Who knows? Ultimately, she felt her love for him was flawed because it made her vulnerable, and she couldn't stand that.

The tight band around her head had loosened its grip. She looked for an off-ramp to get something to eat. Spotting a Bennigan's, she pulled in, parked, and popped four more Advil. She found a booth in the back where there were fewer customers. The professor ordered a chardonnay, checked her cell phone, and was relieved to find no new messages. Sipping her cheap wine, she perused the greasy menu on the table and fixed her eyes on a selection that she thought had disappeared from menus worldwide––Creamed Chipped Beef on Toast. Instantly, she was mentally transported through a culinary wormhole and spat out into a memory of sitting at a dingy kitchen table with her brother and Donner Brooks, a red-nosed alcoholic Mother had married a year after Bilkes fled the scene.

Donner was older, retired, and living comfortably off a pension from Martin Marietta, which was probably the main reason Mother had chosen him after the Bilker drained her bank account. Donner was harmless. He was actually quieter than Carmie, so he blended into the wallpaper. Home from Choate for spring break, Anne once snarkily called him Blitzen and felt the sting of Mother's left palm across her face.

Donner did most of the cooking, while Mother played the role of self-important feminist writer––composing nonsense poems and working on a memoir that no one would read. Every Tuesday and Friday he prepared chipped beef and toast––those tasteless bits of pinkish mystery meat languishing in a pasty white gravy always served over limp white toast. Chipped beef seared into her memory the evening Mother announced at dinner, between bites of Donner's delicacy, that she knew her daughter, then a junior in high school, was gay. This was the first, but not the last time Mother made this pronouncement. When Anne tried to protest, Mother insisted that she knew better and that her insolent daughter needed to listen.

"Angelina, to be successful in this life, you must first face the truth about yourself, dear. Remember your Shakespeare, darling, 'To thine own self be true.'"

Long before the future professor developed her theories about sectionalization and ignoring the idiotic, she would square off with her mother and attempt to go toe-to-toe. That evening, Mother ended what had become an argument by hurling a plate of Donner's chipped beef against the wall. The dried collage remained on the wall long after Donner packed up his pension and left.

She ordered a tuna salad and texted Kitts. She'd forgotten to give her Dihn's contact information. He could be a valuable ally in her investigation. "If it's out there, this very odd little man will find it." She added a double thumbs up emoji.

The droning sounds of the restaurant were pierced by a loud voice. She had yet to notice, while munching on her salad and reading emails, the woman seated in a booth behind her. The woman's voice grew louder as she appeared to speak with someone on her phone.

"NO! No, I'm not goin' there. No...I have ta tell ya again, wanker! Yeah, well, bugger off then!"

The professor turned to see a black-haired woman with a sleeve of tattoos running up her arm slam her phone onto the table and then look up. "And just what ya think yer looking at, ya nosey Nancy? Best ya piss off before I show ya what's what."

Rattled by this unhinged woman, Anne quickly got up and paid the cashier. Another bizarre occurrence in a week that made no sense. The parking lot was crowded. Reaching for her keys, she noticed a thin

TEARS ARE ONLY WATER

scratch running the length of the front door. "Good God!" she gasped. Someone had keyed her car.

The professor stormed back into the restaurant and approached a harried cashier. "I beg your pardon, but someone in your establishment has just vandalized my rental car. I must speak with your manager immediately.

The cashier rolled her eyes and said, "You've just notified her. Sorry, but there's no way of knowing when you got that scratch. You can fill out a complaint, but that won't be looked at for a few days. We're short-staffed." She turned and walked away.

The professor glanced back to where she'd been sitting. The dark-haired woman was still on her phone. She looked up at Anne, waved her keys, and cackled with a maniacal delight.

The gesture felt ominous. Anne had no desire to confront this deranged-looking woman who probably had a gun in her purse. The professor hurried to her car. Back on the road, she turned on the radio and tried to find NPR to calm her nerves. An update about family members anxiously awaiting word about the missing plane brought more thoughts about Carmine.

Were all her remaining days going to be this way? Had she done such awful things that the universe had decided to take its retribution? The professor took a deep breath and attempted to close the door on the unnerving encounter at the restaurant.

The GPS led her to the hospital grounds. She turned onto the tree-lined road leading to Admissions and drove past rows of old red brick buildings. She felt the place was full of ghosts. Something about it seemed eerily familiar.

She parked and purposely looked away from the ugly scratch on the door. The clatter of an early spring landscaping crew grew louder as she looked for signs to admissions. She followed the breezeway that led to an inner courtyard where men in green uniforms were raking the winter kill. Alone in the garden, wearing a white hospital smock, an old woman with long white hair appeared to be dancing with her pruning shears as she snipped at the twigs. Ah, horticultural therapy for the mentally afflicted. She recognized this as standard fare in state hospitals, where patients were exploited to do menial labor around the hospital grounds in the name of treatment. All but the most chronic patients had long been released from these institutions, only to fill the streets with throngs of the homeless mentally ill. *Judging by her antiquity, this woman must have been one of those who'd never seen life outside the hospital walls.* The professor sneered at the sign, Colorado Mental Health Institute–Pueblo. *Ha, it's still a state insane asylum. Words couldn't change that fact.*

The door opened automatically, leading to a generic waiting room adjacent to a reception desk. A woman with an instantly forgettable appearance pointed the way to the Admissions Department. Fortunately, the lobby was not crowded. The professor was grateful there were no lines or take-a-number nonsense at the windows. She gave her name and stated the reasons for her visit.

She spelled out her brother's full name. "I'm his sister, Professor Anne Schivalone. He was mistakenly brought here on Wednesday from the medical facility in Aurora."

The admissions clerk typed at her keyboard. The professor watched the woman's eyes as she searched for a matching name. "Yes, he's in the Kreske Building. I'll call the nursing station there to have someone come talk to you."

Of course, the professor wouldn't hear of this. Her energy restored, she glared at the poor clerk and spoke in a low tone, making her voice both authoritative and menacing.

"You must understand, young lady, I will not move from this spot until you get ahold of my brother's doctor. I won't speak to a resident or intern. I will only speak to the physician in charge of his care. Have I made myself clear?"

The flustered clerk left her station. Her supervisor came out to try to reason with the irate visitor. The professor repeated what she said and insisted she was prepared to make a scene if required. The supervisor told her to have a seat and assured her he would do his best to get someone to speak with her.

She took a seat and checked for emails again. Nothing. She looked at magazines and picked up the Denver Post lying on the table. Skimming the pages, she saw updates on the gas explosion in New York City that killed eight, the drunk driver crashing through barricades in Texas, a mudflow in Washington state killing 43, and still no word on Flight 370. More disappearances, maiming, death, destruction, and lives changed forever. *Yes, Barry, it certainly is the eve of destruction.*

Twenty minutes passed, and the professor grew increasingly impatient. Finally, she heard a commotion in the hallway. She looked up to see the supervisor and clerk walk out, followed by the old woman from the garden, still carrying her pruning shears. What she had mistaken for a patient's gown was actually a long lab coat, which looked far too big on her.

The old woman was considerably shorter than the two admissions staff. Her white hair had been pulled up in a bun. Her dark skin had lines etched deeply around her eyes and cheeks. Her hands were those of an anciently old woman, with gnarled fingers and large tributaries of veins running down the back of each hand. Like a parting of the Red Sea, the admissions clerk and her supervisor stepped aside so the old woman could approach. The professor's jaw dropped as she read the name on the lab coat.

"Hello, Dr Schivalone, forgive me, I was in the garden. I am Dr Hazel Lukachunai. I'm in charge of your brother's care."

PART TWO

AWAKENING

"Trauma is a thief that robs us of memory and places our minds in a sleepy shadowland. Symbols of healing can light the path of awakening and set us free."

–H. T. LUKAS
From the Shadows of the Mind: Traumas & the Symbols that Transform Them, 1980

Chapter 20

Sacred Birds

Saturday, March 22, 9:00 AM

The meeting on Thursday was not what Carmine had expected. Outside, in a garden? He had no data points for such a therapist. Nothing about her felt familiar.

In his long history of patient-hood and shrinkery, he'd come to expect the standard litany of questions about his presenting problems––rarely speaking, no friends, being bullied, and reading obscure books about dead mathematicians. The questions would segue into what he studied in school, if he liked his teachers, and if he had hobbies. Then would come the standard questions about his mental status. "Rate your anxiety, depression, and anger on a scale of 1-10." "Do you hear voices, believe others are out to get you?" And, "Do you wish you were dead?" But now, something was different. There was no set of tired questions, no probing, prompts, quizzes, or tests. Instead, she seemed content just sitting with him, paying homage to the sights and sounds of the garden.

"Yes, I do like b-birds."

"Ah, that's good Carmine. I do too." Dr Lukachunai talked of the sacred birds, the four gatekeepers on the Medicine Wheel––the eagle, hawk, crow, and owl. "They are of the air, you see, and each carries either wisdom or messages to help us understand and communicate our most important thoughts." She explained that the eagle has the most extraordinary vision because it flies highest and connects us to our ancestors. "Crows are storytellers and shapeshifters, while owls carry messages between the living and dead. The red-tailed hawk is a most sacred bird. It is our protector who warns us of danger, not just of things that can harm us in the world, but it also awakens us to what we need to see."

They'd been in the garden for over an hour, and the morning sun was intense. For Carmine, it seemed but a few minutes.

The doctor smiled at him. "I find that this is the right spot to begin listening to what you can tell us and even what you cannot, Carmine. The garden is a sacred space. We can travel at your pace. You'll be here a few weeks, maybe longer, while we listen and help you tell your story."

She motioned to Julio. "Please take our Carmine back to the ward. We can dispense with the restraints. You can help him get ready for his testing and group afterward. Thank you, Mr Garza."

Julio nodded and set the chair in motion as Dr Lukachunai stayed behind. When they rounded the corner heading toward the building, Carmine looked back to see her making movements that reminded him of Tai Chi.

"What is sh-sh- she doing?" he asked Julio.

"Oh, that's her spirit dance, bro. It's an offering she makes to the birds."

Chapter 21

Beelzebuffo

Two Months Earlier....Wednesday, January 22, 2014, 1:00 PM

In the fall of 2013, CMHI-P was stunned by a tragedy that threatened to upend the norms and culture of the institution. When the much-loved Executive Director of Health Facilities, Dr Orin Corvine, died suddenly after his car careened off an icy road, the Board of Overseers needed an interim replacement until a search and selection process could be completed.

Among his many respected accomplishments, Dr Orin had responded, twelve years earlier, to the need to diversify their treatments and broaden their bio-psycho-social orientation to include a spiritual dimension. Given the unique setting in southern Colorado, and the demographics of many of their patients, Dr Orin thought it fitting to integrate indigenous healing methods into their treatment programming. His vision was to identify components of traditional Native practices and, when appropriate, include some of them as ancillary therapies along with the standard treatment protocols. He even had a sweat lodge built on the campus to conduct indigenous ceremonies for some patients. It was Dr Orin who, in 2002, hired Hazel Lukachunai, first as a cultural consultant and then as a staff member and team leader in the Forensics Unit. Lukachunai was an experienced Navajo psychologist who'd directed the San Francisco Jungian Institute. Several features of the traditional healing program proved popular with many, but not all.

Dr Baron Leonid Buffo, a well-heeled physician and heir to Buf-Pharmics, Inc., a mid-size player in the pharmaceutical industry, had originally been named to the Board because of his family's political connections. Now the Board needed an acting director, and Buffo eagerly accepted the interim appointment. B. L.'s pudgy frame was a tailor's worst nightmare because no matter how expensively cut, his suits could not contain his lumpy body. Feared more than respected, B. L. Buffo was often referred to (behind his sizable backside) as the Big Toad--a reference to the extinct giant frog known as Beelzebufo.

An ambitious man in his late 40s, "Beelzebuffo" had lobbied for the interim post before Dr Orin was even placed in the ground. The Board didn't realize Buffo saw his temporary posting as a stepping stone to a permanent appointment. He intended to use his family's power and prestige to ensure he would be Director well into the next decade. The Big Toad also had a clear and self-serving agenda for his administration--ELIMINATE ALL TRADITIONAL HEALING PRACTICES. Medicine in the form of pills, not the rituals of therapy or traditional healing, would regain its dominance in treatment.

In the weeks following his December interim appointment, he moved the Director of Forensic Services, Dr Maurine Tran, to a lesser position. Tran had been an early advocate for integrating a limited number of culturally sensitive diagnostic and treatment practices into their hospital treatment protocols.

In January, Beelzebuffo called an emergency meeting of the CMHI-P Executive Committee to review the status of his plan to scale down and eventually eliminate traditional healing therapies throughout the hospital. The various department heads crowded into the Ponderosa Pines Conference Room.

Buffo cleared his throat and croaked for everyone to be seated. He began the meeting by announcing that "political correctness" and the tilt toward diversity had damaged the reputation of CMHI-P and diluted the effectiveness of proven medical and pharmacological treatments. "Ladies and gentlemen, we've effectively been held hostage to these unproven treatments. Need I remind you that this is a hospital, not the purview of medicine men and witch doctors. So, as of today, we will no longer offer these so-called spiritual treatments as part of our programs. No more drum circles, spiritual healing groups, or any other Native practices that have crept into our treatment regimens. Oh, and that sweat lodge abomination will be dismantled."

His subsequent announcement––a plan to terminate Lukachunai–– was met with pushback from some older members of the Board who respected her but were more concerned that her dismissal at this time would reflect poorly on the institution (by this, they meant the Board). Buffo realized the votes were not there to have Lukachunai fired and that he would have to bide his time until he could remove this last irritating vestige of traditional healing from CMHI-P. Removal would require a meticulous paper trail of noncompliance with new regulations, which he planned to present as malpractice.

When the meeting was adjourned, he called one of the senior charge nurses to his office. "Olive, I have a special assignment for you. We're going to get the dirt on Princess Minnehaha. I can't do it all at once because she has a voodoo-like hold on some of the older Board members. We need to start a file on her so I can begin to shorten her leash. I need your eyes and ears about any peculiar practices that violate our new policies. We need to build a case that she's a quack, unfit and harmful to patient care. I want to hear how she quacks like a duck, Olive, so I can clip her wings and send her ass back to the rez."

Most nurses would have cringed at the blatant racism of the Big Toad's cartoonish comments and been repulsed by the tiny beads of sweat that trickled down his swarthy brow. But there was no cringing or repulsion for Olive Astracides. She was old school. Staff at CMHI-P knew that she had no affinity for the Native programs and no fondness for Lukachunai.

Throughout her well-structured life, Astracides had the reputation of always coloring within the lines. Other nurses and techs knew that anything not conforming to conventional nursing practices was anathema to their charge nurse, who some thought was better suited to the culture of a 1950s hospital ward setting. Medical doctors were in charge. They prescribed medicine. Their authority was not to be questioned. Nurses ran the wards. Lukachunai was both a non-medical doctor and a traditional healer, which did not sit well with the charge nurse. When she returned to her office, Olive Astracides RN began a secret file labeled "FWW" (Fowl Weather Warnings).

Chapter 22

Non Compos Mentis

Saturday, March 22, 2014 10:30 AM

After his garden session with Dr Hazel, Carmine faced a long day of diagnostic assessments, including lengthy interviews and testing sessions, answering repetitive questions, solving mental puzzles, filling out lengthy inventories, and interpreting inkblots. The level of one-on-one attention, social engagement, and questions would be taxing for anyone, but it was torment for a man accustomed to spending days without uttering a word.

Still in his wheelchair but without restraints, Carmine was escorted to each appointment by Julio. The first stop was a psychiatric interview with Martin Oakley, MD, who probed him with more questions.

Oakley's office was overstuffed with books, journals, files, and charts. When the stacks have stacks, things get lost. How many items of importance had fallen between the cracks of the cluttered piles on the doctor's desk? Carmine was taught that unkempt workspaces were the progeny of office dwellers who'd failed to learn a cardinal lesson in kindergarten: Put your damn stuff away. A neat desk means an orderly mind; a messy desk, well....

The doctor squinted as he brushed dandruff off his tie and read through the medical file, which Carmine noticed had grown another inch thick since he'd left the Aurora Medical Center. Dr Martin Oakley was a balding gentleman with an ashen gray complexion and a rumpled tweed jacket. The monotonic droning of his voice could have been successfully marketed as a soporific. Oakley robotically went through a series of questions. None were new. Many were just tiresome repeats.

Oakley's voice hummed on, coaxing sleep. The room grew stuffy, and the light faded from Carmine's eyes. The doctor looked up to see the fluttering of his eyelids accompanied by the gentle buzz of snoring. Heavily medicated patients were frequently drowsy, but none lost consciousness as quickly as this man sitting across from him. Carmine opened his eyes to an elbow jostling accompanied by Oakley's breathy staccato commands. "Hey. Wake up. Wake up. You need to stay with me now, Luedke. This is important. You have to stay awake."

Oakley summoned Julio to get the patient some coffee and take him outside for fresh air "to wake him the hell up."

Julio knelt and said, "Okay, Car-man, you need to stay in the room for this. You got a busy day ahead, so just hang in. Let's get you caffeinated, bro."

Strong coffee helped. In the second hour, Oakley inventoried Carmine's mental functions, his symptoms, and what scant history he could obtain from his laconic patient. When the doctor reached for the mother-lode--the core delusional belief that he'd been visited by a dead woman--Carmine stiffened.

"How could a woman who's long been dead appear, and why would she choose you? Do you really believe this? How is such a thing possible?"

Carmine winced and pounded his fists on the arms of the table. "B-because she was there! I-I did think she was dead, but she wasn't. She *did* come back. I-I can't be here. She is l-looking for me. I have to let her know where I am. She chose me and left a g...g-glove in my office. I held it." His weariness grew. He was tired of the same questions asked by these skeptics and doubters. Raising his voice, he shouted, "THEY'RE ALL IN ON IT! I can prove it was LuCinda.... That's all."

If Oakley had a stamp on his desk, he would have stamped the file: "Non compos mentis." The patient is not mentally competent to stand trial. Instead, they would have to treat his psychosis, which would take at least a month, maybe two, to reduce the intensity of his delusional beliefs. Oakley ordered the restraints back on and finished writing his prescriptions––Quetiapine for psychotic symptoms and Modafinil for narcolepsy. He called for Julio to take the patient back to the ward. He looked at the towering aide and grumbled, "Get him something to eat before he does his neuropsych this afternoon."

Julio took Carmine to the cafeteria line and seated him at a designated table. A nurse with rusty red hair wheeled the medicine cart to him. She dosed out the pills and watched as he took each in sequence. Swallowing on command, Carmine felt a thud in his empty stomach and a rebounding of queasiness. He shuffled the pile of green and orange morsels around his plate. Taking small bites for sustenance, not pleasure, he forced himself to finish a third of what had been scooped up for his lunch as his stomach did an unhappy dance. Seated across from him was Georgi, a gaunt-looking man who had devoured all but his utensils. Georgi's hungry eyes found Carmine's plate as he licked his spoon. "Hey, ya done there, sport? Mind if I...."

Julio signaled it was time for his afternoon appointment. The gentle giant wheeled Carmine down narrow hallways until they reached a faded sign pointing to the Cortical Functions Laboratory. Seated outside, they waited until 1:00, when a young tech opened the door.

"Let's see. Car-Carmine, uh...Ludick. No, sorry. How do you say it, hon?"

"L-lewd-key," he said softly. Single-word responses would be all he could easily muster this afternoon.

"Okay, Carmine. I'm Grace. Let's get you started. Julio, dear, we'll be about three hours then Dr D. can see him. Maybe we can loosen his restraints a tad. He'll need both hands for some of the testing."

These tests lit up the bookkeeper's frontal cortex like an old circuit board. Making designs with blocks, recalling endless strings of digits and letters, and navigating mazes were a smorgasbord for a man who romanced numbers, shapes, and colors. While many were worn out at this point, Carmine came to life.

"Quite outstanding, Carmine. You must've eaten your Wheaties this morning, hon. Think you set clinic records on some of these. The doctor will be in shortly to continue. She's got more testing to do, then she'll make sense of it all."

Dr Lia Dhikavi wore a purple hijab that offset her white lab coat. "Good afternoon Mr Luedke. I heard you've been doing well on many of our tests. So, let's you and I begin, shall we? I've got some questions. I know you've been in answering mode all day, but just a few things to go over before we get started."

Carmine found her voice soothing. It was easy to look into her eyes, which sparkled and brought splashes of color to mind. Her questions were all familiar. Following another two hours answering hundreds of questions on personality inventories, drawing pictures, associating to words, writing down early memories, and making up stories, Dr D. brought out a set of inkblot cards, held one up, and asked, "What might this be?"

The afternoon light was growing dim as Lia Dhikavi rapped lightly on Dr Hazel's door. Their ritual for the last eight years had been to spend quiet time together at twilight, discussing diagnostic impressions or sharing frustrations concerning the new administration. It was no secret that Lia cherished time with her most revered colleague, who brought back memories of her grandmother, Maman Joon.

Hazel still wore her lab coat, adorned with a traditional squash blossom necklace. She gave Lia a warm look and beckoned her to sit. Passing her a cup of greenthread tea, she asked, "What did you think of him? Mr Luedke, the man who is a stranger to words."

"He's complicated, more so than usual," Lia responded. "Oakley has already certified him as non-compos psychosis, but I'm not sure. He wrote an order for continued restraints but left that to staff discretion. To say that still waters run deep seems too trite, Hazel. Carmine is a jigsaw with too many pieces missing. His scores on cognitive measures were nearly off the charts. We don't see too much of that here. It's like

TEARS ARE ONLY WATER

he came to life when he was with Grace. She said she'd never seen anything quite like it. So, no cognitive impairment; actually, quite the opposite. But he was different with me. Slow to respond. A man of few words, to say the least. I could only coax a few words at a time."

Lia adjusted her hijab. "They diagnosed him with a brief psychotic disorder in Aurora—rule-out schizophrenia spectrum—but I don't get that from him. Something else, maybe? They found trace elements of DMT in a hair sample, which goes along with the hallucinations and paranoia described in the police report. The report said he claimed someone had visited him the night before, and now everyone was trying to cover it up. So, this guy was on a hallucinogen and speed when he attacked that woman. But here's the thing, Hazel, I didn't see the kinds of disruptions or illogicality in his thought processes that fit a psychotic profile, even what we see in amphetamine-induced psychosis. Oh, and forget about autism. Some staff wondered if he was on the spectrum, but there was little to suggest that is the case. He's quiet and odd, for sure. Still, the testing showed a deep interest in people and an enhanced capacity to empathize. He responded to my prompts when I asked him to say more, often providing clues that he was holding back."

Hazel nodded. "Yes, Lia. I sensed this yesterday, sitting in the garden with him. The leaves haven't completely fallen from his branches. There is life there, but his roots are starving. Life can't flourish when roots aren't fed."

"But here's another interesting thing. Every time there were explicit or implicit cues relating to father figures in actual or symbolic form, he went dark. Twice during the testing, he even nodded off briefly. For everything else, he was okay. Answers were brief without much elaboration but nothing bizarre like we might find in acute paranoid psychosis. It was only when he heard anything that pulled for images or deep associations relating to fathers that he closed his eyes and seemed to disappear. You've got yourself a Gordian knot, Hazel. He needs you."

It was not unusual for Lukachunai to check on patients following the evening group and community meeting. After PM meds had been dispensed that night, she knocked on Carmine's door.

"Ahhh, Carmine. Such a long day you've had. We put you to work, did we not? Next week we can begin. I'm interested to hear the many stories you have brought to us. You'll likely be with us for a month or longer, so we have time. Now you should rest. Sleep well and listen to your dreams, Carmine."

He nodded. "T-thank you, but I don't really have any s-stories to tell. There aren't any. That's it."

She smiled, turned, and moved toward the door.

"We all have stories, Carmine. You have one I'd like to hear more about on Monday. It's the one about your father."

Chapter 23

Off the Grid

Sunday, March 23, 5:30 PM

Anne checked into Motel 6 Pueblo late Saturday afternoon after her unexpected encounter with Lukachunai. Her room was as she'd expected-- small, cheap, and dank. Her meal at Bingo Burger sat uneasily in her lower quadrant. She purchased two bottles of Barefoot Chardonnay, put one in the tiny fridge, and opened the other, which was now about a glass from being empty. The thought that she would have to wait up to a week to see her brother agitated her indigestion and invited a large gulp of wine. Lying on the bed, she reviewed the insanity--*Carmine had lost it and was being treated by a geriatric shaman. Bad actors in Aurora were lying--why? Noa--who? And now she was about to get fired by that obnoxious little tweedle, Holmes. Fucksake....* She finished the first bottle and passed out.

The following day she awakened to a new sense of dread. Amid the sturm und drang of all that was going on with Carmine, her mother had started banging at her compartment door, demanding to be let out. In her morning fog, Anne recalled a fragment of a dream. She was sitting at the kitchen table with an older woman whose back was toward her. The woman wouldn't turn around. She was mumbling, and Anne couldn't hear what she was saying. Anne tried to run to the front of the woman, who kept turning away until both were spinning like tops.

The metaphor of mental compartments was formed in the crucible of Anne's prickly relationship with her mother. She'd laid the groundwork for managing her mother long before she formulated––or pirated, depending on who you talk to––her theory on adaptive compartmentalization. But before she'd grown a thick skin and broken ground for her network of compartments, she did everything she could to please and placate her mother, always searching for ways to gain her approval, and blaming herself when she could not.

Shortly before escaping to Choate, the professor learned to ignore her mother. When the soliloquies, pontificating, complaining, and criticizing would begin, she pretended she was deaf or dumb like her brother, visualizing a giant claw coming down from the ceiling, placing her mother in a soundproof compartment, and locking the door. The problem was this never worked that well. Then she discovered wine.

For some reason, her mother was raging from her compartment this morning, demanding to be heard. Like most narcissistic parents, Mother had always sought to control others with her symptoms. If the spotlight was on someone else or if they had somehow disappointed her, Mother would cough and develop a *terrible* headache. Over time, Anne perfected her ability to tune her out and place her mother in that special compartment bearing her initials. But then, her mother actually got sick. Her litany of pain and suffering became genuine, but by then, her complaints fell on Anne's highly trained deafened ears. Mother, who had long cried wolf, became subject zero in the professor's theory of adaptive compartmentalization. Yet, on the rare occasion that her complaints escaped their compartment and Anne responded with something approaching human kindness, Mother was quick to parry with a sneering and help-rejecting retort.

Mother held a black belt in turning up her nose at anything Anne offered that did not fit her precise agenda. She made that face and curled her lip at the idea of assisted living or hiring a live-in aid. Yet, for months, her mother continued to call and complain until her calls went straight to Anne's voicemail. Then...she died. *Damn her.*

The professor tried to scrub away the silt from her past by taking a hot shower and refortifying her compartments with a swig from her second

TEARS ARE ONLY WATER

Barefoot companion. Then, it was time to begin her search into Lukachunai's background. So far, the internet had provided few answers but more questions about Dr Hazel Lukachunai. *Who is this woman?*

A deep dive produced several hits for a Navajo psychologist named H. T. Lukas dating back to the '50s through the early '70s––top of her class at Radcliffe as an undergrad and Harvard as a grad student. All the sites referred to this woman as Tallulah––the name Hazel was never mentioned. The last name was slightly similar, though. Could it be the same person? Then, she read how this Tallulah Lukas woman traveled to London to study at the Tavistock Clinic. Anne winced. *The Tavistock–– yet one more glorified temple of the religion psychoanalytica.* Still, the professor found this intriguing.

The next hit identified H.T. Lukas as a student at the Jungian Institute in Zürich. She found a faded image of a young woman with closely cropped dark hair sitting beside a very old-looking Carl Gustav Jung, puffing on his pipe. The professor squinted and studied the black-and-white image, noting a slight resemblance to the old woman she'd met yesterday. *Yeah, same nose and eyes.*

There was a listing of several papers H.T. Lukas authored about child development, early trauma, and repression. Several links described a book she wrote in 1980 titled *From the Shadows of the Mind: Traumas & the Symbols that Transform Them,* about Jungian archetypes and their power to heal psychic pain. The professor poured another glass of chardonnay. *And there it is, folks, more psychoanalytic fiction about repressed trauma and its stifling effect on the developing mind. How quaint and wrong-headed. Pour me another drink, thank you very much.*

Anne continued to read how H. T. returned to the States in the late '70s and became President of the Jungian Institute in San Francisco. The professor frowned. So typical. This woman undoubtedly taught gullible students more about Jungian fairy tales, fiction, and fabrications. The professor liked that––Jungian Fairy Tales, Fiction, and Fabrications. Nice melodic ring. *Ooh, a title for my next book, maybe?*

175

Then, the hits stopped. Nothing more. It was as if H.T. Lukas had ceased to exist. Then, a random hit provided a link to the 1994 directory of the Colorado State Hospital. She saw an unceremonious listing of H. T. Lukachunai as a cultural consultant and staff psychologist.

Had H. T. Lukas effectively disappeared for almost 20 years? Anne downed her wine. *Where had she gone and why? Who the fuck was Tallulah, and what's with the changing of her name? Why would someone fall off the grid unless they had been disgraced or died?* But she saw no obituary. Although Dr Lukachunai looked weathered and fossilized, she was very much alive yesterday. The professor continued digging.

On her 19th page of Google deep diving, she came across two obscure references for a Hazel Lukachunai. The first was a paper written in 2000 titled "Healing with Mountain Grasses." The other a small book published by the Society of Bird Medicine in 2002 called, *In the Way of Sacred Birds--Messengers, Storytellers, and Teachers.*

The professor found all this puzzling, odd, and yet intriguing. Whatever the critics may say about Anne Schivalone--cynic, iconoclast, snob... drunk--few would doubt her tenacity when presented with a formidable puzzle. Noa--*ugh*--used to say that when something didn't make sense, she was like a dog with a bone, gnawing, chewing, and consuming every strand until she'd managed to bury it.

She was startled by the shrill ringing of her phone. It was a Facetime. She answered to hear a loud "GRAAWK," then Nicola's face appeared on the screen.

"No, cool it, Langs! Damn. Shit, I think he knew I was calling you and was trying to tell me to find new friends, sister."

"Well, tell Big Bird I don't like him either, and I didn't realize I had made it onto your friend list."

"Yeah, right. Seriously, hope it's not too early, but I got some news that's gonna rock your brains, so maybe you should sit down."

TEARS ARE ONLY WATER

Instead, the professor stood up quickly, and the blood rushed from her head. "Okay, what's so earth-shattering? I was planning to see Carmine's shrink today but have to wait until next Friday. Just crazy. This place is straight out of Dante's Inferno. I was just doing my homework about this strange lady masquerading as his doctor. But more about that later. So, what have I got to sit down for?"

Kitts recounted how she'd spent the day––first, visiting the high-collared office manager and then the snooty doctor at the hospital. "Totally unhelpful. Stonewalling, if you ask me. Their stories paint a picture of your brother as a lunatic, yada yada. But there was some cleaning lady at Shrenklin's who pulled me aside to whisper that your brother was a good man. But listen to this...she said that the glove *did not* belong to her. So, Big Mama Pelcovey was lying."

Anne had been pacing the room and, at this piece of news, slapped her hand on the dresser, toppling her glass of wine. "I knew it! That horse-collared phony. I guarantee this wasn't her first and will not be her last lie."

The deputy then talked about her visit to Jonas and how she'd seen the same blonde woman in the stairwell at Shrenklin's who later came out of his office with him. "I'm gonna run her down tomorrow after meeting up with this Dihn you told me about. Sounds like a good guy to know. I've got a boatload of questions for him."

"Agreed. He fits the stereotype. An odd recluse like my brother, but he will be useful. Dihn can check into the companies Carmie was auditing. I'll text you a list. But come on, Kitts, did this news require me to sit down? We knew Pelcovey was lying, and I felt Jonas was a scam artist from the moment I first saw him. And this woman in a red dress sounds like a wild goose chase."

"Wait, Sister. I promised you there's more, and it's big, I mean B-I-G, so you should sit your professor ass down *now*."

Kitts told her how she'd met up with an old marine buddy in the lab at the hospital to check out what Carmine's blood work had shown. Anne interrupted.

"But we already knew it would show the amphetamines in his system. That's nothing new. You better not quit your day job, Deputy. You should give careful consideration to this social work thing, Kitts, because your detective skills are about a day late and a––"

"Oh man, I get it. See, that's the thing with you. You think you're so damned smart, got it all figured out, but you don't. I realize, Doctor, that listening is not one of your gifts, so if you'll shut the hell up and let me finish, maybe then we can figure out a plan."

The comment about not listening hit a nerve. Anne had heard this too many times, but before now, it had not penetrated her forcefield. She took a breath and said, "Sorry. Go ahead, Deputy Kitts."

Kitts told her that her friend checked Carmine's lab results, and in addition to amphetamines, they found vast amounts of DMT in his blood.

"You know what that is, sister? DMT? It means that not only was speed goosin' his receptors, but he had this other stuff onboard too. DMT, you know, that shitworthy junk can cause––"

"Hallucinations!"

"Yeah, my buddy Froggie said it's a bad mix with the speed he was taking. But this DMT shit probably caused hallucinations, agitation, and wild paranoia. All the stuff that Books was showing."

"I can't believe this, Nicola. Carmie taking something like that? He took mega doses of Adderall to keep him from falling asleep, but he would never mess with hallucinogens. Dihn would've told me if he had been taking something besides Adderall."

"But wait, Sis, it gets weirder. Froggie said that the tech who'd first entered this was the same person who scratched it from his record. Here's the kicker...ready for it....She's now gone missing. Been off the grid since the day after her last shift when all this came down. Hasn't reported back to work."

Head spinning had become a daily event. Finally, Anne had to sit down. "We have to find this woman! She knows what they're hiding.... You know, the more I poke this steaming heap of malodorous excrement, the worse it gets."

Kitts laughed. "Ooh, Professor, the image of you poking a pile of shit is more than I care to take in, but please send photos. Actually, I'd call all this one giant cluster fuck."

Chapter 24

Tallulah

Monday, March 24, 2:30 AM

Hazel couldn't sleep. Though she tucked most patients into their professional compartments at night, there were the occasional few who refused to be silenced. Such was the case with Carmine Luedke. Too many unsettling thoughts about missing fathers. In a few hours, she would meet with this silent bookkeeper who had untold stories about his father that needed to be told. Her own stories had been told, and all that was left were memories sprinkled with regret.

The tug between Western and Indigenous approaches to healing had never completely disappeared. It had taken too long for Hazel Lukachunai to find out who she was. Earlier, she had lost her way.

Her mother's older brother, her *adá'i*, was a traditional medicine man well-known in her community. When his assistant passed away, Hazel's mother became his apprentice. Her older brothers attended his healing ceremonies, all hoping to follow their famous uncle's path. But not Hazel.

Her family was dirt poor, worse off than most in their small Native community in southern Colorado. Her mother was Navajo, and her father was Ute. She was never told the story of how two people from Nations that had long been enemies found each other. All she knew was her parents had never signed a truce. Their nightly arguments permeated the thin walls of their tiny house.

TEARS ARE ONLY WATER

Hazel remembered her father's rough hands and kind eyes as he lifted the children onto the back of his broken-down truck for those bumpy drives into town. She felt protected by his strength and looked forward to spending time with him. But those innocent trips into town became a source of shame when she heard the hurtful whispers of the White townspeople.

One incident continued to haunt her. Hazel had spoken about it only once years after. She described how she and her brothers always wore tattered clothes from the Salvation Army. They would pile into Pinksworth's Five and Dime with their father. The owner's eyes burned with hate, as he followed them through the aisles.

One day he said, "Well, if it isn't Chief Give-Me-Something with his little Indians in tow."

When they left, he always checked their pockets. But on this day, he made Hazel take her dress off to make sure she hadn't stolen anything. As the Native family left, the shop owner called to his wife, "We need to fumigate the whole damn place again." It took 40 years for Hazel to allow her tears to flow.

As a child, she had been secretly ashamed of her *amá sání,* her ancient grandmother with peculiar odors, an odd assortment of rituals with plants, and morning prayers to the birds. "If I close my eyes, I can make her disappear," she used to tell herself. *Amá sání* had defiantly refused to learn the White man's language. Hazel's mother spoke English but never learned to read. Hazel vowed she would be different. In an act of defiance, she changed her name when she left home. Hazel became Tallulah.

But nothing haunted her more than her *azhé'é.* She adored her father as a child but became embarrassed and frightened by him as she grew older. Struggling with diabetes and alcoholism, he came to embody all the vile stereotypes that Whites had of Native People—"drunk, unedu-cated, savage." Always silent and brooding over the culture-robbing and soul-murdering crimes against their People, her father's morose moods turned to anger, and his actions, fueled by alcohol, became abusive. Life became too much for him, and one night he took his last drink, which he chased down with a bullet to his head. Hazel found him the next morning. His final act of devastating defiance thwarted her grief and deepened her shame, which she'd locked in a secret compartment.

That compartment had been unlocked by the quiet bookkeeper she would meet, in the garden, tomorrow morning.

Chapter 25

Messages From the Dead

Monday, March 24, 4:30 AM

Like a cork bobbing gently on the water, he let the waves carry him away. The spray of salt water on his face, cool and comforting, invited him to close his eyes as the small boat rocked him like a baby. Engulfed in a strange dreamscape, the man who knew only night terrors, numbers, and eyes peering through windows, allowed himself to float and wander. He was puzzled by these uncommon sensations in this unfamiliar place. What was this? Peace? Serenity? Then, something above—far away at first, circling overhead—now moved closer. The stretch of shadow-colored wings cut through the sky as a massive owl approached its target and glided to a soft landing on the side of his boat. With a sharp beak, coal-black eyes rimmed in gold, and horned feathers atop its head, the bird sat motionless and stared intently at the man floating on the sea. The man stared back, puzzled but not afraid. Then with the flapping of its tremendous wings, the sky creature took flight... and the man woke up.

Carmine's room was still dark as he rubbed the dream from his sleepy eyes. He stood, his legs still weak after all that time in restraints and the wheelchair. But it felt so good moving around the room on his own. After breakfast, Julio would take him to the garden for another meeting with Lukachunai.

A cool morning breeze tickled his brow. The sun rode the bluffs of Greenhorn Mountain and was beginning to warm the back of his neck. With Julio by his side, he walked to the garden. There was no way he could match Julio's stride, but it was good to be walking again. The Navajo healer was seated at the same bench every morning, softly chanting words he did not recognize. The two men stopped and waited.

"Uh, s'cuse me, b...b-ut what's she saying?" Carmine whispered, looking up at the giant.

"She's talking to the birds. Always does that in the morning. It's her old Native language called Diné Bizaad, something like that. You can look it up, bro."

"Okay....But I don't have a dictionary, Julio."

When she stopped her morning verses, the two approached.

"Morning, Doctora. Here he is right on time." Motioning to Carmine, "You sit here, bro. I'll be over there in my usual spot."

The doctor sipped her tea. "*Ahéheé*. Thank you, Mr Garza. She watched him walk away. Then, looking straight ahead, she said, "This is my favorite time of day. There's a freshness each morning as light sends nighttime back to its slumber. I sit and listen, listen to the birds, you know. They have many things to tell us if we listen, but we are usually too busy to pay attention. .... I trust you slept, Carmine."

"I don't sleep like normal people. I can't sleep w-hen I try and don't stay awake when I need to. And if I fall asleep––she can't find me."

"Who can't find you?"

He had said too much. "Just...s-something. I get mixed up. It's nothing. That's all. But I guess I did sleep some last night. I have narcolepsy. Did you know that?"

She smiled. "Yes, I did. I believe that there is more to Carmine than Narcolepsy. I want to hear more about the person who is looking for you. But we can wait on this. I am glad that you were able to sleep last night. How about dreams? Any dreams?"

"Oh yeah, a dream. Last night I had one.... W...w-as on a boat some- where, you know, kind of floating around and some huge bird like an owl. I was watching it in the sky. It flew down and sat on the side of my boat. It kept staring at me. It was so close .... That's all."

Lukachunai looked toward the south. "Hmm. Good. That is a good one, Carmine. Now, if you let the owl and boat come back to your mind, what thoughts or pictures do they bring with them?"

He sat in silence, trying to find the residue left from a dream that had almost faded from his mind. "Not much. I was just on my b-ack lying in the boat. I was floating or kind of drifting, I think. Like, you know, rocking back and forth."

"Ah, tell me about the floating and rocking."

The rustiness of his words gave way. He found it easier to speak. "It felt good, peaceful, actually. Its beak was sharp, and eyes were black. I can see them. But I didn't feel scared when it flew to the edge of my boat. It just kind of sat there looking at me. Like it was supposed to be there, you know.... That's about it for the dream. I woke up, and you know, another day in my life. So, there you have it."

"Yes, very good. Very good. Remember the other day I told you that birds are a sacred part of the Medicine Wheel and that the eagle, hawk, crow, and owl bring messages that help us discover important things? We must pay attention and listen. A visit from the owl brings an important window of understanding."

He hung on her words as she spoke, and his mind began to clear.

"The owl of your dream that night has excellent vision. Remember I said that owls are like gatekeepers? They watch the doors between the worlds. They listen to our shadow selves and can help explain messages in our dreams. Those big eyes and great horned ears? They help us look and listen to messages where deep truths lie. Truths that are hidden behind our fears and doubts. Did I mention that owls help us listen to messages from the spirit world, like those who have passed on?"

Startled, his stammer returned. "W-w-wait, you mean like dead p...p-eople are sending me messages?"

The doctor took another sip of tea. She responded, "Maybe not in the literal sense, but we need to learn what these messages are or where they come from. We shall find that out together. I think of these messages as things we need to wake up and pay attention to. Maybe things we're trying not to see. But, Carmine, you ask an important question about those who have passed on and possibly left you with unfinished business. Tell me your thoughts about such messages from the dead."

He hadn't expected this question and began to pull back. Warning. Danger. Moments passed while he tried to encapsulate himself in Euler's cocoon-- $e^{i\pi} + 1 = 0, e^{i\pi} + 1 = 0$--but the doctor was patient and knew how to sit with silence.

Finally, he answered. "Really, dead people? Um, well, yeah, my p...p...p-arents, I guess. They're dead. That's about all. Oh, and E died too. That was the name of this woman I knew. Her real name was Elizabeth, and I was the only one who called her E. That's a long story. Everyone thought she was dead.... Now, I don't know. I mean, I thought she was dead. It was in all the newspapers. But she did come to my office one night last week and is looking for me now." His speech grew more insistent. "You s-s-see, she came to find me. She needs me. No one believes me, but it's true! It's like no one knew she was still alive because she hid her work, you know, on some top secret project with all these scientists.... She found out where I was, you know, in my office. She said they need me on the team. Then...she disappeared again after I cut out, you know, Zzz-- when this fuck brain of mine shorted out like a defective circuit board. I know I shouldn't say fuck." He snored for effect and rapped his knuckles forcefully against the side of his head.

Dr Lukachunai reached up and stopped him from hitting himself, then encouraged him to continue.

"Um, sorry.... I know I shouldn't s-swear. I won't do it again."

"Your language is fine, Carmine, but there is no reason for you to hit yourself like that. I noticed that you do that when you get stuck. You turn your words or fists against yourself."

TEARS ARE ONLY WATER

"But I turned it against LuCinda last w...w-eek. I shoulda choked myself instead. Now, everyone thinks I'm a psychotic killer or something like that. You know, like, 'Oh, Carmine's lost his mind and snapped. Something's always been off with Carmine the Demento.' People think that math heads are weird anyway. Like we live in our heads, talk to numbers, and sometimes just go crazy. Like John Nash, you remember him, right? There's others too. You know, lose their minds and...try to hang themselves.... But I know E was there last week and can't find me now. She looked the same but, you know, older. She said she needed me on her research team because I know a lot about numbers, you know, advanced calculus and algorithms. She said it was important, that it would change everything. Really...that's it."

She gently pressed on. "An owl came to you in your dream, Carmine. Listen to it. To see E again in your mind, your dreams, or anywhere means something with her is not finished. It is a sign she has more to tell you about yourself, that there is more to know."

She paused and took another sip of tea. "There is something else I need to bring up, Carmine. It is about when you came to the hospital. You know when they did all those laboratory tests after you got here? Well, our laboratory found a substance in your blood that can cause hallucinations––DMT. So, you had this and a stimulant in your system, a combination that could have caused hallucinations and made you feel people were coming after you. So, I must ask, did you take DMT the night you believe you saw E?"

His mind swirled, and he jolted to his feet. Julio stood up and began to approach, but the doctor signaled him to stay.

"W...w...w-hat!? Geez. Really? So, wait.... You mean I was imagining that a dead person was talking to me because I dreamed about an owl? Now you're saying it was all a hallucination? Like it was just a crazy thing in my fucked head? Hell, shit, damn." He reflexively smacked the side of his head. "I'm sorry, I'm sorry. I guess I've got Tourette's too. No, Doctor. No D-DMT, no.... Yeah, I know what that is, but I just take methylph-phenidate, you know, Adderall, to stay awake but, no, nothing else, never. Geez.... That's all." He sat and buried his head in his hands.

"I thought as much but needed to ask. Still, that leaves the question about how it got into your system, but perhaps that is a matter for us to explore at another time. Let us agree that there is much we do not know, Carmine. The critical thing to know about hallucinations is that they are not simply a random firing of neurons in the brain. No, they are communications from deeper parts of our minds. They can be frightening and cause suffering, but they can also be clues and valuable guides. Yes, there are medicinals that cause us to see and hear things, but the seeds of those messages are in our minds––out of sight from our eyes. So, I wonder what message your E, however she came to you, needed you to know. Can you tell me more about E? You said you had a long story to tell."

The noisy cawing and clacking of crows filled the air. He looked towards her, shielding the sun from his eyes. An aura of yellow and blue outlined her white coat. Once he started to speak, his words flowed with surprising ease. He told the doctor he'd met E in high school and that she made him feel special because she admired how much he knew about numbers.

"How nice to have had someone see you, Carmine––see how much you knew about numbers. That's something she valued about you."

His words continued to pour out, and before he could stop, he was telling her about the night of E's accident and how it was all his fault because he tried to kiss her.

"She didn't like that. I didn't know what to do, so I just ran away. I'm not just a normal person. I am an idiot. I was even more of one back then. So, she ran after me and called my name. You know, she was looking for me in the dark of night. Then, I hear a car...speeding down the street...and it hits her. That's all I.... The sound was.... She came looking for me...and I froze and...."

"Froze and, what Carmine?"

TEARS ARE ONLY WATER

"Fell asleep. That's what I do. I fell asleep in the bushes right where I was hiding. The same thing always happens. Like my b-brain gets subtracted. A switch just gets flipped, and I cut out. Doesn't matter where I am. But the point is that E came looking for me and...I c-checked out. I left her. There's no more to say. That's it."

Lukachunai listened. "It seems E has always been looking for you––in the past and even now, so it seems.... This was the night you thought E died, Carmine? Is this what happened?"

He looked away. *Too much. Stop!* He needed to narrow his focus and make her disappear. He shut his eyes. Desperately searching for Euler to rescue him, he whispered, "*$e^{i\pi} + 1 = 0$...$e^{i\pi} + 1 = 0$... $e^{i\pi}$.*"

"See if you can let the numbers go and be here with me now, Carmine. Can you tell me what happened to her, to E? I know how hard it is to stay present, to be both storyteller and witness."

Carmine bolted upright. "N-no, not then! She didn't die then. It was years after the accident. She recovered from the accident, and we lost touch. She got back to her life. But one day, she just decided to k...k-kill herself. I never knew why. No one did. She left a note. All it said was, 'It's time.' That's it.... That's all."

Chapter 26

Apache 11 Eagle Down!

Monday, March 24, 7:30 AM

Nicola made her to-do list after talking to Schivalone yesterday. Adrenalin mixed with caffeine focused her mind. First on the list–check out Stenna Marks. The lab tech might be MIA, but Kitts knew tricks to finding people. She'd start by going over to her place to snoop around.

Then, she'd bring a peace offering to Burwinkle to take the edge off. Recalling how he threw her out of his office when she brought granola bars after his heart attack, she thought, "donuts." *Yep, gotta get a box of Krispy Kremes.* She needed to do damage control to get back into his good graces and buy more time. The thought of his big, beet-red face venting his spleen while his meaty hands rubbed his chest wasn't pretty. The LuCinda thing caused enough agitation. But the news about the DMT and the missing lab report––not to mention Marks, who'd gone AWOL––were game changers. Burwinkle would have no choice but to put some real teeth into her investigation. She pictured him chomping on a Krispy Kreme and that look on his face when the light switched on. His eyes would flash with excitement, and he'd bellow, "Ya thinkin' someone drugged the bookkeeper? Well, fer God's sake, Cole, we got us a real crime goin' on here!"

If all went well, the sheriff would greenlight a formal investigation and give her time to put the pieces together. Then, after pacifying Burwinkle with glazed sour cream cakes, she'd pay a visit to the hacker Dihn. Schivalone had texted a list of the companies her brother was working

TEARS ARE ONLY WATER

on. They figured that Dihn could identify anything weird in the companies' records. Follow the money, right? Then, if she had time, she might pay Jonas another visit to see what she could find out about the blonde in the red dress who kept showing up and possibly snoop around a bit more about the sniffing intern.

First stop: Stenna Marks' home. The deputy had no trouble locating the address from the central database. She knew the neighborhood. As she drove up, she read the faded numbers on the mailbox—1312 S. Fairfax. It was an old '60s-style rambler with a sweet little garden out front but no other signs of life. It reminded her of Auntie Rhea's old house. Probably a clothesline and remnants of an old incinerator in the back where they used to burn trash before anyone cared about air pollution. There was no vehicle in the carport, no barking dog. The curtains were drawn. There was an upended garbage can on the sidewalk that no one had bothered to put back.

She found the gate to the back of the house and looked around the yard. Overgrown bushes made scooting through the narrow jungle path difficult. A small sprinkler was on, drowning a tiny flower bed by the house. The lawn was flooded, and the peonies drooped as if to beg, "No more, sir, please." Kitts sloshed through the muddy grass to the patio and checked the back door, which to her surprise, was unlocked. *No one's home but someone's home?*

Checking that none of the neighbors had noticed a cop snooping around, she slinked into a mudroom. A couple of coats hung on the hooks, and a mound of laundry sat atop the washing machine. A stale fruity stench hung in the air of the small kitchen. On the table sat two Kings Soopers bags full of groceries, which put the ex-Marine on high alert that someone *was* in the house after all. She drew her service revolver and inched her way into the hallway. Her eyes were immediately drawn to the mountain of envelopes and fliers piled up beneath the mail slot. *Someone's home, but no one's home? That someone must have been here and left in a hurry.* She checked the rooms upstairs, where she found well-lived-in spaces with closets full of clothes. In one closet, she found a stack of suitcases gathering dust. Someone left in a rush without packing or even putting the groceries away.

Kitts spent another 30 minutes casing the upstairs rooms and unfinished basement.

Confident that no one was in the house, she holstered her pistol. She looked through the pile of mail. Most of it was junk or bills––*wait 'til Stenna gets her next water bill*––but nothing looked out of the ordinary. A well-lived-in house, now vacant. There were no signs of a struggle, only of a sudden departure.

She found an address book that might offer clues about where Marks had gone, but she wasn't hopeful. Flipping through, she found a Crystal Marks––maybe a sister or mother. Kitts pocketed the book and made a mental note to call this person later. She waded through the swampy backyard and turned off the water before returning to her patrol car. *Why would someone leave so quickly that they couldn't even turn off the damned sprinkler? Absent-minded, distracted, or scared?*

She radioed to make sure Burwinkle was in, then her next stop was the Krispy Kreme a few blocks from the station. A few minutes later, Kitts was in his office, presenting the sheriff with a token of her apology and the big news. A box of donuts and a big break in the case played to the sheriff's appetites. His eyes widened as she went through the mounting evidence. Flakes of donut glaze clung precariously to his mustache like icicles on a downspout. Burwinkle slurped his coffee and encouraged his deputy, who had just regained her favored status, to go over the details again.

"Well, I'd be a blind man in a snowstorm if I couldn't see that handwritin' on the wall."

She loved his way of inventing metaphors and jumbling them in the process, another of Burwinkle's endearing qualities.

"This could be big, Niki. You might jes get that transfer and maybe more, girl. Sorry 'bout that business with LuCinda. Here's what I think we gotta do next." He paused as his squat fingers moved appreciatively toward the donuts. "First, lemme try this little fella over here."

TEARS ARE ONLY WATER

As she had hoped, the sheriff was all in. He filled out the paperwork sanctioning a full-time investigation with Kitts as the lead officer. "Ya can handpick someone to ride along or fly solo. I'll leave that up to you."

She told him about Dihn, the woman in the red dress who had shown up in too many places, and her uneasy feeling about Jonas. Then, she leaned in close and said, "Uh, there's one more thing, Sheriff... I don't trust Mama Lu. I hope I'm wrong cuz I know she carries a lot of cred around here, but go with me on this a little while longer 'til I check into a few more things."

"Well, yeah...that is a big ask, but I'm gonna give ya this one, Cole, fer a little while. LuCinda's good people, but I hear ya. This is police work, and we can't let this other stuff get in the way. So that'll remain between us fer now. But all I ask is that ya go easy and let me know what yer findin' every step of the way. And don't go all Rambo and gettin' too up into her business and get people all pissed off again. And check back with me after ya see this Chinese fella Dihn, whoever the hell he is."

Schivalone had told Kitts to leave a message for Dihn that she'd be coming over later in the day because he wouldn't be up until noon. The deputy found the aged geek much as the professor had described––thin frame, straggly hair, aging stubble on gaunt cheeks. She saw the head tremor that Schivalone told her about and thought of Agent Orange. Kitts was reminded of the Lone Gunmen, those computer-hacking nerds on that show X-Files from the '90s. Intrigued that an old White man would go by Dihn, she was tempted to learn his story but didn't have the time to get into it. As a former marine, she recognized the orange and yellow chevron patch on his fatigue jacket.

"Nam?" she asked, to which he nodded,

"Yup. 3rd Marines, Khe Sanh."

She gazed at him. "Semper Fi, Corporal."

"Yeah.... Fidelis. Oorah and all that shit.... You?"

"Gunnery Sergeant Kitts, 5th Marine Regiment, Operation Khanjar."

"Hell shit, that was some meat grinder there."

193

She shrugged. "That shit don't mean nothin'."

"Yeah, right.... Heard all that before."

A wordless bond was formed. Dihn nodded in recognition. He pushed a pile of files off his couch, and poofs of dust filled the air. "Siddown Gunny. I'm partial to ginseng tea at this time of day."

Kitts asked how long he'd known Luedke and said she and his sister suspected some bad actors had set him up. "Did you ever know him to mess around with hard drugs?"

Dihn shook his head, "Nope.... Compared to me and you, Carm's a boy scout. I helped him procure his share of methylphenidate, ya know, Ritalin and some such shit like that he took just to stay awake.... He mighta upped his dosage, poor guy, but nothin' besides stimulants, you know."

His head wobbled even more when she asked about street drugs like DMT, which she shared had been found in Carmine's tests.

"Take it you don't know Carmine very well cuz if you did, you'd know how crazy that sounds.... Listen, the only thing he ever did was the shit I already said. Didn't even drink that much. Carm has a quiet and gentle soul. Lives more in his head than in the outside world. What do they say? 'Still waters run deep?' Yeah, that's him. He come to me the other night all worked up. Had this crazy idea that some dead woman from his past had found him. Yeah, sounds pretty out there, right? I was thinking, man...what's up with this? But you know, he needed something, so hell, I'm all there for him. He asks me to take a look on the dark web to see what I could find out about her. Got some tricks, you know, for doing these deep dives. Musta been ten years ago, maybe more, that he talked about her one night, right here. Got pretty broken up.... Never saw much emotion in him before or since, but I did that day. All I know is, crazy as all this shit sounds, there's no way Carm's going to be putting stuff like that into his body.... Musta got there some other way, if you catch my drift."

She did catch his drift. "What did you find out? What did you tell him?"

"Nada. Just like the papers all said. The woman went and did a swan dive off the Golden Gate. No one knew why. Body was never recovered, but lots of jumpers aren't....Could she still be out there? Maybe? But if you ask me, Gunny, the one-word answer is shit no. That's it. End of story. Comprende?"

Kitts said she and Anne wanted to check on the companies Carmine did the books for. They needed Dihn's hacking skills because Shrenklin's wouldn't release information about their clients. She also mentioned the suspicious characters, Jonas and Pelcovey, who seemed to be hiding something. "Maybe there's a connection between them and your friend, Carmine, or maybe not." She said they were on a bit of a fishing trip—*damn, I could be fishing right now*—that they weren't looking for anything special, just something that didn't look right in the financials.

"Yeah, about that too.... He was rantin' that day about how some of his accounts wouldn't balance, that the numbers wouldn't add up. That's not like him either, ya know, Carm was a wizard with numbers. He kinda come up short on words but numbers, never. Nope, not happenin'."

He said he'd look into the companies and text her when he found something. She thanked him for his help and reached out to shake his hand. Dihn extended his but looked away...*Don't mean nothin'.* Just two ex-marines trying to carry on, keeping their stories to themselves.

It was close to 3:00 when she left Dihn's. Her mind felt cluttered with voices barking out instructions. Go see Jonas. Check into Red Dress. Pick up Langston from the vet's. Check out Books' apartment. Update Burwinkle. She had plenty to do while awaiting word from Corporal Dihn about the bookkeeper's companies.

A vacant sensation in her stomach reminded her she'd missed lunch again. But something else added to that hollow feeling—Dihn. She couldn't erase him from her brain. Unwanted memories competed for her attention. Something about the old corporal had pierced her hardened armor.

Like so many she knew, he was one of those who never really came home. He survived it all, was lucky enough not to come back in a body bag, and found something to do in the world. But he never really came home. Living alone and still in that stupid fatigue jacket after nearly 50 years. She knew people like Froggie––young men who'd aged beyond their years after spilling their blood in the desert for the red, white, and blue, but, other than her bitter father, she'd had few contacts with guys from Dihn's war. She once picked up Pops from a medical appointment at the VA and remembered all those old men in wheelchairs crowding the hallways. Many sat staring off, all wearing blue ball caps emblazoned with their military units. Man, she grew up around that shit––old marines who never made it back and wouldn't let you forget it.

She needed to make sure she wasn't late picking up her bird. Langston always got grumpy when he had to wait. The jumble in her mind distracted her from her mission. Her razor-sharp focus had been diverted. When you take your eyes off the trail, you miss stuff, and bad shit happens, like not noticing the white Nissan parked across the street as she left Dihn's.

Langston gave her the stink eye when she entered the small waiting room. Dogs and cats in their handsome little pet carriers looked warily at the giant blue bird, who hopped onto the deputy's shoulder.

"Sorry, I'm running late. Anything I should know about Mr Langston?"

"No, all's well. Good check-up. He's a healthy boy, yes you are, such a good boy," the vet said as she gave Langston a gentle scratch on his head.

Back home, the deputy wanted to scrounge up something to eat. Unfortunately, the fridge was mostly barren, scarcely populated with edible items, including an expired carton of milk, a large baggie of veggies marked "Langs," a few cans of Coors, and a container from China Delight––*Hmm, how long had that been there?* Soy sauce and Tabasco might be needed to make it palatable.

Langs laid waste to his carrot, and the Lo Mein was better than expected. Kitts dropped her fork when her phone pinged. Dihn.

TEARS ARE ONLY WATER

"Got something. BIG. Not for electronic transmission. For eyes only. Come ASAP. You know where to find me, Gunny."

She gulped down the last of the noodles, strapped on her service revolver, and hurried to the cruiser. Dihn's message sounded urgent. She reached for the siren and flashers and thought, *Screw you, Jerry.*

She could tell right away that something was wrong. His door was cracked open. A loud hum came from inside the dark room. The glow of monitors, most lying in pieces on the floor, illuminated a path to the back of the room. Everything was in shambles. Books, technical manuals, and papers were strewn everywhere. Sparks shot out from a circuit breaker. Revolver in hand, she crept to the back corner.

Dihn lay face down in a pool of blood, an exit wound in his back. Her eyes darted around the room. Gunnery Sergeant Kitts made sure that the shooter was not still there. Looking back at Dihn, she noticed a trail of smeared blood. He must have been shot then crawled to where he lay. In his right hand, he clutched a shred of paper. She bent down and read "2 Kings" and some scribbled numbers. But at that moment, all the gunnery sergeant could see was Wilson, Peters, Gonlin, and Garcia in Musa Qala...all lying face down, blood seeping from underneath.

Kitts reached for her radio.

"APACHE 11 APACHE 11. Please copy.... Apache 11...this is Foxtrot Six.... I have an Eagle down in sector Alpha, building 15! I say again, Eagle is down! Casualty is urgent surgical. I repeat...casualty needs MEDEVAC."

She reached to find a pulse. Nothing.

"Foxtrot Six. Change casualty to Routine....We lost them."

Chapter 27

Woman in the Window

Tuesday, March 25, 7:30 AM

Their early morning ritual continued the next day. Carmine waited with Julio in the garden while Dr Lukachunai finished her morning prayer to the birds. When she was done, she stood to greet Carmine as Julio receded to his bench at the far end of the garden.

The doctor began by telling him that his sister had come to visit. "She came a long way to see you. In fact, I have an appointment with her on Friday."

Carmine nodded, "Oh, then you'll get to meet my m...m-mother, Maimie, too."

Though initially confused, Hazel quickly caught his meaning. She was beginning to appreciate a hidden quality in this man of few words. Carmine Luedke had a quirky sense of humor. "I assume you mean they are alike, your sister and mother?"

"Yes, but Anne is shorter, and Maimie's dead. Other than that, they're pretty much the same p-person. That's all." After a short pause, his words began to flow. "I mean, they were always at war until my sister finally escaped to boarding school. Anne's mission in life was to be as different from Maimie as possible, but the more she worked at it, the more she became our mother. There was a 16th-century monk named Nicholai K...K-Keloskovich, who was an arithmancer. That's the magic stuff with numbers. Keloskovich's First Law states that the more an object tries to change, the more it stays the same, or the farther you

198

travel away from the original source, the closer you get to it, provided, of course, the pathway is spherical....S-sorry, Doctor, I do that too; just go off on stuff and end up saying too much. The crazy math guy who gets lost in his head." He hit the side of his head. "Yeah, I was saying Anne tried to be different but ended up being pretty much the same. I was the main problem for them, you know. But there *is* a difference. Anne worried about me, but Maimie...she worried mostly about herself. I was her little genius or her carnival f-freak. The best and the w...w-worst, you know. Yep. That pretty much sums up what Maimie was all about. In the end...I think she was mostly ashamed of me....That's all." Carmine lifted a fist toward his head.

The doctor laid her hand on his arm. "Stop. These are sad stories, Carmine, and I see how much her words have gotten inside you, how you judge yourself through her eyes. You told me when we first met that you had no stories. I think you have many. It sounds like your mother saw you as her reflection, as you say, the best and the worst of herself–– all she hated and everything she wished to be true. It sounds like she did not really see *you*, Carmine. So, thank you for sharing stories about your mother and E. I know that was hard." She leaned in to hear his whispery response.

"I always dreamed about this woman looking in my window. C-could never see her face. I was s-stuck in a dream and couldn't move. She kept knocking, trying to f-find me... last week, she finally did. Then, it hit me. It was E all along, looking for me." His voice grew louder. "I-I have to tell her where I am!"

The doctor shook her head and sat back. "Yes, I know you feel worried. But something has been unfinished in all of this, it seems. Something with E was left open and never closed. It is like a weight on your mind, always there weighing you down. This idea that she is coming to find you reminds me of how she searched for you that night long ago but could not find you. Like the face at your window, she is trying to get you to wake up, to see something, but I don't know what or why she is looking for you and haunting your dreams....I accept what you're telling me, Carmine, that you believe she was there in the room with you and how real it all felt. It seems, though, that something is missing from the story. This woman who loved what you could do with numbers, who came looking for you because of your extraordinary skill with numbers, has made me wonder how your passion for numbers came to be. Something or someone must have lit that spark in you. I'm curious about your mentor. You must have had an exceptional teacher, perhaps when you were small. So, I ask myself, who taught Carmine about numbers?"

For the second time in two days, the light in his mind was growing dim as he felt pulled in opposite directions––retreat or stay. For five minutes, he squeezed his eyes shut, balled up his fists, and mechanically repeated the same equation. Finally, he looked up and stuttered, "V-Vati...my father....He was a genius. I found his books in boxes, you know. He taught me to count and do square roots. He recited pi to help me fall asleep. He told me he could see colors in numbers, just like me. Uh, really...that's it."

The doctor gave an encouraging smile. "I think there is more to your story. I've wondered about your father. You shared with me some about Maimie and Anne, but nothing about your father. So, may I ask, what about your father, Carmine?"

The titanic battle waged on inside Carmine's head. He bent forward and rocked, squeezing his eyes shut. The voice inside urged him to ignore her. *If you can't see her, she's not there. You have beautiful and meaningful equations to solve.* He opened his eyes. She was still at his side. He looked away again. Too much. *Stop!* He needed to narrow his focus and desperately begged Euler to find him. He chanted, "$e^{i\pi} + 1 = 0...e^{i\pi} + 1 = 0$." His words grew louder and more urgent "e-i-pi-plus-one-equals-zero, e i pi plus one equals zero."

Lukachunai leaned closer and said softly, "It's ok, Carmine. Stay with me. I see now how your mind has found a clever way to protect you by creating such a special place for E and your father. They live inside your equations. E and pi distract you from thinking about those from the past, but this equation also ensures that E and your father are constantly with you.

His words fell like clumps of sand. "He died....I was playing with a w... w-watch they gave him, but I dropped it. I b-b-broke it." Words,

TEARS ARE ONLY WATER

bumper to bumper, halted, then collided with his tears. "He... was.... M-mad at me...then...then he died."

Dr Lukachunai reared back. "Eeeeee. He *died?*.... *How* Carmine?"

"I-I, you know, ran away...hid. Maimie looked...but I hid in the shed."

"Like you hid when E came looking for you and––"

"I c-could see her. Eyes looking in. She was looking for me through the win...win...w-wind––"

And with that, his words stopped as the boy in the shed closed his eyes, dropped his head, and drifted away.

Chapter 28

2 Kings 14

Tuesday, March 25, 10:30 AM

Shit. Another day had been lost between the cracks. With each hangover, each wave of nausea, and each beat of the snare drum in her head, Anne promised herself she was done. Done with drinking––*or maybe just cut back a little*––done with worrying about her brother––*when did he ever worry about me?* ––done with missing Noa––*who?*–– and done with haunting dreams from her deepest compartments––*why are they doing this to me?*

Thoughts swirled like the ceiling above as she tried to focus and summon the will to get out of bed and wash away the self-loathing. Last night, she'd gotten another couple of liters of Barefoot Pinot to keep her company. *Oh my God, how pathetic was that?* There was so much to sift through and file, but it was harder to silence all this noise in her mind. She wanted to retch it all from her system. In moments like this, she didn't know which she hated more: her life or herself.

A hot shower and a black coffee helped cleanse the morning residue of regret and disgust. With everything temporarily stowed neatly back into compartments, the professor could focus on the realities in Pueblo, Colorado. *Just breathe, Anne.* Her rage at not being able to see her brother for a week had been waylaid by news about the DMT found in his blood. Together with Kitts, they would root out the lies and corruption that had put her brother in this situation.

The thought of Deputy Kitts brought more annoyance. *What the hell was wrong with this woman?* Anne was left here rotting away, and Kitts

TEARS ARE ONLY WATER

hadn't thought to pick up her damn phone to call or text. *Goddamn Kitts. Goddamn Noa. What is wrong with you people? And what the hell has she found out about the lab tech who went missing? What did Dihn tell her yesterday? Did she even talk to him? Fuck you people.* Anne pulled out her phone and called the damn deputy.

Four rings, and the message cut in.

"Not in. You know what to do...."

Then, "Braaak."

A third call went straight to Kitts' voicemail.

Anne barked into the phone. "Hey, Inspector Clouseau. Pick up already, for Chrissake! Give me a call, Nicola, before the mind rot sets in. You promised an update about what you've found out. So, please, give me a damn call. WOULD YOU PLEASE!"

She dug through the scribbled notes in her purse and found the number for the sheriff's department. Maybe Kitts was there. If not, they could get her a message, and perhaps she would call. The switchboard placed her on hold.

"Yeah, Miss Shivalun––uh, sorry, Professor Shivalun––this is Sheriff Burwinkle. Was just gonna give you a call 'bout yer brother's situation. We've had some developments you could say––"

She cut him off. "Yes, I've heard, Sheriff. DMT in his blood and the technician who's gone missing. Deputy Kitts told me all that, but I haven't been able to reach her."

"Uh, 'bout Depety Kitts and that fella Dihn.... There was a major incident yesterday afternoon. She was tryin' to track down this woman at the hospital who'd removed those lab results from yer brother's record but couldn't find nothin' much, 'cept she'd disappeared from her house. So then––now I gotta tell ya...better be sittin' down fer this––Depety Kitts went to meet with this Dihn character of yers and found he'd been shot dead at his home."

203

Anne saw stars. The room went gray before coming back into focus. All she could picture was the old man's head tremor. She stumbled over her words. "Dihn...*shot*? And Kitts? Is she.... I need to talk with her, but I can't reach her."

"Well, here's the thing.... First, this is official police business. The case is a homicide, and that's where Denver PD steps in. So, this ain't our case no more. I gave the detective in charge yer name and number, so he'll probly be givin' ya a call. As for Depety Kitts, we had to take her off the case. She was shook up pretty bad. Had to send her to the hospital to get checked out."

"Whaat?! Why?" Her hands were shaking and beginning to feel numb.... *Just breathe, Goddammit.*

"Can't really say much. But 'tween you and me and that picture on the wall, she, uh...got a little confused when she come up on the scene. Radioed in some call signals that...well, let's jes say they ain't what we use around here. In all the commotion, she musta lost track of where she was...like maybe had one of those flashbacks or somethin' to Afghanistan. Lots of folks do ya know. They come back and find a crime scene like that, and boom, they're back there. Happened to Kitts yesterday. Now with Denver PD takin' charge, best thing fer Depety Kitts to do is rest and git away from all this fer awhile. Far as you and that poor brother of yers, ya can work with the detective assigned to the case now that it's in their hands. Pretty clear we got us a serious crime that yer brother got caught up in. Seems he might of got himself drugged too, but they'll be lookin' into all that. So--"

"Wait! That's it? You're going to just expect me to sit on my hands in fucking Pueblo and, what...wait for some fucking detective to decide to call me? To put it in terms that maybe you'll understand, Sheriff, 'That ain't gonna fly.'"

"Ya got a right to be spewin' hellfire at me. I git it. Was a time I felt that way 'bout this brother I had who got in all sorts of trouble cuz of, well, some problems he had. Point is, people treated him pretty bad, and I was angry all the time. So, believe you me, I feel fer what yer goin' through; honestly, I do."

TEARS ARE ONLY WATER

Anne had readied herself for a counterattack and was not expecting this from him. Not immune to words of empathy––even if spoken ungrammatically––she drew in a breath and simply said, "Sorry. And thank you. It's just that I can't sit by and do nothing. If I can talk with Deputy Kitts and find out what she knows, I'd be doing something. Can you understand that?"

"Yep, yep, I do. I truly do, but ya see, she ain't in much shape to talk with anyone. When we got that radio call, we knew somethin' was off. Dispatch sent a cruiser, and my depeties found her curled up on the floor next to the body of Mr Dihn. Pretty unresponsive. Not how we expect to see Depety Kitts. Got her a spine of steel, that one. So, yer a doctor, right? Ya can see she's probly best left to herself now. The hospital released her and said she needed rest and maybe some help at the VA. But tell ya what, I can git her a message fer her to call ya, providin' that works fer her. Otherwise, you just gotta set by. I've already said more than I should have. I know the waitin' is hard, but I'll make sure the Denver PD's got yer number. Sorry, wish there was more I can do."

Anne had never worn helplessness and uncertainty well. That suit never fit. Trusting authority, remaining level-headed in times of stress, and letting go of what she couldn't change were not in her nature. Despite her denial and self-deception, she feared the impostor within. *My ugly little secret*, she told herself in the dark and sleepless nights that had come to define her existence. Noa knew what she had always tried to hide and deny. From the beginning, she saw how Anne played a role–– the important professor was a pretender, starved for attention and validation, lying to the world, but especially to herself. Noa had known the truth but stayed until it became too much. She left when she couldn't stand it any longer.

Anne played a role when she lectured her students. "Take heed, young minds. When confronted with the illusion of stress, don't become sucked into the void by taking mindless action. Remember, it's our neocortex that separates us from lower animals. So, don't just do something. Sit there, breathe it out, secure it in a mental compartment, and let it go." Despite all she preached to others, the reverse had always been true for Angelina Regina Schivalone. When the glaring lights of emotion were switched on, she was like her mother, who'd say, "For God's sake, Angelina, don't just sit there, do something!"

The professor threw on some clothes and found her keys. Time to move. She pulled up the address on her phone––445 Happy Canyon Road.

Her mind was blank as she sped towards Denver. The radio blared to distract her from her thoughts. She hadn't formulated a plan for how she'd approach Kitts––whether or not to tell her that she knew what happened yesterday and that the sheriff had placed her on medical leave. She stood on the front porch and wondered whether Kitts would refuse to answer the door. Her thoughts turned to the menacing-looking gun and giant parakeet. What if the deputy was unresponsive or, worse, unstable?

Thoughtful decision-making would have helped Anne figure all this out, but at this moment, she could only knock. She heard faint sounds of the blues playing inside but no footsteps coming to the door. She rooted herself to the porch for ten minutes, maybe more, frozen in place as she waited. Without Kitts, she'd be lost. Her knocks grew louder as the numbness spread through her legs. Feeling defeated, she was about to leave when the door opened.

"I guess you can't take a hint. Never learned that one, huh? When people don't answer your calls or call you back, it's cuz they don't wanna talk to you. But you don't get it, do you? You just can't act like a normal person and let it be. So, did Burwinkle tell you to come or to leave me the hell alone?"

Anne's typically well-oiled words weren't there. Another secret that few, besides Noa and her mother, had ever known was that the sharp-tongued professor could suddenly stumble over her speech. She looked down at her shoes and couldn't feel her legs. "H-he told me. T-told me all of it. I-I'm so sorry for––"

"What you got to be sorry for? It's done! Don't you get it? Someone's killing people now. This thing's a whole lot bigger than you even know.

TEARS ARE ONLY WATER

They killed that old man, and they won't stop at killin' just him. Shit, you're probably next for all I know or care. What do you say about that, hmm? You should go the hell back to Pueblo and then pack your sorry ass up and go home. It's over. Can't you see? DPD's got it now. Christ, just go home, Anne."

"I-I can't leave. I'm not really sure I have any p-place to go, but––"

"Well, shit. So you decided to come over here. Shiit. Some White people got no sense.... Well, you're here now. Might as well come in."

She stepped in, stiff-legged with numbness spreading up her calves. Langston lifted his head from his bowl with a giant Brazil nut in his beak. He cracked it and glared at the woman he only knew as an intruder into his domain. "BRAAK!"

"Chill, Langs. Yeah, I know, it's her again, but be cool."

"Listen, I-I'm sorry to come here again, but you wouldn't pick up. I left messages, and the sheriff told me what happened, and I-I-I just had to talk to you, see you."

"You doing that now? Sounding like your brother with that stutter stepping. Yeah, well, since you don't take a hint, let me help you. When someone doesn't call you back, there's probably a reason."

The deputy's words knifed deeply. Anne thought of Noa not answering her phone and her final voicemail. Kitts couldn't have known what she'd said, but her words cut to the core. The wound was raw. Anne cleared her throat, "Um, can we sit and talk, please? I-I won't stay long."

Rolling her eyes, Kitts motioned to the couch. "Okay, but I got the timer running. Shit, now I guess I gotta offer you something. I think I can find some toilet water."

A half-empty liter of Jameson was on the coffee table. "Uh, maybe something a little stronger?"

The deputy looked at the bird and shook her head. "Damned, girl, you better get your ass over to AA after all this shit is over. Yeah, now that you've snooped my Irish whisky, okay, but just a quick drink. Say your piece and then get your ass—"

"Okay, yes. I've never had that before, but I-I'll try some. Thanks."

They sat silently, sipping whisky, not looking in the other's direction. The only one looking at anyone was Langston.

Eventually, Anne dared to speak. "Listen, um...about uh Dihn. Oh my God, poor Dihn. You'd just seen him, right? I mean, you were going to see him. That's what you told me on Saturday. And checking on the woman from the hospital to see if you—"

"Yeah, let's just cut to the chase, Sis. The woman's gone. Something must've spooked her cuz she got the hell out of Dodge in a hurry. Maybe she's been killed and dumped somewhere by the same guy who offed Dihn. And yeah, Dihn, he texted that he'd found something and for me to come over to check it out. Probably had to do with one of the companies your brother was checking into. Said it was for my eyes only. Didn't want to text it to me. Some top secret bullshit."

The silence that followed was thick and painful. Kitts stared off, downed her glass, and poured another. Anne looked at the back of the deputy's clenched fist. "Listen.... Burwinkle told me what happened, I-I mean with the radio call you made. That—"

Nicola dropped her head. Anne sensed a moment of shame, which quickly flashed to anger when the deputy turned back to her.

Kitts stiffened. "What the hell you trying to do here, Sister?! I don't need that. You trying to shrink-rap me? That why you came over here? Check on the ex-grunt who lost it? Well, I don't need that s-h-i-t. You got that? That shit, I mean all that shit, belongs over there. In the past, done, isn't that what you tell people? Just put it away. Don't forget, I read those shitty little books that you and your mother wrote."

Anne cleared her throat. "Well...I just think that maybe—"

"Look, it don't mean nothin'! You understand that? It happened, and it's done. Everyone loses their shit. Tell me, nothing like that ever happened in your perfect, little White princess, Ivy League-ass universe?

So, if you came here to get all sad-eyed about what happened, playing the doctor in my home, you can just walk the fuck out the door! Better yet, Langston, attack her sorry scrawny ass on my command. One word from me, and he shreds your jugular like a play toy. And he'll do it too. You know, once they get the taste of blood.... Shit, I'll just bury your sorry ass in the garden, you know, cheap fertilizer for my pansies."

Kitts stared with the look of a stone-cold killer. The bird inched closer. Anne put down her glass and shifted uncomfortably. They held each other's gaze. Then, without warning, the deputy burst out with laughter.

Langston looked up. "Braaak?"

"Oh, I got you good. Hahaha! Should've seen your fuckin' face all pruned up like that." Kitts wheezed as she doubled over in laughter.

Anne cracked a smile then laughed until the tears ran down. The release felt good.

"Really, my bird doesn't know how to hurt people. I do, but not him. Still haven't decided if I'm gonna shoot you. I'll just dump your body. Hell, they'll pin it on the guy that shot Dihn." She topped up their glasses. "Now, what does your stupid book say? Just find a compartment, right?" Kitts turned serious. "Listen, we gotta talk about some stuff. Yeah, DPD's got the case now, and Burwinkle's got me on a medical leave thing, but he don't know shit about what's goin' on. See, your man Corporal Dihn left us a little surprise on a piece of paper that they don't know jack about."

Dizzied by the abrupt change in the deputy's mood and the effect of the whiskey, Anne struggled to keep up. "What about Dihn? He was a Corporal?"

"Story for another day, Sis. Try to keep up. See, a bullet hole wasn't the only thing I found on him." Kitts explained that she'd found in his hand a bloody scrap of paper with scribbles, which she pocketed before she passed out. "We just gotta figure out what's on it."

Anne scrunched her face. "What's to figure out? Why didn't he write it out? Doesn't make sense."

"You're not listening. He left us a fucking note. *Damn* girl. Way I see it, Dihn was some kinda ex-spook. You know, the type who loves secrets and all that shit. Those cats always leavin' codes and clues and whatnot. You know, things not being what they're supposed to be. I don't know, Sis. I can't get into the dude's head. The point is, he was dyin'. Maybe the shooter was still in his house, and Dihn figured this was the best way to tell us what he'd found. "

Anne sat up. "What is on it? Will you show me? Maybe I'll——"

Kitts pulled the shred out of her pocket. Blood stains dotted the back. "He left a message for me. See, he knew I was on my way over. So, the shooter comes in, pops him, takes him for dead, and leaves. Except Dihn must have crawled to find paper and then scribbled something about a king."

"How come you didn't give it to Burlinkle? I mean——"

"Don't trust him. Not with this. I mean, he's okay, but Miss loud-ass Mama Lu has her spies around, so I figured I'd check it out. Just need to decode the damn thing. Know any professors who can help?"

Anne leaned in and squinted. "It looks like maybe an address. See.... It says...2 King something. Is there a King Street around here? We should check the phone book."

Kitts grabbed the note. "Phone book? What century did you come out of? No, don't think it's an address cuz he tried to write somethin' after King, but the blood marks have messed it up."

Anne snatched it and held it close to her face. "2 Kings with maybe some numbers. Like 2 Kings, something...something. Is that your fingerprint in the blood?"

Stealing it back, Kitts said, "Yup, it was still wet when I pulled it out of his hand. And it ain't no address, least no place round here." She paused and then looked up. "Ya know, my Auntie Rhea was a good Christian

TEARS ARE ONLY WATER

woman, unlike her niece. She'd be turning over in her grave to hear me ask this, but isn't there a Bible book 'bout Kings?"

Anne Schivalone, avowed atheist and secular iconoclast, shrugged and reached for the Jameson, draining it into her glass. "You got one? I mean, a Bible?" She held up the empty bottle. "Another bottle would help us too, but if you have a Bible, you better hold it because I think it will surely catch fire and burn your house down if it comes anywhere near me."

The deputy smiled. "Yeah, I can believe that about you. I got my aunt's old one." She disappeared and came back with a shabby looking Bible. Leafing through it, she said, "Let's just see.... Yup. Book of Kings. Better than tryin' to track down an address on a nonexistent King's Street in Timbuktu. You're really not as smart as you look."

Anne seized the paper and held it close to the lamp. "Wait. Looks like... maybe 2 Kings.... Then a 17 or could be 14 and...."

Kitts thumbed through the Book of Kings, scanning chapter by chapter. "For you heathens, the first number is the chapter and the next a verse, so let's see what ol' 2 Kings has to tell us. Let's try 14 first."

As Anne shut her eyes, she heard Kitts' voice. "Wait...what's this? Says here in 14:25 somethin 'bout Jonah."

Anne opened her eyes, and they stared at each other. "My mother taught all her children to be good atheists, but isn't there a Bible story about Jonah?"

Kitts' fingers raced through the pages of her aunt's old Bible. "Dear Auntie Rhea never imagined that her wayward niece would finally turn to the Lord's word, not for solace but to hunt for clues left by a dead, White, ex-marine named Dihn."

Kitts read down the page. "Yep, here it is. The Story of Jonah." She froze. "Holy shit. Sorry, Auntie. Right here. Jonah 1:17 says, 'Now the Lord had prepared a great fish to swallow up Jonah. And Jonah was in the belly of the fish for three days and three nights.'.... Wait. Dihn was getting the names of

J. HERMAN KLEIGER

Carmine's accounts and looking into anything funny with Pelcovey and Jonas, right? So, what's with Bible Jonah and the whale thing? Unless one of your brother's companies has something to do with a fish."

Anne shot to her feet. She reached for her purse and took out a piece of paper. "Here's the list Dihn sent." Tracing her finger down the page, she said, "Look, there's a fishing company called Tawney-Banks."

"But Jonah? Wait a minute. Not too subtle, Dihn," said the deputy.

"Yeah. I think he was trying to tell us something about the one and only Roger Jonas, the quack who couldn't wait to ship Carmie off to the state hospital. You talked to him, right?"

"Yup, Jonas sure is one pompous ass. Quite unconscionable if you ask me. This whole damned thing smells like rotten fish, and ol' Jonas might be in the belly of the goddamn beast."

Chapter 29

The Magic of Pi

Thursday, March 27, 11:15 AM

Powdery snow covered the ground. Early Spring in Colorado could not be trusted to be any more than Winter's fickle child. Though she welcomed all seasons, Hazel missed her morning sessions in the garden. Her aging bones ached when she spent too much time in the cold. Warmed by a cup of tea, she looked through her appointment book. She had to see Carmine later than usual because of a last-minute staff meeting.

The meeting topic, a status report on the elimination of Traditional healing practices, was no surprise––an unwelcome reminder of the recent losses and changes at CMHI-P. Hazel's heart was heavy each time she thought about Dr Orin. He had a deep respect for nature and for all people. His vision of healing––broad and compassionate ––stood in marked contrast to the views of those in power now. Baron Buffo, with his blatant contempt, clouded her mind. She struggled to find compassion. *It is true; there is good in all people. Even young Baron was once a helpless babe who must have had someone who cared for him, but more likely, this vile man had been a child who got little love and attention from his family.*

Some of her colleagues viewed Hazel as an enlightened being, unencumbered by base human instincts. This was not the case. She tried to hide her wry smile whenever she heard him referred to as Beelzebuffo. Nurse Olive Astracides had aligned herself with Buffo and had been making notes on Hazel, waiting for the opportunity to file a formal complaint to get her fired. Because of this, the doctor had decided, with great sadness, to suspend all use of Native healing rituals. Instead, she felt forced to limit her therapeutic work to more conventional methods that she learned long ago when she was H. T. Lukas––Tallulah.

Her first supervisor at the Jungian Institute, Erich Neumann, taught her the limits of talk therapy with patients like Carmine Luedke, whose trauma was layered and almost inaccessible with words. At the institute, Tallulah had been struggling to reach one of her patients, a traumatized young woman who'd retreated from the world. Neumann suggested she walk with the patient in the clinic gardens instead of sitting in an office cluttered with books and papers.

"Ach, Tallulah," her supervisor said. "With some patients, we need to find the universal content to help unravel stories behind their symptoms. Remember, Herr Jung taught that mythology and ritual are pillars for such contents. To heal her soul, I think your young lady needs to have this kind of experience with you and not just hear your explanations."

Carmine retreated after he had opened up in their Tuesday session. Since then, he refused to speak to anyone. Each time Hazel looked in on him, he was on his bed with his back towards the door. Julio said he'd gone into a shell. The nursing staff said he had stopped eating and refused to leave his room. This man who had begun speaking up and peering out at the world had, once again, sought refuge in a sleepy shadowland. Hazel viewed it as a desperate clinging to what he felt had kept him safe throughout his life. Safety for him meant unplugging his consciousness and placing himself in a self-induced coma, surrounded by numbers and symbols. Now when they met, Carmine remained silent. The weather had turned colder, and their warm connection had chilled. She tried to see him in the evenings, but he'd fall asleep as soon as she began to speak.

Hazel sensed his commitment status would end soon. Oakley had changed Carmine's diagnosis to reflect the role that DMT had played in his symptoms, making the case for a shortened length of stay. Knowing the pressures to return patients to their communities, she felt the urgency to act. Previously, she would have been free to initiate a healing ceremony for retreating patients like Carmine, especially when time was a limiting factor. But the new administration eliminated this option. Sessions in the garden and therapeutic walks were acceptable, but nothing more. A Traditional prayer ceremony was out of the question.

Sitting with Carmine in her office was yielding little. The warm room was stuffy and had a soporific effect. Perhaps if they had more time, she could eventually reconnect with words to forestall his retreat, but she didn't have that luxury. She needed to get him outside to move. Cold fresh air was what he needed. Yes, time for a medicine walk to wake up his senses.

There was a soft tap at her door.

"Ah, come in, Carmine."

He looked tired and wan. She motioned for him to sit and asked if he had slept and dreamed. He shrugged and looked away.

She offered tea.

He shook his head.

"You know, Carmine, you began sharing your stories a few days ago.... That was a brave beginning, and I'm honored by your trust. But often, when people begin to tell the stories they have kept hidden for so long, they become scared and get stuck. I do understand that none of this is easy. It is too cold to sit in the garden, but let us walk together through the snow."

They went down to the garden, white and pristine. The air was more arctic than brisk, and her hip had stabbing pain. They walked in silence, she with her limp and Carmine with his drooped head. Lukachunai's voice broke the silence and hung in the frigid air. "My ancestors took Medicine Walks to seek signs and omens. Nature always speaks to us about ourselves and our place in the world. Can you hear the sounds of snow, Carmine?"

He tried to be aware of his senses––the feel of snowflakes on his face, the scent of the pines, and the sounds of birds high overhead.

"See if you can pay attention to the images that each of your senses brings back to you."

They trudged through the snow for thirty minutes, mostly in silence. Finally, she led Carmine back to the garden. She'd brought a blanket and brushed the snow off their bench.

They sat for a minute in silence. She hoped their walk had awakened Carmine's senses and helped clear his mind. Measuring her words, she began. "I think that what you told me was so important, and I do understand that when a man lives in darkness, the flare of a match can be blinding.... You've been through so much...too much Carmine, and have taken refuge in the comfort and protection of numbers. Your father left you, and your mother could not find you. Then, your sister went away, and after that, E. There was no one to help you walk through all that you lost, all the hurts. You lost a father, your precious Vati, someone to teach you what it means to be a man. You lost the connection to his people and culture. Then you lost your special friend-ship with Elizabeth, your dear E."

To her surprise, he nodded. A reassuring sign that he was with her and an invitation for her to continue. "You have blamed yourself for all these losses, and you sought refuge in numbers––a creative connection to the father you lost and to E.... But numbers also helped you try to forget, Carmine."

He spoke. His voice, low and hard to hear, suddenly pierced the cold air. "Vati taught me about p...p-i, the number, you know. He said it had magic in it.... So, after he died, I thought if I could memorize 100 digits, maybe he'd come back.... So, I c-closed my eyes and said as many numbers as I could. Then, I waited for the magic, opened my eyes, and looked for him. That's all.... I just looked."

TEARS ARE ONLY WATER

An opening indeed. The doctor had touched the slumbering man inside. "Oh, Carmine, I think you're still holding onto this magic, hoping. Can you tell me more?"

But it was too late. Carmine's head bobbed under the weight of slumber.

Back in her office at the end of the day, she sat down to have tea with Lia Dhikavi.

Lia pursed her lips. "They made it pretty clear again this morning about Native healing. They're watching you, Hazel. The Big Toad's out to get you. Everyone knows that. I'd tell you to keep a low profile, but what does a girl from the streets of Masouleh know."

Hazel smiled. "You know, Lia, I spoke with Jung once before he died. Did you know that? He was very old and seemed fascinated that a little Diné girl would travel all the way to Zürich to study in his institute. He was still puffing that pipe of his. He told me, 'Fidelity to the law of your own being is an act of high courage.' I have held onto that, Lia. The law of my being is my work here, regardless of where that path may lead."

"Wait, I know you.... You have something in mind, don't you, Haz? You're cooking up something."

"Is not the work we do cookery? Aren't we chefs of the mind and soul, Lia? Carmine has retreated into somnolence as a refuge. His trauma is thick and old. He not only retreats to the impersonal world of numbers and abstract symbols to hide from his grief, but he also falls asleep--the ultimate suspension of the mind. My presence and my words only scratch the surface. The layers of his trauma are so deeply entrenched that I fear I cannot reach him. With each step forward, his mind becomes as frozen as the winter ground. I fear he will not be here much longer. I must walk a path of courage to reach him.... I'm going to talk to Julio about arranging a five-night healing ceremony."

Chapter 30

A Long Blue Feather

Thursday, March 27, 12:10 PM

Nicola didn't get up until 10:00. She put on her uniform, brewed coffee, then drove to the station around noon. If Burwinkle objected, she'd tell him she needed to finish her report on Dihn. Depending on how she read his mood, the deputy might lay out her evidence implicating Tawney-Banks in Dihn's death. She hoped to sweet talk him into temporarily assigning her to DPD Homicide to work the case.

The office was quiet. Most deputies were out on calls. Kitts saw the secretary.

"Hey there, Marlene. Sheriff in?"

"Hi hon. How you feeling? I thought you'd be out for a while. Yeah, the sheriff is in shuffling papers on his desk. Should I tell him you're here?"

"No, thanks. I'm doing fine. Just here to finish up some paperwork, then I'll pop in to say hi."

After the incident at Dihn's, the sheriff had wanted her to take extended leave, but two days were enough for Kitts. She was released from the Emergency Room on Monday evening and planned to rest on Tuesday but then got that call from Schivalone. What began as an annoying intrusion became a shot of adrenalin as the two sleuths made the link between Jonas and Tawney-Banks. She just had to find the connection to Dihn's killing.

With the case being transferred to DPD Homicide, Nicola knew that Burwinkle was done with all matters concerning the bookkeeper and Shrenklin's. But she wasn't. Dihn had left them something as he bled out. Though campy and over the top, his clue about Jonas and Tawney-Banks would be hard for even the sheriff to ignore.

On Wednesday morning, the deputy had contacted Det. Jodie Griggs, an old buddy from the academy. Kitts considered her a loyal and resourceful friend. She told Griggs about trying to get a temporary assignment so she could investigate the connection with Tawney-Banks. Jodie said they had recovered information from Dihn's hard drive about Tawney-Banks and offered to send a copy.

Nursing a hangover, Nicola spent the rest of Wednesday searching Dihn's files on Tawney-Banks Commercial Fish Company. With offices worldwide, T-B CFC was headquartered in Aurora, CO. It even had a whale as a logo. Bingo. There was a CEO in Delaware, but the CFO, Misha Horwath, was in charge of daily operations. Kitts Googled Horvath and identified her as the woman in the red dress. Another connection to Jonas.

The deputy burrowed into the files on Dihn's hard drive until her eyes became blurry. T-B CFC listed a Board of Directors with pictures and bios. As expected, Roger Jonas, MD, was listed as a member. His photo showed the trademark smugness, that curled-up-lip-stench-sniffing look she'd encountered during her visit to his office. There were other doctors, including Baron Buffo, heir to the pharmaceutical company. But the surprises didn't end there. She found the name and headshot of a grinning LuCinda P. Pelcovey among a handful of other community figures on T-B's Board. Kitts imagined the acrid scent of her perfume vaping off the page. The deputy also recognized Julius Rainsford, the local judge who had signed the bookkeeper's commitment papers. The last name on the list was strange--someone named BOB--just three letters with no last name, picture, or bio. The address was a PO box.

J. HERMAN KLEIGER

She was exhausted and bleary-eyed after reading through Dihn's voluminous files. She lay on her bed, hoping to get a few hours of sleep. Her nightmares had been intense since she had found Dihn, face down in his blood. Like her father, she had always managed to bury unwanted thoughts about their wars with a double shot of bourbon, chased down with a "Here's to cheatin', stealin', fightin', and drinkin', Oorah!" But everything changed on Monday. Dihn's death had flipped a switch. Musa Qala was reeling through her brain. Her compartments were leaking.

Back at her desk, the deputy typed her report on the Dihn homicide and placed it in a file folder. She liked it when the office was quiet. None of the annoying banter from the boys. Kitts pulled out another piece of paper and typed notes she would show Burwinkle. The evidence will scream from the page as he reads her notes.

- Something was not right about a company the bookkeeper was working on
- The company was Tawney-Banks Commercial Fishing
- Someone drugged Luedke that night
- The hospital found DMT in his lab work, which disappeared from his record
- The bookkeeper gets suspiciously shipped off to Pueblo at record speed
- Judge Rainsford, a Board member of T-B CFC, signs the commitment papers
- The tech who discovered the DMT is missing
- Dihn gets killed while looking into Shrenklin's accounts
- Dihn leaves a coded message linking Dr Jonas to Tawney-Banks
- A list of Board members includes Jonas, Pelcovey, and Judge Rainsford
- Track down identity of BOB?

TEARS ARE ONLY WATER

Kitts shut the folder when she heard a commotion behind her.

"Shit, well, I'll be. Hey, Jerry, take a look see at who's here."

Jerry walked up behind Boggs. "Hell, Gunnery Sergeant Cold Kitts is back on duty to serve and protect. Hey there, partner. You feeling okay? Glad you're seated because we wouldn't want you to lose your balance or nothing. Guess you'll be taking some refresher training on our call signals."

Ignore them. Auntie Rhea's words echoed in her mind. But Kitts never could. Bullies had to be confronted. She shot to her feet and glared at Jerry.

He stared back...then blinked. "Come on, Boggs. She ain't worth breaking a sweat over."

Kitts held her stare. "Fuck off, Jerry, and take little Boggs with you before he wets himself."

The two walked over to their desks and continued to mutter nonsense. Kitts sat and placed her notes in the folder under her incident report on Dihn. She went to the restroom, splashed water on her face, and got a cup of coffee before picking up the folder. Burwinkle's office was down a narrow hallway. She saw him at his desk, looking out the window. Knocking softly, she opened his door and peeked her head in.

"Hey, Sheriff. Got a minute?"

"Damn, Cole. What in tarnation are you doin' here? Thought I told you to stay away from this place fer a while. What is it about an order that you can't seem to get into that thick skull of yers?"

The deputy explained how she'd spent the last two days resting up–not true–and felt fully recovered–also not true. She had to finish the report on the Dihn killing and didn't want to put that off any longer.

"I know, Sheriff, you're looking out after your deputies and want us all in good shape. I'm fine, really. Here's the report, along with some notes I've made about the whole thing with the bookkeeper, Shrenklin's, and the thing with Dihn. I wanted to talk about getting a temp assignment

221

to DPD to assist in their investigation. As you can see, I've done a lot of digging already. Figure it'd be good for our department to have some fingerprints on this case as it moves forward."

She handed Burwinkle the folder.

He hesitated and shook his head. "Cole, I thought I told you--"

"I know. You did. But please, Sheriff, look at my notes."

He opened the folder....His eyes widened as he looked up from the empty folder, which he tossed on the desk. "What the hell is this? Cole, now I know you've lost yer shit. Ya need to get the hell out of here and get some help. Startin' today, yer on official medical leave. I'll decide when, or, better yet, if ya can come back here at all. Shit, Nicola."

Kitts was stunned. "But...." She had no explanation. No more words. She turned and walked out of his office and back to her desk. Her thoughts were jumbled but then sharpened. Jerry and Boggs must have taken her papers out of her folder when she was in the restroom. Quickening her pace, she passed her desk but came to a full stop. Something sitting in the middle of her desk drew her attention. Out of place, yet familiar. Something she'd seen every day but never here. A long blue feather....*Langston!*

She ran past Jerry and Boggs' empty desks and past Marlene, who looked up and said something Nicola didn't hear. She ran to her car and slammed it into gear. Tires screeched as she sped away. Panic rose as her heart pounded in her throat. *Someone's got Langston!*

She parked and sprinted toward her house, leaving the car door open. Her front door was ajar. On high alert, the deputy pulled out her pistol and inched her way through the living room. Walking point. On patrol for the second time in a week. Her possessions were strewn across the floor. Slashed paintings hung on the walls. Her medal case smashed. She looked up to see an empty perch and cage. Her bird was gone! Someone had taken him or...worse. She heard a scratching sound, faint at first, grow louder as she approached the hallway closet. She pointed her pistol and slowly opened the door. "Langston, oh my God."

TEARS ARE ONLY WATER

"It's okay, boy." He was freaked out but calmed by the sound of her voice and the familiarity of her touch. She lifted him, cradled him in her arms, and noticed his tail feathers had been clipped. Nicola continued speaking in soft tones and carried him into the garden. She sat on the bench and petted him. "Shhh. S'okay boy. S'okay."

Sitting with her back to the garden, she hadn't noticed that someone had chopped down her dogwood tree.

Chapter 31

Bob

Thursday, March 27, 8:30 PM

Kitts was shaken. She didn't report the break-in. Who could she trust? She left a message for Jodie Griggs. "Hey, something's come up. Call when you can." She had promised Schivalone an update but found talking to her exhausting. She thought about calling Burwinkle. He was thinking she was crazy, but the ransacking of her home and terrorizing of her beloved bird proved she wasn't. She dialed his number and left a message.

Around 9:00 PM, Langston alerted her that someone was at the door. Her first thought was it had to be Schivalone again. *Damned liquor-mooching professor. Totally her MO to come skulking around at the witching hour, except she's supposed to be back in Pueblo.* Kitts got her Glock and opened the door. A tall man stood before her, looking down at the ground.

"Hey, excuse me, um, Deputy Kitts?" He eyed the menacing-looking blue bird on her shoulder and the pistol in her hand. Cautiously reaching for his ID, he said. "Sorry, I know it's late to just show up like this. I'm Lt Micky Aarveen, special agent with the CBI. Got a tip from a detective, who said she knows you. Something to do with a company called Tawney-Banks Commercial Fishing. You know of them, right? Detective Griggs remembered I'd been looking into them for a while, so she phoned me. I left a message for your sheriff that I'd be contacting you about this. Wanted to follow protocol, you know."

224

TEARS ARE ONLY WATER

Kitts studied his ID while Langston reached out for it with his beak. "Stop! Damned bird gotta poke his nose into everybody's business." The picture looked like the man standing before her, and she had enough familiarity with Colorado Bureau IDs to know this was legit. "Yeah, that's right. Jodie G. and me go way back. Come on in."

Aarveen's eyes darted around the ransacked room before honing in on the smashed medal case with an eagle, globe, and anchor insignia. "You Corps?"

"Yeah, got out a while back, you?"

"Nope, I did my time in the Navy. Then NIS."

"Yeah, well, figured you for a squid."

Aarveen smiled. "Yep, that's me. Hey, this Tawney-Banks operation is a big deal. I've been on a task force looking into them for close to a year for possible RICO violations. How much do you know about them?"

Kitts nodded. "Only that they have some local dirtbags on their Board and that some of them might be mixed up in a murder and maybe some other shit."

"No surprise there. T-B is basically a shell company for a criminal operation. They got their hands in a whole lot of bad stuff––drug distribution, bribery, trafficking, maybe some gun running, and definitely money laundering. You ever see Godfather? Well, T-B is to fishing what the Corleone family was to importing olive oil. So, murder pretty much fits the bill. Wouldn't be the first. How'd you get roped into this in the first place?"

"Okay, well, might as well take a seat, Lieutenant, and I'll run through what I know. It's been a fucked up week. As you can see, I had a break-in today. I'm not normally this messy. Think it's all connected to this shit with the fish company."

She was telling him about being called to an assault on an office manager by a bookkeeper when Langston squawked again. Another knock at the door. "Guess the party's at my house tonight."

She opened the door. "Sheriff! My God...what are you doing here? I'm goin' over the Tawney-Banks shit with this special agent from the Colorado Bureau. Come on in."

Burwinkle appeared frazzled and out of breath. He rubbed his chest and put on his folksy face. "Yep, yep, I figgered he might be comin' by. Wanted to check in on you too, Cole. Got yer message. What the hell happened here?"

"Had a break-in earlier. I think it's all connected to what I've been looking into."

Burwinkle gave a sympathetic look and put his hand on her shoulder. "As long as yer okay, Cole." He nodded at Aarveen, who'd stood up when the sheriff entered the room. The sheriff held out his hand. "Pleased to make yer acquaintance, Agent, uh––"

"Aarveen. I left you a message earlier that I'd need to speak with your deputy. She was just going over what she knew about Tawney-Banks. I told her we'd been tracking them since last summer. They're into a ton of crap. Got their fingerprints all over the place."

"Yep, yep. Figgered that might be the case. What all ya got on them?"

Kitts jumped in. "Like I was trying to tell you today, I've got a list of folks on their Board who might have been involved with the case against that bookkeeper last week, and, who knows, maybe Dihn's murder."

Burwinkle looked down and shook his head. A second later, he drew his Smith & Wesson M&P and shot Aarveen between the eyes.

Langston flew from his perch and crashed into the wall. Kitts stood motionless. Smoke trailed from the barrel of the gun.

"Goddammit, Cole! Damn you! Look what ya had to get mixed up in." He raised his revolver and pointed it toward her while reflexively rubbing his chest. "I let ya run with this. Figgered ya'd get tired of it all and move on. But ya just couldn't let it go, could ya. Damn nosey, sociologist, badass, ex-marine. Ya fucked up here, Kitts, and it breaks my heart. You were like a daughter to me, girl. And, my God, Nicola, it

TEARS ARE ONLY WATER

breaks my heart that ya had yer nervous breakdown and went to killin' yerself after you mistook this fella here for some intruder and shot him. Damn, damn, damn. I will cry at yer funeral, and I promise ya that all yer fellow officers will be decked out in blue fer a 21-gun salute at the cemetery."

Kitts stumbled back onto the couch as the sheriff came toward her. She stared wide-eyed as Burwinkle got closer.

"See, Cole, ya should've gone on that damn campin' trip with this crazy hawk of yers. And dammit all, ya should have gotten help fer this PTSD stress thing. Hell, everyone down at the department could see you were wound too tight, girl...chasin' ghosts, like a twig ready to snap, and goddammit, then ya did! Another vet goes off and kills herself. Couldn't take no more killin' after ya nailed this here intruder."

The sheriff's breathing became shallow and rapid. He rubbed his chest vigorously, the color drained from his face.

Beads of sweat formed on his broad forehead as he now clutched his chest. "Oh, and 'bout that Bob feller in those notes of yers, ya weren't thinking too deeply 'bout that one were ya. Didn't think they might just be a feller's initials, did ya. Dadgummit, how I hated that name, Burwell. Now what would make a mama name her baby boy Burwell? Can you imagine? Burwell Oliver Burwinkle. I wanted 'em to just call me Bob. *Not* Burwell, not Oliver. But *no*, Mama B said it was Burwell or nothin'....But enough jawing 'bout the past. Ya know too much, Cole, and we can't have—"

Bob never had a chance to finish his sentence. From his left, an angry blue bird careened onto him, sinking sharp talons into the sheriff's meaty neck, while the mighty beak clamped down on Burwinkle's ear. He dropped his gun, bobbed, and weaved as he tried to get the attack bird off his face. Langston's ear-piercing squawks drowned out Burwinkle's screams. The sheriff pulled a hand away from his attacker and gripped his chest. His knees buckled.

The overstuffed sheriff fell like a downed oak right next to Special Agent Aarveen. Langston strutted over, mounted his prey, and dropped a severed ear onto the floor.

"GRAAWK"

Chapter 32

Tears Are Only Water

Friday, March 28, 10:00 AM

The professor left early for her appointment with Carmine's doctor. The sky was gray, like her mood. She hadn't heard from Kitts and wondered if she'd discovered more about Dihn's murder or anything that connected Jonas to one of her brother's companies. Such questions were a welcome distraction from the uneasiness she felt about her upcoming meeting with the Navajo healer. It was time to open that compartment and confront her brother's doctor. She'd been left long enough in this dingy motel in Pueblo, Colorado, so she packed her quiver of arrows and set out to meet the enemy.

Piles of dirty snow lay on the sides of the streets. Last night, the temperature had dropped to below 30 degrees Fahrenheit. As she drove down the tree-lined road leading to the main building at CMHI-P, she was gripped by something ominous yet oddly sad. Something familiar yet forgotten. Her stomach tensed, and her fingers began to tingle. *Diaphragmatic breathing, now. Too much cheap wine. Only water from now on...maybe.*

The professor arrived 20 minutes early. The secretary, whom Anne saw as a typical mousey-looking clerical person, instructed her to wait in the doctor's office while Dr Lukachunai completed her morning rounds.

Anne was shown into a sparsely furnished room, uncluttered and neat. A colorful painting made with sand and other earthen materials was on one wall. She thought of her own commodious office adorned with expensive art and fine furniture. Lined with bookcases, her walls were papered with every certificate or award she'd received since Choate. The professor looked closely and saw a nominal certification from the Colorado State Board of Psychologist Examiners, the requisite license that appeared in all shrinks' offices. Next to it hung a more extensive certificate with an intricately patterned border and calligraphic lettering:

The International Council of 13 Indigenous Grandmothers

There was a list of women from all over the world. Anne squinted and found Hazel Tallulah Lukachunai listed among a dozen other names. *Tallulah. Gotcha. So, you are the notorious H. T.*

Anne scanned a shelf that was home to a handful of books. An oversized volume by Carl Jung, *Mandala Symbolism,* and another called *The Great Mother* by E. Neumann stood next to a small volume by D. W. Winnicott's *The Piggle.* She recognized the old 1980 volume by H. T. Lukas, *From the Shadows of the Mind: Traumas & the Symbols that Transform Them,* and next to it, a small book by Hazel Lukachunai called *In the Way of Sacred Birds––Messengers, Storytellers, and Teachers.* The professor wrinkled her nose. *Such nonsense. More psychoanalytic dumplings and twaddle. Ooh, note to self, Psychoanalytic Dumplings and Twaddle is another great name for a book.*

She reached for an odd-looking book with a worn leather cover. *Beyond Madness: Mystery and Meaning in Reflex Hallucinations,* written by someone she'd never heard of––Anton Zellinsky. *Ancient tomes by dead clinicians standing at attention next to the healer's little bird book. This is who they placed in charge of my brother's care? God save us all.*

Anne jumped as Lukachunai opened the door and entered her office.

"Well, hello there, Dr Schivalone. So nice to see you again. I was looking forward to our meeting. Tea? We could get coffee or water if you prefer."

Anne was struck by the snowy expanse of the old woman's hair, tied in the back and flowing to her waist. A bright turquoise necklace framed the unspoiled crispness of her lab coat. An herbal scent reminded her of the old woman dancing about the garden the day she'd arrived.

"Some coffee would be nice."

TEARS ARE ONLY WATER

Lukachunai alerted her secretary and motioned for Anne to sit. "I think we can help your brother. Though slowly, he has begun to adjust and take his first steps. I understand that he's been through a great deal."

The professor leaned forward and shot her first arrow. "What do you know about his life? My brother shouldn't be here. This has all been a horrible mistake. You probably don't realize it because you've been so busy psychoanalyzing him, but he was drugged! Someone put DMT into something he ate or drank. Bet you didn't even check on that, hmm? A police officer and I have tracked down the people responsible. It was a terrible mistake for him to be brought here, and I'll see to it that those responsible are held accountable. Now, when can I see him? Better yet, when the hell can I get him out of here?"

A rap at the door. Coffee arrived.

Lukachunai handed the cup to Anne and then poured her own tea. "Yes, how awful that was. We found trace elements of DMT when Carmine arrived. He has denied using it or any other hallucinogen, so you're probably right that someone else was responsible. I am speaking here not only of the behavior that got the police involved but also of his hallucinations."

The sharp tip of the professor's arrow was blunted, but only for a moment. She slammed her cup to the table, spilling coffee. "So, if you know all this, why in God's name are you keeping him?! This is clearly a police matter, not a psychiatric one or whatever you call what you're doing. Oh, and don't think I haven't read about you, Dr Hazel Tallulah Lukachunai or H.T. Lukas, or whatever you're calling yourself these days. Psychoanalyst, shaman, or bird doctor. Lord only knows what you call yourself, but I don't care. I demand you bring my brother to me right now so I can take him home!" *Whoosh!* Another arrow launched.

"Psychoanalyst, yes. Shaman, no, but I am a healer who loves birds. I do claim that. Wisdom comes from many teachers. And thank you for your interest in who I am. As for your brother's stay here, there are two issues at hand: First, he was brought to us by a judge's order, so he will have to be discharged by the same. So, you are correct, it is a legal matter. But more importantly, Carmine has suffered terribly, not just because of what he has been through in the last two weeks, but because of a layering of trauma that has defined so much of his life. He has begun to talk and do some meaningful work. We can help awaken his mind."

The professor squared her spine. "Touché about the court order. You can be sure I'll check into that. But how do you think you'll be able to help him? Nobody else has. My brother is unique. He's different and always has been. You can't help him with your Native herbs or psycho-analytic fairytales. I know my brother, and I've spent decades studying what helps people cope, and it's not by digging up a lot of crap from his childhood."

Lukachunai smiled. "Oh, I guess we have both spent some time learning about one another. But truthfully, I came across your book a year or so ago. Though I believe the human mind has a basic need to be whole and not split, I found your ideas interesting...refreshing."

Taken aback, another arrow blunted. The professor stuttered, "Oh, w-well. Um, so you r-read it."

"Beliefs, Misbeliefs, and Aberrations: Unmasking the Cognitive Orches-trator of Maladaptive Thought and How to Silence Him. Yes, interesting title, 'Unmasking the Cognitive Orchestrator'. I found·it quite enlight-ening, actually."

Her narcissism stroked, the professor softened. "Thank you. I feel that too much time is spent dwelling on the past, trying to recover hidden memories, everyone's victimhood, and feelings...feelings everywhere. Can't we just breathe? Can't we just keep unnecessary compartments closed?"

The powdery-haired healer smiled softly. "Go on, Doctor."

Leaning in, the professor continued. "Here's a case in point. I know someone. Just met her, actually. She's a deputy in the Arapahoe County Sheriff's office. I met her through this dreadful ordeal with my brother. Anyway, this woman is a war veteran. She was a marine in Afghanistan. I saw that she'd gotten a Silver Star over there. So, this woman, who has seen more awful things than the two of us put together, is tough as nails. She doesn't let anything get to her." Anne paused and pushed away thoughts about Kitts' recent flashback. "Um, this woman doesn't waste time dwelling on what can't be changed. She doesn't cry and feel sorry for herself, and she is *not* a victim! No, she proudly wears this tattoo on her forearm for the world to see. We should all proudly print these words on our foreheads. It reads, 'Tears are Only Water.' You hear that? Tears are only water. Well, boo fucking who, if you'll excuse my fucking French, Dr H. T. Hazel--whatever your last name is--Psychoanalyst-Spiritual Doctor. Tears. They are an irritation of the mucous membrane in the cornea. The cornea emits salinized water. It runs down our cheeks. You wipe them up and toss the tissue. End of story."

"*C'est bon.* Your French is fine." A ray of sunlight peeked through the window, illuminating a patch on the sand painting. Lukachunai's eyes brightened. She searched her mind. "'Tears are only water'...That comes from a poem. I believe it is from a wonderful children's book called *Taggerung*. You know the author, Brian Jacques? It has always been a favorite. In his story, he writes about how we should never be ashamed to weep and that it is good to grieve. Jacques wrote that 'tears are only water' and that all things--plants and trees--cannot grow unless they have water. But all living things need sunlight too. I think the final line is something like 'in time, a wounded heart will heal, and the memories of those we have lost will be sealed inside forever to give us comfort.'"

The professor shook her head blankly. Her last arrow had fallen to the ground, and her quiver was empty. Her arrows, barbs, and darts had been dulled. At that moment, all Anne Schivalone could do was stare at one of the 13 Grandmothers who sat before her.

Lukachunai continued. "Another great writer, Victor Hugo, I believe, told us that 'those who do not weep do not see.' I think your brother has cut himself off from his deeper vision and so, too, from his tears for many years, perhaps since your father died. He was only five, is that right? What can you tell me about your father, Dr Schivalone?"

Anger had always been Anne's companion, her guide, a protector that sharpened her spears. Throughout her life, she'd kept her edge. Always angry. The flame was held at a low burn. Now, she felt an unsettling numbness. The floor seemed to move, and her eyes began to sting. She stared down at her feet and took a deep breath. Her voice was soft when she said, "Yes, Carmine was only five....My father was a brilliant physicist and mathematician. He knew everything, but then...he started talking to himself."

Lukachunai looked towards her. "Your father talked to himself?"

"Mother had him shipped out to the state hospital." She motioned around the room. "This place, I think. I visited him one time. After he was gone and I was a grad student, I tracked down his records. It turns out that Vati wasn't just muttering to himself. He was conversing with the Others, or *Andere*, as he called them. They were the lost children of Bergen-Belsen, where he spent four years of his life as a boy. He was tormented by their screams. Both of his parents were killed in the ovens there, as were most members of his family. He never saw any of them again. He watched as they took his only sister away... Anne."

"Such a monstrous tragedy for any person to endure, unspeakable for a small child.... Do you recall what your father was saying to them?"

Anne rubbed her eyes, willing the stinging to stop. She tried to clear her throat. Her chest felt tight. "He spoke in German. His voice wasn't soft like I remembered, but it was seized by fear. I was a child. I didn't know what his words meant or why he was chanting them over and over...so, I wrote them down and memorized the phonology. Later, I discovered they meant, 'Please...you have to stop doing this to me. Please, you have to stop doing this to me.'"

Hearing her voice speak the words out loud penetrated Anne's armor and unlocked a hidden compartment, a place inside she'd spent a lifetime guarding. She crumpled in her chair.

The tears came in sudden, spasmodic torrents––suppressed by a lifetime of denial and a knack for looking the other way. The sharp edge of disdain for anything soft and sentimental collapsed. Her tears swept her away on a rickety raft in a river swollen by a deep ache and longing she'd spent a lifetime hiding...in the shadows of her mind.

TEARS ARE ONLY WATER

Lukachunai passed a box of Kleenex and waited silently. After several minutes, she gently asked, "Carmine told me that Vati died. Can you tell me how?"

Gulping for air to still her tears, Anne formed the words, "He-he hung himself. Carmine found him."

"Eeeee....Your *little brother*? *How*? *Where*?"

"He went looking for Vati....He thought he was mad at him.... Carmie found Vati hanging in the basement.... He ran away...Mother finally found him asleep in the shed."

"Your brother said something about that, a shed that had a window."

"She was looking all over for him.... I was only 13, and she sent me away to boarding school. When I returned that summer, it was as if Vati had never existed. All his clothes, his books, and pipes were gone, packed away in that old shed. Mother had another man living with her, and my brother had stopped speaking."

The healer nodded. "Dear Dr Schivalone, I must say you are as strong as this deputy you've told me about, maybe even stronger. You have shared so much. Some I suspected and so much I did not know. If you permit me, Carmine is my patient—you are not. But as I've listened to him... and to you today, I understand there are two lives buried beneath layers of trauma. You see, sometimes there *are* victims. Both of you have managed that trauma in the best ways you know how. Forgive another reference to a poet, but they are the true seers. Longfellow said, 'There is no grief like the grief that does not speak.' I believe you and Carmine have not spoken of your grief and trauma."

Anne listened, her raft drifting far from familiar shores. Her swollen eyes welled with more tears.

Lukachunai spoke carefully, "Your brother was the child of a concentration camp survivor. His father committed suicide. His mother could not see him or help him. He formed an attachment to a woman he thought valued him. She rejected him and later killed herself. He was tricked and assaulted a woman. Now, he is accused of a crime and has been sent here. Whether his civil commitment was the right decision or not, he is here now. Your brother suffered through so many losses. He lost a father, a mother, and a connection to the outside world. He lost a connection to his Jewish ancestry. He lives in the shadows, and it is time for him to come out. I can help Carmine, Dr Schivalone. I can work with him while he is here until we are told he must leave. Then it will be up to you and him."

Anne nodded. The stinging was gone as her tears fell softly like water. She felt comfort in this uncomfortable moment.

"I work in Native healing ways, sprinkled with the powder of Jungian symbols. I understand how the mind--your cognitive orchestrator-- can retreat to protect itself from light that is too painful to see." She smiled softly, "I can help your brother begin to see and bear that pain."

Chapter 33

Hijo Prodìgo

Friday, March 28, 4:50 PM

The session with Anne Schivalone inhabited the healer's thoughts for the rest of the day. She was reminded of narcissism's brittle edge and was saddened by how this woman, like her brother, had been so severely damaged. Each in their own way, both siblings tried to live by not fully seeing their truths. What to do now? Looking at the snow out her window, her thoughts turned to Julio. She would need his help...and his discretion.

Julio Garza was twelve when he first came to the hospital. His mother had abandoned him. Probably the youngest crack addict they'd ever seen, he was made a ward of the state. Dr Lukachunai, who had recently come on staff, was assigned as his therapist. At first, he was unreachable––violent, nonverbal, and brooding. He only tolerated her presence when quietly working on sand paintings or when taking silent walks around hospital grounds, with security following close behind. Over time, they widened the course of their walks, which Lukachunai called "our Medicine Walks." She taught Julio how to be still, how to listen, and to understand that he was truly part of something larger than himself.

As the years passed, Julio grew in size and maturity. He remained in the hospital system for five years, got clean, and eventually completed high school. Then after his high school graduation, Julio disappeared. No one, not even his doctor, knew why he had left or where he'd gone.

Hazel was surprised to see him four years later when he applied for a job as a nurse's aide at the hospital. At the time, she served on the committee tasked with interviewing applicants for patient care workers. Julio was 22 and had grown to the size of a house. When he walked into the interview room, she was struck by his size and by the proliferation of tattoos adorning his arms and neck. There had been rumors that he had returned to the streets after he left CMHI-P. Staff reported seeing someone who looked like Julio running with a gang called the *Norteños*, but no one was sure what had happened to him.

He took his seat, the chair too small for his frame. A monochromatic sleeve ran from the back of his right hand up his arm, leading all eyes to the spiderweb tattoos on both sides of his neck. The committee members fell silent. Surely a man of his size with those tattoos must be affiliated with a gang. But Hazel wasn't so sure. She had a keen interest in symbolism; she'd studied tattoos and their psychological and cultural meaning. Even if he had been in a gang, bilateral neck and throat tattoos were often seen as symbols of communication and openness to people and new experiences. Hazel spoke first.

"Hello Mr Garza, Julio. It's a pleasure to see you. It has been a very long time. I am curious why you have returned. You left many years ago, and now you are back. The art on your body is quite intricate and beautiful. It must tell a story, but I think it's left some of my colleagues speechless, perhaps worried that you belong to a gang. Please forgive me, but I believe that it is always best to state the obvious. So, can you tell us about your life and why you have chosen to return?"

The quiet in the room was deafening. All eyes were on the giant as the committee members leaned forward to hear his response.

"Okay.... You know a boy needs a family, Doctora. When he has no family, he finds one. With no mama, no papa, and an abuela who died, you can always find a family on the streets. I found that family when I was a kid. It's true that some in my found family were not good people. Then I came here. I hated you people and trusted no one.... But people here, especially you, Doctora, took care of me. But it was hard. When you haven't had caring, it can hurt when you get it. I didn't feel I really

TEARS ARE ONLY WATER

belonged, so I had to leave. I knew I should not go back to the street, but my head was thick. I had to learn this myself. One thing I learned was we are not given only one familia. Me, I had three. The first one rejected me, the second cared for me, and the third one used me. What I found back on the streets was empty––people using people, hurting people. It's true, I have been wild in my life. I was a cholo, but I am not in a gang now. I was, si, but now, no. I'm here because I believe a man grows by giving back to become part of something more important than who he is. I took a lot when I was here. So, I came here to walk a path of giving back. Maybe I can be of service, Doctora. That's all I got to say.... Oh, and I need a job."

After he'd spoken in front of the committee, the room was silent. Then, Dr Orin asked, "When can you begin?"

Julio had been an aide ever since. Hazel's respect and affection for him deepened in the ten years they'd worked together. He was written up in a *Psychiatric Times* article about the effectiveness of mental health services for ex-gang members. *The Pueblo Chieftain* featured him in an article, heralding the return of the prodigal son, "El Hijo Prodìgo." Julio came to be known as a symbol of compassionate treatment at CMHI-P. He was smart and loyal, but his true gifts were the connections he formed with patients, some of whom were so closed off and allergic to human contact that they never opened up to other staff members. Hazel found that Julio's understanding of Native healing was deeply intuitive. He was assigned to Hazel's team and was frequently by her side, assisting with her most difficult-to-reach patients.

Sitting in her office, she waited for him to arrive. She'd left her door cracked open. He stuck his head inside and smiled.

"Donna said you wanted to see me."

She smiled and nodded, "*Yá'át'éh*, Julio."

"A good afternoon to you, too, Doctora."

"Sit, please, Julio." She motioned him in. "Tea?"

Rubbing his hands together, he said, "You know it...but only if it's your homebrew."

She stood, fetched the kettle on the burner, poured, and passed a mug, which disappeared in his massive hand. "As you know, sometimes our patients are stuck and hard to reach, Julio. We cannot reach them. You know who I have in mind."

"That would be Carmine, the bookkeeper. Si.... This man is a strange bird, but I think his heart is good. I've taken some Medicine Walks with him, like you told me to, Doc. He doesn't say much. Yes, there is something deep inside that stops him."

"And that's why we need to do something different. I am thinking of a five-night traditional healing ceremony with a sweat lodge like the one they made you take down but smaller. He will only be with us for a short time, and then he will be gone. We *must* provide a healing ceremony, Julio, an experience, not simply a series of interpretations and explanations. Those things can follow, but he needs something else now. I am afraid that words alone cannot reach him. I believe nothing short of this will free him from the darkness that grips his mind. Talks in the garden, medicines, group sessions, and building birdhouses in the woodshop are fine, but we need stronger medicine for him."

"Not a good idea, if you're asking me, Doctora. I think you are––asking me that is––so I have to tell you, not a good idea, Doña. That fool, the Big Toad Beelzebuffo, will cut you off. It's against his law now, Doc. You know this."

"All true, Julio. But it is necessary. We cannot reach Carmine any other way. He will not be here much longer. I will cover for you. I will place in writing that you were working under your team leader's orders and that you registered your dissent."

"They won't fire me. Es muy escandaloso to fire poor Julio, Pueblo's hijo prodìgo. The papers would call it a big scandal. No, I'm not worried about me. But you, la medica of the thirteen abuelas, they will burn you. Olive is keeping a book on you. You know that, right? They are waiting,

TEARS ARE ONLY WATER

Doctora, looking for the chance to swoop in like a big Red-tailed hawk and take you out. But I worry for other reasons, too."

She began to protest, but he held up his hand. "Please, let me finish. With full respect for you, Doctora, let me just say this. These chants and ceremonies...I've seen what they take from you. When you last did this kind of ceremony, it almost killed you, Doña.... And now you want to try it again. I can see that it is harder for you these days. You can't hide your limp so well as you think. A five-night chanting ceremony with *this* patient at *this* time of the year will take too much from you. That's what I fear most."

She shook her head. "Yes, yes. Thank you, Julio. I appreciate your concerns for me. But I will be okay with Carmine, really.... Funny that you should mention the Red-tail. The *Atseeltsoi* is my spirit bird and protector. I have taught you they are truth-tellers, warriors of truth, so I will trust the hawk."

He buried his head in his hands. "What this thing will take from you and what they will do with you.... Maybe you can't reach this man. Then what? I don't think I can do what you ask, Dr Hazel."

"What is right usually is not the easy path, and what is easy can put us to sleep. Carmine needs to wake up, Julio." She stood up and faced him, her eyes at his level, though he remained seated. She reached for his hands, winked, and said, "We can do this. Let's just *do it*, bro."

241

Chapter 34

Hall of Mirrors

Saturday, March 29, 8:00 AM

Anne sat up in her hotel bed, clutching her cell. The phone rang six times before she answered in a low and raspy voice.

"Good morning. This is Hazel Lukachunai. I am so sorry to have awakened you, Dr Schivalone. I know the hour is early."

She blinked. "S'okay. I needed to get up. Is there something wrong?"

"Nothing has changed since we met, but I need to speak with you about Carmine's treatment. Time is short, even shorter than I first thought. I received word last night that he will probably be here for just another week, ten days at most, as they sort out legal issues surrounding his commitment. I feel I can still help him, but that help will need to take a different form. I want to perform a healing ceremony with him."

Anne rubbed her eyes. "A healing what? What are you saying?"

"A traditional Native healing ceremony. It is well-suited to people with grief and trauma so deep there are no words. I know that this will sound strange to you, considering your background and the concerns you raised yesterday. And no doubt, it will play into your ambivalence about me being a psychoanalyst *and* a Native healer. I know you have contempt for the first and mistrust of the second."

Anne moved to the side of the bed, where she'd been since their meeting the day before. She had purchased a bottle of wine after their meeting, intending to numb herself by draining it as soon as she reached the

TEARS ARE ONLY WATER

hotel. But the wine had an acrid taste. She ended up pouring it down the drain and going to bed. All that remained was an odd and unsettling feeling, a sour stomach, and a fuzzy brain. She'd exposed her soul to this old woman, leaving her feeling raw and emotionally spent. But she felt different. She was not angry...sad and empty, but not angry. Forty-eight hours ago, she would have launched into a rant as she had done throughout her life. She would have fired one arrow after another to vanquish her foe, especially if they were asking things that caused discomfort or made her feel vulnerable.

She finally spoke. "Um, I'm not sure what you're saying. How will a healing ceremony help him? You know how all this sounds?"

Her mind was still in a fog while she listened to the easy cadence of the Navajo healer's words about the symbolic process. Hazel explained how Carmine needed to experience the death of his old and the rebirth of a new self.

"Your brother's mind has been split. Like the sun that sets, Carmine must plunge into the darkness of his unconscious to heal so he can then experience renewal."

Lukachunai laid out the plan for evening ceremonies to take place over the next five nights. She paused, her voice breaking stride. She shared that earlier administrations had sanctioned Native healing ceremonies but the current group in charge wanted them "to be, uh...used more sparingly."

Anne was on her feet and began pacing around the room. When she stopped and faced herself in the mirror above the bureau, she saw her mother looking back at her disapprovingly. She shut her eyes tightly and tried to listen to the explanations about how each evening would begin with traditional songs and stories. Lukachunai would conduct the ceremonies with help from those who'd assisted her previously.

"Some call it a Holy Way Chant, but it is a prayer ceremony for healing. This is right for Carmine. I have done these ceremonies many times over the decades. They go far back in time, passed down by the Elders. I will speak and sing in my Native language, present sand paintings, burn sage,

243

cedar branches, pollen, and tobacco, and make other herbal offerings. There are woods located behind the cement pillars at the old 11th Street entrance. A grove of cottonwoods makes this area private. We will build a structure for Carmine's ceremony. I understand that all of this will seem strange to you. Please trust me to do what is right to help your brother in the little time we have left. Of utmost importance, Dr Schivalone, I would like you to attend. *Carmine* has asked for you to be with him."

Anne looked again at the face in the mirror and this time wondered about the frightened woman staring back at her. She looked little and lost, a 100-year-old woman whose compartments had all been flattened by an emotional tsunami. But she was still standing...and continued to listen. Hearing that her brother wanted her to be present for this voodoo ritual further penetrated her already porous armor and brought tears to her eyes.

"I'll have to think about it...but okay, okay. Carmie asked that I be there? If that's true, then alright.... It's strange, but I suppose not all that different from other magical rituals masking as psychotherapy. Frankly, at this point, everything in my life has become a distorted image of real-ity. I feel as if I've been lost in a fun house at a sleazy carnival, trapped in a hall of mirrors for far too long and can't find the exit. But what you're talking about sounds...."

Lukachunai waited.

"Never mind. I'll do it. Just tell me what I must do.... Oh, and Doctor, I still think you're a crazy shaman, but nothing else has helped my brother...so why not."

Chapter 35

Myth of the Sleeping Boy

Saturday, March 29, 10:00 AM

Hazel planned to place several other calls that morning, but there was an intense moment of soul-searching before she contacted the few people she could trust. Thoughts swirled as she poured her tea. Tea was comforting, but she wished she had stronger medicine now. She rubbed her aching back, trying to warm the chill in her bones, feeling a mixture of sadness and uncertainty. Here she sat, an old woman at the end of her eighth decade. *Am I that arrogant, single-minded, and foolish to think I must do this and put others at risk by asking them to help with this last forbidden ceremony? I must be all three.*

The bookkeeper had touched and rattled the wise healer, the sage grandmother whom others looked to for guidance. Was it his silence and imprisonment that she couldn't reach by customary rituals of psychotherapy...or was there something else?

Ambitious but ashamed of her heritage, Hazel Lukachunai had squeezed much of her past into padlocked compartments. She had been determined to learn the ways of Western medicine and leave her ancestral traditions, her shame, and the rawness of her grief behind. Thus, she ventured far from home, severing her roots, as she studied in Cambridge, London, and then Zürich--in each place, passing for someone she was not. In college, people assumed her family were educated professionals from India. In England, she tried to pass as Persian, though some jeered "Paki" under their breath. She hid behind a new name to draw attention and scrutiny away from who she really was and from where she came. So, she became Tallulah Lukas, hoping to blend in. She wore drab Western clothes, kept her hair closely cropped, and never did anything to celebrate her culture. Her waking hours were spent in dark libraries studying science and the teachings of European doctors. Her family never understood.

In one of their last meetings before his death, Erich Neumann, her cherished supervisor at the Jungian Institute, asked her who she was. "Tallulah, to heal splits in the minds of others, you must first awaken those parts of yourself that have fallen asleep. I do not believe that you are fully awake. I think you are not sure of who you really are."

Neumann's words confused and disappointed her. She tried to protest by telling him she had discovered many things about herself in her own analysis.

"Ach, Tallulah, yes, yes. Your analysis has been very important, but I am talking about something else. I think you know yourself on the outside, but what about the inside? We all know Tallulah, but who is Hazel? I have never heard you use that name. And Lukas? There must be a story about Hazel and where she has gone, no?"

That comment lit a spark that continued to smolder after she left Zürich and moved to San Francisco. It burned during her tenure as president of the Jungian Institute until, one day, she realized she had lost her way.

After her mother died, she resigned from her position. Feeling lost and depressed, she started drinking. She couldn't sleep at night and wondered if life was worth living. She had been playing a role for far too long, and now the performance was over. She stopped working and stayed in bed all day. Finally, with nowhere else to go, she returned to her home in Southern Colorado. Her uncle told her she had a sickness in her soul and invited her to help him with his healing ceremonies. On her first day of her training, she was late.

"I'm sorry, *Adá'í*. I overslept."

"I can see that, Hazel. I think you have been asleep for a very long time."

TEARS ARE ONLY WATER

After a year of working together, she continued to struggle. Recognizing this, her uncle prepared a five-night ceremonial rite to help her awaken. This changed her life. She became his apprentice the following year and immersed herself in traditional healing songs and prayers.

For the next two decades, she disappeared into obscurity, losing ties to her former colleagues and students in San Francisco and Zürich. She devoted herself to studying Traditional ceremonies, toiling in the heat of a sweat lodge, making sand paintings, learning ancient stories, prayers, and songs, and becoming an expert on the spiritual properties of birds. And through it all, Hazel Tallulah Lukachunai woke up to who she really was. She didn't forget who she had been, for she was now an Indigenous healer *and* a psychoanalyst--a student of the Medicine Wheel *and* the institutes of Cambridge, London, and Zürich. Accepting a job at the state hospital allowed her to be herself and offer all she'd learned from her Western *and* Indigenous teachers.

As she sat in her office, she reflected on Julio's words. Much of what he said was true. She knew that they were eager to remove her from the staff. Rumors that they'd started a special investigation were probably true.

Her tea had cooled. She shook off her wisp of sadness and lingering doubts. She had to do this. *There is one final ceremony to be performed for this n'diilgaazh, this man who is sleepwalking through his life. It is decided. It is time to wake Carmine Luedke.* She had chosen the story for his ceremony--Myth of the Sleeping Boy.

The healer wrote the names of those she would contact. Then, she put in writing that each would be acting on her orders and that she alone was responsible for this healing ceremony. Then she dialed Julio, who didn't pick up. She left a voicemail for him to come to her office at noon.

Hazel called George Schmidt from the Grounds Department and Gina Rivani, the red-haired art therapist on her team, to come to the noon meeting. She invited Benjamin Franklin Joseph, an Indigenous artist who had helped patients create sand paintings. He could help Gina create these for Carmine's ceremony. Finally, she had a more extended call with her most trusted colleague, Lia.

The last name on her list was Berti Schwartz, a retired staff RN who'd lost her job to Astracides the previous fall. A Brooklyn transplant who could never explain how she ended up in Pueblo, Colorado, Bertie lived with four cats and maintained connections with many of her former co-workers. A gritty woman with colorful expressions, she'd challenged the mandate to reduce the Native healing practices in the hospital. At her retirement party, she cornered Lukachunai and declared, "The Fat Frog and his reptiles are crawlin' all over this place. Call if you ever need me. I got your back, sister."

Bertie still worked shifts to cover when other nurses were away. The plan was to get her on the schedule for the nights of the prayer ceremonies so she could verify that Carmine hadn't left the ward.

The Navajo healer needed all of them for this final ceremony. George would assist Julio with building a modest sweat lodge, smaller than they used in the past. Gina could help Benjamin Franklin with sand paint-ings. She was forever grateful to Dr Hazel for performing a healing cere-mony on her daughter when she was not responding to treatments from the hematologist.

Hazel brewed more tea while waiting for the group to convene. She felt a twinge of guilt about what she told Carmine's sister about how the administration had asked for Native healing practices to be used––how had she put it––"more sparingly." Perhaps she should have said nothing about this. She realized that her white lie was both an admission and an attempt to cover up the truth that Indigenous healing practices were no longer allowed.

George arrived first. A thin man in his 60s, he had worked at CMHI-P longer than Hazel. George was quiet by nature and, like many, felt a certain reverence for the Navajo doctor. He had attended her lectures and drum circles when the administration still sanctioned them. George had worked with Julio on the construction of the original sweat lodge and then its subsequent dismantling.

TEARS ARE ONLY WATER

Gina and Lia arrived at the same time, bringing bagels. Bertie brought homemade babka. "So, what else I gotta do with my time but bake and eat? Mother used to say, 'Now that you're getting to be an old bag, you better learn to bake.'"

Gina chuckled. "What kind of mother would say that to her daughter?"

"Same kinda mother who'd name her daughter Bertha."

"Bertie, you always bring the light wherever you go. I'm glad you're here. Same for all of you." Lukachunai looked around with a smile. She took out her list and began reviewing her group's assignments.

Gina said, "You need me to get started on Jungian mandalas. You called Benjamin Franklin about the sand paintings, right? I can help him work with Carmine starting tomorrow during art therapy. I'll sit with him while Benjamin mixes the sand and colors and blends it with corn meal, ground-up flowers, charcoal, and anything else you want."

"Perfect, Gina. Benjamin Franklin will tell you we need five colored *Iináájí* paintings for the patient to sit on each night. We will need black for death and white for renewal. Benjamin and I can tell you where the yellow and blue coloring should be arranged."

They listened intently as the healer sketched a plan for each of the five nights. The paintings, songs, and prayers must follow the story about the ceremonial hero.

Lia spoke up. "Have you chosen a story hero for the ceremony for Carmine? I remember the ones you had before, like the Rain Boy and Big Star. Were you thinking about one of those or something else?"

Before the doctor could answer, Julio lumbered in. "Sorry, Doctora. Change of shift was slow today."

Aware of his reservations and concerns, Hazel looked at him, her eyebrows raised. He held her gaze, smiled, and nodded, "S'all okay, Doc."

Relieved, she turned back to Lia. "You have a good memory, Lia. It has been a while since we've done a ceremony, but the one we will do with

Carmine will be different. Aside from the unique nature of his suffering, this will be the last one we ever do. His sister has agreed to come each night, so I need you to coordinate that with her. Julio, George will help you build a smaller sweat house this time. We only need a small one. I was thinking by the cottonwoods behind the old cement pillars. There is a spot that will be perfect for our final ceremony. We shall begin at sundown and continue until 10:00 PM. The last night, we shall go until dawn. Since Bertie used to be the night nursing supervisor, they will welcome her back with open arms. She can explain how she misses the hospital and wants to help out. Once she is on the schedule, she can help with nighttime bed checks. It is not ideal, but it will have to do. We all need to be careful. Like I've told each of you, I have put in writing that you are acting on my orders as I am the team leader."

Hazel waved off their protests. "No more discussion about that, please." This is my decision as team leader. You are not responsible, any of you. I shall meet with Carmine later today to go over his ceremony. Then I'll speak with his sister again to make sure she understands when and where to meet you, Lia. So...I think we are set. Benjamin Franklin will be at the ceremony. Gina, you may attend, too, if you like. Any questions?"

"Doctora, what myth have you chosen for this?" asked Julio.

"Oh right, sorry I never answered you, Lia. No, the ones you mentioned are good, but I have found a *háábóyátééh* of particular significance for our patient. This is a restoration prayer that will continue over the five days of Carmine's ceremony. It is called Myth of the Sleeping Boy, something you have yet to hear. It's very old, and I know of only one time it has been used with someone who needed to be awakened. But I think the story is the right one. I know it will work. The story...."

The healer closed her eyes.

"It is about a boy who was tasked with watching over all the animals in his village. At night, he fed them and led them into their hut, where they slept through the night. But while watching over them, the boy fell asleep. It began to storm, and lightning hit the hut, which burst into flames. The boy awoke and was frightened because the flames were so bright they burned his eyes. All the animals perished. The boy ran away, found a place to hide, and fell back asleep."

Hazel stopped to catch her breath. She sipped her tea, closed her eyes, and continued. "The boy never opened his eyes again and left his village in shame. He wandered through the years afraid, stooping and crawling through the thicket. He ate what he could find with his hands and drank water that gathered in the hollows of logs. The boy grew into a young man."

Her voice grew soft, her eyes misty. "One day, he came upon a magic pond. He knelt to drink, and his eyes opened. The young man saw a frightened-looking face staring up at him. He blinked, and the man in the water blinked back. The young man thought, 'This poor man is trapped under the water. I must set him free.' Disregarding the danger to his life, he dove deeply, wrestled with the submerged vines, weeds, and branches, and shook them, hoping to save this drowning man."

The storyteller spoke in anguished tones. "When the young man surfaced, he crawled to the shore and looked for the stranger. He saw nothing but murky water swirling around. He grew sad and wept, fearing that the man in the water was lost. Next to him sat a crow.

'Why do you weep?' asked the crow.

'Because the man has drowned,' said the boy.

'No,' said the crow. 'You were brave and saved the man, and now he is free.'"

Pantomiming the story, Hazel continued. "Wiping the tears from his eyes, the young man gazed deeply into the pond once more. This time, he saw the reflection of a red-tailed hawk circling high overhead. The young man stood up and faced the sky. With the warmth of the sun on his face, he found his courage. He felt a longing for home and decided to return to his village. Along the way, he encountered animals who followed him."

The group listened and then signaled their approval.

"It's perfect. Really fits him," said Lia.

Gina nodded eagerly.

Bertie always spoke her thoughts out loud. "What? He sleeps all the time? I'll take some of what he's drinkin'. Myths, schmyths. I don't get it. What happened to the guy in the water? And where'd that crow come from? But I guess you know what you're doin'. You always have, Dr Hazel. I'll make sure that next week the log says Carmine stayed in bed. Asleep."

Lukachunai gave Gina a few more instructions about the paintings and mandalas. Then they stood, hugged each other, and moved toward the door.

Julio lingered. "Your story of the sleeping boy is a good one for this bookkeeper you want to wake up." He winked. "It's a good story, bro."

She smiled as he exited and left, "Yes, it is a good myth for our sad, sleeping hero, the *n'diilgaazh hastiin.*"

No one noticed the two unit nurses who rounded the corner of the hallway just as the band of accomplices was exiting Hazel's office.

"That's weird. Such an odd group to be here on a Saturday," one of them said. "What's up with that?"

Chapter 36

Song of Death and Renewal

Sunday, March 30, 10:00 AM – Saturday, April 5, 6:00 AM

The plan was set. Lia would contact Anne Schivalone later that morning. George and Julio would quietly begin erecting a simple sweat lodge. So as not to arouse suspicion among the nursing staff, Gina had several patients coming in to work on sand paintings, and tonight would be Bertie's first graveyard shift. Hazel remembered the line from that show she watched in the '80s, *The A-Team*––a guilty pleasure she was sure no one knew about––when the George Peppard character, Hannibal something, would always say, "I love it when a plan comes together." *So yes, Hannibal, this one feels good.*

Hazel shuffled through the report she'd received on Carmine. With so much going on, she had only glanced at it before pushing the folder to the side of her desk. In the file was a copy of a chart note from Oakley concerning, among other things, changes he'd made in Carmine's medication. Oakley changed the provisional diagnosis of a schizophreniform disorder to a medication-induced psychotic episode. He lowered the dosage of antipsychotic medication, upped the Modafinil to target Carmine's daytime sleepiness, and would add Sodium Oxybate to reduce his nighttime cataplexy. All well and good. But she took particular notice of Oakley's order for Carmine to be discharged within the week, noting that "the patient is mentally competent to face his criminal charges." She was right. They had little time to act.

· · ·

Carmine followed her to the garden. The morning chill was made more bearable by the bright sunlight, but the doctor was shivering beneath her heavy coat. His mind was in a haze. He had seen her daily but remembered little from their sessions.

"Carmine, it is important that you try to stay with me this morning. We will begin a special ceremony tomorrow to help with the deep pain I believe you have been carrying. I don't know if you remember, but your sister is in town and has agreed to attend our ceremony."

Her words cut through the haze. *Anne.* Her name lingered in his mind. He wasn't sure he wanted to see her but, at the same time, felt something approaching desperation to be with his sister. He strained to return to the doctor's words.

"And you will see Ms Rivani and my friend Benjamin Franklin in the art studio every day to work on sand paintings that we shall use each night. Julio will come for you after supper and take you to a place we have prepared in the woods, and then we shall begin."

He tried to take in what the doctor said but noticed she was shivering. "I don't need to be out here, Doctor. It's c-cold. We can go inside if you like."

She agreed to move their session back into the warmth of her office. Once there, she poured tea, which Carmine accepted. This was the first time he'd received her offering. They sat together in silence until she signaled that they needed to stop.

"Tomorrow, we begin.... It's time, Carmine."

Monday, March 31, 6:00 PM. Night 1

There are times when you're embarrassed even though no one sees the reason why. This was one of those moments for Anne Schivalone. Going along with this ridiculous ceremony ran counter to everything she believed and preached, but she was going along, nonetheless. She purchased a heavy parka and knitted cap, hoping that no one would

TEARS ARE ONLY WATER

recognize her, even though no one knew her or even cared. She wore sunglasses even though it was dusk. Participating in a healing ceremony seemed irrational, but this might be the last opportunity to reach her brother.

She waited in the hotel lobby for her ride. When they met for coffee the day before, Dr Dhikavi insisted she call her Lia. Anne liked this doctor with her colorful hijab. Lia pulled up in front of her hotel at 5:30 sharp. Right on time.

When Anne got in, she couldn't help but say, "This is crazy, you know."

"Ha, yeah, many times I've thought that about Dr Hazel, and as many times, I've been wrong. She's dialed into something, like an energy plane most of us don't understand. It's not the way we were trained as scientist-practitioners. Anyway, I think it's so good you agreed to be part of this. I've seen this work before with other patients here. I brought blankets and hot coffee. There will be a fire inside the hut, so it will be warm enough, but I'll bring blankets to put on the ground. Let me just go over again what to expect."

Lia drew a breath and continued. "Dr Hazel believes that a Holy Way Ceremony will help restore Carmine to health. You have to suspend your Western brain and understand that these Native healing rituals have been practiced for 20,000 years, probably longer. Part of the ceremony involves a hero's quest, which the doctor has chosen especially for your brother. I know it sounds strange, but the quest is based on the symbolism of death and rebirth, which means that Carmine will have a chance to reconnect with the parts of himself that he has deeply repressed. Dr Hazel calls these the 'shadows of his mind.' She wrote a book about this decades ago, even before she began doing healing ceremonies."

Anne listened, her disparaging inner commentary temporarily on hold. Along with her usual skepticism, she experienced an odd mix of new and unnerving sensations––warmth, curiosity, and vulnerability. Without her cynical snark, she felt naked.

Lia, with her flashlight, led the way through the brush until they came to a clearing. They saw the glow of light from inside the small domed structure and smelled a sweet smokiness. "Stay by my side," Lia whispered. "Just let your love for your brother wash over you, and everything will be fine."

The lodge was about fifteen feet long and seven feet high. The frame was fashioned out of thick-cut branches and covered with a black tarp. Under the round opening in the dome, a fire illuminated the darkness inside. Lia took off her shoes, and Anne followed. The dirt floor was cold. Anne was happy to have those blankets to spread on the ground. The fire's welcoming glow warmed the air and radiated the sweet, earthy fragrance of sage and tobacco. Lia nodded to a red-haired woman wearing a shawl. To the right of the fire sat a long-haired Indigenous man wearing a red plaid shirt with a dark-colored bandana tied around his forehead. Lia picked a spot, spread the blanket, and motioned for Anne to sit.

Lukachunai sat across from them, eyes closed, mouthing words that Anne strained to understand. The healer wore all black, her white hair draped over her shoulders and down her back. On the ground next to her was a large, textured, multi-colored painting. The flap to the hut was open. An enormous man carrying an old drum walked in with her brother trailing behind. He closed the flap, and they both took a seat.

Anne's eyes stung, blurred by the smoke and the sad image of her brother, who looked little and lost. Wrapped in a colorful blanket, Carmine was directed to sit in the middle of the painting next to the healer. He sat cross-legged and slumped. He was pale and stared vacantly at the fire. Anne recognized that look––and that achy feeling–– she had always tried to ignore when she saw her brother looking so vulnerable.

The healer stood, stepped forward, and spoke.

"With strong hearts, clear minds, giving and brave spirits, we seek to enter this sacred space. We request that our spirit mother provide clarity and direction to help this man awaken from his prison so that he may become whole again."

She angled her head toward the sky and began to sing in a language Anne didn't recognize. Her voice rose and fell in waves as the large man drummed. The heat from the fire, pitch of her voice, smoke of the burning sage, and resonant beating of the drum excited the senses.

Anne looked to Lia, who whispered softly. "Everything from now on will be in her Native tongue. She's beginning with a prayer to the sacred birds, starting with the smallest and ending with the largest and most powerful, the eagle."

Anne watched her brother's face. His eyes were shut. The bright timbre of Lukachunai's voice pierced the air as she swept the smoke toward Carmine with a large feather.

Anne inhaled deeply and felt the warmth inside.

"A purification," Lia whispered.

The air was filled with a thick aroma as the healer placed offerings into the fire––first the grasses, then pollen, sage, and lastly tobacco. The man wearing the bandana tended the fire. The healer continued her chanting prayer as she knelt by the side of the painting. She gently rubbed the mix of herbs and sand onto Carmine's head, neck, chest, arms, and legs. The king-sized man sat quietly and softened his drumbeat, never taking his eyes off the Navajo doctor. The songs were repetitious and droning. Anne's eyes closed, and her mind grew hazy. Lia nudged her gently. But Anne hadn't fallen asleep. She was floating above the fire, drifting toward the top of the sweat lodge.

Lukachunai stopped chanting, and Anne came back, startled. Beside her, Lia began to move, signaling that the first ceremony had ended. Time, the eternal trickster, had fooled her into believing that they had been sitting for minutes, not for four hours. The giant tattooed man wiped the painted herbs off her brother's body. Carmine's eyes were open now. The healer mumbled her last words, and Lia said, "That's it. One down, four to go. We need to leave now." Anne caught her brother's eyes as he stood and prepared to exit. He had a hollow look. But did she detect a slight smile?

. . .

Friday, April 4, 6:00 PM. Night 5

There are two meanings of the word ritual––a stereotyped pattern of behavior and a healing or religious rite. Anne thought the events of the last week satisfied both meanings. The subsequent ceremonies followed the same routine: The Iranian doctor picked her up at 5:30; they made small talk and then trudged out to the sweat lodge. Anne was confused and couldn't completely silence her inner scoffer, but some things had changed. She'd slept better the last three nights than she had in three years. In addition, she hadn't had a drink...or even wanted one.

Most importantly, she thought Carmine had smiled at her at the close of each ceremony. Still, this was all beyond the pale, challenging the foundation of her rigidly rational, condescending mentality. If this madness really helped her brother, then it made a mockery of everything she'd believed and held in contempt.

This final ceremony was supposed to go through the night. She forced her mocking cynic back into its compartment.

On the drive over, Lia further explained how the myth and the hero's quest were supposed to link everything together. "Clearly, this whole ceremony is based on traditional Native symbolism. The story heroes are figures, usually guys, of course, who were initially lazy or careless. Sounds about right, huh? The kind of people we think of as losers. But they're transformed through an unanticipated event that leads to the death of the old self and the renewal of a new one. You probably think this really sounds crazy, but we've come this far, right? These myths have been the backbone of these chants for longer than we'll ever know. Tonight, it all ends, and then...we'll see."

Anne thought she heard a trace of skepticism in Lia's voice. But by now, it was clear how much she revered the old woman.

Lia shared with Anne the myth about a sleeping boy.

Anne uncharacteristically acknowledged, "That sounds like a good one for my brother."

TEARS ARE ONLY WATER

"All the chanting you hear links back to this story, which connects to your brother. This is all integrated into the paintings and songs. On Monday, the rituals had to do with purification. The paintings each night identified the powers that would heal Carmine. It's all very spiritual. Tonight, Dr Hazel will take into herself all the bad parts that have been causing your brother's illness or keeping him asleep to his own mind. She will perform a prayer to release him from all these forces that have been summoned over the past week, so he can return to a, let's say, normal state of being. So, that's what we're hoping for. He'll probably be discharged next week. And sad to say, this is most likely Dr Hazel's last healing ceremony."

These last pieces of news came as a surprising appendage. Anne wanted nothing more than to get her brother out of this place and take care of his legal charges. Still, it had been several days since she'd thought about Deputy Kitts or Dihn's murder. That nightmare seemed distant. When they returned to Denver, she would find a good lawyer to get this matter settled. But Anne had also heard what Lia said about this being Lukachunai's last ceremony. There was no time to ask why. They had arrived.

Seated in the sweat lodge for the last time, Anne sipped hot coffee and huddled beneath her blanket. The fifth night was the coldest. She felt she'd been in a strange trance for the last week or maybe even month. Could she have been sleepwalking through much of *her* life? Suddenly she thought about Keanu Reeves in *The Matrix*, where all those people thought they were living in reality, but it was really a computer simulation. Reality was actually darker and more dangerous. She tried to ignore a thought on the edge of her mind: Had she been like the sleeping boy trying not to look too closely at her darker compartments, and had she shut her eyes to what Noa had tried so hard to get her to see?

The healer was dressed in white tonight. She looked gaunt and pale, no doubt exhausted by five intense nights of chanting, singing, and praying. The attentive giant washed Carmine's chest, neck, arms, and legs and returned to his corner. Lukachunai's singing and chanting grew louder and continued for several hours. With no warning, her brother began to retch and vomit. Instinctively, Anne tried to reach out to him, but Lia gently held her back.

Despite the vomiting, the ceremony continued as the healer painted dark rings around Carmine's weary eyes. Anne thought about the stages Lia had mentioned--evocation, transformation, and release. Lukachu-nai's voice became strained, her intonation raspy and harsh. She used a large eagle's feather to brush smoke from the fire toward her brother. Carmine embraced it as it wafted around his arms, then his chest, neck, and finally over the top of his head. The drumbeat grew louder. Lia's eyes closed. Anne thought she saw blood on the healer's hands as she cut pieces of sage and cedar branches and placed them into the fire. The flames intensified in unison with the transcendent spirit in the sweat lodge.

Sweat flowed from her brother's face. The healer's hair was drenched as if she had plunged her head into a pond of water. She stood, pale and unsteady, chanting her urgent plea for Carmine to awaken more force-fully and rapidly than before. She pulled him to his feet and then collapsed to her knees like a puppet whose strings were cut. With the final thunderous beat of the drum, her brother wailed as if trying to match the thunder.

The ceremony was over.

Lia motioned to Anne that it was time to leave. "He will rest all day, as we should. We'll know more by tomorrow." Lia pulled at Anne's sleeve, "We need to go...*now*."

The healer remained on the ground. Anne looked back at her brother. He still looked small and thin, but something was different. As exhausted as he was, Carmine, gaunt and pale, held his head high as if searching for something overhead.

Dawn lit the eastern sky. The air was crisp and clean. The two walked briskly up the path as their breath hung in the air. Still dazed by the power of the last chant, Anne didn't notice the stirring and whispering in the bushes to the left of the sweat lodge.

"Did you get that on tape?"

"Oh yeah, the kill shot. We got more than enough to drive a spike through her heart."

Chapter 37

Balancing The Books

Monday April 7th, 8:00 AM

The day of Carmine's discharge came more quickly than expected. As Lia predicted, Carmine slept soundly through the entire weekend after the final healing ceremony while Anne dozed on and off in her hotel room.

On Monday morning, she was awakened by a phone call.

"Aw, come on, Dr Hazel, you couldn't wait til at least 9:00? How's Carm--"

"Oh, I'm sorry...Dr Schivalone? This is Miranda Morales from the Director's Office at CMHI-P. We're hoping you can meet with the Director and your brother's new doctor at 10:00 this morning. It's about his discharge today and...the events that came to our attention at the end of the week."

Discharge now? New doctor? What the hell? After a pause, she agreed to come in at 10:00.

Sipping weak coffee in the Director's waiting room, Anne wondered why the head honcho wanted to see her and why Lukachunai herself-- or at least Lia--hadn't called. Her thoughts were interrupted when a smiling man in an ill-fitting suit opened the door.

"Oh, Dr Schivalone, what a pleasure it is to meet you. I'm Dr Baron Buffo, the Director of the Mental Health Institute." He gestured behind him. And this is Dr Oakley, Carmen's psychiatrist. So good of you to come in on such short notice. We've got your brother in the office and would like to discuss his discharge and other matters of mutual concern."

She followed him into the office where Carmine sat looking small and out of place in an overstuffed chair. Next to him sat an officious-looking nurse who held a large file on her lap.

"Carmie, how...how are you feeling?" Anne blurted out.

He nodded and looked like he was about to answer when the nurse interrupted. "Hello, I'm Mrs Astracides, the Charge Nurse on your brother's ward. He slept through most of the weekend, but I think he's doing quite well on his new medication regimen, wouldn't you say Carmine?"

Oakley interrupted and spoke in an annoying monotone.

"Your brother is ready to be discharged. He does have this legal matter to clear up, but his civil confinement here is no longer needed. Since we do not see him as an imminent danger or a flight risk, the sheriff's department in Arapahoe County has notified us that he can return there on his own recognizance. In fact, you may drive him back there today."

God help his wife sitting across from him at the dinner table or, God forbid, lying next to him in bed.

Nevertheless, Anne was taken off guard. "Today? Really?" *Why this sudden sprint to the finish line?*

She asked what had happened to Lukachunai, and they shifted uncomfortably in their chairs. The nurse mumbled something about her taking emergency leave. When Anne inquired about Dr Dhikavi, the nurse said she was also unavailable.

Oakley excused himself and said Carmine's prescriptions would be brought to the ward. The nurse said that Anne could come for him at 1:00 PM. As the nurse left, a grim-looking man, whose complexion was indistinguishable from the matte of his gray suit, entered and sat at the conference table behind them.

Buffo returned to his desk and signaled to the gray man who then pulled a file from his briefcase and handed it to Buffo.

"This is Mr Samuels, from our legal department."

The grim looking man explained that they had been informed about a serious breach in clinical protocol that, unfortunately, involved her brother's care. He coughed. "It appears that unproven and...possibly harmful practices which have been banned at our facility were foisted on your brother without our knowledge or the legally mandated informed consent."

Director Buffo leaned over his desk––close enough so Anne could smell the stale aroma of morning cigar on his breath. He took his handkerchief and mopped beads of perspiration from his brow.

"Dr Schivalone, we only want what's best for our patients and are concerned that your brother could have been harmed by these unorthodox practices. For this reason, we are prepared to offer a settlement to resolve whatever untoward effects that may result. Of course, there will be a nondisclosure statement to ensure that this matter is handled as discreetly as possible. The clinical staff and Dr Oakley assured us that your brother has responded well to our milieu treatment and medication regimen. We're all very fond of Carlos here and have every confidence that his recovery will continue...but want to provide a payment to help with any future treatment needs...should they arise."

He signaled to Samuels, who handed Anne an envelope. She opened it and pulled out a check made out to Carmen Luedke. She gasped at the substantial five-figure amount.

"Oh my.... I'm not sure I.... Perhaps we should consult our own attorney and take some time to process all of this but––."

But Carmine cut her off mid-sentence and reached for the check. He studied it and looked up at the director. *Buffo*....He had seen his name before on a Tawney-Banks invoice. The numbers didn't add up.

TEARS ARE ONLY WATER

"My name is Carmine, not Carmen, not Carlos...and, uh, I'm the b... bookkeeper.... I know the numbers in calculating accrued legal reserves in m-m-malpractice cases. Respectfully, this amount is quite low... $250,000 is fair compensation and will b-balance the books." He shrugged. "Oh, and I remember n-names. That's it."

Stunned, Anne stared at her brother....For the first time in her life, she was speechless. *Really? $250,000? Balancing the books? I remember names? WTF?*

The lawyer began to protest. Buffo silenced him with a glare and instructed him to issue another check with...a corrected name and a corrected amount.

And that was it.

Chapter 38

Kelly, Casey, Bowman, & Young

Wednesday, April 9th – Thursday, April 24th

Anne was reeling after their shockingly lucrative meeting in the Director's office. During their drive back to her hotel, she wondered if she had hugely underestimated her brother, who had always seemed remote and disconnected from reality. *Carmie negotiating three times the settlement that had been offered? Who is this person?*

After a day of rest, they would leave Pueblo, spend a few weeks in Denver, then return to the East Coast. Anne had put a rental deposit on a rundown townhouse on the outskirts of Denver. The first order of business was to clear up Carmine's legal charges. Then she had to decide whether to return to Amherst, swallow her pride, and curtsey to the twit Holmes or to sever her ties with the university.

Carmine had barely said a word since they left the meeting. He slept through the days and responded to Anne's questions with short answers and wordless shrugs. She'd grown weary of trying to engage with him and remembered the relief she felt decades earlier when she left home for Choate. It hadn't just been the need to escape her self-absorbed mother and disgusting stepfather, it was the loneliness she felt in her brother's presence.

Her GPS took them to the shabby townhouse that would be their home for the next couple of weeks. She needed to contact the sheriff about resolving Carmine's charges. Surely, they would acknowledge that her brother had been drugged and set up. She hoped that there would be a plea deal with an offer of probation, and that they would agree to transfer his case to the Northampton District Court in Amherst.

They unloaded the car and entered a cramped living room with tattered furniture. Anne held her nose and began to tidy up. It was easy to see why the place was cheap and rented weekly.

Carmine found a bedroom and shut the door behind him. Later, when he emerged to shower, Anne peeked inside the sparsely furnished room and thought it looked as barren as his life. As she was about to leave, she noticed a feather hanging from the ceiling.

The next day, Anne went to a nearby Safeway for groceries and bought a Denver Post. Back in the townhouse, she poured a mug of coffee and started to take a sip when her eyes were drawn to the headline, "Local Company, T-B CFC investigated for racketeering." She dropped her mug when she read the names of board members listed as persons of interest––LuCinda P. Pelcovey, Roger Jonas, MD, and Judge Julius Rainsford. She was startled to see Dr Baron Buffo listed as the new chairman of the board. *"I remember names. This will balance the books."* *My God, Carmie.*

Anne thought about Kitts. Why hadn't the deputy returned her calls? While the previous week in Pueblo had been a blur, she'd left several messages for Kitts. Each time, her calls went to voicemail. Anne called Burwinkle. A receptionist with a disinterested nasal voice answered.

"The sheriff isn't available to take your call. Give me your name and number and I'll have someone contact you."

"No. Not satisfactory, Miss. Please connect me with Deputy Kitts right away. I need to speak with someone to clear up charges concerning my brother, Carmine Lued––"

"She is not available either, ma'am. Neither the deputy or the sheriff can help you. Best I can do is take your––"

Anne slammed down the phone. "Bitch."

She hadn't heard Carmine walk up behind her.

"Guess it's t-time to get a lawyer, Sister. That's it."

They looked through the phone book together, calling firm after firm where they navigated menus, were put on hold, and spoke with annoying receptionists or paralegal gatekeepers. Her patience wearing thin, Anne placed one last call to Kelly, Casey, Bowman, & Young Esq. Attorneys at Law. She was surprised when someone answered on the second ring.

"Good afternoon, This is Nicolas Kelly speaking. How may I help you?"

Anne explained that she and her brother had several legal matters to discuss, starting with resolving Carmine's assault charges. "Oh, and I read something about an investigation into a fishing company called Tawney-Banks that might have set my brother up for the charges he's facing. So, I want to hold this company responsible, two of its board members in particular––a LuCinda Pelcovey and Dr Roger Jonas. I think they drugged and framed my brother. They have caused enormous pain and suffering to us both."

The attorney said, "Yeah, there's a lot of buzz about Tawney-Banks these days. Why don't you come in this afternoon."

Kelly, a bearded man in his 30's, greeted them with a broad smile. The office was small and simple, nothing like the ornate, walnut-paneled suites of top legal firms. There was an older secretary hunched over her keyboard and another man sitting at a desk in a side office.

Anne asked about Casey, Bowman, & Young.

"I'm the managing partner. The others have retired, but we plan to expand, isn't that right, Dorine?"

The secretary uttered a disinterested response. "Sure, Nick. If you say so."

Inside Kelly's small office, Anne laid out their twofold agenda: Deal with Carmine's legal problems and take on Tawney-Banks. Carmine sat and stared out the window.

TEARS ARE ONLY WATER

Kelly listened and took notes. "Considering what you're saying happened to Carmine here, we'll need to speak with someone in the District Attorney's office about his assault charges. I used to work there and have plenty of contacts. As to this other matter with Tawney-Banks, I think a lot of pieces are starting to come together. Did you hear about the killing of that CBI agent a few weeks ago? T-B CFC has left some huge fingerprints. Oh, and in case you didn't know, that sheriff from Arapahoe County––the guy that killed the agent––was at the center of all this."

Anne lost her breath. "What? The sheriff?"

Kelly picked up his phone. "Yeah, can you come in here?" The man they'd seen in the side office entered and took a seat. "This is Lucius Griswald. We call him Lucky G. He's our investigator."

Anne was about to make a sarcastic comment when Carmine spoke for the first time. "Tawney-B-Banks was one of my companies. Their numbers wouldn't add up. They b-blamed me. I want to sue them to hell. All of them. That's it."

Things happened quickly. The following week, Anne and Carmine met with an assistant DA, a former colleague of Kelly's, about Carmine's charges. Given the link to the Tawney-Banks scandal and evidence that he had been drugged, along with hospital reports that he was not a danger to himself or others, the DA was willing to reduce the charges to a misdemeanor Class C Assault. No jail time but a year's probation and community service.

Anne blurted out, "Great news! We'll need to see about getting his probation and community service transferred to Northampton District Court where we'll be relocating. It will be best for my brother to be with me."

The assistant DA was about to speak when Carmine cut in, "No. Not gonna happen. I-I'm staying here."

When Anne tried to protest, he held up his hand and said, "This is where I live. That's it."

Over the next several days, Anne tried to get Carmine to come to his senses and return to Amherst with her. Each time, Carmine shook his head and walked away. She decided to let it go for now and concentrate on the lawsuit against Tawney-Banks.

Over the next two weeks, Lucky G unearthed notebooks full of material on T-B CFC. News broke about the indictments of L.P. Pelcovey and the judge. LuCinda's picture was in the paper, and there were news clips of her walking with her attorney to the courthouse. She was still wearing her neck collar. According to her lawyer, Ms Pelcovey claimed she was an innocent victim of a deranged psychopath who was fooling the authorities.

The shocker was that one of the persons of interest was cooperating with the prosecutors. It was none other than Roger Jonas, who named Pelcovey and the CFO of Tawney-Banks, Misha Horvath, as key players in the scheme to drug and frame Carmine. Jonas began cooperating after a key witness from the hospital came forward with information about a conversation he'd overheard between Jonas and Horvath. The witness swore he'd heard Jonas tell the CFO that Carmine would be seen as a psychotic bookkeeper who was skimming funds from the companies Shrenklin's was managing. The witness was identified as an intern named Kaspar Kashimi.

Jonas went on record about Pelcovey drugging Carmine, knowing he would pass out and give Horvath time to make changes on his computer, showing that the bookkeeper had embezzled $250,000 from T-B CFC and deposited it in an offshore account. They hadn't counted on Carmine's attacking LuCinda, which strengthened their contention that he was mentally ill, dangerous, and needed immediate involuntary confinement. Burwinkle and Rainsford ensured a quick commitment to the state hospital.

TEARS ARE ONLY WATER

Anne scoffed at how a lowly intern's testimony had gotten the almighty Jonas to flip and supply ample evidence against Pelcovey and Tawney-Banks. But the announcement that the doctor would have to surrender his medical license was her sweetest revenge.

Details about the scandal appeared in the daily paper and national news. A link between Tawney-Banks and the director of the state hospital resulted in Dr Baron Buffo's swift resignation. Stories suggested that his stepping down as director of CMHI-P was the least of his worries as he was being accused of profiting from T-B's criminal enterprises.

One afternoon when Anne was napping and Carmine had gone out for a walk, she was awakened by a knock at the front door. *Damn, Carmie's left without his key again.* She got up and peered through the window to see Lucky standing with a short, dark-haired woman.

"Hey Anne, sorry to drop by like this but there's someone I think you should talk to."

He introduced the woman as Det. Jodie Griggs from the Denver Police Department.

Anne led them inside as Carmine walked up to the townhouse. Lucky patted him on the back. "Hey Carmine, got someone who wants to talk to you."

Over the next two hours, the four sat around the dining room table. Griggs pulled out a file and said she had information about what had happened to Burwinkle and Kitts.

With all that was happening with Carmine's charges and the lawsuit, Anne hadn't thought much about Kitts. She figured that the case had been transferred to higher authorities and that she'd gone on that vacation she was talking about. Plus, she was angry that Kitts had dropped her. Anne knew they weren't friends. Still, she had lowered her guard and felt a connection with the deputy, only to be reminded that trusting strangers is risky.

"You apparently haven't been following the news about a string of homicides we've had around here that we think are linked to the fishing company. We have one woman in custody but think a trigger man is still at large." Griggs spoke as she pulled out two pictures from her file.

Anne immediately recognized the loud woman with tattoos who had keyed her car at Bennigan's. "Oh my God. This crazy woman was following me."

Carmine spoke for the first time. "I-I know them. I think they were following me too."

Lucky said, "Wait, there's a lot more going on than just you two being followed, right Jodie?"

"Yep, we think they were involved in two homicides, maybe more. We've been looking into them for a while. There's been a task force investigating Tawney-Banks for over a year now and these two characters have been ID'd as suspects in a couple of other shootings. We think this guy killed a lab tech at MCA and a computer hacker named Carl Carothers. I think you might know him."

Carmine sat motionless. He looked at the others, slumped, and buried his head in his hands.

Because they'd spoken so little since his release from the hospital and with the flurry of activity around the lawsuit, Anne wasn't sure if Carmine knew what had happened to Dihn. She placed her hand on her brother's. "I'm so sorry Carmie, I––"

He looked up at her. "It wasn't y-your fault, Anne."

She saw water pooling in his eyes and squeezed his hand. "I met him. He was your true friend, Carmie."

The group took a break. Griggs and Lucky talked and made some calls. After 20 minutes, they sat down again.

"Kitts and Burwinkle," said Griggs. "I guess you don't know the full story?" She laid it all out––the investigation by Agent Micky Aarveen and his visit to Kitts on March 27th.

Anne was stunned as Griggs told about Aarveen's meeting with the deputy and how Burwinkle had shown up and killed the agent in front of Kitts.

"The sheriff was in on it all along––had been on Tawney-Banks' payroll for some time. He was about to kill Deputy Kitts too, but I guess her bird attacked him, and the fucker dropped dead of a heart attack. Yeah, can you believe that? A parrot attacking a crooked sheriff? This was the last thing Kitts needed, you know. Sad part was she really trusted the guy. So, let me tell you what happened to Nicola."

Chapter 39

Must Mean Somethin'

One Month Later....Monday, May 26, 10:00 AM

Anne waited impatiently for him to finish his shower and polish his shoes. *Oh my God, he spends way too much time polishing those awful shoes.*

"Come on, Carmine! For the love of God, you're such a snail. We can't keep her waiting."

She paced the living room, reflexively reaching for a can of Febreze and dousing the room with a thick spray to cover up stale odors that had seeped into the threadbare furniture. Anne knew something about covering up the unpleasant. She had hidden stench from the past with expensive perfumes, designer clothes, advanced degrees, and affected speech. Since the surreal week in Pueblo, she'd had too many ruminations about her early years, which pried open rusted compartments with their foul odors from the past. *Don't go there. Not today.*

Their time in Denver had begun to feel stale. Thick red tape prevented a speedy disposition of Carmine's charges and the arrangement of his probation. Slower yet was the case against Tawney-Banks. *You can sue the shit out of someone, but the wheels of justice moved like a slug.* Kelly had told them that the case would likely take over a year to come to trial and that they should feel free to leave town during all the discovery and whatnot.

Anne looked around the living room. Her eyes landed on her suitcase by the door gathering dust and stopped at another eagle feather Carmine had hung from the broken ceiling fan. When she questioned him about the feathers' significance, he shrugged and turned away.

She hadn't decided what she would do about Amherst. The thought of groveling to Holmes gave her hives. Maybe she would take a break from teaching or try to teach just one class at the community college. Staying too long in Denver wasn't just about Carmine's probation, their lawsuit, or her uncertainty about the future. Anne hadn't entirely accepted that he would be staying behind. She wanted to escape from him but wasn't ready to leave him again. Carmine would remain in Denver doing his community service and living off the hush money from CMHI-P. She had reluctantly accepted $50,000, which Carmine insisted she use to get her life together. "That's it," he had said. End of discussion.

She was startled when he appeared behind her. "Come on, Sister. W...w-e don't want to be late."

It took about 25 minutes without traffic. They sat silently, and her mind began to wander.

Carmine seemed different. He was still a man of few words, but they had actually shared a few moments of genuine connection. On their walks together, he pointed out birds whose songs he recognized. They laughed while recalling stories about the Bilker and their mother's dreadful poetry. One evening, they wept together after he mentioned their father. The day after their shared tears, they drove to Boulder and took a long hike.

Fighting back more tears, Anne said, "I abandoned you. I just couldn't stay in that house, and you...you wouldn't....But I left you with them. I've been an awful, controlling, and know-it-all bitch of a sister. I'm so, so sorry." She broke down and sobbed when Carmine scooted closer and gave her a long, comforting hug.

They hadn't talked about what had happened during the nights of his healing ceremony. She had so many questions. What was it like for him? Who was that colossal man beating the drum? And what had become of

Hazel Lukachunai, who vanished as if she never existed? Maybe it had all been a dream after all. The Navajo healer had been canceled––fallen off the grid once more. When Anne made inquiries, no one would say what had happened to her. Carmine was not ready to talk about anything related to the hospital, especially the events of his last week there. Like his responses to her questions about his eagle feathers, he went dark and grew distant whenever she brought it up.

Anne thought about returning to Amherst. She rehearsed calling Noa about meeting for coffee or drinks. Even though she'd had only a few glasses of wine over the last month, Noa would still think she was a drunk, so going to their wine bar wasn't a good idea.

She even thought about phoning her old therapist, Salma Kahn, who now would rival Lukachunai in age, but Anne wasn't ready for anything like that. Reaching out to Salma, if she was still alive, would further chip away at the crumbling edifice of cynicism and denial that had insulated and sustained her.

Still, she couldn't shake the dramatic and curious week in the wooden hut. Like vapors that hung in the air, present only in the slight haze or subtle scent they left behind, traces of the healing ceremony lingered. It was as if both siblings had entered a trance and emerged different from who they had been. Like both had been teleported somewhere and returned, but their molecules had been slightly rearranged. This idea embarrassed her, but she couldn't shake it.

Her life had changed since she'd boarded the plane to Denver that March morning. Aside from feeling her molecules had been jostled, Anne felt her relationships and professional life lay in ruins. Not only had she been dumped by her girlfriend and placed on administrative leave by the university, but the publisher canceled the contract for her *Trick or Treatment* book because Anne hadn't met their deadlines. She had thought about a new book and pitched it to her agent. Anne had thought of a title: "Finding the Key to Hidden Compartments––When to Open Them and When to Let Them Be," but her agent poo-pooed the idea.

TEARS ARE ONLY WATER

"Honey, you've got a brand. You're the brash, in-your-face slayer of all things Freudian. Any talk of opening compartments now is a non-starter. Let's keep them closed, shall we? And talk about another book attacking the billion-dollar pharmaceutical industry. That'll sell, hon."

They arrived at their destination, parked, and walked through the large glass doors of the Rocky Mountain Regional VA Medical Center.

It had been three weeks since Jodie Griggs told them what had happened to Kitts. When Burwinkle shot the agent and then aimed his gun at her, she lost it. Yes, the bird attacked the sheriff, who died on the spot, but the deputy had a severe flashback and then disappeared in a fugue state. A neighbor called about hearing a gunshot, but when the cops arrived, they found two dead guys and a crazed bird standing on top of one of them. No Kitts. She had left the house with her hunting knife and Glock. A massive search turned up nothing for days. They found her in the foothills a week later, 25 miles from her house. She had not slept and had eaten only what she could scavenge. Kitts was severely dehydrated, mute, and had a wild look. After being treated in the acute care ward, she was transferred to the PTSD unit at the VA.

The detective had been looking after Langston and visiting Kitts daily. Jodie said that Nicola was finally ready to see them.

The elevator took them to the 8th floor, where they entered the doors marked PTSD and Trauma Rehab Unit. Kitts was waiting for them in the community room.

Anne was struck by how the deputy seemed smaller than the bronzed statue she'd encountered that first night--how her "tears are only water" toughness had softened. Kitts was sitting by herself, looking out the window. Dressed crisply in Marine fatigues and combat boots--a requirement for patients on the ward--she had braided one side of her hair with brightly colored beads. Kitts was always a conundrum. What you see is not always what you get. Anne remembered how she was initially struck when she first walked into Kitts' living room by the incongruity between the combat medals and chiseled biceps, the pistol and menacing bird, versus all those scented candles and Monet prints on her walls. Anne had shaped her image of Kitts to shore up her own brittleness, never seeing the whole truth behind the cliché.

Kitts brightened up when she saw them enter. "Well, if it isn't the Bobbsey Twins, Sis and Books."

She eyed them as they cautiously approached. "I won't bite you. It ain't like I got a disease that you're gonna catch." She stood and gave Anne and Carmine a hug. "Man, it's good to see you. Yeah, some crazy ass shit, huh? Jodie's been filling me in on you two and what y'all got going on with the Tawney-Banks shit. And Mama Lu? Sheeet. That one didn't surprise me, but this other crapola? Man."

Anne hadn't been sure about the visit, but Kitts seemed glad to see them. The professor reminded her of Dihn's murder and Burwinkle's betrayal, but the deputy still couldn't talk much about that.

Anne spoke first. "Well, you're looking good, Nicola. Yes, it's all been incredibly insane. Uh, I mean everything that happened with Jonas and Pelcovey. We couldn't have done any of this without--"

Carmine interrupted. "I'd probably be dead if it hadn't been for you. I n-never thanked you D-Deputy Kitts. Really. That's it."

"Well, I'll be. You can talk Books, after all. Damn boy, good to hear you speak up. And you're welcome. Was just doin' my job. But I'd be lying if I said it's been easy. Been pretty rough, you know, not dealing with your shit. Like my counselor, Jerome, said in group today, 'You fools can try to run from your pasts, but it's faster than you all, and it's gonna catch you and punch you in the gut. Count on that. Just a matter of time.' Well, shit. It sure as hell chased me down and beat the crap out of me."

Anne repeated that they couldn't have done any of this without her. That Carmine would probably still be in the state hospital. "And with those killers out there stalking us, I would have gotten killed and ended up as fertilizer for your garden."

Kitts laughed. "No shit, Professor, they would have killed you...if I didn't shoot you first."

After an awkward silence, Nicola spoke in a softer tone. "Man, I thought I was done with all that shit. Had left it over there. Don't mean nothin', just like my pops had taught me. But I tell you, that shit just ain't true. Should've listened more to my auntie instead of those damned old marines in the house."

They sat quietly as Nicola began to cry. "Ever tell you I had a little brother too?"

Carmine leaned in and said, "B-Blue. Right? You said his name in the car when you drove me to Pueblo."

Anne offered Kleenex from her purse while Nicola told them about what had happened to Blue. "You know, Books, when I first picked you up that day, you kinda reminded me of him."

Carmine blushed, shrugged, and squirmed in his seat. "T-thank you for your kindness to me, Deputy Kitts, but I don't think that's fair to Blue."

Kitts laughed. "Damn, so he speaks again, and he's funny too. Sounds like Books has finally found his voice. But don't put yourself down like that. You're a good dude, far as I can see."

Then Kitts shared the story of her first encounter with Anne. "You're fully aware, little brother, that this sister of yours is certifiable. I have never met such a tight-assed kook, but I love ya, Annie."

Kitts told them how she'd found Dihn. "Sorry, man. I know he was your friend." Nicola saw the tears in Carmine's eyes and brought up Mama Lu to lighten the mood.

When Anne asked about Burwinkle, Kitts said she couldn't go there. "Oh, I've cried plenty about that one. But not today."

Visiting hours were almost over. Anne asked Kitts what she planned to do. "Gonna stick around here for a bit longer? You told me you knew all this shit about graduate schools. I think you owe that to me."

"Sure. Maybe we can talk about some of those schools when you get out. You serious about leaving the police?"

"I'm still thinking about that. Not sure what I'm gonna do. Graduate school costs a boatload, you know, upwards of 100K, and last I checked, my dogwoods don't got money growing on them. But Langston and me will figure that one out. And what about you, Sis?"

Anne told her about their plans. "Carmine has to stay here for the next year while on probation. As for me, I'm not sure what comes next. I will probably return to teaching. Might try to teach at the community college. Could write another crap book. Maybe I'll start a garden. I have to find something meaningful to do with my life. Who knows? Because I sure don't."

"Well, Anne, you know that sounds pretty good to me, finding somethin' that must mean somethin'. I think we both got some catching up to do with all that."

She turned to Carmine. "And Books, glad you're not in jail, boy. No, really. Hey, I remember when I dropped you off at the hospital and fed you that BS about how they'd help you see what was wrong with you, and then you asked me in that quiet mumbly little ass way of yours, 'Who will help you see?' Yeah, it took me a while before I was ready to see. You know, I'm trying to get right with all those ghosts I've been running from. But I never said thanks for that. So...thank you, Carmine."

Chapter 40

Colorful Constants

Five Years Later....Wednesday, May 15th, 2019 6:00 AM

He always loved walking and listening to the sounds of nature. May was his favorite month. If someone asked, "Why May?" Carmine would say he enjoyed everything, especially the sunrises. The world felt new again like the Earth was giving everything a second chance. Between the spring's chill and the summer's heat, May air made breathing easier.

While walking this morning, he remembered he hadn't called his sister. Anne bought a small house in Upstate New York. After the Tawney-Banks settlement last year, money wasn't a problem for either of them. She never returned to Amherst and stopped teaching altogether. But she was writing her memoir. Anne had a new partner, Katie something, and seemed as happy as she could be. Carmine was relieved because she had seemed lost and lonely for most of her life. They didn't talk much, but he promised to call with an update on his exhibit and interview with Taos Magazine and the reception next month. Not surprisingly, Anne was most impressed that he was being interviewed for a feature article.

Anne never accepted that he wanted to stay in Colorado. She was even more confused--no, upset--that he moved back to Pueblo after she left. He could still hear the disapproval in her voice when he told her.

"You're doing what? Why on God's earth would you return to that hell-hole? What is it, Carmie, Stockholm Syndrome? I just don't get it. But, in truth, I've never really understood you."

J. HERMAN KLEIGER

Anne persisted with her interrogation. Carmine, never a match for her polemical skills, did as he always had done: Remained silent and ended the conversation.

But he wasn't sure why he'd moved back to Pueblo. He knew it felt right, like something he had to do. With the money he'd gotten from the hospital, he had enough to live on while completing his community service. Getting the lawyers to transfer his case to the Pueblo County Probation Department was easy. They were laid back and gave him names of places he could complete his mandatory community service. He didn't know why, but he chose Sangre de Cristo Arts Center. Little did he know where that choice would lead or who it would lead him to.

As he waited for his big interview today, he wondered where the last five years had gone. As far as his tormented relationship with sleep, medication helped some, but he still got sleepy in the afternoon. The good news was he hadn't had cutouts for a while, though sleeping through the night was still a problem. Carmine didn't dream much, though he sometimes saw the woman looking in his window. He'd fought against accepting that this was only an ancient memory fragment of his mother trying to find him. For a long time, he'd privately clung to the belief, no, hope, that Elizabeth Covington was still looking for him. However, he accepted he was holding onto pieces of the past. But he hadn't completely let go of Elizabeth. *Maybe she really was out there...searching for me.*

When Anne left, she made Carmine promise to stay in touch with Kitts. But it only happened a couple of times that first year. He took the bus up to Denver, and they met for coffee. Deputy Kitts was still in group therapy then and hadn't decided what to do with her life. Carmine thought that when she looked at him, Nicola was really seeing her brother, Blue. He could tell that she was still drowning in all the pain she'd endured. He felt, in his heart, that he owed her. She'd seen something in him others hadn't. He knew she was a deeply good person who was stuck in her pain. Carmine wanted to help her get free, so he sent her, by certified mail, a cashier's check for $150,000. The donor was anonymous. That was four years ago. Kitts would be in town next month. He was looking forward to seeing her.

TEARS ARE ONLY WATER

. . .

Carmine walked to Gus's Tavern, his favorite breakfast place in town. He was early, and Noni was always late. He ordered tea and had started to write in his journal when he saw her walk through the door.

"Hey, you, sup? Been waiting long? Ooh, I see you've got your journal. Have you started it yet? You should write your memoir, you know, Carm."

Carmine stood to hug her, then fell silent....

"Hey, dude, you're in yer head again. Come out, come out, Carmine."

She was excited about the show and his big interview today. They had gone out shopping for clothes last week to make sure he looked sharp for this important event. Top of the list was a blue blazer and a pair of brown wingtips, which Carmine polished as soon as he took them out of their box.

"You nervous about all this attention, you know, having to talk about yourself? Cuz it's okay if you are. Just speak from your heart. Oh, and remember, ya still got me, Carm."

Before he could answer, she reminded him they were celebrating with Roo, Max, Sloanie, and the Brookster at Parise's tonight for karaoke. The exhibit and interview didn't bother him as much as the thought of karaoke. These people were Noni's posse, so he guessed they were his too. All he knew was that it had taken four years for him to agree to get up on stage, and tonight was the night.

She always ordered bubble tea, which she sipped slowly and never finished. Talking was more important to Noni Kwon than drinking or eating.

"Hey Carm, did you ever think that maybe you're on the spectrum, something like Asperger's? Cuz if you are, that's cool. Betcha didn't know that Rena, Margaret Ann, and Jess Hooper say they aren't neurotypical either."

After a long pause, he told her he wasn't sure, but that others had thought he might be.

Carmine shrugged. "D-don't know. Just know I always felt different. That's all."

"But listen, that's okay. I might be too, Carmine. Point is, I could give a crap if you are. Just wanted you to know that. Oh, and don't forget, we're going bike shopping this weekend. I think it's time you got back on that horse again, don't you?"

She took another sip of her drink and said she had to run. A kiss on the cheek and she was off.

"Dude, You'll be great today."

Noni had lived in Pueblo most of her life. If it were the '60s, she would have been a hippie. She seemed to have a new tattoo or piercing every time he saw her. She practically had to drag Carmine to the Dragon's Lair for his first tattoo--an eagle's feather on his right forearm. Their friends thought that was cool--everyone likes eagle feathers. But his second trip to the tattoo parlor freaked them out when he had them engrave $e^{i\pi} + 1 = 0$ on the underside of his forearm. No matter how normal Carmine tried to act, he couldn't escape how different he was.

Kathleen Corvus and her crew from Taos Magazine had set up in the exhibit area. She was a pro, friendly and personable enough to put Carmine at ease. The interview was scheduled for one-hour. It lasted two.

She began with "Okay, Carmine, I always like to ask people for three words that best describe their life, now and in the past."

Without his usual pause, Carmine blurted out, "WAKE UP. WAKE THE HELL UP! Wait, am I-I allowed to say that? And sorry, that was a little loud, huh? Oh, you asked for three words to describe me in the past, and I technically gave you six. So, sorry for that too."

TEARS ARE ONLY WATER

"No worries. Hey, just relax, Carmine. Now, I think people want to know when all this began. You know, like the year you started doing all of this," Corvus asked, motioning to the walls.

"The year? .....I guess that would b-be, um, 2014. That's it."

"2014? Interesting. Tell us what you were like in 2014 and before that and then what changed."

"I-I was different. Mostly alone, kind of living in a box. I thought a lot but didn't feel much or touch anyone. I guess you could say I was drowning. People didn't even know my name. They just called me the b-bookkeeper."

The time melted away as Carmine walked her down the strange path he'd been on for the last five years. He held back little.

They had been talking for almost an hour when Corvus closed her notebook and suggested they take a short break.

He felt oddly invigorated from telling his story. A crowd had gathered around them.

After a 15-minute break, the interview continued. "Well, that's quite a backstory, Carmine. I see why you chose 2014. A mind-blowing year, right?" Motioning to the exhibit, she asked, "Is that when all this began?"

Carmine told her that when he'd started his community service at the art center, they had him moving boxes. He said he enjoyed the physical labor because he didn't have to think about things.

"One d-day, I moved some boxes out of their accountant's office. Her name was Laura Jane, but most people called her LJ. She did all the books for the center. I could tell she was having trouble with the program she was using. I told her I'd done some accounting before, was pretty good with computers, and could help."

"Ah, always the bookkeeper, eh? What happened next, Carmine?"

"I r-remember she rolled her eyes and said, 'Okay, so everyone's an expert now. Well, be my guest.' Her mistakes were easy to pick up, and she was impressed. She asked if I could help with odds and ends around her office. I even helped LJ with her taxes—they were way overdue."

Pointing to the paintings, Corvus asked, "But how did that get you to start doing all *this*?" "Uh, she, LJ, sent me over to the art studio to pick up invoices for their supplies. That's the day I met the art teacher."

Carmine glanced at the crowd and saw her smiling at him.

"Her name is Noni. She was between classes and asked if I was into art. I said I didn't know but that I saw c-colors. She thought that was weird but cool, even though I didn't explain it too well. So, one day, Noni sat me in front of a c-canvas with all sorts of paints and trays of beads, sand, and feathers, and said, 'Just let yourself go. See if you can channel your inner mind with all those colors you see, but don't overthink it, Carman.' She calls me that sometimes. I told her I couldn't paint anything. And Noni brought up T-Tupac. You know Tupac? He said that you should celebrate life by splattering color on paper and how it would set you free. So, that's what I did."

Scribbling notes, the interviewer asked, "So that's how all this got started?"

"Yeah. I shut my eyes, picked up a black sharpie and wrote an equation. Then, I got c-colored sand and a few feathers and glued them to the canvas. Next, I took out the paints that matched the colors of the equation and began to paint. I thought of something from a line in a dream that Ramanujan had written in his lost notebook. Do you know Ramanujan? He was a g-great mathematician. He said, 'While asleep, I had an unusual experience...S-suddenly a hand wrote in red flowing blood a number of elliptic integrals.' I didn't use blood because I didn't want Noni to think I was crazy, but I used some dark red paints. I thought it was an awful mess, but she had a d-different reaction. She said, 'Oh man. Wow, this is amazing, Carmine! See, you found something inside that has a deeper meaning. Congratulations, dude, you just created art.' That's how she t-talks."

TEARS ARE ONLY WATER

Carmine told the interviewer how Noni showed his painting to TJ O'Brien, the art center's director, who thought they'd discovered a unique voice.

"So, Mr TJ O'Brien told me to keep painting. That was three years ago, and I haven't s-stopped painting since."

Corvus smiled and put down her notebook. "Wow, thank you Carmine Luedke. You have a remarkable story, and your work is...well, I've never seen anything quite like this. What do you call these pieces?"

"Colorful Constants."

"Interesting. There's a double meaning of constants and colors, right?"

Carmine agreed. "Yeah. T-there's the mathematical definition and another meaning about things in life that don't change. You know, a tension between the colors, which always change, and those things that stay the same...that's all."

Corvus thanked him and gathered up her things while her photographer snapped a few final photos of Carmine and his paintings.

Carmine needed some time to clear his head, so he walked back to his apartment. He was exhausted but had promised Noni he would show up for the celebration and dreaded karaoke-ing. The interview had been wearing. Talking about the past had awakened a mix of memories. He thought about how numbers and equations had clogged his brain for so long. They didn't inhabit his mind like before, but they were still part-time residents.

Numbers and colors. That first painting remained in the storeroom. For his second, he painted Bernoulli numbers in 3D and used different colored feathers with a black and white sand border. That painting sold, and word got out about a bookkeeper...who became an artist.

Chapter 41

Ahéheé

One Month later...June 15th*, 2019, 6:00 PM*

Sangre De Cristo held a reception after the magazine article was published. The gala event brought much-needed publicity and donations from the arts community. Since he was featured on the cover of the current issue, Carmine was told to invite as many guests as he wished. He asked only Anne and Nicola Kitts.

Anne sent her regrets from a small village in Provence where she and Katie had been staying for the last three weeks. The settlement with Tawney-Banks had given her financial freedom to do what she wanted. She felt so proud after reading the article that she immediately purchased one of her brother's paintings. Anne had completed her memoir, "Conversations With My Mother: What I Never Said." Her inward-looking work detailed the sorrows and turmoil of their troubled relationship. Anne was even rewriting some of their mother's poems. When Carmine expressed surprise, she responded, "Well true, some are still ghastly, but Mother had a raw talent. That has to mean something. It's what I want to focus on."

Still ready with a snarky comment, Anne continued to think her inner thoughts out loud. But during their recent phone call, Carmine heard a lightness in her voice––something approaching acceptance and quiet joy. He didn't know when he would see her again but looked forward to her letters and occasional calls.

Kitts––no longer Deputy Kitts––flew in for the gala during a break from Smith College, where she had begun working on her doctorate in social work. She never returned to law enforcement and, after long camping trips with her blue companion, Langston, she applied to graduate schools. Even without Anne's connections, Kitts had been a strong candidate for top social work programs. She and Carmine tried to keep in touch but that rarely happened. It hadn't taken her long to figure out that he was the benefactor for her graduate school tuition. They haggled over this in their calls.

She would say, "Books, I know it was you. You're always up to something sneaky like this. And I will pay you back, got that? Been saving up my money."

To which Carmine would typically answer, "S-sure. I know that. But I did it for you and for Blue, right? That's all."

The night was magical. Everyone from the center turned out. Noni, her friends, and their families were all there. The music, food, and weather made for a perfect evening. The public relations director, Debra Lerner, pulled Carmine aside with news that *The New Yorker* wanted to interview him.

As Kathleen Corvus said during their interview, his story was amazing. He had friends, talent, success, and financial security. He had everything he wanted and wanted everything he had.

And yet....The numbers didn't add up. His accounts were not balanced. Amid the abundance of good fortune, he felt an echo of absence. How could his life be so full while he felt so hollow? For five years, he'd tried to silence this nagging feeling. It began as a distant droning, then a drum beat, faint at first, that something was missing. He heard it while painting. He also heard it with Noni. But the drumbeat only grew louder. While sitting outside one day, he listened to crows cawing in a nearby tree. Messengers....That's when he realized he needed to look for Julio and Hazel Lukachunai.

. . .

Noni had gone to Denver for the week, so he took time off as well. He relished time by himself. He got up at sunrise and returned to the trails around CMHI-P, which was not where he usually walked.

When he first moved to Pueblo, he had walked around the hospital every day. He made clumsy efforts to talk to everyone he saw entering the building, asking where he could find Dr Lukachunai and Julio. He sensed that people were uncomfortable, wondering if he was a patient who'd escaped from one of the wards. Later, he started going into the garden, hoping to see her talking to the birds. But by then, the security guards viewed him as a nuisance and quickly escorted him off the campus.

Back then, Carmine walked the nearby trails hoping to see Julio. He had imaginary conversations with him, thinking that they might become friends. Eventually, he gave up any hope of ever seeing them again and started thinking that the whole time in the sweat lodge might have just been another dream-like hallucination.

His time at the hospital was a distant memory, and he never fully understood what had happened that last week. But something had changed. New variables were introduced among the constants. He felt the same but different. The droning in his mind became the words of her song. He imagined her sipping tea and talking to birds in the garden. Though he'd forgotten much about those two weeks, he remembered what she'd said about holding onto his father. She told him he'd suffered enough and nothing that happened to Vati or E was his fault. She said he needed to let go. Though *so much* of that time was a blur, he still heard her words before the healing ceremony, "Carmine, you must wake before you can sleep." And imprinted in his mind forever was "hope is something with feathers that sings songs without words and perches in your soul."

The dusty trails looked the same as they did so many years ago. He walked them each day, hoping to see Julio or Dr Hazel. By the end of the week, he was resigned to not finding either of them. *People move on from the past, right? People leave, too.* So, he decided to take a final goodbye walk. As Dr Hazel had said, it was time to let go and move on.

TEARS ARE ONLY WATER

The sun radiated from a cloudless sky. As usual, he saw no one on the trail. Then, after an hour, he saw something 400 yards up ahead. At first, he thought it was a huge boulder or tree stump on the side of the path. As Carmine got closer, his heart raced when he saw the object move. It was neither a tree nor a boulder but a huge man standing by the trail.... He'd found Julio Garza.

Julio waved as Carmine approached. The gentle giant hadn't changed. Studying Carmine, Julio said, "Hey, sleeping man. You look different. I see you got new shoes. *Nice.* Didya wake up, bro?"

The two walked for several miles, much of it in silence. Carmine shared that he'd moved back and now worked at the art center. Julio said he helped his uncle, who owned a farm. Finally, Carmine asked the question he'd wondered about every day for the last five years.

"W... w-what happened to Dr Lukachunai? Is s-she...?"

Carmine heard the sadness in Julio's voice as his words took on a somber tone. Julio now referred to her as Grandmother, not Doctora. He told how she had suffered a stroke and was hospitalized after the last night of the chant. Then, Julio filled in the pieces about how the healing ceremony was not supposed to happen. Everyone who participated was suspended, except for Dr Hazel, whom they fired.

"Yeah, bro, they fired her. It's a dark story. Dr Lia decided not to come back. Same with Gina. They didn't want their jobs back after their suspension. Beelzebuffo and his *matones* read Grandmother's letter saying that the ceremony was her decision, so they blamed everything on her. They asked, no, begged me to come back, bro. I said, 'Naw, no way. Fuck you, esse.' Then the fools wrote out a big check if I swore not to tell the papers what had happened."

"W-what did you do, Julio?"

"You think I'm a fool, bro? I took the cash."

"Is Dr Hazel...I mean, is she--?"

Julio cut in. "Oh, Grandmother? She lives with her niece in a little house. You know, a couple of folks from the old days take turns coming by to spend time with her, like Gina and that nut job Bertie. Sometimes Dr Lia drives down from Denver to spend the day with her. Grandmother, she's okay but doesn't talk too good. You know, her words are broken. Strokes mess that up, but her mind is still as sharp as an arrow. Still got her spirit bird. Can see it in her eyes when she watches you like a hawk. That hasn't changed.... She asks about you. We all figured you disappeared somewhere after they let you out of the hospital, but she still asks sometimes, bro. Yeah, she does."

Carmine asked if he could see her. Julio said he'd check and let him know. Carmine had a pen and wrote his phone number on a space between the tattoos on Julio's arm.

Months passed and no call. Then one day, Julio showed up at the art center.

"Lost your number, bro, but remembered you said you worked here. So, you wanna go see her now?"

Carmine asked Noni if he could take the rest of the day off. He went into the storeroom and found his first painting he'd placed in a bin four years ago. It was a sand painting of Euler's identity.

Julio had his truck in the parking lot. It dropped to a few inches off the ground when he

got in.

Pointing to the painting, Julio asked, "What's that?"

"It's just s...s-something I did. That's all.... I thought she might like it. I don't know."

"No, *nice,* nice touch, bro. Betcha Grandmother will like this." The radio blared a loud, syncopated beat. "You like Latin trap, you know, Conejo, maybe some Sick Jacken, bro?"

"Sure, I g-guess." Carmine wouldn't tell him that it hurt his ears.

TEARS ARE ONLY WATER

Julio veered off the highway onto an unmarked dirt road with nothing in sight. He turned again and drove up to a small, plain-looking house with a colorful garden in the front.

She was sitting in a rocking chair on the porch, watching as they drove up. Another woman came out and said, "She's been waiting for you."

And there she was...looking much the same but older and frailer than he'd remembered. Her right arm hung at her side. She nodded and gave a crooked smile. His heart began to pound in a way he hadn't expected.

"It's her stroke, bro, like I told you."

The old woman motioned for Carmine to approach and sit beside her. Julio stood by his truck while her niece brought tea. The old healer reached out her left hand and squeezed Carmine's fingers. Her eyes brightened as she looked into his.

"Eeee. Ah, um... Car-nime! *Yá'át'ééh*, W...w-welcome. A, ah... a good afternoon. I see you, um...are waking up. You woke up Carmin!" The right half of her face hung low as the left side raised into a smile. "Tell me how, um...are you still liking the wings...overhead, um, the birds?"

He nodded and quietly said, "Uh huh. I do," because he didn't have more words for what he was feeling. She saw the eagle feather on his arm, touched it, and smiled again. Then, Carmine awkwardly handed her the Euler painting, which her niece placed on her lap. "Here, I made this for you. It's not much, but I w-wanted you to have it."

Her niece said, "Oh, Auntie, look! He made you a nice sand painting full of numbers."

Her eyes widened as she studied the painting, then looked back at Carmine. She felt the textures and feathers and reached for his hand to help trace the numbers with her fingers. She smiled when she saw the Euler tattoo on the other side of his forearm. Carmine sat with her for over an hour that afternoon in silence, for words did not come easily to either of them. Finally, when he felt lost for what to say, he reached inside and found her words.

"*A-ahéheé*. Thank you, Grandmother. Thank you for seeing me."

She gave a bent smile in recognition and nodded her head. "Yes, *Ahéheé*, Carn, em...Carmine. Thank you, too."

Her niece quietly whispered that her aunt was getting tired and that they should leave. She looked to Julio, who nodded and got into his truck. As Carmine walked away, he heard the old woman who had awakened him say, *"Hágoónee'."*

Julio said, "It's her way of saying goodbye, bro."

During the drive back, the beat of the music and the cadence of the rap reminded Carmine of songs he'd heard her singing during the healing ceremony. Julio dropped him off at the arts center. He wished Carmine well. His last words were,

"You did good, bro. Stay awake, okay?"

That's it....Carmine knew he would never see either of them again. But that was okay. They had become constants in the equations of his heart and mind.

The artist dreamed of writing numbers in the sand that night when a woman appeared at his window.

"Hey Carm...ya gonna ask me in?"

The dreamer spoke the words, "No, not tonight, E...but it is time for me to tell you, *Hágoónee'.*"

The artist's dreamscape opened to a trail that led him to a meadow with a magic pond. Feeling asleep but fully awake, he knelt at the water's edge and gazed deeply. He saw a man looking up at him. He smiled, and the man smiled back. The water cleared. Then he saw a reflected speck in the sky. He looked up and watched as a lone Red-tailed hawk soared high overhead, dancing in flight.

Acknowledgments

Few books are born without a team of midwives offering love, encouragement, support, and expertise. I've had a tremendous team in this lengthy birthing process, and I'm grateful for their help.

My parents will never read this book, but their spirits live in the words I write. Thank you, Mom and Dad. Same thanks to my dear sister Margy, who reads my work and provides lifelong support. This same gratitude extends to my always supportive Brothers-in-Law, Larry and Greg.

A major shout-out to my kids Nike, Colleen, Katie, Lucky, Jodie, Nicole, and Tom for your love and support of my writing. Nike, you eagerly read early drafts and provided accounting expertise to lend authenticity. Katie, your help was measured in the time and care you devoted to expertly proofreading and consulting on the manuscript. Jodie, as always, you were there enthusiastically sharing your legal expertise with relevant concepts and terminology. Nicole, thank you for creating for me a wonderful private writing nook in your home with a soothing view of Back Creek. And Tom, how could I exist without your patience and generosity with technical support when I'm in need? Of course, to Riley, Brooke, Sloane, and Max, thank you guys for the joy of being Popi and for keeping me young(ish).

Thanks to Jericho Writers. Their constant fostering of the creative spark has been an incredible support. I've benefitted from their great webinars and courses that have enhanced my never-ending journey as a writer. I've been fortunate to have had two teachers––actually, two phenomenal Debi/Debbie's––who taught brilliant courses, the first on Self-Editing and the second on Self-Publishing. Both are warm and witty teachers who provided inspiration and encouragement.

Two editors lent their time and expertise to turn sometimes tortured prose into sparkling language. To Debi Alper of Jericho Writers, I'm grateful for your painstakingly detailed and occasionally painful developmental editing of my manuscript. Your questions––always respectful and encouraging––helped me rethink characters, plot, and voicing. Your words, "Make every word earn its keep" helped guide me through multiple re-writes. My second editor was my wife, Nannette Bowman. It is so much like you to take something pretty good and make it so much better. And how true to form that you've helped me see what I did not. You were a patient partner, coach, and editor. You helped each word earn its rightful place. Thanks to both of you!

My friend Steve Lerner, one of my favorite people in the world, introduced me to Dr. Debra Bolton, who served as a valued consultant, teaching and guiding me as I wrote about Indigenous culture and helping me bring Hazel Lukachunai to life. More than a cultural consultant, Debra, you became a valued friend. *Ahéheé*.

I appreciate input from Dr. Thomas Gray a former staff psychologist at CMHI-P for his interest and sending old photographs of the state hospital. Thank you, Tom.

Kathy Koviac of Blackthorn Studio designed a beautiful cover and patiently worked with me during the creative process. Thank you for reading an earlier version of the manuscript, which contributed to your artistic vision. I love the cover! Thank you.

Thank you, Rachel Thompson for your help with social media and marketing. Thanks also to Steve Bennett and Laura Spinelli at Authorbytes, who designed a beautiful website. And thank you, Charlie Levin at Munn Press for helping turn the manuscript into a book and with the subsequent marketing campaign on Amazon.

I'm fortunate to have had a group of advance-release readers who took the time to read this story. Thank you Barton, Debra, Tom, Mark, Jed, Diane, Joni, and Laura.

I'm grateful for my years at the Menninger Clinic, which connected me to teachers, fellow Rorschach travelers, and supporters of all things psychoanalytic and psychodiagnostic. And a special thanks to the Topeka Men's Group for being there with unconditional support and friendship.

And in the end, there she was....

It always comes down to one person——a muse, perhaps——and that is you, Noni. Wise and loving partner, soulmate, wife, friend to all living creatures, and teacher of how to live a fruitful life, this is for you. I think it's a good story, bro. Thank you for always being there, and thank you for helping me wake up.

Author Notes

Tears Are Only Water fictionalizes people, places, events, and psychological theories. The main characters are products of my imagination. However, Leonhard Euler was an 18th-century Swiss mathematician. Carl Jung is also a historical figure. Erich Neumann was a student of Jung's, but his role as Hazel's supervisor was, of course, fictional. CMHI-P, Aurora Medical Center, and the Arapahoe County Sheriff's Department are real places that have been altered for the story. Describing corruption in the Sheriff's Department is not based on actual events. It is in no way meant to convey disrespect for law enforcement.

Native American mental health practices are well established (e.g., Native American Counseling & Healing Collective in Denver, CO), but I know of no such program ever existing at CMHI-P. The character and name of Hazel Lukachunai were my creations. I consulted with Dr. Debra Bolton (Ohkay Owingeh/Diné/Ute) about Hazel's name and Native healing. Debra's suggestions about Indigenous language and culture helped lend authenticity to my story. I also relied on several sources about Native healing ceremonies. These included: "Indigenous Native American Healing Traditions" (Koithan, M. and Farrell, C., 2010, *Journal of Nurse Practitioner, 6(6):* 477-478*)*, Donald Sandner's *Navaho Symbols of Healing. A Jungian Exploration of Ritual, Image, &* *Medicine* (1979, 1991, Healing Arts Press), and Evan Pritchard's *Bird Medicine. The Sacred Power of Bird Shamanism* (2013, Bear & Company). Finally, I came upon a fascinating article by a psychoanalyst, Farrell R. Silverberg, Ph.D., N.C., Psy.A., on "Ancient and Indigenous Roots of Psychoanalysis: A Psycho-Anthropological-Shamanic Treatise" based on his paper presented at the 2010 International Forum for Psychoanalytic Education Annual Conference in Nashville, TN. I used several internet sources for Diné vocabulary, including a *Navajo-English Dictio-*

AUTHOR NOTES

nary (Leon Wall and William Morgan, 1958, University of Northern Colorado Scholarship & Creative Works @ Digital UNC https://digscholarship.unco.edu/navajo/1) and Glosbe.com (https://glosbe.com/en/nv). I take responsibility for any errors, misrepresentations, or simplifications that may have occurred in my translations of Diné words and expressions. My intent was to represent Indigenous culture and healing practices respectfully.

Wikipedia was a primary resource for references about all things mathematical. Included were references about constants, proofs, and renowned mathematicians such as Leonhard Euler and his identity equation, $e^{i\pi} + 1 = 0...e^{i\pi} + 1 = 0... e^{i\pi}$ https://en.wikipedia.org/wiki/Leonhard_Euler.

Information about narcolepsy was based on the webinar "Detect and Defeat: Improving Awareness of the Differences in Narcolepsy and Novel Strategies for Treatment." https://www.mycme.com/courses/awareness-of-the-differences-in-narcolepsy-and-treatment-8288

Anne Schivalone's theory of adaptive compartmentalization was my creation, and its clear limitations were exaggerated to fit her character. I set up a strawman tension between the positions ascribed to Hazel and Anne, which I inflated for effect. As a psychologist and psychoanalyst, I believe (as many who would read this book) that processing loss and trauma from the past is far better (and necessary) than trying to ignore it. At the same time, Anne's position on "adaptive compartmentalization" has some merit as a means of coping, depending on the type and severity of the stresses we decide to ignore.

I acknowledge the story reached the height of improbability with Carmine's rushed commitment to the state hospital, as well as the extended time Lukachunai would spend with an individual patient in such a setting, including conducting weekend sessions. These exaggerations were created to further the story with the knowledge that this is not how things generally work in the real world.

I made multiple literary references throughout the book. Some were ascribed to the appropriate source. Here is a list of references for quotes and music mentioned.

AUTHOR NOTES

Mississippi John Hurt *The Complete Studio Recordings* (2000). On Amazon Music https://www.allmusic.com/album/the-complete-studio-recordings-mw0000105748/credits

Barry McGuire. "Eve of Destruction (1965)." *BarryMcGuire.com.* Retrieved September 5, 2010.

Hazel's quote "There is no grief like the grief that does not speak," was attributed to Henry Wadsworth Longfellow.

BrainyQuote.com. Retrieved October 14, 2023, from BrainyQuote.com Web site: https://www.brainyquote.com/quotes/henry_wadsworth_longfello_379337

Victor Hugo's quote "He who does not weep does not see" is from *Les Miserables,* first published in 1862.

Carmine recalls Hazel speaking about hope as "something with feathers that sings songs without words and perches in your soul." This is from Emily Dickinson's 1890 Poem "Hope is the Thing With Feathers" published on Academy of American Poets (https://poets.org).

Carmine mentions Tupac's message about "celebrating life by splattering colors," which is from the album *The Rose That Grew From Concrete,* released in 2000 after his death.

https://www.goodreads.com/quotes/11071762-celebrate-life-through-the-music-through-the-spoken-word-through

Finally, the title, "Tears Are Only Water," is taken from *The Taggurung* by Brian Jacques, published in 2001. I thank him for his inspiring words that gave birth to this novel.

Made in the USA
Coppell, TX
18 January 2024

27868559R00184